Earth, Beast, Metal

The AIS Files

Book One

A Chronicle from Alku

Recommended Reading Order

The Final Keeper Trilogy
Keeper's Reign - Book 1*
Keeper's Secrets - Book 2
Keeper's Prophecy - Book 3

The AIS Files
Earth, Beast, Metal - Book 1*

*Either of these books can be considered an entry point into the Chronicles from Alku universe.

Contents

Foreword

Greetings from the Alii Interface Syndicate, also known as the AIS.

When I first realized that the Alku Universe would span multiple books, spin-offs, side-stories, and locations, I knew I needed a second way to dive into the series. Earth, Beast, Metal is that second entry point.

While I would still classify this book as urban romantasy, I would add a stronger science fiction sub-genre to it than The Final Keeper Trilogy. Here you'll meet Crow, a character created by my partner in the word mines, Ander C. Lark, and learn more about how the magical community protects and polices itself.

Crow isn't the only newcomer you'll meet. In fact, you'll meet characters from future books who will become integral in the Keeper's life and adventure, along with the two main characters from the second AIS novel—and no, I'm not telling you who they are. I have to keep some secrets.

For now, I hope you enjoy this alternate look into the hidden world of magic and a deeper exploration of three races of beings that were not highlighted in Alku.
Yet.

For now...from our world to yours, happy reading, and welcome to the Alku chosen family.

For those of us who have lost someone...
...and wished for more time with them.

Acknowledgements

Thank you to my chosen family who gave me the confidence to fly my rainbow proudly.
And to Ander, who introduced me to Crow and their intriguing coffee shop.

Pronunciation Guide & Glossary

Note: The following <u>does</u> contain spoilers

Eliza Leone (e-lie-za lee-o-knee)

Names/Characters:
Alexander (Xander) Yoru (zan-der yo-rue) Paranam/Panthenam: Adoptive brother to Ashton and Eileen, son to Sue and Arthur Giri.

Arthur Giri (r-th-er gear-ee) Human/Trans-Mechanite AI: Grandfather to Ashton, Eileen, and Alexander; spouse to Sue Giri

Ashton Giri (ash-ton gear-ee) Mechanite: Brother to Eileen Giri and Xander Yoru; agent in the Invisibles Department of the AIS, and partner to Thenia Loris and Serena Ainsley.

Crow (???) ???: ???

Eileen Giri (i-lean gear-ee) Mechanite: Sister to Ashton Giri and Xander Yoru.

Josephine Roma (joe-seph-een row-ma) Mechanite: Best friend to Sue Giri and leader of the Invisibles Department at the AIS.

Lucus Garv (lew-cus gaar-vh) Human: Ex-fiancé to Thenia Loris.

Serena Ainsley (sir-ee-nuh ai-nn-s-lee) Paranam/Serpanam: Green snake shifter and partner to Thenia Loris and Ashton Giri.

Stephan Athan (ah-thahn) Sanguiste: Ancient sangusite, owner of the Day Night Cafe.

Sue Giri (gear-ee) Mechanite / Trans-Mechanite AI: Grandmother to Ashton, Eileen, and Alexander; spouse to Arthur Giri.

Thenia Loris (th-en-ee-ya lore-is) Elemental Witch: Earth and Water elemental witch, and partner to Ashton Giri and Serena Ainsley.

Wyatt Zareb (y-at zz-err-ebb) Mechanite: Agent at the Invisibles Department at the AIS.

Locations:
Alku (al-coo): A sanctuary city for those of the magical world located in the forests of Washington State, USA. The current location of the Keeper and the world's archive.

Crow's Nest Coffee: ???

Species / Races:
Angel of Death: Humanoid beings with differing physical and personality traits depending on which direction they ferry a soul after life.

Elemental Witch: A race of humans who inherit magic from their ancestors and have an affinity to one or more elements.

Keeper: A being chosen to protect the world's knowledge in an endless archive.

Mechanite (meh-caw-night): Humans who have evolved the capability to speak with mechanical objects and machines.

Paranam (pair-ah-nam): Humans with two souls: one human and one animal. Can shift into the soul's animal form.

Sanguiste (sang-whist): An immortal being, once human, but traded their soul to a demon upon death. Consumers of blood, emotions, or bodily fluids for sustenance.

Trans-Mechanite AI (trans-meh-caw-night a-i): A combination of coded programming and living soul into a being of ones and zeros.

Transmogromorph (trans-mog-row-morph): A group of beings that can shift their physical form into that of another human if acquired first. Naturally good, relatively rare, and highly secretive.

Other:

Alii Interface Syndicate (AIS) (al-i in-ter-face sin-di-kate): The governing, protecting, and shielding body of magic users and non-Outsider humans who work to keep the magical community safe and hidden.

Outsider: A human ignorant of the magical world and its inhabitants.

Do you know about Campfire?

Campfire is a website and ebook storefront with a novel addition to standard ebooks. (Sorry, I couldn't resist.) Campfire allows the author to provide readers with extras that unlock as they read or can be purchased separately.

Character bios and backstories, location descriptions, recipes, maps, magic, species, and item encyclopedias exist. And that's just the start!

Explore all the books in the Alku universe for updated and new information as the series progresses!

https://campfi.re/EBM

The Chronicles from Aku
Tiefen Hool
AIS NA
Aku
Pacific City
Nisi Dakry

mechanite script key

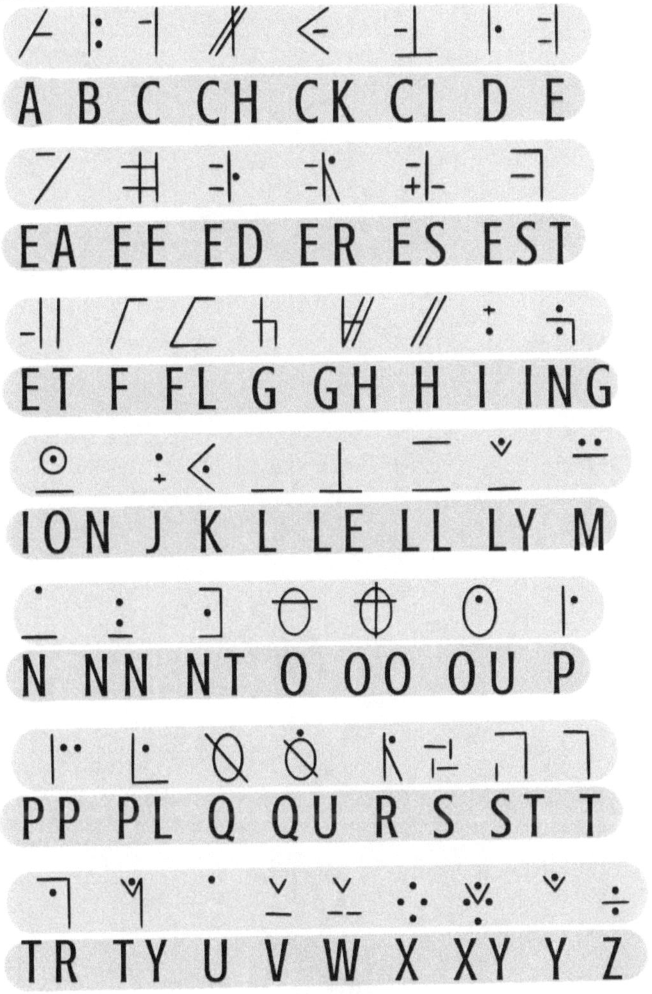

A B C CH CK CL D E

EA EE ED ER ES EST

ET F FL G GH H I ING

ION J K L LE LL LY M

N NN NT O OO OU P

PP PL Q QU R S ST T

TR TY U V W X XY Y Z

created by Eliza Leone

The story so far...

The Final Keeper Trilogy

Note: The Final Keeper Trilogy can be read *before* or *after Earth, Beast, Metal.* In my opinion, it is better to read the trilogy first, but you can also consider EBM as an alternative entry point into the universe.

If you read EBM first, here's what you need to know from The Final Keeper Trilogy:

A young woman named Onnie moves to a quiet, cozy town named Alku, nestled in the forested mountains of the Pacific Northwest, when her grandfather requests that she inherit his bookshop.

She is told of an ancient prophecy that may refer to her, and eventually comes to pass, proving that Onnie, the Final Keeper, will either be the destroyer or savior of magic.

Earth, Beast, Metal

The AIS Files
Book 1

Chapter 1: Starting with the Unexpected

May 2024, Maine, USA | Thenia Loris

Thenia sat at a little metal table pushed against a wood-paneled wall in a quiet coffee shop. She was in a small town in Maine, a state she was slowly getting to know and becoming more comfortable with over the few weeks that she'd been house-sitting for a friend. While most of her days had been lazy, and Thenia was more of a homebody, today, she'd felt the urge for something different and went out to explore. After wandering from street to street for a few hours and completing some errands, she was in desperate need of a snack and something caffeinated.

Thankfully, Thenia had, quite literally, bumped into a chalkboard sign on the sidewalk in front of The Crow's Nest and pulled open the glass door while rubbing the bruise forming on her thigh. The rich smell of freshly roasted coffee beans and buttery pastry invaded her senses, along with how well-kept and cozy the place was. She'd practically sighed in happiness.

The shop's interior had an antique feel, and everything gave off an older vibe, but nothing felt outdated. Instead, it perfectly fit the semi-steampunk atmosphere. When Thenia first stepped inside, a person behind the counter greeted her with a friendly smile and a slight beckoning gesture.

They introduced themselves as Crow and then took her order, happily accepting her cash while looking relieved that they hadn't needed to ring up a credit card. The register was the single piece of modern technology visible within the shop, aside from the few coffee-related contraptions gleaming with clean and polished reflections.

From behind dark lashes, Crow's dark eyes seemed to observe her as they prepared her order, their color shifting in the light as they moved. Their ebony hair did the same from where it was pulled into a long ponytail, effectively keeping it out of their way. The purples, blues, and deep greens seemed to shimmer, and Thenia found herself amused at the crow feather coloring and wondered if the name came first or the person's hair and style had.

With her order ready, Thenia claimed a table and dug into her simple but delicious grilled cheese sandwich and a huge cup of iced tea.

She'd nibbled and scrolled through her phone for a while, relaxed and happy to be out of the heat. At one point, she had begun spacing out when the coffee shop's door jingled for the second time since she'd made it jingle herself. When she glanced towards the sound, Thenia was surprised to see that she was the only remaining patron, aside from the newcomer.

A young man in a graphic T-shirt and well-loved jeans drew Thenia's attention as he entered. His blond hair fluttered in the slight breeze, and his face lit up when he saw the barista.

"Crow! Long time, man!"

"Hello, Ashton. It has been."

Crow looked slight compared to the newcomer, but their face nearly glowed as they fist-bumped Ashton's outstretched one and returned his smile.

"How you been?" Ashton asked.

"I've been well. Yourself?"

Ashton must have felt Thenia's stare as she studied him, and he glanced in her direction. She flushed, eyes darting back down at her food, and tried harder to ignore the conversation she was most definitely not a part of.

"Not bad, but you heard about Gram and Pops, right?"

Crow sighed sadly. "I did. You have my condolences."

"All good. They were together and happy. Couldn't ask for more."

Thenia inferred the man's grandparents had passed, but by his tone, he evidently processed grief differently than most. He practically sounded happy for the pair.

"True," Crow responded, "and Eileen and Alexander?"

Ashton chuckled, "Still off protecting the weak and saving the innocent."

"Good, good."

"Well, before I forget," Ashton said, "Sure you don't mind if I hang this on your notice board?"

"Of course not. May I inquire as to what it is you have decided on? Pure curiosity, I assure you."

Ashton scoffed. "Curiosity…sure. But yeah, I'm going to hire a groundskeeper. With the other two off doing their thing and me taking over Gram's house, I also have all of Pops' gardens to manage."

"Ah, I see," Crow said, and something in their tone compelled Thenia to reflexively glance toward the pair.

The barista was indeed looking at her from the corner of their eye, while Ashton strode across the room and over to a corkboard on the wall opposite Thenia's table.

"You never were one with a green thumb, were you?" Crow asked, focusing away from Thenia once more.

"Nope! That was Pops all the way, but I'd hate to kill what he tended for so many years. That, and it's going to take me a while to go through Gram's things, so I won't have enough time to learn either."

"Understandable. Well, I'm sure the right person for the partnership will find you soon," Crow said with a sneaky smirk.

"Hope so. The guest house and the garden are both missing the man's vibrancy."

Ashton glanced at Thenia a second time, his gaze making her feel warm and also marginally uncomfortable.

Thenia concentrated on her tea and started playing with the beads of condensation that rolled down the side of the cup. She smirked at them and whispered under her breath, watching as two of the drops twirled and danced with one another, up and down the cup, around the lid, and back down the side.

After distracting herself for a handful of minutes, she looked up to find Ashton gone and Crow leaning on the counter. Their eyes were cast down, but they wore a knowing smile on their lips, and they flicked their gaze over to her and then away again.

"Crap," she mumbled knowing she'd been caught.

Thenia rarely used her magic and never in public, but for whatever reason, she felt safe enough in the coffee shop to use it. After so many years of hiding her capabilities, Thenia's stomach sank at how unsteady it made her to acknowledge that she'd used it so reflexively.

She hastily ate the last few bites of her sandwich and got up from the table to throw away her trash. Purposefully, she went to a bin on the other side of the room, which happened to be closer to the noticeboard. In the center was pinned a single sheet of paper with a few sentences and two pictures under the header, "Groundskeeper wanted." One of the images was of a large manor house in the hills, with an absolutely breathtaking garden surrounding it. It was of typical Maine architecture with columns and round rooms accentuating the dark shingled roof and crisp white siding. The second image was of a tiny home, designed to be unique but still cohesive with the main house. Both pictures made Thenia's heart race, and she mindlessly reached for the paper, but when her fingers grazed it, she jerked her hand back and lowered it.

"It looks to be a perfect opportunity, don't you think, Miss Loris?"

"Ah, yeah. Someone will be very happy there," Thenia lamented as she returned to her table for her bag.

"But not you?"

She scrutinized the observant barista, who hadn't moved from their position behind the counter; not even their eyes had shifted from the floor in front of them.

"No. Not me. I have other obligations right now. I can't be settling anywhere."

She was lying to the stranger and herself, and they both knew it. After separating from Lucus, Thenia decided to uproot herself from her childhood home and all the expectations that came with it. Her parents had moved to Australia years prior, so there was no reason for her to stay in the place where she had lost herself so completely.

So she hadn't.

Since then, Thenia had traveled to Greece, France, and Ireland. She'd visited temples in Japan and the jungles of Africa. While in New York City, an old friend called and asked if Thenia could apartment-sit for her while she went on a multi-week work trip. With nowhere to be and nothing stopping her, Thenia agreed and spent the last six weeks in Maine. Next week, Sara would be home, and Thenia would have to find another location to explore.

Crow's patient tone returned, and Thenia's focus returned to the present. "Roots are just as important to people as they are to plants. Just because they were once rooted in the wrong soil does not mean they should never try to put them down a second time."

Thenia blinked a few times, Crow's words ringing in her ears. "What do you mean by that?" Her body tensed, and the crippling fear of someone finding out she was an elemental witch locked her in place. No one could know what she was. If Lucus found out, he'd—

"Nothing more than what I said."

Crow finally lifted their gaze, and when she looked into their endlessly deep eyes, she swore their dark hair had been feathers, not strands, but only for a second. Then she blinked, and everything was normal again.

The stranger added, "Withholding water from a plant will teach it strength and resiliency, but only because you've taught it through abuse and neglect, not from a place of love and well-being. Don't you agree?"

"Well, um…yes. I suppose…." Thenia babbled, but as she did, Crow walked away from the counter and over to the notice board, where they removed Ashton's flyer. Crow crossed the cafe to stand in front of her, folded the paper into quarters, and held it out to her.

"You will not heal while running."

Thenia was mesmerized by the paper Crow held out to her. She wasn't sure how long she'd stared at it, but when she finally reached out and hesitantly took it from them, she found herself admitting, "I'm… tired…of…."

A chill washed through her, and she shivered. When Thenia lifted her head, Crow was behind the counter again, resting against it in the same position they had been minutes prior. In her hand was the folded flyer, and she squeezed it tighter for a second before she shoved it into her purse and picked up her iced tea.

"Enjoy yourself, Miss Loris," Crow said when she reached the door.

She paused but didn't turn around, nodding, "I will try."

"That's all we can ask for."

With that, Thenia pushed open the door and left The Crow's Nest, not realizing until she was half a dozen blocks away that she'd never told Crow her name.

Thenia unlocked the front door of her friend's apartment and stepped into the brightly lit and airy space. The tension in her shoulders eased, and she had to admit that she was still mentally in the coffee shop with its mysterious owner and the intriguing Ashton. She shut the door behind her, settled her bag on the table beside it, and locked up. While she walked further into the space, Thenia couldn't refrain from looking over her shoulder at her bag and the pocket that still hid a flyer tucked within it.

"Stop it, Thenia," she scolded and made her way into the sky-blue kitchen to fill a watering can she'd left on the counter.

Sara's apartment was bursting with houseplants, which was partly why she asked Thenia to house-sit. Sara trusted very few people with her little green babies, and when Sara confessed that Thenia was whom she trusted the most, Thenia couldn't have said no if she'd even wanted to.

She placed the container under the filtered water faucet and left it to fill while she moved further down the counter to three pots with clippings that required a bit more attention than the others.

"Hello, little ones," Thenia greeted the three pothos cuttings. "Let's check those roots, shall we?"

With delicate fingers, Thenia gently pinched the base of the plant right above the soil line and whispered her request in the language of the elementals.

A soft hissing sound, barely audible, came from beneath the soil, and a few seconds later, Thenia was able to extract the plant—roots and all. It took zero effort as the soil voluntarily released the plant as it moved away from its life support system. The result was that she was able to examine the pristine, dirt-free roots without causing the slightest distress to the plant while she did so.

"Oh, look at you! You look wonderful!" Thenia beamed and praised the young plant as she lowered it back to the pot, where the soil shifted to make room, and then reclaimed the roots with the same careful movements. "Let me check your siblings, and then we can see about getting you all a drink and some food."

Thenia repeated the process with the other two pots, and when all three were replaced, she turned off the faucet and retrieved the watering can.

Before she watered any of the plants, she requested more information from the soil with another set of hushed words. This time, when Thenia rested her pointer finger on the surface of the soil, she could deduce how much water each plant needed and identify any imbalances in the soil composition.

She moved through the apartment, and the numerous plants all received the same level of care. She refilled the watering can half a dozen times before finally placing it back where it belonged, her task finished for the day.

"Alright. That's taken care of. What's next?"

Thenia's gaze wandered over to her purse, and she rolled her eyes before throwing her hands up in the air.

"Fine. Fine!"

She stomped to her bag and brought it over to the glass-topped dining table, and set it beside her laptop, which had been set up in that spot since she'd arrived. Her eye stalled on the half a dozen stickers on the device, and she traced her finger over an adorable potted succulent sticker and then over to a beautiful daffodil.

"His gardens are breathtaking..." she mumbled, recalling the photos on the flyer.

When Thenia finally tore her attention away from her stickers and inner musings, she opened her laptop. Once she logged in and opened her email, Thenia pulled the flier out of her bag and studied it again. Her eyes roamed over every detail for a few minutes, until finally she sighed, giving up and giving in.

"It really does look too good to be true. There has to be a catch." She frowned but set the flyer aside and opened a blank email anyway.

Hello Mr. Giri,

My name is Thenia Loris. I saw your flier for an on-site groundskeeper and would like to inquire if the position is still available.

I have worked as a florist in the past and have a degree in botany with a focus on plant propagation, cross-breeding, and soil composition. If you are interested, I'd like to discuss the position more. I can be available for a call or in person if that suits you better.

Thenia paused and re-read the message before she groaned and, with more force than necessary, hit the backspace key repeatedly.

"Yeah, let's try that again, and this time, don't sound like such a plant snob."

She wiggled her fingers above the keys and nibbled on her lower lip before typing again.

Hello Mr. Giri,

My name is Thenia Loris. I saw your flier for an on-site groundskeeper and am interested in learning more if you've yet to find anyone for the position.

Looking forward to hearing from you,
Thenia

She read the email a few dozen times and then stood and paced behind her chair before plopping back into it and quickly hitting send without giving herself more time to overthink it. She heard the computer's email sending sound, and she slumped in her chair, suddenly exhausted.

"Why the hell was that so difficult? Honestly, the coffee shop owner was right. It would be good for me to put down some roots in a new place."

She peeked over at the three pots on the kitchen counter and smiled.

"Yeah, how about I follow your lead?" Thenia wandered over to the first one she'd checked on and leaned on her elbows on the counter, putting her eye level with it. "What do you think? Good idea?"

The plant remained silent, but talking to it made Thenia smile and immediately feel better.

"I missed this," she said with a frown before mumbling, "Manipulative asshole."

Thenia shook the intrusive thoughts of her ex from her head and skimmed the apartment.

"It's been a long time since I've had so much free time. What do I want to do?"

In one corner of the living room, Sara had set up a folding table with neatly organized paper and scrapbooking supplies. Thenia narrowed her eyes at it but then shook her head.

"Nope. Not my thing. Besides, it's not as if I have photos to scrapbook anyway."

She walked over to a thin bookcase beside the bedroom door, tipped her head to the side, and scanned the spines.

"A few I recognize. Dante's Paradiso?" Thenia snorted. "Really, Sara?" she giggled. "What else?"

Thenia pulled a book out and read the back. "The Color of Blood. Looks like a romance novel, but judging by the title, there's probably more to it."

After she had replaced the book on the shelf, one at the far end caught her eye, and she pulled it out. "Starting with the Unexpected. Interesting."

A faint chime came from the dining table, and Thenia's entire body froze. She slowly pivoted to stare at the device for a few seconds before swallowing roughly.

"It's fine, Thenia. It might not even be him. Could be Mom and Dad."

On shakier legs than she'd like to admit to, Thenia went to check her messages, and sure enough, the only unread message in her inbox was in reply to the one she sent Ashton. The one she'd sent less than five minutes earlier.

She clicked on the message and skimmed it, ripping the band-aid of rejection off.

Miss Loris,

The position is still open, and I'd be happy to show you the grounds and accommodations and answer any questions you may have. Would you be willing to stop by this weekend? Maybe 2 pm on Saturday? I'll include the address and my cell. If you have questions before then or need directions, don't hesitate to reach out.

Ashton

Thenia blinked a few times and then felt her cheeks raise as she involuntarily smiled. She placed the book still in her hand on the table, quickly replied that she'd be there, and then closed her laptop.

"Well, looks like I got a bit of my own unexpected start."

She grinned at the book before picking it up and taking it over to a squishy armchair in front of the sliding glass door and the balcony beyond it.

"Let's just hope it's a positive start to something."

Thenia cracked open the book and flipped to the first chapter, content with losing herself in the pages for the rest of the afternoon.

Ashton Giri

Ashton sat back in his desk chair and stretched his arms above his head. On his main PC's screen was an email from the woman he'd seen in Crow's earlier that day.

"Thenia, huh?"

He smiled at the email, and the window open beside it, displaying the woman's file from the Alii Interface Syndicate's database.

"Thenia Loris. Age thirty-two. Born to Regina and Joseph Loris in New Jersey. Elemental witch with an affinity to Earth and Water elements. No siblings, no children, no spouse. No criminal or punishment record, human or magical."

There was a candid image beside the data of a beautiful woman gazing off into the distance. She had dark hair past her shoulders, dark eyes, tan skin, and a spattering of freckles on her cheeks. Her smile was radiant, but Ashton couldn't help but think it looked…off. Practiced, maybe, or guarded.

"Aren't we all?"

His email chirped when he received a response from the current object of his attention.

That works for me. Thank you, and I look forward to seeing you on Saturday.

Thenia

Ashton grinned but was quickly distracted when a command window popped up over his open applications. It quickly began filling with a blue set of characters that continued to appear as if he were watching someone typing them. The language wasn't English or any other well-known language—at least not to humans. It was the language of the mechanical and one that only a mechanite would know —and Ashton was most definitely familiar with it. He wasn't the only one in his family who could read it, either. His sister, Eileen, was also a mechanite and the only person who could access his system without triggering alerts and snares. Not to mention that anyone else accessing his system in this way would be breaching the mechanite code and that was exceedingly unlikely.

Ashton relaxed as the content of the message verified it was indeed from his sister.

Ashton, are you sure you don't need me to come back? Xander and I will come home if you need us. Stephan will understand. He sends his condolences to you, by the way.

Ashton clicked into the window and pulled out a second keyboard tray over top of his standard QWERTY one. The new one had significantly more keys, and the characters matched those currently blinking on his screen.

Thanks, Eileen. Tell Xander I said hi and Stephan, too. I'm good, really. Went to visit Crow today. They say hi to both of you. I put up a flier for a groundskeeper, as they suggested. Actually, an elemental witch seems interested and is coming by on Saturday: earth and water. No record, and it looks like she could be a good option. On paper, at least. We'll see. Don't worry about me. Gram and Pops' house is fine. I'll get the garden handled, and then when you're back on this continent, you two can come home for a while and help me sort through her data.

Before he was finished with his response, Eileen's reply had already begun to appear, symbol by symbol, popping into existence beneath the ones he was still typing.

Ashton, you don't have to do this alone.

"Really, Eileen?" he pursed his lips and tapped faster.

I know, and I'm not. Don't think I'm not going to be driving you crazy as I go through Gram's files. There's an absolute fuck ton of it. Partly why I am looking for someone to watch over Pops' garden. It's going to be a while before I have time to get out there. I promise I'll ask for help. I'm going to need it. Trust me. But you don't need to stop your life for this, we have time. Besides, you'll get bored here.

Eileen didn't respond for a few minutes, but once she had, Ashton would have bet his grandparents' house that it wasn't until after she'd talked to Xander.

Fine. I'll drop it. Xander and I will finish up this job for Stephan and then come by to see you. I also want to pick up Gram's wedding ring.

Ashton glanced at a photo of his Gram and Pops on the wall across the room. The two of them were in the gardens out front with the sun shining above them, and they were laughing with dirt smudges on their faces. Without taking his eyes off the photo, Ashton replied again, his pale fingers flying over the keys.

Thank you, Eileen. I'll keep it safe for you, and I love you. Stay safe, both of you.

We love you, too, Ash.

Ashton snorted at his sister's nickname for him. Only Eileen, Xander, and his grandparents had ever shortened his name. As he thought about it, he realized that the list had been reduced by half, and his chest began to ache.

The window he'd spoken to Eileen in disappeared, and Ashton pushed back on the desk and rolled his chair backward. He leaned his elbows on his knees and dropped his head into his palms.

"Damn. I already miss you," Ashton whispered into the lonely room that was only filled with a dull hum from the machines surrounding him.

Ashton's parents were killed when he and his sister were still practically babies, but it hadn't been only theirs. Alexander's parents also never made it home after that final mission. None of them had memories of their parents. But they'd ended up fine when Sue and Arthur Giri took all three of them in to raise as their own.

Gram and Pops had been their sole family, except now they were gone, too. They'd died a few months earlier, quietly, in their sleep, and together. Ashton couldn't have wished for a better passing for them, but now he, Eileen, and Xander were alone.

His siblings had left home long ago, following in their parents' career footsteps. They took on various jobs, ranging from espionage to physical altercations to security. The only difference was that they only worked for private clients, not the organization that had sent their parents to their deaths.

On the other hand, Ashton had decided to work for the division tasked with tracking and assisting the magical world's inhabitants to keep them safe in an era of technology—the Invisibles Department of the Alii Interface Syndicate.

Just like his Gram had.

His Pops had been human.

With his grandparents gone, Ashton had moved back to Maine and into their childhood home. His first day back, he's taken one look at the gardens and burst into tears. His Pops' essence was in every leaf and petal. When Ashton finally worked up the courage to enter his grandmother's office a few days later, he'd broken down a second time.

Eileen and Xander never settled in one place for long and had left Maine a week after the funeral, leaving Ashton alone, with no one for company except the machines, the flowers, and the memories.

"I hope you know what you're doing, Crow," Ashton muttered.

Then he sniffled, got to his feet, and left the room, the soothing glow of the mechanical at his back.

Chapter 2: Putting Down Roots a Second Time

May 2024, Maine, USA | Thenia Loris

Thenia shut the rear door of the electric car she'd hired and bent to wave into the open front window.

"Thank you. Drive safe for the rest of your day."

A petite older woman smiled back at her. "I will, my dear. Good luck, though if you ask me, he'd be crazy to say no to such an intelligent woman like yourself."

Thenia felt her cheeks flush, but she smiled a bit wider. "Thank you."

The woman waved, and Thenia stepped back so she could head off to pick up her next client. Once the car was out of sight, Thenia pivoted and stared at the hefty gate blocking a driveway leading further into the property.

The gate was a stunning art piece of intertwining flowers and vines made of dark metal and attached to a stone pillar on either side of the paved driveway. A stone wall continued into the distance around the property on both sides. Even with only a cursory glance at the foliage that crawled over or hung onto the exterior of the wall, Thenia could see how much they were flourishing. What she could glimpse through the gate further confirmed the previous tender's unmistakable adoration for their plants. While slightly overgrown, everything was healthy and trellised, potted, and supported if needed.

"Well, that answers one question. Not a scam. Anyone would need help with these plants, especially if they weren't a native green thumb."

Thenia strode to the small keypad beside the driveway, but before she had the opportunity to press a button, there was a faint beep. The gate mechanism whirred to life and began opening on its hinge. She drew her hand back and quickly reviewed her outfit to confirm she was presentable.

Her lightweight canvas bag was slung over one shoulder, her jeans were clean and tucked into worn but sturdy boots that were practical and stylish enough to be worn outside the garden, and her dark hair was pulled up into a ponytail. She seldom wore makeup anymore, but she'd lined her eyes and applied a simple combination of mascara and sunscreen. Lastly, Thenia smoothed her t-shirt down her torso and then stepped through the gate that was open just enough for her to slip past.

Ashton had instructed her to follow the driveway to the main house, and he'd meet her there. She hadn't even realized when she'd reached the house, considering she'd been too enthralled by the plants she'd passed and was hardly watching where her feet carried her.

"Incredible, isn't it?" a male voice greeted from the porch.

Thenia reluctantly tore her eyes from the verdant beauty and gazed up the short distance into Ashton's pride-filled smile. His honey-colored eyes sparkled, and she had to admit that he was just as captivating as the foliage. He wore jeans, a t-shirt, and a canvas coat with a warm-looking flannel underneath it. In Thenia's opinion, he was dressed far too warmly considering the temperature, but it didn't appear to be bothering him.

"Ah...yes, it is," she managed to reply, pulling her eyes away and internally scolding herself for her prolonged examination of who would hopefully be her boss if she behaved correctly.

"Would you like something to drink, or a tour first? Or, if you have questions before any of that, I will answer what I can."

In the distance, she spotted a rose garden. She'd always had a weakness for them, and it piqued her curiosity.

"Would you mind walking? Honestly, whether you give me the job or not, I'd be incredibly disappointed if I never got to see the rest of this before I leave."

Ashton chuckled and skipped down the few porch steps in his Converse. "I don't mind at all, and I promise, even if you decide against taking the job, you can wander until you've seen your fill."

She stupidly nodded before glancing at Ashton's outstretched hand and then up into his face again.

"Thank you. I'm Thenia. Obviously."

She shook his hand, which was soft and callus-free compared to her own, which wasn't rough, but there was no way to conceal that she worked with her hands. Or at least, she used to.

"Ashton. It's nice to meet you." After they let go, he stepped back, turned his head away, and scratched his neck, his expression pinched and uncomfortable. "Ah, I have a confession to make."

Thenia stiffened, utterly unaware of what he could be confessing to, but she felt the pit in her stomach expand into a chasm. The last time she heard those words, her ex left her after a decade together and a marriage proposal. All because he thought she was crazy and worried she couldn't repress her witch delusion well enough for him and his career.

"I work for the AIS and looked you up after you emailed."

Thenia closed her eyes and pivoted around to walk back to the front gate. "I understand. Thank you for your time."

"Wait!" Ashton dashed around her and stepped into her path. "I didn't tell you to upset you or make you uncomfortable. The opposite, actually. I know you're an elemental witch with an affinity for earth and water."

She braced herself for the lecture. Being called a freak, or crazy, or what was worse—to have him turn his back on her for merely being herself.

"I'm a mechanite."

Thenia's eyes snapped up to meet Ashton's, and she narrowed them as she attempted to evaluate if he was lying. Even if he did know what a mechanite was, it didn't mean he was one. Lucus knew elemental witches were real, whether he believed her or not, but he was nevertheless an Outsider.

"I just wanted you to know I knew. That way, neither of us has to hide who we are or what we can do. Honestly," he scratched his neck again, "Not sure I could hide it with someone living so close anyway. You'd be bound to notice, so I figured I'd confess early."

She knew she was standing there, essentially gawking at him, but she was floundering to find what words to say.

"Ah, so..." Ashton started, but trailed off when his eyes darted to the ground. Then, his lips began to curl into a slight smile. "Oh, I was wondering if I'd ever see you."

Thenia shook herself from her thoughts and glanced down where Ashton had squatted next to a shrub and was squinting into it. He beamed up at her, his smile back and his earlier discomfort gone.

"My Pops was the gardener. Human. My Gram was a mechanite, so this was his sanctuary while she worked up in the main house." Ashton pointed into the plant a few feet from them. "He told me of a friend he'd met in the garden one day. A small green snake that would sun itself while he worked. He said he used to talk to it and hoped it would be alright without him when his...time came."

Thenia knelt on the stone driveway beside Ashton and followed his finger's indicated direction. Sure enough, tucked into a little daffodil plant was a small green snake with a tiny yellow mark on its nose, and it appeared to be observing them with intelligent eyes.

"How do you know it's the same snake?" she asked.

"The yellow marking. Pops mentioned the unique trait once when he was talking about it."

She nodded and studied the creature more. "Well, sounds like it decided to stick around."

"Maybe you could talk...to...it?" Ashton said hesitantly, and Thenia glanced at him from the corner of her eye.

"Meaning?"

He shrugged. "I don't know. It probably misses Pops, too. Maybe while you're out here, you could talk with it, like he did."

Thenia crossed her arms in front of her chest but smirked. "You haven't given me the job yet," she said.

"You haven't run screaming for the hills, either," Ashton teased. "This place is a lot of work. I wouldn't blame you if you didn't want it on that fact alone."

She stared at him for another few seconds before pushing herself back to her feet and smiling down at him.

"Shall we continue with that tour?"

The relief on Ashton's face had her chest filling with butterflies, but she squashed them down as he stood and waved goodbye to the snake.

"Stay safe, little one."

Thenia watched the snake flick its tongue at him, and she'd swear it nodded in reply.

"Well, let's head over to the guest house then. It's most definitely a tiny house, but it's comfortable." Ashton gestured for her to step onto a side path ahead of him.

"Works for me," Thenia said, giving the green snake one final look before letting Ashton direct her.

Ashton Giri

The last thing Ashton had wanted to do was make Thenia uncomfortable. He understood that a substantial portion of the stories about the AIS among their kind weren't the best. It made sense, considering the scope of responsibilities the organization carried out, which included everything from resolving disputes, law enforcement, and treaties between species, to the more mundane work of his department. In general, the Invisibles Department was regarded positively and was more reactionary than combative. Modernizing magical kind and concealing them among humans while still being in plain sight was incredibly important, and he took pride in his career.

"You said your grandfather tended all of this?" Thenia questioned from in front of him as her eyes wandered over each and every plant, one by one.

"Yup, he did. Gram worked from the house, like I do, which left him with a lot of time on his hands." Ashton chuckled at the memory of his grandparents teasing one another. "Apparently, one day, Gram told him to get a hobby and stop distracting her. He started with a single jasmine vine in a pot."

Thenia stopped to stare at him, wide-eyed in disbelief. "Wait, you can't be serious?"

Ashton grinned. "One hundred percent. Way before I or my sister were born, but yeah, that's how all of this started."

"Damn." Thenia's mouth snapped closed, and when her eyes returned to the garden, her expression was filled with even more respect than before.

He followed the route her gaze took and tried to view the garden as she did. The spectrum of colors was wide, and while predominantly green, splashes and pops of vibrant pinks, yellows, and rich purples were scattered throughout the vines, shrubs, and trees. By now, all of them were overgrown, but they were still lush and full of life. Bees and butterflies flitted amongst flowers, and hummingbirds and finches played tag around the tree branches. All of it was...breathtaking, and Ashton's heart ached as tears pushed at the backs of his eyes.

He swallowed down his rising emotions, and they resumed following the dirt path. When they reached a point where a second trail made of pea gravel branched off, Ashton directed Thenia to follow it instead.

"So, how much land does this all cover?"

Ashton quickly flipped through his memory before responding. "Um...I think the entire property is nearly twenty-five acres, and a portion is forest and coastline."

"Wow, okay then."

Thenia stopped to scrutinize a leaf the size of her palm, and Ashton truthfully had no idea what plant it was. Then she swiveled to look up at him, head cocked to the side.

"What's up?" he asked.

"Why is there a tiny house if he was the groundskeeper? I assume he lived in the main house."

Ashton grinned. "He did. They built it for me, my sister, and a family friend who's basically my brother. Something about when we came to visit, having our own space or something." He shook his head. "Not that we cared if we stayed in the main house with them or not. I've only stayed in it once, and my sister and Xander haven't at all."

Thenia nodded and stood back up, dusting off the knees of her jeans and returning to their walk. She was stunning. There was no way to deny it. From her photograph in her AIS file, Ashton had known what she looked like, not to mention the few glimpses he'd stolen at Crow's, but up close, Thenia was gorgeous. Her glossy, brown hair was pulled back, revealing her slender neck and sun-kissed skin.

"They sound like they really loved you," Thenia said, breaking Ashton's, hopefully subtle, admiration of her.

"They did. Raised the three of us after our parents were

killed."

He noticed her flinch, and he continued before she could say anything. If it was one thing he and his siblings were tired of, it was pity over the deaths of their parents.

"All three of us weren't more than three, so we don't remember them. As cold as it sounds, it didn't really affect us much. Gram and Pops were our parents."

Ahead of him, Thenia nodded as they continued to walk predominantly in silence, with her periodically pausing to study something or ask him a question. After a few minutes of meandering, Ashton saw the roof of the tiny house coming into view.

"Ah, there it is."

Both of them slightly increased their pace, and when the house fully came into view, Thenia gasped and placed her hand over her mouth.

"Oh, my god, it's beautiful."

"It is," Ashton agreed, proud of his Pops, who'd built most of it. "Would you like to see the inside?"

Thenia nodded vigorously, and he chuckled before gently nudging her forward with a hand on the small of her sun-warmed back.

A smallish gate separated the more extensive gardens from a simple one that led up to the thousand-square-foot home styled after a modern cottage. He'd made sure to check the condition of the space the day before and did a quick dusting while opening the windows to air it out. A delicate breeze drifted past them, and the sheer curtains drifted in and out of the open windows, playing keep-away with a few nearby plants and vines.

As they ambled up the path, Thenia grazed her fingers over the black lanterns with solar candles inside them. When she reached the front door, she hesitated and glanced over her shoulder at him.

"Go for it," he smiled.

She grinned and made an adorable squeak before opening the door into the entryway, which doubled as the dividing space between the cooking and wash areas ahead of them, the left and right living spaces, and a pair of staircases.

"This can't be real?" Thenia hadn't even stepped inside yet, her feet frozen on the outer threshold.

"I hope it is. I dusted the place yesterday. Either that, or I've had some really vivid dreams." Ashton said, teasing her, but he immediately shut his mouth, hoping his humor wouldn't offend her.

To his relief, she practically snorted and then smiled and finally stepped into the house. He followed her inside, and the room was comfortable for the two of them to fit. A third would make it cozy, but anything beyond that, and the space would feel cramped, which was what his Pops had intended. He'd build the home so that his children would have their privacy, not so that he and Gram would hover.

Thenia's eyes roamed the grey wooden floor, the dark paneled walls, the warm lights, and the soft fabrics and furnishings. He followed her as she meandered into the kitchen with its large windows, quartz countertops, and open shelving. She grazed the stainless steel fridge with her fingertips and ran her palm over the edge of the farm-style sink and onto the counter.

Ashton let her wander and gave her as much freedom as he could while remaining nearby to answer any questions that may come up as she explored. Due to the square footage of the tiny place, it naturally felt more intimate, and he, once again, didn't want to make her feel awkward, especially since he intended on begging her to accept the job if he had to.

Between her credentials, how she treated the small snake, and her curiosity about all the plants as they walked, he knew she was perfect. Not to mention, they seemed to get along reasonably well, at least after his earlier mistake. He could see himself feeling comfortable with her around, which was priceless to him. Ashton was the introvert of the family, and being able to exist with someone comfortably, even without talking, wasn't something to undervalue.

Thenia leaned into a small room off the kitchen, where the washer and dryer were located. Beyond that, another door led into the bathroom. He didn't have to follow her to know that it contained a walk-in shower, a claw-foot tub, and other necessary amenities.

Once she'd seen what she wanted, Thenia skipped past him, a blush on her cheeks as her eyes darted away from him. It almost felt like she was ashamed of being excited. Her file contained standard information, and beyond that, he refused to look up anything else or invade her privacy, so he was basically guessing.

She bypassed the narrow sets of stairs tucked on the left side of the front door and went up the flight of stairs on the right that led to the study. Half of the cozy room was at standing height, and the other half was beneath one side of the home's slanted roof line. Another large pair of windows looked out over the rear of the house and the cliff beyond. The room was furnished with relaxing seating, a small desk flanked by bookshelves, and a tiny wood-burning stove for warmth.

He heard Thenia gasp again, but it was only a minute or two longer before she bounced down the steps and proceeded to the other side of the house to explore the living room, outdoor patio area, and finally, the second-floor bedroom up the second flight of steps.

When she'd eventually had her fill of exploring, Thenia returned to the kitchen, where he'd sat at one of the three stools under a short bar counter to wait for her.

"What do you think?" Ashton asked. "Not too small?"

"Small!" she exclaimed. "It's perfect. This house will seriously spoil me for the rest of my life."

Something flashed in Thenia's eyes before she snapped her

mouth shut and glanced away, physically shrinking and closing her body off as she had earlier.

Ashton didn't want to pry, so he opted for what he hoped was a friendly laugh and said, "Well, good. I'm hoping you'll stay for a long time. This garden needs someone who cares about it and can care *for* it, and it's obvious that you can do both."

She nodded without turning back to him, so Ashton stuck out his hand a second time. "You in?"

There was a brief moment of hesitation before Thenia finally met his eyes and accepted his hand. The paleness of his sun-starved skin contrasted with her darker one, and her soft and slim fingers squeezed him gently.

"If you'll have me, I'd be honored."

He shook his head. "Nope. The honor's mine, Thenia. Thank you for taking my flyer."

She flushed but dropped her head slightly before murmuring low enough that he almost missed it.

"Try to put down roots a second time...."

Thenia Loris

It was nearly dark by the time Thenia unlocked Sara's apartment and shut the door, slumping against it. When she'd left that morning, Thenia hadn't expected her day to be as long and exhausting as it turned out to be. On top of that, she'd scarcely slept the night before due to nerves about meeting Ashton and her impending job interview. Now, she felt wrung out.

After they agreed that she'd accept the position, she roamed the gardens with Ashton, and he told her more about the grounds and how his grandfather had tended them. Truth be told, she had begun to get overwhelmed with all of it when Ashton mentioned there were a few books in the main house where his grandfather had written down notes, instructions, and other information. He promised to get them together for her and put them on the desk upstairs in the tiny house before she was scheduled to move into it the day after tomorrow.

Thenia groaned and dragged herself from the door, hauling herself further into the apartment, and greeted the plants before flopping onto the couch with a second groan. Eventually, she pulled her phone from her pocket and checked her messages. There was one from Sara, verifying she'd be home late in the evening tomorrow, and Thenia was free to go to bed without waiting up for her.

The second message was from Thenia's parents, checking in to see if she'd decided on her plans once Sara returned home. Thenia was too exhausted to respond and made a mental note to do it in the morning before she began packing.

She tugged off her shoes and got more comfortable on the couch. It was late enough that she should probably get up and eat something, but it could wait a few more minutes.

Her phone beeped, and she noticed a text message from Ashton.

I hope you got back to your place safely. I found the books Pops left. One looks like a planting schedule, and the other looks like a bunch of formulas, so I'll leave that one for you to decipher.

Thenia snorted. "Likely fertilizer mixtures or soil compositions."

Thank you. That will be extremely helpful.

She hit send, and her phone beeped again less than a minute later.

I'm sorry if I offended you today or made you uncomfortable. I was trying to do the opposite, but I forget that my job often has a certain...connotation for others. I just wanted you to be able to be yourself and not have to hide like we have to so often. I'm sorry again.

Thenia closed her eyes and sniffled.

She wasn't even sure who Thenia was anymore. After so

many years of existing, stifled and smothered by Lucus, she'd lost everything. It had taken her weeks to figure out something as uncomplicated as what coffee she enjoyed.

The answer was none. Black tea iced, no matter what the weather was. That's what she preferred, but even a detail that meaningless took so much effort to figure out. What clothes did she like? What did she like to do in her spare time? Did she like baths or showers?

Each decision she encountered required her to stop and evaluate it. Otherwise, her reflexive answers were whatever Lucus had wanted or, *No, thank you, I can't.* Well, now she could, and she would.

Her phone beeped again.

And here I go, bringing it up again and sticking my foot further in my mouth. Thank you again, Thenia, for accepting. I'll see you in a few days. I'm here if you have questions.

"Questions, huh? Fine, how do I get myself back? Where do I learn what I think?" she sighed, dropped her phone on her chest, and flung an arm over her eyes.

She must have dozed because a handful of grow lights clicked on when their timers were activated, and Thenia blinked into a darkened room. Her phone was still on her sternum, and she glanced at it before pulling up her chat with Ashton, now with extra guilt over falling asleep on him and causing him to second-guess himself.

You surprised me, not offended. I've had to hide what I am for most of my life, and it's only recently that...well, it doesn't really matter. Just know I appreciate the acceptance, and I'll work on not making you feel like you did something wrong.

Thenia tossed her phone on the couch before sitting up and rubbing the sleep out of her eyes. Then, she wandered into the kitchen to find something to eat.

It wasn't until she retrieved her phone on her way to bed that she saw she had another message.

Thenia, when will you stop this and talk to me? Are you really going to throw away over a decade because of a small misunderstanding? I told you I thought about it and changed my mind. Call me. Tomorrow. Or I'll come to get you myself.

She immediately recoiled from the device, which tumbled from her hand and clattered on the wood floor before the screen dimmed. After what felt like two seconds and two years simultaneously, she approached her laptop, abandoning her phone where it landed. She opened the new email she'd created after leaving Lucus, and the only one she currently used. Her thread with Ashton was up, and she immediately typed him a message.

I broke my phone. If you need me, I have my laptop and will continue to check my email. Sorry.

After hitting send, she proceeded to get ready for bed, moving pointedly around her cell phone and leaving it where it was. At one point, she stopped to throw a towel over the camera that was still facing up. Then, she crawled underneath the covers, turned off the lights, and buried her face in a pillow.

There was one thing over the last few months that Thenia had learned about herself, and she was one hundred percent confident of something that she didn't like.

Lucus.

Chapter 3: Lonely and Alone

May 2024, Maine, USA | Thenia Loris

Thenia pulled her suitcase and backpack from the trunk of the sedan she'd taken to Ashton's before gently dropping it shut. The driver was a quiet, balding man who was more interested in listening to sports radio than carrying on a conversation with her. He waited until she stepped away and then drove off without a word or backward glance. She wasn't in the mood to talk to anyone anyway, so the silence hadn't bothered her.

As on the other day, before she could enter the gate code, it began to open once she was near enough to it. Now that she knew that Ashton was a mechanite, she was less surprised, and he'd likely seen who was in his driveway and opened it himself. He'd already told her the property had various cameras and sensors, and that he'd show her everything after she settled in. Even though he'd assured her that the security was mostly a precaution for him due to his job and his grandmother's before him, Thenia was relieved to know it was there all the same. She didn't expect Lucus to find her, but it made her feel better either way. Especially after his message two days prior.

When she heard soft footsteps, she glanced up and saw

Ashton jogging toward her, his charming and cheery smile on his face.

"Thenia!"

"Hey," she smiled and hiked her backpack higher up onto her shoulder.

"Sorry, I was planning on being out here when you arrived, but I got distracted."

"No problem. I've only been here a minute. My car just left."

Ashton's eyes flicked between her two bags, and he frowned slightly. "Is this all you have?"

"It is," she said, turning her face away from the disapproving stare he'd likely give her.

It felt like Ashton was going to comment, but he reached for her backpack strap instead.

"Then let me carry this one?"

She looked from his hand to his genuine expression and then nodded slightly before relinquishing the bag to him.

"Thanks," she said softly, inwardly admitting she'd been wrong in her assumption.

"Of course."

They began walking up the driveway together, their only conversation consisting of the scuffling of their shoes and the clacking of her rolling suitcase. When they reached the dirt path, Ashton reached out and touched her forearm, shaking his head.

"There's a paved path connecting the back of the main house and the front of yours. It will be much easier on your suitcase and arm if we take that one. Besides, I can show you the best place on the property on the way."

His eyes sparkled with delight, and Thenia had to admit she was completely curious about what he was talking about from his child-like glee alone.

"Okay, lead on."

"I'll show you more of the main house later, and you're

welcome to use it as your own, by the way. Kitchen, library, whatever. Think of it as an extension of your own."

"Oh, are you sure you're okay with that?"

"Absolutely. You'll see. The few rooms we were in the other day were a small portion. Gram and Pops realized very early that two mechanite children and one panther paranam kid needed a lot of space to grow, not to mention get into mischief. I swear, half the rooms we have are duplicates because they needed one that was livable while they cleaned up after our chaos in the other. Then we'd swap and do it all over again."

Thenia smiled slightly. "I don't have any siblings, so I don't quite understand, but I can imagine."

"Only child, huh?"

"I am."

"Sounds..." Ashton trailed off.

"Lonely," Thenia offered.

"I was going to say boring."

She chuckled. "Well, yeah, a bit of that, too, I guess. I'm not much like my parents. They are more like you, so it wasn't boring for me."

"Like me?" Ashton asked, leading her up the porch steps and smirking at her over his shoulder.

Thenia felt her cheeks flush, and she kicked herself for saying aloud what she'd been thinking.

"Ah...yeah. Um, energetic. Bright. Personable."

Ashton didn't respond, but she saw him frown in one of the window's reflections as they passed it, and she quickly shifted her eyes away from the vulnerable display of emotion.

He led her around the front and side of the main house, and when they were at the back, she saw another small set of steps that led down to a path paved with stones that matched the driveway. It was a few feet wide and snaked off into the gardens and into the distance.

"Here," Ashton said, stopping at the top of the steps but

facing toward the house, not into the gardens. "Eileen and Xander spent a lot of time out here. Especially when he was in his panther form."

Thenia followed where Ashton was looking and saw a wooden platform hanging from the rafters by four thick chains. On top of the platform was a mattress with sheets, pillows, and what looked like a remote sticking out from under a throw blanket.

"What do you think?"

She left her bag where it was, walked over to the bed swing, and gently ran her fingers down one of the slightly warm chains.

"This is...."

"The best spot in the house. Reading, conversation, nap, whatever. All of it's good. Eileen used to read to Xander while he had paws."

Thenia chuckled at Ashton's silly humor.

"I studied out here for most of my school years, rain or snow. Didn't matter. And Gram would often read while Pops worked in the garden on her days off."

"Sounds wonderful."

"It is, and I hope you'll use it. Being selfish..." Ashton trailed off, and Thenia glanced at him and saw his bright smile had been swapped with a sorrowful frown. "It's a bit disused these days."

She walked over to him at the top of the steps and smiled. "Thank you. I will."

Ashton studied her for a few seconds and then nodded ever so slightly. "I'm glad." Then he cleared his throat and gestured for her to go down the steps and to the path. "It only goes to your place, so lead on."

Without giving herself time for second thoughts...or twelfth thoughts.... Thenia lifted her bag down the stairs and began the last leg of their walk to her new home.

Ashton Giri

Ashton stared at Thenia's ponytail, swaying as she walked down the stone path to her new house. When he'd seen how little she had brought with her, he'd momentarily wanted to question her about it, but again, she closed herself off as if he was planning on scolding her. It felt like she was mentally and physically preparing for a lecture when he only wanted to reassure her that anything she had was welcome. With her reaction, he did the only thing that came to mind and brought her to the outdoor bed swing his Pops had installed decades earlier.

Ashton wasn't exaggerating when he said it was the place in the house that the five of them fought over. It was also true that it'd been rarely used lately, and when he did use it, reality would seep in again, reminding him of all he'd lost, so he never stayed long.

"Oh, Ashton, I have a question," Thenia said, pulling him from his mind.

"Hmm?"

"Groceries. I don't have a car. Would it be alright if I had supplies delivered?"

"Doesn't bother me at all. That said, you're welcome to go with me when I head into town, or you can use the car whenever you need to. I'm pretty much a homebody and have to set a reminder to drive it around the block occasionally. Well," he winced, "that's assuming you can drive. Sorry, I should have asked, not assumed."

She shifted only a little, but he could see her soft smile. "I can, yes. Thank you, and please let me know when you go. I'd love to join you."

"You got it."

He glanced past her as they neared the house, and she followed his eyes to see what had grabbed his attention. When she saw the house, she paused for a second. Then she took a deep breath and continued down the path and up to the small dividing wall, but she abruptly stopped short and smiled down.

"Oh, hello, little one," Thenia said, and Ashton saw the tiny green snake on the wall, curled up in the sun in a tight coil. "Sunny day, huh?"

The snake flicked its tongue, and Thenia chuckled.

"Well, I'm going to unpack, but if I finish before it gets dark, I'll come say hello if you're still here. Okay?"

Ashton watched as the snake flicked its tongue again and then blinked a few times before settling down to rest, apparently willing to wait for Thenia to finish what she needed to.

Thenia smirked at him and then continued up to the front door.

As he approached the snake, Ashton glanced down and saw it staring at him, but it hadn't lifted its head to greet him like it had Thenia. "Hey, friend," he said as he passed it. "Give her a good welcome, would you?"

He heard Thenia open the front door, holding it for him as he followed her inside. Then he settled her backpack on the kitchen counter and stepped out of the way.

"Thanks for carrying that," she said with a smile while she tucked her suitcase as close to the stairs up to the bedroom as she could so neither of them would trip over it.

"No problem. I put a few things in the fridge and pantry for you. Some staples and produce, but I hope you're not allergic to anything because I just realized I'd forgotten to ask."

Thenia stared at him again for a second and then shook her head adamantly. "No, I'm not, and thank you. I prefer to stick to vegetarian food, but only if it doesn't cause trouble."

"Won't bother me. Do what makes you happy. Ignore the meat in the freezer, and I'll put it back in the main house eventually." What he said must have been the wrong thing again, and she nearly suppressed a flinch, but not fully. He quickly added, "You should be set for a day or two. We can go into town and pick up what you'd like whenever you're ready."

"What I like…" she trailed off, staring at the fridge.

Not for the first time, he wanted to ask what had made her upset, but he didn't. It felt like nothing he said was right, but he didn't know what was wrong to avoid it.

"Oh, ah, did you need to get a new phone? Or is it something I may be able to help with?"

He'd forgotten until then that she'd emailed and said she'd broken it a few nights prior. Something about the whole thing felt off when she'd emailed him, and he wanted to be careful when bringing it up. But again, he clearly said the wrong thing and must have stumbled into another one of those difficult conversations when Thenia abruptly stiffened and lowered her head before she shook it.

"No. It's fine. I have my computer. Thank you for the kind offer, though."

"Thenia?"

"Yes?" she answered, her eyes still lowered to the floor.

He stepped closer and raised his hand to touch her arm, but then he dropped it and stepped back. His words seemed to hurt her, so until he knew more, he needed to be careful. He had no idea how she'd react to touch, even benign ones, and he couldn't risk running her off.

"Let me know if that changes. I'm happy to help."

She nodded, but whatever he'd brought up had darkened her mood, and he gritted his teeth at the entire situation.

"Alright, well, I will get out of your way. Come get me if you need me, or send me an email. I'll come right down."

"Thank you."

She still wouldn't look at him, and Ashton could feel himself getting upset at who or whatever had made her feel so…small? Intrusive? He wasn't sure what she was feeling, but her discomfort was evident, and the last thing he'd wanted was to be the cause of it.

He nodded once and walked to the front door. Before he pulled it open, he stopped to look at her one more time.

"Thenia, thank you for being here."

He didn't wait for her to reply and hoped that giving her space would erase whatever thoughts he'd brought to the surface. Instead, he pulled the door shut behind himself and shoved his hands into his back pockets as he walked down the front path, but he stopped at the snake, still curled up contentedly on the wall.

"I'm not sure if you can understand this, but," he glanced back at the house behind him and then back to the snake, "come get me if she needs anything and won't come herself."

The little snake flicked its tongue and tipped its head to the side.

"She's...guarded. I don't know who or what hurt her, but I'm afraid she won't ask for help if she needs it."

The snake blinked once and lowered its head to rest on its body once again.

"Gonna take that as a yes." He sighed, "Thanks."

Ashton didn't want to leave Thenia in the state of mind he'd unintentionally put her in, but he made his way back through the gardens and up to the main house anyway. When he was back on the porch, he stopped at the foot of the hanging bed and rubbed his face roughly with his palms. Then, he shoved his emotions down and went inside via a door just off to the side of the swing.

That specific patio door led into the living room, and he walked over to a well-loved couch and sank into it. His phone dug into his hip from inside his jeans, and he retrieved it and sent a message to his sister and Xander.

Thenia's moved in. One suitcase and a backpack and...there's something she's...dealing with. I don't know what it is, though. Oh, and we saw the snake again. Was on the wall by Thenia's house, waiting there to greet her, I think.

Ashton dropped his hand into his lap, and his eyes slowly surveyed the large room. There were family photos on the walls, framed art from their childhood, and handmade pottery, boxes, and other odds and ends tucked into shelves. Two sturdy oak bookcases flanked the fireplace, and a television hung above it. One side was filled with DVDs, and the other had an extremely eclectic grouping of books.

When he reached over and pulled a pillow into his lap, it was one that Gram had embroidered. He ran his fingers over the beautiful threads that depicted some plant his Pops had been fond of.

The screen of his phone flashed, drawing his attention, and he saw a message from Eileen.

Don't pry, Ash. I'm glad she's settled, though, and Pops' snake is with her. It sounds like they both may need some company.

Ashton unlaced his high-tops, dropped them to the floor, and swung his legs onto the couch. He stared at the pillow he held one more time before he flopped it over his face so he could hide beneath it.

Something beeped extremely loudly in Ashton's ear, and he nearly yelped as it woke him from his unintended self-pity nap.

"Shit."

He blinked several times and checked the security cameras scattered around the property when they continued to nag him about an oddity. A few sensors around the perimeter of the property had been triggered, and he pulled one of the camera feeds up in an application on his phone and selected a recorded clip from a few minutes earlier. He hit play and saw Thenia walking among the gardens with a notebook in her hand, scribbling furiously in it. She stopped and looked closer at a few plants before sketching them quickly.

After a quick check, he confirmed that all of the other notifications were from Thenia triggering them. Calmed by the fact that nothing was amiss, Ashton used the footage the system had captured to teach it that the newest resident wasn't a threat and to treat her as it did him. That would quiet the alerts specific to Thenia, and he would feel less like a creeper every time he checked on any of the system's oddities.

Ashton pushed himself into a sitting position and was shocked to see he'd been asleep for a few hours, not just a few minutes. With a groan, he got to his feet and wandered into his bedroom, checking his email as he went. A message from Thenia surprised him, and he stopped in the middle of the hallway to open it.

Thank you again for today and...I'm sorry for how I acted. It won't happen again.

Ashton gritted his teeth and ran his fingers through his blonde hair. "What the hell does that mean?"

That was the second time she'd apologized or implied she had done something wrong—which she hadn't. He replied, knowing she was in the gardens and wouldn't see the message until she returned home.

Thenia, you did nothing wrong. You don't have anything to apologize for, and you're welcome. Do you need anything?

After sending the message, he took screenshots of their conversation and sent them to Eileen.

See. What the hell do I do? The last thing I want to do is make her uncomfortable or have her leave because of a misunderstanding.

Ashton finished the short walk into his room and tossed his phone on the large bed as he walked past. It sank deeper into the dark blue comforter and nearly disappeared amongst the fluff. He went directly into his closet and got undressed. Then he went to shower in the bathroom attached to his room, which Jack-and-Jilled with Xander's on the other side.

Gram and Pops' house hadn't changed since they'd passed.

Neither he nor Eileen nor Xander had been up to it yet, but Ashton knew it was something he couldn't put off forever. Eventually, he'd have to go through each room and make some decisions. Realistically, he should take the master bedroom and move out of his childhood one, but that was another thing he wasn't ready for yet.

He stepped into the bathtub and, under the water, which he hadn't checked the temperature of in his mental wallowing, he hissed as the ice-cold water contacted his skin.

"Oh, for fuck sake."

He flinched back and hastily adjusted the taps, failing to suppress a shiver. Once the water wouldn't give him hypothermia, he quickly showered and got out. With the bathroom quiet, he heard his phone chime in the other room. He wrapped a towel around his waist and then grabbed a second one to dry his hair as he walked.

Ash, have you looked her up? You're going to need to be patient with her.

After reading his sister's message, Ashton's skin went colder than when he had stepped under the frozen spray.

I did a check in the database for her, but that was it. Didn't want to invade her privacy.

He didn't put his phone down. Instead, he stood in the middle of his room, dripping on the carpet while staring at the screen, waiting for a response.

I agree. Look into Lucus Garv. If you stay on the surface, you'll find enough. I don't recommend saying anything to her about what you see, but it may help you understand how to approach her.

Thanks. I appreciate it.

As he walked by, he set his phone on a table and quickly threw on a clean pair of jeans and a long-sleeved t-shirt before hanging up his towels. No matter what the temperature was outside, he kept the office chilly to counter the heat his rigs gave off, so he retrieved a hoodie and his phone on his way out the door. He went further down the hall to what was once his Gram's office but was now his own.

The blue glow of the various screens greeted him, and he shut the door behind himself, blocking out the yellow-tinted light from the hallway. He slipped into a comfortable desk chair and swiveled to face his computer tower.

"Let's do this the fast way."

Ashton grinned and reached up to rest his palm on the side of his machine, making sure to contact an exposed section of the motherboard with his fingertip. A slight shock raced up his palm and through his blood as he connected with the machine, and then he heard the familiar hum in his mind. He closed his eyes, more out of habit than necessity, and pictured the name Lucus Garv in the language of the mechanical.

Instantly, his mind filled with images of a well-dressed man and a beautiful Thenia on his arm. Picture after picture surfaced. One was from a hospital fundraiser, one was from an awards ceremony, and a few were from what looked like high-profile dinners with government officials. Lucus was smiling like a jackal in all of them, and Thenia was a few steps behind him, her smile forced and empty. She never looked at Lucus, and her eyes were more often downcast than visible.

Ashton switched to newspaper and internet articles and was buffeted with dozens of articles about the wealthy malpractice attorney and New Jersey's most eligible bachelor. There were gossip columns mentioning Thenia, the quiet, plain-looking woman Lucus often had with him, and who most theorized was his personal assistant or secretary—until the last article. It was a wedding announcement for the two of them that had shocked many and angered even more.

After that, the media attention shifted to Thenia, focusing on her history. Ashton skipped those and pivoted back to Lucus. The date on the announcement article was less than six months earlier, and there wasn't anything after that except speculation pieces about the wedding having been called off because Thenia was an adulterer, gold digger, or many other defamatory assumptions.

Ashton was about to stop when an internet blog page flashed to the front of the metaphorical pile, specifically about Thenia. He ignored it, but it was brought to the front again—twice more.

Fine, I get it, Ashton replied in the language the machines understood.

He checked the blog but didn't recognize it, assuming it was small or local to New Jersey. The article had no pictures and only mentioned Thenia by her first name.

While those out there seem to pine over the wealthy "eligible bachelor," Lucus Garv, only one knows the truth behind that white smile and smug exterior. The woman always in his shadow—his fiancée, Thenia. A quiet and highly intelligent woman....

The blog provided more background on Thenia, so Ashton skipped most of it.

The truth behind the well-covered windows is, in fact, a relationship based on control and gaslighting. The young woman is forced to follow a strict diet and exercise plan, with her every decision chosen by Mr. Garv, and with no regard for her own wants or opinions, leaving her alone with a version of herself that he has so carefully constructed.

Ashton felt the edge of his computer case cut into his palm from where he'd squeezed it tighter in his anger. He skimmed the rest of the post and stopped on the last section.

While the relationship may appear idyllic on the surface and to any outsiders, these well-crafted circumstances only benefit Lucus Garv, who has manipulated this vibrant woman and remolded her into the image he desires. There is no evidence that this abuse extends to physical harm, but in my opinion, that line is not far from the current ones he has already crossed.

Ashton thanked the machine and pulled himself back into

his office, where his body sat in the chair. When he pulled his hand away from the computer, he saw a thin slice along two of his fingers.

He clenched his fist closed and sent Eileen a message by merging with his watch just far enough under the surface that he didn't have to type.

I understand.

Chapter 4: Better Understanding

Thenia finished drying the bowl she'd used for breakfast and replaced it within the cabinet before hanging the dish towel on the hook to dry. She picked up a glass of water as she left the kitchen, went through the living space, and out a glass door leading to a small patio with a two-seater outdoor couch and two matching armchairs. A small table sat on one side of the couch, with a low coffee table between them. Thenia placed her cup on the side table before sitting down and pulling a book from the cushion beside her into her lap.

Ashton had done as he'd promised, and when Thenia went upstairs to the lounge space the day she moved in, she found three handwritten journals filled with garden notes and information on the small desk. The content was so dense that she'd spent the last two days reading one of the books and was barely halfway through it.

She'd gotten into the habit of taking one journal with her, along with a blank notebook she'd found on the bookshelf, and wandering the grounds getting to know what was planted where and checking on anything needing urgent attention. Thankfully, it hadn't been too hot, and the mornings had been dewy enough that very few plants needed watering or tending. Grateful for the weather's buffer, she'd tried to study as fast as possible.

Only once had she run into Ashton since the day he walked her to the tiny house. They'd not been near enough to talk, but he smiled and waved at her, and she managed to wave back without screwing up again.

By the time she'd pulled herself from her head that first day, the man was already gone. She immediately realized what she'd done and emailed him to apologize.

She hadn't spoken to him since.

Movement at the edge of Thenia's vision made her glance down to where her laptop was resting, now uncovered since she still held the record book. The small green snake slithered onto the cushion and over to the center of the computer, before curling up and looking at Thenia.

That was another thing she'd been getting used to. The little creature visited her several times during the day and seemed to be checking in on her. It didn't bother her, but it was new, and truthfully, Thenia had spent most of the previous seven years with only herself and occasionally Lucus for company. Though the latter basically didn't count. Hell, even *she* didn't count. The version of Thenia that was with Lucus was blank. She'd been blank.

Something tickled the back of Thenia's hand, and she glanced back down to see the tiny tongue of the snake brushing her skin, the creature staring up at her.

"What's up?"

The snake lowered its tiny chin to her skin and continued to stare at her.

"Worried about me?" Thenia smiled and carefully rubbed the top of its head with the tip of her pinky finger. "I'm fine. It's over now."

The snake closed its eyes, but quickly opened them again when Thenia's laptop chimed beneath it.

"Oh, it's an email. Do you mind?" Thenia held out her hand, and the snake slithered into it, letting her move it to the back cushion of the couch instead.

Thenia opened her laptop and saw a message from Ashton.

Hey, were you still up for a run into town for groceries?

"Oh, I forgot about that."

Thenia quickly agreed and said she'd get ready to go and would meet him whenever he was headed out.

She looked at the snake again and smiled. "Guess I'm going into town for a while. You gonna stay here?"

The snake curled into a tight little coil and closed its eyes, answering Thenia's question.

"I'll see you in a bit, then. If you've not left by the time I get back."

She took her laptop, glass, and book back into the house and put them all on the counter in the kitchen before heading upstairs to quickly change her clothes and grab her boots. Once dressed, she went downstairs to the bathroom and finished getting ready. Ashton knocked on the front door just as she was putting her hair into a clip.

"Come in, Ashton," she called over her shoulder and turned off the light in the bathroom as she walked through the laundry room and back into the kitchen.

"Hey."

Ashton was leaning on the doorway wearing a pair of light jeans, tennis shoes, a hoodie, and a backward black hat.

"I didn't mean to rush you."

"Not at all. We were on the porch looking through the books you left."

"We?"

Thenia chuckled. "Sorry, yes. Seems your green snake needed company. It's been coming by a few times a day. I swear it's checking up on me."

Ashton's surprise was evident, and he smirked. "Interesting.

Maybe there was something more to Pops talking to it. Well, I'm glad you had company then."

She smiled and rinsed out her glass, and when she turned around, she saw Ashton staring at the stickers on her laptop. When he realized she'd caught him, he flushed, looked away, and rubbed the back of his neck.

"Sorry. I wasn't doing anything or anything."

"Didn't think you were," Thenia reassured. "Can you do anything without touching it anyway?"

"Ah, technically, yes, but only because it's connected to the internet, but I'd still need to touch something else. Cell phone, router, something like that."

"Glad I had my facts right. Sorry, I've only met a single mechanite before you."

He nodded, and she grabbed her laptop and slipped it into a drawer away from the prying eyes of possible intruders—not that she expected any.

"I, uh, like the stickers. My sister, Eileen, has a few on her own. A quote from her favorite book and a flower from her favorite video game."

Thenia grinned. "How neat. They probably make her smile when she sees them."

Ashton nodded. "Yeah. Eileen tends to appear as a blank slate to others, mostly when she's working, but those stickers are a small glimpse into her personality that she lets creep out."

Thenia paused, her hand hovering over her wallet, and she studied Ashton for a lie.

"Really?"

He nodded again. "Yeah. She and Xander work for some pretty influential people and are often sent into situations where being unobtrusive is ideal. At least in her case. She's more the hidden-in-plain-sight operative, and Xander is the clear protector."

"Sounds...lonely."

"They have each other."

"And you stayed here?" Thenia asked, knowing she was being nosy.

Ashton shrugged, but his warm smile returned. "Their life is too...chaotic for me. They visit."

Thenia nodded, but she couldn't help feeling sad that Ashton had been left all alone in the big family house, filled with nothing but memories for company.

"Well, ready to head out?"

"Yes," she nodded, stuck her wallet into her back pocket, and followed him out the front door. She'd already locked it, so she pulled it shut, knowing her key was buried in a nearby flower bed two feet down, and she'd retrieve it when she got back. Between not needing to carry keys and not having a cell phone, it meant all she needed was her wallet, and she could skip the whole purse thing.

"Do you mind me driving?" Ashton asked as she caught up and walked beside him.

"Nope. Thanks."

"No problem. Anywhere you want to go besides the grocery store?"

She shook her head. Even if she had wanted to go somewhere else, she'd not have bothered Ashton with it.

"Okay, well, if you think of anything, let me know. I don't mind."

When he smiled at her, she returned it but quickly stared back at the path ahead. She needed to pick up supplies and let him return to his day. He had better things to do than drive her around town for soap.

"Thanks for helping carry, Ashton," Thenia said as they reached the front door of her house, each of them carrying half a dozen bags.

"It's a pretty long walk, I don't mind."

She put her bags by the front door and stopped to look at him. "Do you have a key?"

"Uh, yes? But not on me, why?" he said hesitantly.

"Yours would have been faster to use, but that's fine."

She smiled and walked over to the flower bed where her key was buried, but when she knelt, she felt Ashton watching her, and she went still. When she peeked at him without turning her head, she was right, though if his expression was honest, it was one of confusion rather than annoyance.

Thenia stared at the soil, looked at her upturned palm, and then at the soil again.

"Do you want me to head back, or would you like me to stay and help unload?" Ashton asked calmly.

When she looked up at him, he wore a relaxed expression, and she narrowed her eyes. It felt like he knew more about her than he had the day she moved in, and she tried to recount their conversations to remember if she'd said anything she shouldn't have.

"Uh, it's fine. Um...either. Whichever you want, I mean." She continued to trip on her words until his shadow crossed her face before he crouched beside her.

"If you're uncomfortable, I can leave, but as you mentioned earlier, I've only met a handful of elemental witches. Considering it was for work, I've never seen one interacting with their element. Would you teach me?"

Thenia continued to stare at her palm, and after a full minute of trying to talk herself out of it, she nodded and placed her shaky hand on the dirt. Her voice cracked when she said the words that would shift the soil, and after she cleared her throat and tried again, she heard the soil respond.

"Is that a good sound?" Ashton whispered, but then covered his mouth with his hand. "Shit, sorry. Shutting up."

His outburst snapped something within Thenia, and she erupted into laughter as she reached into the soil for her key. The dirt moved away from her skin while simultaneously pushing the key toward the surface. When she had regained the key, she held it out in her palm for Ashton to see while she tried to catch her breath.

Ashton had started to laugh with her, but when he saw the key, he gently lifted her hand above him so he could investigate the back of it without forcing her to drop the key.

"There's no dirt."

She shook her head. "Nope. I basically aerated it so I could remove what was in it cleanly. I do it to plants too, so I can inspect their roots without damaging them."

He met her eyes with his own, and she was shocked silent by the awe in them.

"It's not very exci—"

"That's amazing. Not to mention, very helpful considering your work with plants. Seriously, that's really cool, Thenia."

She shut her mouth, and when she glanced at where he was still holding her hand with his own, he noticed and carefully let her go.

"Thank you for showing me. Really."

She could only close her hand around the cool metal and nod.

"Come on," Ashton said, getting to his feet and offering her a hand up. "We should get stuff put away before it gets too warm."

Thenia swallowed roughly and let him pull her to her feet. Once she unlocked the door, mostly in a stupor, she returned the key to the soil. They brought bags in without conversation, and while Ashton unpacked everything onto the counter, she put things away. It didn't take them long, and she was grateful for the help.

When they were finished, Ashton declined her offer of reciprocal assistance and thanked her for going with him. Before he left, he packed up what little meat he'd tucked into her freezer earlier in the week, and then he rushed back to the car to take his own purchases into the house.

After putting her wallet away and pulling off her boots, Thenia poked her head onto the back porch and checked to see if the snake was still there, but there was only a slight indent from where it had slept.

Thenia smiled and closed the door before going back inside.

It would be back.

Ashton Giri

After six hours in front of his keyboards, Ashton cracked a few knuckles in his fingers and rolled his neck.

"At least that's finished."

He pushed his chair back and groaned when he tried to stand and found that his left foot had apparently abandoned him at some point. With a few taps of the toe of his shoe on the floor, the tingling receded a bit, and he could limp toward the door and out into the hallway.

It had been a long time since he'd been given an assignment with that much work and such a tight deadline. Apparently, there had been a paranam who tried to suppress their beast's soul for too long and was forced to switch forms in the middle of their commute to work that morning. The whole situation had caused quite a mess, and the only saving grace was that the woman had been an avinam, or bird shifter. Even if Ashton was only responsible for scrubbing cameras and social media, and identifying Outsiders who needed to be visited by his more in-person colleagues, it was a lot to clean up. It also forced him to deprioritize his outstanding ID creation backlog, which meant he would have another long day tomorrow. That list never seemed to end, and it made sense considering there were quite a few magical species that lived much longer than humans and often needed updated identification to conceal their true age.

As he half walked, half limped, Ashton's limbs began to tingle less, and he made his way down the hallway and into the kitchen. He'd barely finished putting his shopping away from his outing with Thenia earlier in the day before work had called him in.

When he thought back to watching Thenia dig her key out of the ground, he grinned for the hundredth time since it happened. Ignoring the fact that what she'd done was just fucking cool, he was ecstatic that she'd done it in front of him in the first place. Her reaction when she realized he was still beside her and she needed to use her magic had him biting his tongue. He'd been torn between leaving her with her privacy and asking to stay and see what she would do. Ultimately, he left the decision up to her and was glad she'd let him observe her.

Ashton entered the kitchen and froze when he saw one of the exterior lights was on outside one of the windows. None of his alarms had triggered, so it was most likely that Thenia had turned it on for some reason. It wasn't worth chancing, though, so he left the interior lights off and crept into the living room and closer to the back door. When he was nearer, he saw the reading light was on above the swing bed, and Thenia was sitting cross-legged on it. One of his Pops' books was in front of her, and her notebook was in her lap where she was scribbling furiously.

He couldn't help but watch as she swapped between writing or sketching, with tapping her pen on her knee. When she stilled, Ashton held his breath and hoped she hadn't noticed him and wouldn't freak out, but instead, she muttered roughly to herself and robotically set the pen down in front of her. Then, she laced her fingers together and settled them in her lap while she returned to reading.

The entire series of movements felt raw, and he could see how much tighter Thenia was now holding herself as she worked. What surprised him the most was how angry he was about the entire change in demeanor. She was wearing a hoodie and what looked like pajama pants, with her hair in a messy bun on the top of her head. Why the hell did she need to be so poised?

Then he remembered what he'd read about her ex and his manipulation of everything she did, down to how she held herself publicly. He went from angry to feeling powerless so quickly that he knew he needed to leave her alone before he did something stupid.

It took every ounce of his willpower to back away from the window and not disturb her. Ashton continued backward until he felt his back hit a wall in the hallway, and he slid down to the ground. He tucked his knees to his chest as his heart tried to escape, and his emotions started to overwhelm him.

Whatever Thenia's ex had done to her, Ashton wanted to erase it. The woman he was getting to know was vibrant and full of life, and when she switched off, he wanted to beg her to switch back on. *That* Thenia smiled and laughed freely when they made small talk, she cared about a small green snake, and had listened to him when he'd asked her to use the swing bed.

The swing bed....

He hadn't expected seeing someone using the family's favorite spot would have affected him so strongly, but when Ashton stopped to think about it, he dropped his forehead onto his jeans.

"She was right. I was lonely being here alone."

He squeezed his eyes shut and sniffled, refusing to lose his shit over something so small. The light filtering through his legs dimmed, and he glanced up to see that the porch light had been turned off.

Ashton used his watch and merged with it to see through the cameras scattered throughout the property. When he saw Thenia walking home, he pulled himself from within the machine.

At least he wasn't alone anymore.

Chapter 5: Choices Made

June 2024, Maine, USA | Thenia Loris

Thenia ran the back of her hand across her sweaty forehead and sat back on her heels among a patch of wild strawberries. It was warm, the sky was clear, and when she glanced at the sun, she'd estimate she'd been in the garden until far past lunchtime. She studied the plants around her and was heartened by how much straighter they stood or how glossy their leaves were. Even some of the blooms looked fuller.

"I'm glad I did all that reading. Even if it took weeks to get through it."

The flicking of a small tongue brushed her cheek, and Thenia giggled at the tiny green snake who'd taken to curling around her ponytail while she worked in the garden.

"You think they look happy, too?" she asked, and the snake flicked its tongue a second time. "I'm glad. They were far from ncglcctcd, but they felt…sad."

A bee buzzed past Thenia, and she followed its lazy path with her eyes.

"Hey! Thenia!" Ashton called from where he appeared at the edge of the horizon.

She smiled and waved as he approached her.

When he got close enough, his eyes were drawn to the green snake, and he grinned even wider and laughed. "Well, that's one way to keep her company, that's for sure. Can't say it ever hung out in Pops' hair."

Thenia raised her pointer finger, and the little snake rested its chin on the fingertip. "Yup, I've had a beautiful hair tie most days these last few weeks."

"I'm glad." Ashton stopped on the path nearest her and slipped his hands into his jeans pockets. "I'm sorry about that, by the way."

"About what?" Thenia asked, getting to her feet and dusting off the knees of her jeans.

"Leaving you on your own for so long." He groaned. "That really makes it sound like I'm your boss, and that's not what I meant." Ashton rolled his eyes but still wore a smile. "Work's been crazy. I've been at my desk for fifteen hours a day pretty much constantly."

Thenia's eyes widened. "Wow, really? Are you eating at least?"

He chuckled. "Actually, that's why I came to find you. I've got some free time this afternoon and wanted to make one of my Pops' recipes for dinner, but it's formulated to feed an army of teenagers. Care to join me?"

"Oh," Thenia hesitated for a second, but before she could make an excuse, Ashton stopped her train of thought.

"Please? I really could use the company, and it's vegetarian."

She met his stare and felt her neck heat, and not because of the afternoon sun. "You remembered that?"

"Of course. It's important to you, or at least it seemed like it."

Thenia slowly nodded. "Alright. I'd love to. Thank you."

"Sweet, well then, I'll let you get back to it, and I'll see you at..." he trailed off and checked his watch, "Six?"

"What time is it now?"

"Three fifteen-ish."

"Perfect. I'll finish up here and then go clean up."

Ashton slipped his hands back into his pockets and waved at the little snake. "See you soon then. Have fun, you two."

Thenia saw the snake's tongue flick in her peripheral vision. Then Ashton left for the house along one of the dirt paths that Thenia now knew meandered around most of the grounds before finally arriving at the building. Once she could no longer see him, she picked up the small gardening shears from beside her foot and tucked them into her back pocket.

"Well, I think this area is good for today. Just needs water."

She carefully stepped over the plants and back onto the path before walking in the opposite direction from where Ashton went. The garden had water spigots at various intervals on the grounds, and Ashton's grandfather had a hose he'd transfer to each one when he needed to water a specific section. Thenia, on the other hand, didn't need the hose.

When she reached the nearest spout, she raised her hand for the snake to slither onto it.

"If you stay on this side, you won't get wet."

Thenia lowered her palm to a warm rock nearby, and the snake curled up on it to watch. When she turned on the water, it splattered directly down into a small section of drainage gravel. She recited the words to control the water, and instead of splattering on the floor, it began to drift upwards and hover above the plants as she indicated to each of them. Then, the water broke into smaller droplets and rained down over the foliage, gently hydrating the disturbed soil without flooding anything. Once everything was tended to, Thenia turned off the tap and yawned before laughing at herself.

"Well, maybe a shower and a nap are on my to-do list."

The snake blinked at her before it tucked its head into its coils, apparently agreeing with the nap idea.

"I'll see you later, I'm sure."

Thenia carefully ran her pointer finger over the snake's back before collecting her remaining supplies and walking to her house. She inspected plants as she wandered past them, but everything looked vibrant, and she was proud of herself. The last few weeks had been difficult, but she seemed to manage, even without Lucus.

When her mind drifted back to her ex, she realized her parents had emailed her a few days prior, and she'd forgotten to respond. Again.

"Shoot. After my shower," she mumbled, crossing into her home's small garden and putting away her tools in a small bin by the wall.

It was one of many that Arthur, Ashton's grandfather, had scattered through the property, though less regularly than the water spigots. Ashton had moved this one into her yard after she'd mentioned needing a closer place to put tools in one day, and every time she saw it, she still warmed at the sweet gesture.

Once everything was where it belonged, she entered the house and put her water bottle on the kitchen counter. Then, she went straight into the laundry room, stripped off her sweaty clothes, and shoved them into the washer on her way into the bathroom. She groaned when she caught her reflection in the mirror and saw the dirt smudged on her forehead, the leaves in her hair, and a small scratch on her cheek that she'd gotten at one point and not noticed.

"Presentable. Good job, Thenia. A mess, just like he always said you were."

She turned on the shower, and when the water was warm enough, she stepped under the spray and let it work some of the stress out of her shoulders as it washed away the dirt, leaves, and shame hidden beneath it all.

Thenia stretched and glanced at the clock on the wall opposite the bed.

"Five-thirty, damn. I got lucky."

She scooched over on the bed and out from under where the

roofline slanted above her, sat up, and brushed the sleep from her eyes. When she'd first moved in, Thenia hadn't moved any furniture around except in the bedroom. The space was tight, and since she wouldn't have a bed partner again anytime soon, she'd shoved the bed against the wall where the roof slanted. The juncture between the wall and the ceiling met at her chin's height, so she barely had to duck if she stood against the wall. With the bed moved out of the way, she had shifted other objects around to give herself a more extensive section of floor space at the foot of the bed. It was the only ample space in the tiny house, and she used it to stretch, do yoga, and spread papers and Arthur's journal entries around her.

Thenia drug her fingers through her damp hair and saw her laptop on the bedside table, from where she'd put it after her shower. She'd intended to email her parents, but apparently, she fell asleep instead.

"Let's just do this before I forget. Again," she said, rolling her eyes at her incompetence.

The message from her mom was still the top one in her inbox, and Thenia opened it to reply.

Hey Mom,

Sorry, everything's fine. I'm getting used to the various plants, and the house is perfect for me. I haven't seen much of Ashton, but he asked me to eat with him tonight. I guess he's been swamped with work the last few weeks.

I'm fine, really. I'm happy here. I hope you and Dad are having a great time. I'll include the address for the main house. Please don't send me anything extravagant. Just a postcard would be perfect.

I love you, Thenia

She hit send and closed her laptop with a soft snap.

"That should placate them for a little while, and I hope she doesn't send anything like the last time."

Thenia remembered the last letter her parents had sent her, along with the handmade table they'd shipped from Australia.

She'd left the table and everything else she owned when she'd walked out on Lucus and her former life. It was a beautiful piece of furniture, and it was a shame she'd had to leave it, but at least it was safely in her family home and not at the apartment she'd shared with Lucus.

"It doesn't matter," she scolded, and then went downstairs and into the bathroom to fix her bedhead and apply a little makeup.

She wore comfortable jeans, flats, and a nice sweater. Nothing fancy, but better than her gardening clothes. By the time she was ready, she had only a few minutes to make it up to the main house without being late, so she skipped out the front door and headed down to the paved path that led to the bed swing and the back porch.

When she walked up the porch steps, the smell of garlic washed over her, making her mouth water instantly. Thenia stopped, closed her eyes, and grinned as she took a deep breath. Since she hadn't eaten since breakfast, her stomach screamed, and she opened her eyes and knocked softly on the back door.

"Come in," Ashton called out.

Thenia opened the door and entered a room she'd not seen yet. It was a living room decorated as if a large family full of kids still lived within it. Pictures lined the walls beside handmade artwork, and the durable but cozy furniture all but begged for her to sink into it. What caught her eye first, though, were the two dozen pillows tucked around the room, embroidered with differing plants and flowers.

"Hey," Ashton said, but stopped short, and she turned to find he was staring at her.

"What?"

He shook his head and smiled. "Sorry. Nothing. Come this way, it's almost finished."

She followed where he led, which was into a large kitchen with a beat-up table that had seen many meals over the years, from what she could tell. When she saw a few bite marks on one of the table's wooden legs, she had to suppress a giggle, knowing the family had never owned a dog.

"I hope pasta is alright. Garlic, broccoli, shallots, and a cream sauce with cheese."

Thenia nodded and tried not to drool. "Yes, it smells amazing."

Ashton smiled and stirred a large pot on the stove.

"Can I help?"

"Sure," he pointed to a cabinet near her. "Wanna grab plates and cups? If you'd prefer, there are wine glasses in the one to the left."

Thenia did as requested, but she hesitated when it came to their drink choices. Lucus hadn't allowed her to drink. Instead, whenever they were in public, she had to carry around the glass to be polite, but she was never allowed to drink it.

"Do you like wine?" Ashton asked from the stove where he was still stirring.

"Um," Thenia didn't turn around. "I...I've.... It's been a long time since I've had any alcohol, so I'm not sure."

"No problem. Would you like to try a glass? If you don't like it, we can pick something else. I'm not a big drinker, so it's up to you. I can take it or leave it."

She didn't answer right away, but she heard Ashton approaching her. When he stopped beside her, he held out a bottle of white wine.

"How about this, try smelling it first. If you think it smells worth a try, I'll pour you a little."

He opened the bottle and held it closer to her, but he didn't encroach on her space or make her uncomfortable. Without looking up at him, she leaned forward and inhaled. The fragrance was crisp, fruity, and slightly tart. It tickled her nose a bit, too.

"What do you think?"

Thenia stepped back and nodded slightly.

"I'm glad you like it. This is Eileen's favorite, and there is one bottle left from the last time she and Xander were home."

Ashton opened a cupboard, pulled down a wine glass, and poured little more than a tablespoon into it. Then he put the bottle and the glass on the counter and walked back to the stove, his back to her.

"Feel free to try it if you want. This is almost finished."

She watched his back as he left her space to decide what she wanted to do, and then she stared at the glass. This wine did smell good, unlike any of the wines that she'd had to use as a prop. Her hand shook as she reached for the glass, and she lowered it back to her side. No, Lucus would—

"Stop it, Thenia," she whispered and reached out for the glass, putting it to her lips and downing the small amount of wine before she could stop herself.

It tasted like it had smelled, but the grape flavor was a little stronger, and it was slightly astringent on her tongue. She...liked it.

"Thoughts?" Ashton said, carrying over the pot and beginning to serve up their two portions in the bowls she'd pulled out.

She nodded and replaced the glass on the counter.

"I'm glad. You can have as much as you want, though I would caution, if you've not had any alcohol in a long time, you'll probably feel it harder, with less." He smiled, "Up to you, though." He held out the ladle to her. "Want to finish serving, and I'll pour us each a glass?"

"Sure," she said in a small voice, but did as he asked.

Then she realized he'd left the decision to drink up to her. Ashton hadn't told her what to do. The epiphany had a slight smile creeping up to her lips, and she felt butterflies in her core.

She'd made the right call to accept Ashton's invitation to dinner.

Ashton Giri

A crack of thunder made Ashton jump, gripping the plate he held tighter. He was washing dishes at the kitchen sink after Thenia had left nearly an hour earlier. They'd shared a meal, a glass of wine each, and talked for a while. She seemed to handle the alcohol relatively well, but Ashton had used the cameras to keep an eye on her when she walked home to make sure she made it back alright.

Then he'd flopped on the couch and replayed the night in his head—at least three times.

Eventually, he'd gotten up to clean the kitchen and put away the mountain of leftovers.

The sky outside flashed, followed by another crash of thunder, but this time he was ready for it.

"Damn. Summer storm."

He couldn't help but smile when he remembered a teenage Eileen running around the driveway with Xander in his panther form chasing behind her. Ashton stayed on the porch with his Gram and Pops and watched them get soaked to the bone. Eileen had ended up sick a few days later, but she swore it was worth it. Xander had felt guilty and didn't leave her side for a week, not that he would have even without the guilt. They had always been inseparable.

With the last dish washed, Ashton dried his hands and leaned against the counter while he texted his sister.

Dinner went well. She had a glass of wine. Apparently, all those pictures at fancy parties where she had a glass in her hand were staged. She hadn't had alcohol in years. The more I learn about that bastard, the more I want to kick his ass.

Another flash filled the room, and Ashton looked out the window as the sky finally opened up, and it started pouring.

It had been nearly a season since anyone had needed the generators, so he probably should go out to check them. He pushed away from the counter and put his phone into his back pocket. He exited the house via the back door, and while he was beneath the overhang, shielded from the rain, Ashton inhaled the specific smell that the first summer rain always carried with it. He loved the rain and felt himself relaxing as he followed the porch around to the front of the house. The last portion of the walk forced him to jog through the rain a short distance to reach the area behind the garage. Even though he was only out in the open for less than a minute, Ashton ended up drenched, but he only grinned up at the clouds harder.

It didn't take him long to flip on the generator's circuits and check the program to ensure the main house and Thenia's were covered in case of an outage. Both could run at full capacity for an hour with minimal fuss if they lost main power, but if he only used the necessities at the main house, they could stay powered for twelve hours before he needed to switch to the primary solar backup.

When he was satisfied that everything was hooked up correctly and they'd make it through the night if necessary, Ashton dashed back to the front porch and went inside to dry off and warm up.

Once the door was closed and locked, he sent Thenia an email.

I've made sure the generators are ready in case we lose power. If you need anything, come up to the main house or email me, and I'll come down. Thank you for coming for dinner. I had a great time. Sleep well, Thenia.

Once he'd sent the message, he read the reply from his sister, except this time it was from Xander.

Be careful, dude. Guys like that don't let go of what they have so easily. Keep the cameras on. Eileen agrees, but she's passed out after our thirty-six-hour assignment.

Ashton chuckled at the pair and wondered if they'd ever get over their sibling mentality and get together. Even if they didn't,

Xander was family and always would be, but at this point, Ashton hoped they'd hurry up already.

Will do, man. Stay safe and whack her with a pillow when she wakes up for me.

Ashton pressed his palm on the smart light switch beside him and turned off everything in the house except the office, essential appliances, and low-power guide lights along the floor in the hallways.

He looked down at his wet jeans and pulled his soaked long-sleeved shirt over his head as he walked through the dark house to his room and a warm shower.

Thenia Loris

Thenia had been dozing on the couch in the upstairs lounge area when a clatter of thunder and her own yelp woke her. She pressed her palm to her racing heart as the dark room was lit for a fraction of a second when lightning filled the sky. Less than a dozen seconds later, the thunder rattled the windows again, and she gazed up at the ceiling. When the rain started, it was so heavy that even she was impressed with her elemental partner.

"It feels like hot chocolate weather. I wonder what Ashton's do—"

She rolled her eyes at herself.

"It doesn't matter what he's doing, Thenia. Leave it alone."

As she continued to scold herself, she went to the kitchen and poured milk into a small saucepan to heat up on the stovetop. Then, she dug through the cabinets and looked for chocolate. She'd seen a tin of hot chocolate mix, a few boxes of tea, and a bag of coffee beans the day she'd moved in, but hadn't thought about any of it since that first day.

Once she found what she was looking for, she pulled out a large mug and a spoon, then leaned against the sink and stared out the window into the rain.

"It's pretty...in a violent way," she muttered to no one.

When she realized she was alone, she froze, and her heart began to race.

"Oh no, the snake!" Thenia started pacing in front of the sink and frantically attempted to remember how snakes behaved in rainstorms.

"Think, Thenia. Do they like rain? Yes, I think, but this one seems to like to stay dry. What about thunder and lightning?"

She bumped her hip on the edge of the counter, and the dull pain refocused her.

"Okay, I'll go look for her."

Thenia turned the stove off, yanked her coat from beside the door, and stomped into her boots. Neither were waterproof, but they were better than nothing and would have to do. As soon as she stepped out from under the roofline, she knew the jacket was a waste of time, as the rain immediately saturated it.

"It doesn't matter. Now, where would it be?"

She jogged down the path, her eyes scanning for a slight pop of green color hidden amongst the dark foliage.

"Check the usual places first."

When she reached the garden wall, Thenia extracted one of the solar candles from its holder and bolted into the rain with it.

Thenia had been searching for nearly an hour but still had no idea where the little snake was. She, on the other hand, was shivering, soaking wet down to her underwear, and exhausted. It broke her heart, but when she sneezed and realized that she couldn't feel her fingers, Thenia had to admit that she wouldn't find it.

"I real...ly hope you...re okay."

Her teeth chattered so violently that she bit her tongue and clenched her jaw closed to prevent herself from doing it again. As she slogged along the last bit of the path back to her house, her search having taken her in a loop, Thenia was thankful she wasn't far from home.

She replaced the candle in the holder as she passed it, and once she was under the eaves of the house again, she admitted her shoulders were sore from huddling into herself against the cold, not to mention the headache that was noticeable now that the bright lights were in her eyes.

Could she have blocked the rain from reaching her? Yes, except she had brushed off how hard it was storming. Now that she noticed the size of the drops and their strength, which was extremely apparent by her soddenness and lowered body temperature, she acknowledged that it had been raining like that for a while.

Once inside the heated house, she hustled to the bathroom and peeled off her sodden boots, jacket, and clothes. She was too cold to deal with them, so she pitched them all into the bathtub, ran up to her bedroom with a towel wrapped around her, and slipped into bed and under the blankets.

It took a few minutes, but she started to warm up, and eventually, sleep overtook her. Her dreams filled with her, and Ashton as they searched a garden for a little green snake caught in a storm.

Chapter 6: Woozy, Weakness, and Worry

June 2024, Maine, USA | Thenia Loris

When Thenia felt the sun's warmth on her cheek, she blinked her eyes open, and it took her a moment to remember where she was. She was still cocooned in a towel underneath her blankets, but when she sat up, she felt light-headed and pressed the heel of her hand against one of her temples and moaned.

"Damn, I hope the snake fared better than I did last night."

A sudden sneeze caught her off guard, and her head began to throb even harder.

"Clothes," she mumbled.

When she threw back the blankets, a shiver rippled through her, and it felt like her groan echoed off the walls around her.

It didn't take Thenia long to get dressed, and she slowly made her way down the stairs to the kitchen. When she saw that the milk from the night before was still in the pan on the stovetop, she frowned at the waste. She poured the spoiled liquid down the sink, washed the pan, and filled it with water before positioning it back on the burner to boil. She swapped the hot chocolate mix with a box of black tea from the cabinet and then opened her laptop to check her messages. There was one from Ashton about their power situation, and she decided to reply after a cup of really strong tea that would, hopefully, clear her head.

The water wasn't boiling yet, so Thenia got up to poke her head out the back door and see how the surrounding area fared after the storm. Everything glistened with drops of water that rested atop every surface, and when the low light refracted off the water, it looked like the land was covered in shimmering diamonds.

"Wait, the sky?"

Thenia rushed back into the kitchen and checked the clock over the stove.

"Oh, my god. It's nearly six!"

She returned to the back door to close it, but a splotch of color caught her eye, and she saw the tiny green snake on one of the couch cushions.

"You're safe! I was so worr—" Thenia quickly twisted her head away and sneezed multiple times. "Worried."

The snake lifted its head and tipped it to the side.

"I couldn't remember if snakes liked the rain, and you seem to avoid the water in the garden, so I went looking for you, but I was searching blindly."

The snake's eyes seemed to widen, and then it slithered over and popped its body up until Thenia lowered her hand for it. Then it curled up in her palm and rested its chin on the pad of her thumb.

"It doesn't matter. You're safe. That's the important part."

Thenia heard the water on the stove boiling, glanced over her shoulder towards the kitchen, and then returned to the snake.

"Would you like to come in? I'm not feeling very well, and I'm making tea."

The snake lowered its head, and Thenia brought it inside before closing the back door and relocking it. She carried the little creature into the kitchen and set it on a portion of the counter far from the stove. When Thenia pivoted to attend to her hot water, she had to reach for the edge of the counter to steady herself, her knuckles white with the effort it took.

"Wow, that sucked," she laughed softly. "Note to self, no sudden movements."

She began to move again, this time more carefully. It didn't take long to brew herself a cup of tea, and she took it to one of the bar stools. Thenia blew on her tea and drank it under the watchful eye of the small green snake, who seemed content to keep her company. When she'd finished the cup, Thenia rested her head on her arms, and the coolness of the countertop on her skin felt amazing. She groaned and rested her cheek directly on the quartz.

"I must have a fever."

As if she'd called it by name, a sneeze snuck up on her and was so forceful that her ribs protested, and she clutched her side.

"Ow." She sniffled and picked up her empty cup. "Okay, more sick than I thought. Another cup of tea, and then I go back to bed."

The snake was still watching her closely, and Thenia tried to smile reassuringly at it. However, it didn't seem to buy her false reassurance, and it continued to stare with narrowed eyes.

Thenia got to her feet, but the world spun around her as a wave of light-headedness washed over her again. She reached out to stabilize herself against the counter, but her vision had doubled, and she missed it, grabbing for the phantom version instead of the real one. Instead, she stumbled forward, the mug flying from her hand and shattering when it hit the cabinet in front of her.

When Thenia's knees hit the floor, she was able to catch herself with one hand, but it was too late to help much. The last thing she saw was the grey hardwood rushing up to meet her cheek.

Serena Ainsley

The world slowed around Serena as she watched helplessly when Thenia lost her balance and grabbed for the counter. Then everything sped up, and the mug that Thenia had been holding shattered on the other side of the kitchen as Thenia fell to the kitchen floor.

It only took a handful of seconds for Serena to fling her snake form off the counter and to the floor, where she landed with a quiet thump. She concentrated on her body and willed it to shift into her human form. Her snake's soul warmed in thanks as it took a backseat to her human body's control.

"Thenia!"

Serena's voice cracked, and she skid to her knees beside the unconscious woman. She checked to make sure Thenia was still breathing and then tried to roll her over. The other woman wasn't very heavy, but Serena glared at her own exposed forearms and, not for the first time, she loathed what she saw. There was no way Serena, with her scrawny body, could move Thenia on her own.

"I'll go get Ashton," she told an unconscious Thenia before Serena stumbled to her feet and raced from the house.

Serena shivered in a t-shirt and jeans, but thankfully, she was still in Converse from the last time she shifted and could run without worrying about the ground cutting into her feet. It had been months since she'd been in her human form, and even longer that she'd stayed that way for more than a few minutes. Serena found herself tripping multiple times as her brain and legs struggled to work together after so many months of disuse.

It didn't take her long to reach the back porch of the main house, where she slipped on the first step, caught herself, and ran to the back door. When she glimpsed the reflection that stared back at her, it made her instinctively want to shift back into her snake form. Her blonde hair was wild around her shoulders, and her face looked sunken and hollow. The only thing she admitted that she enjoyed was the small gold hoop in her nose.

"Ashton! Ashton!"

Serena frantically pounded on the glass, but it only took a few seconds for him to open the door, and she practically fell through it and directly into him when he did.

"What the hell? Who—"

She gazed up at him and pulled away to steady herself. When he saw her face, he froze.

"Ashton, you have to com—"

"Wait, are you the snake?"

"That's not important. Thenia! She's sick. She fell—"

"What!" He gently nudged Serena back out to the porch and pulled the door closed behind them. "Where?"

"Kitchen!"

Serena didn't wait for him and began to run back to Thenia, positive that Ashton was on her heels.

"What happened?" he asked when he was again at her side.

"She went out looking for me last night. Got sick. Slept...all...day...." Serena started to pant, her human body incredibly out of shape and neglected. "Fever. Passed out."

"Got it. Stop talking and focus on breathing."

Serena noticed he was examining her, his gaze focused and curious, and he looked worried. She answered him with silence and continued to run. When they got closer to the house, Ashton sped up and flew past her, rushing up to the door without bothering to knock, and then rushed into the kitchen.

"Thenia!"

Serena jogged in behind him, watched him slide to the floor beside Thenia, and confidently checked her breathing.

"She was breathing when I left. Is she...."

"She's breathing." He pressed his fingers just below her jaw. "Her pulse is fine, too."

"Thank goodness," Serena gasped, bending forward and bracing her palms on her knees but not taking her eyes off Thenia.

"It looks like she split her lip when she hit the floor, but it's already stopped bleeding. Her chin will probably be bruised, too." Ashton looked up at her. "Would you get her some ice, and I'll carry her to her room?"

Serena nodded, still wheezing.

"Can I ask you for help so I can get my arms under her? Steady her, basically."

"Sure."

Serena helped brace Thenia, while Ashton got a better hold on her and stood up.

"Thanks."

"Yeah."

Serena watched them go upstairs before turning to the fridge and hunting around the freezer for something moldable. She saw a frozen bag of carrot cubes and grabbed it, and after opening nearly every drawer, she found a dish towel.

When she took them upstairs, Ashton had Thenia settled into bed and beneath the blankets. He was inspecting her lip and looked up when Serena handed him the carrots.

"Will this be okay?"

"Perfect, thanks." He took them and gently pressed them to Thenia's jawline. "I think she'll be fine, but she has a fever. That's probably why she fainted. Lightheaded or something and wasn't aware of how sick she was."

Serena nodded but continued to stare at Thenia. She'd been so nice to the little snake since she'd moved into the tiny house. Whenever she saw Serena, Thenia always seemed happy to see her. Then, Thenia went to search for her in the storm.

"Are you alright?" Ashton asked warmly.

"Hmm?"

"You're crying."

Serena raised one hand to pat her cheek and then gazed at the moisture on her fingertips. "Ah, yeah. Fine."

"Are you a paranam?" Ashton asked.

Serena lowered her hand and then her eyes until eventually she nodded.

"Did Pops know?"

She nodded again.

Ashton was quiet for a few minutes before he cleared his throat. "What's your name?"

"S-Serena."

"It's nice to finally meet you, Serena. Thank you for looking after Thenia these past few weeks. Not to mention coming to get me today."

Serena crossed her arms in front of her and nodded once.

She heard rustling, snuck a glance at Ashton, and saw him get up from the bed. He stopped in front of her and held out the bag of carrots.

"Would you hold that for her? I'm going to run back to the main house and pick up a few things. Are you hungry?"

Serena hesitantly accepted the carrots from him, took a chance, and met his gaze, which, to her amazement, was warm and matched his bright smile.

"I can, and um...yes."

"I have leftovers from last night. Can I bring you some, too? It's pasta."

She turned away. "You don't have to do that, I'll be—"

"Serena. Please, let me bring you something to eat. Pops would be pissed at me if I didn't."

When she looked back at Ashton, who was smirking, her lips pulled up on their own ever so slightly.

"Thank you."

"Never a problem. I'll be back in less than ten."

She nodded, and he lightly rested his palm on her shoulder as he walked past her and skipped down the stairs. Serena placed her free hand where he'd touched her. Then she remembered Ashton had told her to help Thenia, and Serena quickly rushed to the bed and resumed icing the woman's face.

The tiny frown and creased forehead looked out of place on Thenia's features, and Serena liked it better when the witch smiled—like when she made water from the hose rain on the plants she'd tended or when she was reading Arthur's journals about the garden.

Before Thenia moved in, Serena was lonely. Ashton wasn't outside often, and even when he was, Serena was always too shy to show herself. She wasn't very good with people. Truthfully, she preferred her snake form.

Thenia shifted in her sleep, and Serena brushed her hair away from her damp forehead.

"Ashton and I will take care of you. Don't worry, Thenia," Serena whispered.

She stayed with Thenia until Ashton returned, and after he'd heated them both food, he brought it upstairs to her.

"Here. I figured you wouldn't want to leave her," he said, handing her a warm bowl of incredible-smelling pasta and a fork.

"Thank you."

Serena set the carrots down and began to eat while Ashton ate his meal from where he sat at the foot of the bed.

"Serena," Ashton asked after a few minutes of quiet chewing.

"Yes?"

"I brought you a change of clothes. Eileen's. I figured they'd be more comfortable for you than mine. Would you like me to watch Thenia, and you can shower after you eat?"

Serena flinched and looked at the pasta in her bowl. "Sure. I'm sorry. I haven't been in my human form—"

"Serena. There's nothing wrong, and you don't have to if you don't want to. I just know that after Xander had been in his panther form for a few days, the first thing he wanted was a shower. I'm sorry if I offended you. I made an assumption, and I shouldn't have."

She glanced over at him from beneath her lashes, and his body language projected calmness, not that he was upset with her.

"Okay. You're...right."

"Can I ask the last time you were in your human form?"

Serena sniffled. "Sure. Um...the day your grandparents...." She swallowed roughly. "Before that, a few years."

"Years?"

She nodded. "I, um, prefer my snake form. I'm more...comfortable that way."

"I understand. If you'd prefer to shift back to it instead of the shower, I can give you some privacy."

Serena shook her head emphatically. "No. Thank you. I want to stay with Thenia until she wakes up. If you don't...mind."

"Why would I mind? She's your friend, isn't she?"

She nodded, but tears splashed into her bowl.

Ashton got up to put his own on the dresser and came to sit beside her. She barely looked at him as he held out his hand as if waiting for permission. When she finally nodded, he drew her into his arms and held her against his chest while she cried.

She missed Arthur so much. He was her first true friend, but now she had Thenia and maybe even Ashton.

"It's alright, Serena. She'll be fine. She just needs a little rest. You'll be fine, too. I know I'm not Pops, but you can stay here as long as you want. Human or snake. Whatever makes you comfortable."

Serena sobbed harder into Ashton's shirt and didn't stop until long after both of their dinners had gone cold.

Ashton Giri

It was nearly midnight when Ashton finally settled Serena, who was curled up as a snake on the pillow next to Thenia's. The younger woman had decided to stay with Thenia, as he'd expected, but Serena insisted on remaining in her snake form so that she didn't scare Thenia if she woke up next to an unknown stranger in bed with her.

Ashton snagged the blanket he'd brought from the main house from the kitchen counter as he climbed the second set of steps up to the lounge area. He didn't feel comfortable leaving the two women alone for the night without a cell phone or a fast way to reach him. The last thing Serena's human body needed was another sprint to the main house and back.

He relaxed on the couch, pulled out his cell phone, and texted his sister.

You have a second? Too much to text, but can't call.

Once he hit send, he dropped the phone on his sternum, placed his palm over the screen, and merged with the machine. The shock ran through his blood as it always did, and he waited for Eileen in a space between the ones and zeros.

Ash?

Hey. Sorry, I'm not interrupting, am I?

No, and even if you were, the fact that you wanted to talk here means I would have figured it out. What happened?

Ashton laughed. *What didn't?*

Highlights?

Pops' snake is a paranam who hasn't been in her human form more than once in the last few years. He knew about it, and tonight, she ran from Thenia's to the main house and pounded on the back door to get me. Thenia was apparently out all night in a storm looking for the snake version of Serena, and Thenia's now sick. She passed out on the kitchen floor, and Serena came to get me for help. She's incredibly shy, and I get the feeling she stays a snake, not just because she's physically more comfortable with it. Now I'm sleeping in Thenia's loft while a snake sleeps on her pillow.

He paused, and for a second, he was concerned that Eileen had left.

Um...Ash?

Sorry, he added.

For?

Dumping all of that on you.

I'm going to make Xander bite you. As a panther. Knock it off. I wanted to say thank you. For calling me.

I miss you.

I miss you, too, Ash. We both do.

I know.

You said Pops knew? About...Serena?

Yeah, she confirmed it, but the system triggered when she was running to the main house. Except it wasn't the intruder alert—it was specific to her, so Gram must have known too.

Wow. Okay. Well, look what they did for us. I guess it shouldn't surprise me that they wanted to help her.

Me either. I wish they'd told us, though. He wanted me to keep talking to the snake, but that's all he said.

Yeah, but it was enough.

Ashton chuckled. *Yeah. Guess it was.*

So, what are you going to do?

About what?

Both of them?

What can I do? Serena deserves to stay here as much as I do, and Thenia will be fine with some rest.

That's a lot to take on, Ash. It sounds like both of them have some heavy baggage.

And we don't?

Yes, but they aren't your responsibility.

No, but...they need someone. Serena is already very attached to Thenia, but....

You care about her, too.
I do.
Alright, we'll support you, but Ash?
Yeah?
Ask for help. Please. From them, us, whoever.
I promise.
Fine. I love you, Ash.
Love you, too.
Get some sleep, but let me know how Thenia is doing in the morning.
I will.
Sleep well.
You too.

Ashton severed his connection to the machines and opened his eyes, staring up at the ceiling of the tiny house.

His day had ended very differently from what he'd been planning. When he saw Serena's nose ring earlier, he remembered the yellow mark on the snake's nose and instinctively knew it was her. Then, he recognized how terrified she was. When she told him that Thenia had fainted, his body had moved on its own. It wasn't until they were halfway to Thenia's that Ashton noticed how hard the woman beside him was struggling with the exertion.

Serena was far too thin, and it was clear she wasn't used to her human form. She'd tripped a few times, and thankfully, she'd regained her balance, but when he saw how out of breath she was, he knew Serena would need some of his attention too, once they'd dealt with Thenia's condition.

He was relieved when Serena ate two bowls of pasta. After she showered, her skin glowed a bit more, and her cheeks took on a rosier hue.

Eileen was right. Both women had baggage, and there was no way they could keep it to themselves, but as far as Ashton was concerned, he had two hands free.

He'd gladly help carry them. Then maybe, one day, each of them might be able to unpack a few.

Chapter 7: Vulnerability

Thenia's eyelashes fluttered, but it took her more effort than expected to open them fully. Then she yawned, but a sharp pain seared through her jaw, and she pressed her palm to the side of her face.

"Why— Wait," she bolted upright, and her eyes darted around the room. Her bedroom. "How did I—"

She felt the faint tickle of a snake's tongue on her arm, and when she glanced down, the little green snake was gazing up at her with noticeable worry in its tiny features.

"Oh, hi. Do you know how I—"

"Thenia, may I come up?" Ashton called from the bottom of the bedroom stairs.

"Sure, um...."

She glanced down and realized she was wearing the same clothes as the day before, but she was decent. When she heard Ashton's footsteps on the stairs, she looked up. He carried two mugs and walked over to hand her one. The steam drifted around her, and Thenia immediately felt calmer after inhaling the delicate aromas of lemon and honey.

"Black tea. Lemon and honey. I'm not sure if you like it, but considering you're sick, I honestly don't care." He smirked at her and then smiled at the snake. "Morning, Serena."

Thenia's eyes flew to the snake, "Serena?" but the snake turned away.

"It's a long story. Drink your tea, and I'll catch you up." Ashton reached forward and pressed the back of his hand to Thenia's forehead. "Good, fever's gone. Your jaw hurts, I assume?"

"Yeah, why?"

"Do you remember being in the kitchen yesterday with Serena?"

Thenia tried to recall what she remembered last, and she saw a mug shatter in her memory.

"Oh, yeah, I fell."

"You passed out. You were more sick than you thought. Serena was with you, and when she realized that you needed help, she ran to the main house and came to get me."

Thenia smiled down at the green snake, although it was a tiny smile due to her aching face. "Thank you. I'm sorry I worried you."

Ashton chuffed. "You did more than that, but drink your tea."

She looked at him, hoping he'd say more, but his eyes flicked between her and her cup a few times before he grinned.

"You want to know more, drink. Be careful, though. You split your lip, too, but it doesn't appear very swollen." Ashton nodded to the snake. "Good call on the carrots."

"Carrots?"

"Drink," Ashton prodded more firmly.

Thenia lifted her cup as requested, but she hesitated for a second when she realized Ashton was telling her, not asking her, as he usually did in the past. For some reason, it felt nothing like when Lucus had mandated something to her, so Thenia did as instructed.

"So, Serena came and got me. We brought you up here, iced

your cheek, and kept an eye on you. She slept in here, and I crashed in the loft. Hope you don't mind."

"Not at all. I'm sorry I was so much trouble."

"Hey." Ashton's voice was stern, but when Thenia met his eyes, his expression was still pleased and friendly. "You weren't trouble, so don't apologize for that. You want to apologize for worrying us? Fine, but we care about you and were happy to help."

Thenia blushed and dropped her gaze into her tea. "Alright. Thank you for taking care of me, and I'm sorry I worried you."

"Better."

Ashton rested his palm on one of her knees, still under the blanket, and Thenia saw him refocus on Serena. "Are you feeling up to it? Or would you rather do this another day?"

Thenia glanced between Ashton and Serena and then back again. When he smiled, Thenia saw Serena slither off the bed and land on the carpet with a soft thud before she continued out of the room and down the stairs, making a soft thunk with each step.

"Ah, would you mind, um, catching me up?" Thenia whispered to Ashton once they were alone.

"Yeah. She and I talked about it last night, and she asked me to explain. Then, if you're comfortable, she will come back up."

"Okay…. Why wouldn't I be comfortable?"

Ashton smirked. "Serena is a paranam. When I said she came to get me, I mean in her human form."

Thenia's eyes widened, and then she gradually smiled and facepalmed. "Of course she is. What kind of snake understands an elemental witch and a mechanite?"

"I didn't know either. I guess Pops did, but he never said anything. After meeting her, I understand why."

"Why?" Thenia said coldly, lowering her hand and eyeing Ashton warily. She had a feeling she wouldn't like his answer.

"Serena prefers her snake form. She'd not been in her human form for a few years other than a rare instance."

"Wait, really?"

Ashton nodded. "Truthfully, it was obvious once I got over the shock of a stranger pounding on my back door and the anomalous alerts my system was throwing. She told me what happened and then helped me get you settled. We had dinner, talked a bit, and she showered. Oh, her clothes are in your dryer, by the way. Along with yours from the bathtub, which, considering how wet they still were...makes it no surprise you got sick."

Thenia winced. "Sorr—"

"Nope." Ashton tipped his head down to be in her lowered line of sight. "No apologies."

She chuckled at the absurdity of his action, and he grinned before righting himself.

"Better. Your smile suits you better than that worried expression."

Thenia's heart beat faster, but she was saved from embarrassing herself when there was a faint knock from the bottom of the stairs.

"Thenia," Ashton asked. "Are you comfortable with Serena coming back up? In her human form?"

Rude or not, Thenia ignored Ashton and answered Serena's knock directly. "Serena, please. You've not offended me or made me uncomfortable. Come back up?"

Thenia was watching the stairs, but she could see Ashton's pleased smile from the corner of her eye. There was no movement or sound for half a minute, but eventually, an extremely thin woman with blonde hair timidly climbed the stairs. She was staring at her feet and had her hands in front of her, picking at her thumbnail.

Thenia glanced at Ashton before handing him her cup and carefully testing her legs as she got out of bed. When she felt stable, Thenia crossed the room and stopped before Serena. She was a few inches shorter than Thenia, and considering Ashton was a few inches taller than Thenia, they made a varied group.

"Serena..." Thenia tested.

"Hmm?"

Thenia smiled but opened her arms. When Serena didn't step away, Thenia closed the last few feet between them and hugged her as tightly as she dared.

"Thank you. Thank you for going to get Ashton, for helping him, and for keeping an eye on me last night. And for keeping me company this past month. It's nice to meet this version of you, too."

Serena nodded and hesitantly wrapped her arms around Thenia's waist.

"Thank you...." Serena's voice was quiet, and it cracked from disuse, but she cleared her throat and kept going. "For looking for me during the storm."

"I'm glad you're safe."

Serena stepped back but eventually looked up and met Thenia's eyes.

Thenia grinned. "Ah, the yellow mark."

Ashton chuckled behind them. "That's the same thing I thought, too."

Serena smiled tentatively, but the slight change lit up the woman's features, and her cheeks flushed. "I, um, got it done to match."

"I was wondering about that," Ashton said, standing with them and handing Thenia back her mug. "I didn't think a beast form carried over traits from the human one. At least not a non-biological marker."

"No. The yellow mark was on my snake first."

Serena's cheeks tinted even darker, and Thenia mentally admitted the woman was beautiful, but when Serena smiled, she was breathtaking.

"Glad I was right," Ashton said, "because otherwise, I would have missed way too many chances to screw with Xander when we were kids."

Thenia nearly choked on her tea while Serena giggled sweetly beside her.

"You did that on purpose." Thenia playfully glared at Ashton and gently nudged him in the side with her elbow.

"Can't prove anything," he smirked, but then looked at Serena. "Would you help make some lunch while Thenia does what she needs to?" He looked back at her. "Figure you might want to change, shower, or whatever."

"Thanks, yeah. I'd love to change clothes and brush my teeth." She tentatively ran her tongue along the back of her teeth. "They taste a little coppery still."

He nodded. "From your lip, I'd guess. Did you cut the inside of your mouth, too?"

She nodded.

"Makes sense." Ashton glanced back at Serena, "Help me out?"

"Yeah," Serena replied with a slight nod, but then she looked at Thenia. "Do you need anything?"

Thenia shook her head and suppressed a wince from the action's pain. "Nope, but thank you. I won't be long."

Serena nodded once and then headed back down the stairs, Ashton following behind her.

Once they were both gone, Thenia exhaled as quietly as she could but found herself grinning—a paranam. Of course, she was a paranam. Thenia felt like an idiot, but simultaneously, she was relieved and happy that she'd attempted to find the tiny green snake during the storm, regardless of the resulting sickness or not.

Ashton was right, though. It wasn't difficult to see that Serena wasn't in her human form often. From what little Thenia knew about the race of humans, staying in one's beast form for that long was exceedingly rare. Paranams typically spent most of their time in human forms and switched only when their beast's soul was restless. She'd never heard of one staying in their beast form nearly permanently.

Thenia set her cup on the dresser and changed as quickly as she dared, not wanting to get dizzy and risk passing out again. Once she was in a fresh set of baggy sweatpants and a soft cotton shirt, she meandered downstairs and found Ashton stirring a pot of what smelled like soup on the stove. Serena was nowhere to be seen, and Ashton must have seen that Thenia was looking for her.

"She's grabbing bread from the main house. Don't worry."

Thenia was relieved to know the young woman was still in her human form and returning.

"I know. I felt the same way last night," Ashton said, agreeing with what Thenia was thinking. "We talked a little, but besides how quiet she is, all I learned is that she's lived here as a snake for a long time."

"I wonder why? What about her family?" Thenia asked, sitting on a bar stool.

"No idea. She didn't mention them."

Thenia nodded but didn't know what else to say. She was worried about Serena but wasn't sure why or how to express it.

"I gave her some of Eileen's clothes and told her she was welcome to stay on the property for as long as she wanted. I'll even make space in the main house for her if she wants it."

"I can't see her agreeing to that," Thenia frowned.

"Nope, she basically said as much yesterday, but the offer's there. I think she'll likely prefer to stay with you, though. As a snake, if I had to guess."

"She's welcome as long as she wants—in either form. It's a small house, but there's more than enough room for both of us. You saw my suitcase. Most of the drawers are still empty."

Ashton turned the stove off and leaned on the counter to study at her. He must have found what he was looking for, though, because he sighed. "Thenia, I'm sure this will make you uncomfortable, but I need to tell you something."

Thenia's entire body tensed, and she squeezed her eyes closed, waiting for Ashton to tell her to pack. She'd been too much trouble or—

"Thenia," Ashton said empathetically, but she couldn't speak. Then she heard him move closer to her. "Thenia, can you look at me? Please? Whatever you're thinking, it's not that."

It took her quite a bit of effort to open her eyes, but she managed to do so. Ashton was leaning on the counter in front of her, a smile still on his lips.

"Thenia, I hope you believe me when I tell you that you're an amazing woman, which is unrelated to why I'm saying this, but I also want you to know that."

She watched Ashton's face harden, and one of his fists clenched for a second before it relaxed again.

"I know about Lucus."

Thenia had hoped he'd never find out about her past, but Ashton was a mechanite. Of course, he'd look her up. He'd already known she was a witch the day they'd met. It hadn't seemed like he'd known about Lucus then, but people always lied and concealed the truth. Why had she expected anything different from Ashton?

She released her mug, leaving it on the counter as she got to her feet. "I'll get my things," but Ashton took one of her hands into both of his before she could take a step.

"Thenia, I don't want you to leave—the opposite, in fact. I saw how uncomfortable I made you in the beginning. I asked my sister for advice. All Eileen told me was his name and that if I only looked on the surface, I would find what I needed to understand the situation better and be less likely to hurt you unintentionally."

Thenia felt dread pressing against her eyes and squeezing her chest. She struggled to hold both her breath and her tears back as the humiliation threatened to drown her.

"I didn't look deeper than that and avoided any information about you. I didn't want to invade your privacy more than I already was."

He hadn't known since the beginning. It had only been the night they'd eaten together that he'd been different, and she lowered her head. "The wine," she stated, her voice cracking with emotion.

"I wasn't testing you. I saw how you reacted to the alcohol and assumed it had something to do with that bastard."

Thenia attempted to choke back a sob, but she didn't manage to do it well enough, and Ashton was suddenly at her side, where he tentatively pulled her into his arms.

"Thenia, I won't mention it again if you don't want me to, but I want you to know that I'm here if you want to talk or if I can help."

She struggled to suppress the tears again, but felt a few roll down her cheeks as the front door opened with a soft squeak.

"Thenia?" Serena asked tentatively.

"She's alright, Serena," Ashton answered. "I brought something up that made her upset. It's my fault."

Thenia shook her head against his chest, and he held her tighter.

"Not your fault," she croaked out.

She saw Serena's feet when she stepped up beside them and felt when Ashton removed one of his arms. Then Serena was part of their group hug. The pair's genuine concern for Thenia broke the last of her control, and she allowed herself to sob into Ashton's sweatshirt while he held her, and Serena ran her fingers affectionately through Thenia's hair.

Ashton Giri

When Ashton reached the top of the stairs leading to the bedroom side of the small house, he stopped. Thenia and Serena were both sleeping, the latter surprisingly still in her human form, her body curled around one of Thenia's arms. The pair looked exceptionally comfortable, and he was surprised by how much he wished he were lying beside them, not standing on the other side of the room.

After Thenia cried herself out, Serena held her while Ashton finished making their lunch. The three of them had eaten and talked a little, and then Thenia admitted she was tired and went upstairs for a nap. Serena had gone with her, but if Ashton had to guess, the younger woman probably hadn't recognized how drained she was and hadn't planned on sleeping, too.

Now, it was just him, and he was alone again, quietly creeping away from them and back downstairs. He retrieved his blanket and extra clothes from the loft and slipped out of the house. When he reached the path to the main house, he checked his phone and was pleased to see that work was still quiet and neither Eileen nor Xander had messaged him. The events of the last twenty-four hours had been a rollercoaster, and he was perfectly happy not dealing with the outside world for a little longer.

When he reached the porch, he stared at the swing bed and remembered finding Thenia reading his Pops' notebooks on it. The memory brought a smile to his lips as he continued past it and inside the house. He went into his room and put away his things, then went out front to put out the trash cans and get the mail. Both were chores he hadn't done in a while, which was evident by the mailbox and the bins being overly full.

"Junk, junk, junk," he categorized as he walked. "Bill, bill, boring."

When he neared the bottom of the pile, he saw a plain-looking envelope with his address handwritten on it and nothing else except the postage. Ashton flipped it over, ripped it open, and pulled out a note card with more handwriting.

Return what she took. Return what is ours.

"What the fuck?" Ashton flipped the card over, and unsurprisingly, it was blank. "Return what?"

Ashton had no idea what the card was referencing or even who *she* was. When he entered the kitchen, he plopped the stack of mail on the counter to deal with later, taking only the card and envelope with him into his office.

Ashton dropped the message on the desk and sat down heavily in his desk chair while he continued to inspect it. After a few minutes, he texted Eileen and tried to ask how her job was going in the most generic way possible. He was pretty sure whatever these mystery people wanted wasn't related to her, but he still wanted to rule one "she" out. Then he pulled out his keyboard with the mechanite characters and logged into the system his Gram used for the house.

"Maybe they are talking about her?"

Ashton did a few searches through the household archives that the deceased woman had meticulously maintained, but as he'd expected, he found nothing. Switching back to his system, Ashton searched using the limited information he had in the AIS database and again found nothing.

"Shit. Okay...."

Ashton rubbed his eyes and leaned back in his chair, staring at the ceiling above him.

"Who the hell are you, and what do you want?"

Thenia Loris

Thenia was standing in her kitchen, drinking a glass of water by the sink, when Ashton opened the front door and jumped when he saw her in his peripheral vision. She laughed softly but put her finger to her lips and said in a hushed tone, "Serena's still asleep."

Ashton nodded and gingerly closed the door, making nearly zero sound. "What are you doing awake?" he whispered back.

"I've slept a lot the last few days," she shrugged. "Woke up thirsty, and now I'm just awake."

"Would you like to take a walk?"

"Sure." Thenia put her glass in the sink and told Ashton as she passed him, "Let me grab a sweatshirt. I'll meet you out front."

He nodded, and she tiptoed up the steps into her room. Serena was sleeping peacefully atop the blankets, and even though Thenia had just met human Serena, she already felt connected to the shy woman. They'd spent a lot of time together the past few weeks, and even if Serena was in her snake form, it didn't seem to make a difference.

After Thenia tugged a sweatshirt over her head and slipped on her tennis shoes, she joined Ashton outside, where he was waiting, leaning on the garden wall with a smile.

"She still asleep?" he asked.

"Yup. I don't think she slept much last night."

"Assume not. She was extremely concerned you'd get worse overnight."

Thenia frowned, scanning the footpath in front of her as they exited her small garden. "What do you think happened to her? She has to be what, upper twenties?"

"Probably a good guess, and I have no idea. I haven't had a chance to check the database. Even then, I'll only get surface-level information. Age, parents, species, or race. Things like that. I won't dig further than that. Same as I didn't for you when you emailed that first time."

"I guess that makes sense. If you've got the ability, why not use it?"

Ashton shook his head, "Nope, not why I did it."

"Oh?" Thenia asked, peeking sideways at him.

"If you had been an Outsider, I would have looked up police records and been more invasive. Considering my job and Eileen and Alexander's jobs, I needed to ensure we were safe. I know it doesn't mean much, but it wasn't personal."

"I understand and I get it. Granted, you surprised me, but you didn't offend me. I relaxed a little once I realized you were telling the truth about being a mechanite and not a well-informed Outsider."

"I'm glad."

She wasn't trying to make Ashton feel better. She was only being honest with him. It had taken her some time to settle and think through why he'd researched her, but when she had, it made sense. Not to mention, she'd have done the same if their roles had been reversed—granted, significantly slower and less effectively.

They strolled contentedly for a few minutes, Thenia occasionally stopping to check on a plant or clear debris from where the storm had tangled it amongst the foliage surrounding it.

She knew she'd eventually need to address the human-sized elephant named Lucus in the room, and as much as she didn't want to, she'd put it off for long enough already.

"We were together for over a decade. I was young and stupid."

Thenia saw Ashton nod beside her, indicating that he was listening but not agreeing.

"I lived in my family's home after my parents moved to Australia. I was lonely and exhausted from school, and trying to figure out life in my early twenties. Lucus and I met by chance at a fundraiser I went to on behalf of my parents, who couldn't make it back to the States in time. We talked and seemed to hit it off, and it evolved from there. Everyone said we were a good match, and though I can't say I was happy, but I guess I was content. More importantly, I wasn't alone anymore."

Ashton sighed. "I can understand that."

A small smile crept onto Thenia's lips. "Yeah, I imagine you do. Well, that's where it started to shift, I guess. He wanted me to attend more and more of his work functions with him. Then, award ceremonies and parties. Charity events and business dinners. I was never to speak, nor was I spoken to. I was simply there to prove he was a kind and generous man worthy of someone's devotion. Everything I did, he controlled. What I ate, what size clothing I wore, and...."

She hesitated but figured she had nothing to lose by telling Ashton everything. She'd already gone farther in trusting him than anyone else.

"Lucus is an Outsider. After a few years, I told him what I was, but he never truly believed me. I was forbidden from using my magic or anything perceived as odd or different. I was allowed one single house plant, and the rest were silk. Day after day, I had to watch strangers, Outsiders, tend to my family's lands instead of me."

Ashton cleared his throat, but then he spun away from her, and she saw him take a deep breath. "Sorry. Mad on your behalf. Not at you."

She laughed, one full of self-loathing and regret. "Yeah, well, I'm mad on my behalf, too. Thankfully, I had finished my degree already because he would have made me drop out if I hadn't. It didn't matter much, though, because I still wasn't allowed to use it."

"So what made you end it? There was an article saying you two were engaged."

Thenia smirked. "What makes you think I was the one to end it?"

Ashton's eyes widened. "Wait, he did all that to you, then bailed?"

"Yes, and no. You're half right. A few months ago, he decided that what he needed in a wife was someone more outgoing and personable. The exact opposite of what he'd turned me into over the years. Someone he didn't need to worry over whether they would randomly start shouting they were a witch at parties. So, I let him walk."

"Better than he deserves," Ashton muttered.

"Yes, it is, but I got my life back."

"What did you do next?"

"Where do you go when nowhere feels like home?" Thenia said with a melancholy smile. "I left my hometown and traveled alone, all over the world. I told my parents we broke up, and considering they had only met him a few times over the years, they accepted my story about us growing apart."

"So, how'd you end up in Maine?"

Thenia chuffed. "An old friend called. She had to go out of town for a few weeks for work, and she's a houseplant mom. She said I was the only person she trusted to care for them and asked me to come apartment sit."

"Wow. That's one hell of a coincidence." A few seconds later, Ashton scoffed, "Or not."

"Know something?" she asked.

"Maybe. I'll look into it."

"So, yeah. That's my story," Thenia sighed.

"And your phone?" Ashton asked, searching her face.

"Ah, yeah. He texted me that night. It bothered me, and I dropped it." She shrugged. "It's fine. I'm happy with my laptop, and he doesn't know my new email address. Besides, other than my parents and Sara, I pretty much lost all of my friends when he drove them away."

"Do you want me to block him or something? Just in case he figures it out?"

She bumped his arm with hers and smiled. "Thanks, but I'd rather know if he's trying or does manage to contact me. Better than being blind, I think."

"I can understand that, but don't forget, I'm here if you need any help."

"Thanks, Ashton. Really." She leaned her temple on his shoulder, and he put his arm loosely around her waist.

"Anytime. Thank you for telling me."

She nodded as they continued to walk, the roof line of her house coming into view just over the horizon.

"Ah, about his message..." Ashton asked.

"He said he changed his mind. Wanted me to call him, or he'd come get me."

Ashton tensed and stopped walking.

"Don't worry. The only people who know where I am are my parents. Well, and Sara, but he's never even met Sara."

Ashton was silent for a few seconds, his brow creased with worry, but then it eased, and he nodded. "Alright. Well, we have the cameras, so even if that changes, I'll know the instant he steps on the property."

"That makes me feel better. Thank you."

"Course."

They walked the remainder of the way in silence, side by side again, and when they reached her yard, he stopped.

"You should go in and rest more."

"Yeah, you're probably right. I feel fine, but I really can't chance it getting worse."

"Do you want me to stay again?"

Thenia thought about it, and when she saw he was patiently waiting for her to convey to him what she wanted, she smiled and shook her head.

"No, I'll be alright. Besides, that couch can't be very comfortable. Go sleep in your own bed. I'm sure your back would appreciate it."

He chuckled. "I can't argue with you there. Come get me or email me if you need me. Otherwise, I'll see you tomorrow then."

She nodded, and when he tipped forward and kissed her

uninjured cheek lightly, Thenia held her breath. He smiled again and walked back toward the main house, but called back over his shoulder when he was a few feet away.

"Tell Serena I said goodnight if she's up."

"I will," Thenia managed to answer, her eyes locked on Ashton's back until she couldn't see him anymore.

It was another few minutes until Thenia had recomposed herself enough to go back into the house, and when she entered, she saw Serena on one of the bar stools, frowning down at the counter.

"Oh crap, I'm sorry, Serena. I didn't think you'd wake up, or I'd have left you a note or something. Are you alright?"

Serena nodded but said nothing.

Thenia pushed her shoes off with her toes, leaving them by the front door, and sat on the stool beside the bashful woman.

"What's up? Talk to me."

"Nothing," Serena answered, but then she looked away.

"It doesn't feel like nothing, but I won't push. Just know that you can talk to me if you want to, okay?"

Thenia reached forward and clutched one of Serena's hands, and to her delight, Serena shifted to hold on more comfortably.

"Would you like to watch a movie with me? I'm not quite tired enough to sleep, but I should probably be good and not overdo it."

"Sure."

"Okay, why don't you go find something to watch, and I'll make us something warm to drink? Do you like tea, coffee, or hot cocoa? Or none of them?"

Serena finally lifted her head, and her dark eyes seemed to evaluate Thenia's intentions. It didn't bother her, and she let the young woman do what she needed to.

"Not coffee. Too bitter."

Thenia laughed and nodded before getting to her feet. "I agree. I'll make hot chocolate. I was making some the other night but stopped when I went to look for you and then forgot about it."

Thenia squeezed Serena's hand gently, released it, and walked around the breakfast bar and into the kitchen to begin heating the milk.

"Anything you want to watch?" Serena asked timidly.

"Nope. I don't watch much TV or many movies. So, pick whatever you think looks good. Though nothing gory, please. Blegh."

She heard Serena's sweet giggle, and Thenia grinned at her own reflection in the window over the kitchen sink.

"Okay. I'll go find something."

She watched Serena's reflection as she left the room. Once alone again, Thenia raised the hand she'd been holding Serena's with and stared at it. Then her fingers grazed her cheek where Ashton had kissed her. Thenia's chest warmed, and she felt herself flush from top to toes.

"I'm...happy."

She nodded, and when the Thenia in the window nodded back, she returned to making her and Serena hot cocoa, feeling safe in knowing that Ashton wasn't far either.

Chapter 8: Dinner for Three

June 2024, Maine, USA | Thenia Loris

Thenia nearly drank her entire water bottle in one go as a smiling Serena stood beside her in the warm summer sun. That smile had been making increasingly more frequent appearances over the last week, and Thenia's stomach had yet to cease doing flip-flops every time she witnessed it.

"Do you feel better?" Serena asked, holding her hand out for Thenia's glass bottle.

"Much, thank you." Thenia groaned, pressed her palms to her lower back, and bent to the side. "I have no idea why I thought doing the entire rhododendron section at once was a good idea."

Serena tried to hold back her soft laugh but gave up and pivoted away from Thenia to let it out.

"Hey," Thenia grinned and tickled Serena's side, "don't laugh at me."

The woman effortlessly squirmed away, in a move reminiscent of Serena's snake form. Her laughter was light and carefree, and when Thenia glimpsed Ashton walking towards them, his expression said he'd been noticing the woman's changes, too.

"Now, what fun am I missing over here?" he shouted. Serena's blush was immediate, and Thenia took pity on her and ceased her tickling.

"No fun, just back-breaking work," Thenia replied, taking back her water and finishing what little was left.

Ashton examined the nearest rhododendron, another one, and then another. Then his eyebrows raised, and he stared back at her in disbelief. "Wait, did you do all of this? Today?"

Thenia snorted, and Serena nodded emphatically.

"I brought her water and," Serena turned to Thenia and handed her a green apple, "a snack."

"You're my hero," Thenia said, accepting the apple and taking a loud crunching bite.

Serena's ears turned pink, and she looked at the floor.

"Well, now I am craving Gram's apple pie," Ashton whined, eliciting a laugh from both women.

"Um, I could..." Serena trailed off.

"What's up, Serena?" Ashton asked casually as he openly eyed Thenia's apple.

"When I was a...kid...there was this bakery...."

Ashton and Thenia stopped teasing one another over the apple and looked at Serena. She'd told them nearly nothing of her life before she came to live on Ashton's land with his grandparents, but they'd agreed not to push the subject and let her open up to them if and when she was ready to.

Ashton plucked the apple from Thenia's hands while she'd been distracted and winked at her.

"Wanna use the kitchen?" he asked Serena. "You should know you're welcome to anything in the main house."

"Or mine," Thenia added, pulling her apple away from Ashton with a smirk, who continued to eye it.

"Well, I've never actually...."

"I could pull out Gram's cookbook for you? Her instructions

were always very detailed, so they should be easy to learn from. If you want?"

Serena nodded but stayed quiet.

"You're welcome to use whatever you want from it. If you need anything copied, it's in the office. The only thing I ask is to leave my rig alone. Too much paperwork for the AIS to explain why someone other than me was using it."

Thenia snorted. "I can't even imagine. Serena, you're welcome to borrow my laptop if you need it. I promise I won't make you fill out endless paperwork if you do."

Ashton narrowed his eyes at Thenia and then practically pouted at her apple. This time, she laughed and willingly passed it to him. He grinned before taking a bite, the crisp crunch filling the quiet garden, before he handed it back to her.

"Damn, where'd you find that?" Ashton said, wiping a bit of juice from the corner of his mouth.

"Your grandfather planted a tree in the far west corner of the property a few years ago. We used to...share them."

"I had no idea," Ashton admitted. "Will you show me where it is sometime?"

Serena's timid smile reappeared, and she nodded more energetically this time.

"How's your day going?" Thenia asked Ashton.

He stretched onto his toes, his arms over his head, and his multiple layers of shirts rising just enough to expose a *very* pale strip of skin. Then he exhaled dramatically and dropped back to the flats of his feet with a huff.

"Fine."

Serena chuckled, and Thenia rolled her eyes. "That," she waved her hand in his general direction, "is what fine looks like?"

Ashton grinned. "Yeah. Normal day job stuff, nothing's on fire, and I've had time to look into something when it's slow. So, yeah, it's fine."

Serena narrowed her eyes at Ashton and cocked her head to the side. "What are you looking into?"

She must have asked the question before thinking about it because as soon as the words left Serena's mouth, her eyes widened, and she immediately stared at the floor again.

Thenia peeked at Ashton, who'd also seen the woman shut down, and he was frowning at her.

"Actually, maybe you can help me, Serena."

She slowly raised her gaze to look at him, but she was still mostly closed off.

"I got this odd letter in the mail the other day," he said, pulling a small piece of paper from his pocket and handing it to her. "Any ideas?"

Serena inspected the front side, flipped it over but saw it was blank, and flipped it back to reread the message. Thenia leaned her chin on Serena's shoulder to see over it and quickly read the small amount of handwriting.

"Who is *she*?" Serena asked.

"No idea," Ashton shrugged. "It came in the mail a week ago. All handwritten, no return address."

"You have no idea who they are referring to? Eileen or your Grandmother, maybe?" Thenia asked.

"Nope," Ashton slipped his hands into the back pockets of his jeans. "It was addressed to me, so I don't think it's either of you, and no one is stupid enough to come through me to get to Eileen."

Thenia nodded.

"So, you think it's Sue?" Serena asked.

"Assuming so. I have no idea what she took or even who to return it to, though. I've been doing some research and trying to find a hint, but there's nothing on the dark web, in the AIS's files, or even on Gram's personal system. Granted, I don't have access to much of that. At this point, I couldn't return whatever *it* is, even if I wanted to."

"Please don't be offended by this, but I assume your Gram wasn't involved in anything shady?" Thenia asked.

To her relief, both Ashton and Serena shook their heads before the former responded.

"Nope. Gram was as straight-laced as they come. Eileen and Xander got their hero drive from her."

Serena nodded in agreement. "She was a very kind woman."

"Hmm. Well, I see why your fine was so...lackluster," Thenia teased before finishing her apple.

"Is what it is," Ashton shrugged. "That aside, the main reason I came out to find you two was about dinner. I'm feeling like junk food. Join me for takeout pizza and root beer floats?"

"How oddly specific," Thenia chuckled.

"Sounds yummy, though," Serena nearly whispered.

"I agree. I'm in," Thenia said gently, poking Serena's side with the tip of her finger. "You?"

"If it's alright with you two that I tag along...."

Ashton snorted. "Who are you tagging along with? We want you there as you, not as a tag-along, Serena."

"What he said," Thenia added before she hip-bumped Serena just enough that she had to move one foot to catch her balance, and then she smiled again.

"Okay," Serena agreed shyly.

"Settled then. Preferences?" Ashton asked.

"Black olives?" Thenia requested.

"Mushrooms?" Serena added.

"Mind if I add green peppers?"

Both women shook their heads.

"Sweet. I'll order in an hour or so. Is that enough time for you two to finish up here and get cleaned up or whatever you need to do?"

Thenia put her fists on her hips with a silly smile. "Who needs cleaning up?"

Serena snickered and brushed her finger over Thenia's cheek and the smudge of dirt there.

Thenia smirked before muttering a few words under her breath, and couldn't help but laugh when all the dirt on her clothes and skin dropped to the floor, leaving Ashton and Serena with open-mouthed expressions.

"I stand corrected," Ashton said after he recovered.

Thenia dropped her arms and giggled. "I'm kidding. I do need a shower, but at least now I won't track dirt through the house."

"Nope," Serena smiled.

"Handy."

"It is," Thenia agreed. "Alright. Let me finish up here and then go get cleaned up."

"Sounds good," Ashton said.

He took the paper back from Serena and gently squeezed her upper arm before nodding to Thenia and heading back to the main house. Once he was out of earshot, Serena's hesitant tone made Thenia stop collecting her tools.

"Are you sure I won't be in the way...."

Thenia stood in front of Serena and met her anxious eyes. "Serena, we both want you to be there, too."

"Yeah, but..." She looked away again and then said, in an even softer voice, "he likes you...."

"And?"

Serena shrugged.

"Serena, he likes you, too."

"Not the same way."

Thenia crossed her arms. "You sure about that?"

Serena didn't say anything else, nor did she look at Thenia again, so she continued to clean up from the day's work. Eventually, she was ready to head back to the house, but Serena said she'd meet her at the main house later. Then she headed off into the gardens, leaving Thenia smiling on her front walkway, shaking her head at the unsure woman's back.

"Why is that so hard to believe, Serena?" Thenia said to no one before going inside the house to get ready for dinner.

Serena Ainsley

Serena pulled her...no, Ashton's sweatshirt tighter around herself, and she rubbed the cuffs of the sleeves on her nose. She was a bit warmer than she liked, but she'd never been given someone's clothes before and didn't want to take the sweatshirt off. Well, technically, she'd borrowed Eileen's clothes the day Serena found Sue and Arthur, but other than that.

The last week had been one of the best in Serena's life, and that was not an overstatement. She'd still spent most of her day in her snake form, but she'd either been with Thenia in the garden or with her and Ashton eating meals, talking, or watching movies in the evenings.

Even now, Serena found herself walking to meet Thenia so they could eat dinner with Ashton. Except this time, Serena couldn't stop thinking about what Thenia had said about Ashton. Serena knew Ashton had feelings for Thenia. It was easy to see in the way he looked at her, mostly when she wasn't paying attention to him. Serena had never seen him look at her with that look, no matter what Thenia claimed.

Then there was Thenia. Serena selfishly wanted to keep her new friend all to herself, but more than that, she wanted Thenia to want that, too.

"Serena!" Thenia cried from the tiny house's front door.

"Hi," Serena replied softly, waving a hand from where she'd stopped to wait by the entrance to the tiny garden.

"Let me grab shoes, and then I'll be ready."

"Okay."

Serena fiddled with one of the cuffs of the sweatshirt and

wondered what a root beer float tasted like. She knew what they were, but she'd never had one before. A life alone and mainly as a snake made things like that impossible. She'd seen a lot of things, sure, but never experienced most of them for herself.

Thenia pulled the front door closed behind her and smiled as she practically skipped down the narrow path toward Serena.

"Are you hungry?"

Serena nodded, but before she could say anything, she felt her cheeks heat when Thenia took one of Serena's hands in her own.

"I haven't had a root beer float since I was a kid."

They started walking to the main house, but Serena could see that Thenia was observing her from the corner of her eye.

"Have you ever had one?" Thenia asked.

She shook her head, "But I know what it is."

"You liked the sugar cookies the other night, right?"

"Yes."

Thenia had felt like baking a few nights prior, and though the cookies were a bit chalky, they had a good flavor, and Serena enjoyed them.

"Then I think you'll like this. Similarly sweet, though." Thenia chuckled, "Not as dry as my cookies, thankfully. I think I should leave baking to you from now on."

Serena smiled at the ground in front of her.

They continued to walk, hand in hand, quietly but comfortably, until they saw the main house's back porch. Then, Thenia slowed down, and Serena was forced to either let go of Thenia's hand to keep walking or slow down.

"Serena?"

"Yes?"

"I hope I didn't make you uncomfortable or upset with what I said earlier. About Ashton."

"Did I hear my name?" Ashton sassed from the porch where

he'd stuck his head out of the back door. "Hurry up, you two. Pizza will get cold."

Thenia smiled at Ashton. "Be right there!"

Once he went back inside, Thenia released Serena's hand, leaving it cold and feeling empty.

"Serena, I wish you saw what he and I do." Thenia held open her arms, and Serena stepped into them for a hug. "Truly, Serena. You're an incredible woman with a big heart and a bright smile. Try to remember that."

Serena nodded against her, and Thenia gave her one more gentle squeeze before stepping back.

"Come on, I'm only eating the pizza, so I can justify having had dinner before I eat dessert." Thenia laughed. "I should probably pretend to be an adult."

She retook Serena's hand and led them up the steps and into the main house. The smell of which immediately made Serena's mouth water and her stomach cramp.

"Oh, how does the entire room smell like a pizza oven?" Thenia asked, rushing over to take a stack of plates balancing on top of the pizza box that Ashton carried.

"Trust me, I wish I knew. Now I have to figure out how to get it out of the house, or I'll be ordering every night for a week."

"Aw, too bad," Thenia teased.

Serena held open the door for the pair and was surprised to see Ashton taking the box to a small table beside the swing bed.

"Any objections to eating here? Weather is nice, and I'm tired of light bulbs."

Thenia looked at Serena, who shrugged in response to the woman's unasked question.

"Works for me," Thenia said, putting the stack of plates on the mattress. "I'll grab drinks and napkins. Be right back."

Serena watched Thenia's back as she walked away, but Serena caught Ashton watching her in the window's reflection, not

Thenia.

"I'm sorry," Ashton said, opening the pizza box and beginning to plate slices for each of them.

"For?"

"Making you two eat with me and taking your alone time with Thenia."

Serena felt her brow crease. "What do you mean?"

"What you said earlier. I don't want to intrude, either." Ashton handed her a plate with a slice on it.

"Oh," Serena stared at the plate while she spoke, afraid to look up and see Ashton's eyes when he answered her next question. "You like her, don't you?"

When he didn't answer right away, Serena risked a glance at him and was surprised to see him deeply in thought. "I assume you mean more than as a friend? Because, yeah, as a friend, I care a lot about her."

"But, you want more?" Serena said softly.

Ashton's eyes met her own. "Don't you?"

"I hope this is alright?" Thenia said, exiting the house and effectively stopping their conversation. She handed Ashton a can of soda and then Serena a bottle of water.

"Perfect, thanks!" Ashton swapped the soda for a plate with Thenia.

Thenia pointed to the swing bed and looked at Serena. "Come sit?"

Serena nodded and followed Thenia to the other side of the swing. They helped each other climb up and get settled while Ashton kept the platform steady. Then he sat on the opposite side and took a big bite of his pizza.

"Ug, I haven't had pizza in years," Thenia said, putting it in her mouth. When she realized she'd spoken out loud, Thenia blushed and then laughed into her palm.

"I'm glad I got the good stuff, then," Ashton said and then cocked his head at Serena. "Not hungry?"

"I am." She took a bite and admitted that the gooey cheese and crunchy green peppers were amazing, and the olives and mushrooms blended well. "It's good."

Ashton smiled at her, but before he took another bite, he asked Thenia about his grandfather's garden journals. Serena had been with the older man for most of the time he'd written them, and she missed his company. He was always calm when he spoke to her, and he'd tell Serena stories about Ashton, Eileen, and Alexander from when they were growing up, or about how he'd met his wife and learned what a mechanite was. Arthur had told her about his child and their spouse, dying tragically with their friends and partners, leaving three incredibly young children behind, and parentless.

Serena liked to think she kept Arthur company while Sue was working and helped him feel a little less alone now that his home was empty of children for a second time. In reality, he'd been the one who had helped her.

Her family had no time for her when she was growing up, and being one of the youngest, Serena was often overlooked. Most of her childhood was spent alone, and once she admitted that no one noticed when she was even there, she remained in her beast form and wandered wherever she wanted to.

It was by chance that Serena had found herself in Maine after having stowed away on a truck crossing the country with its cargo. She'd hopped around then, switching from car to car until she'd hidden on a mail van that delivered to Sue and Arthur's home.

When she'd been resting under a rose bush a few days later, Arthur had seen her and treated her kindly. The next day, she couldn't bring herself to leave, nor the day after, nor the day after that. Years went by, and then, one morning, Arthur didn't come to the garden. By that evening, Serena was worried, and after significant reluctance, she switched to her human form and went into the main house to see if anything was wrong. She'd found the couple still in bed, holding hands and no longer breathing. Serena had stayed, rooted in place for a few minutes, tears on her cheeks, mourning her lost friend.

Then she'd called Ashton.

When she reached his voicemail, Serena left a brief message, borrowed a more appropriately sized set of clothes for her current age and size from Eileen, and returned to the garden as a snake. Alone once again.

Ashton, Eileen, and Alexander had returned home to care for their grandparents, while Serena watched from the garden. Then Eileen and Alexander left for another job, but Ashton stayed behind.

Then, Thenia had arrived.

"Serena?" Ashton asked softly. She looked up from her plate and saw that he and Thenia were watching her, both with worried expressions.

"Yes?"

"Are you okay?"

"Yes."

Thenia put her plate down and scooted closer to Serena's side. "You don't look okay, Serena."

Ashton put his plate down and moved closer to her other side.

She patted her cheek and felt tears. "I was...thinking."

"You don't have to share if you don't want to," Thenia said, putting her arm around Serena's shoulders.

"But we're here if you want to talk," Ashton added, resting his palm on her forearm closest to him.

Serena looked at both of them, and eventually, she lowered her plate and nodded. "I just miss...your grandfather."

Ashton smiled and nodded. "Me too."

"Will you tell me about him?" Thenia asked. "I'm sad I wasn't able to meet him. Or his wife. They both sound like wonderful people."

"They were," Serena said, brushing her tears away but unable to say anymore.

Chapter 9: The Snake that Eats its Tail

June 2024, Maine, USA | Thenia Loris

Thenia groaned, rubbed the back of her neck, and then rolled her head from side to side in an effort to relieve the slow ache that had begun creeping into her muscles. She was hiding in the shade on the bed swing, a handful of Arthur's notebooks open in front of her, and her own notebook lay atop her lap. Pens and sticky notes were everywhere, and there were so many page flags in the notebooks that they were starting to look more like porcupines than books.

She had spent the last week trying to make sense of the scattered information now that she'd read each book at least once, cover to cover. Most of the content made sense and only needed cross-referencing from another passage in the same book or one of the others, but there were a few sections that she still couldn't figure out how they fit into the rest.

One of those passages was open in front of her, the book lying on a pillow next to her knee. The page was filled with sketches of flowers, notes on their scent, blooming season, and even what animals Arthur had seen take an interest in them over the years. In the bottom corner of the page was a doodle that

Thenia had never seen before, and she had no idea what the drawing was of or for.

"Maybe planting patterns?" she mumbled as she rubbed the sore fingers of her right hand with her left. "But why would you plant them that way? Unless maybe it was so they would bloom in a pretty pattern years down the road?"

Thenia gazed out into the garden and frowned. "But why only this flower? Roses are pretty, but with the thorns, that seems like way too much work for such little reward. Not to mention, you'd only see that pattern from the sky."

Behind her, the back door to the main house opened, and Thenia saw Ashton exiting the house with two large glasses of iced tea in his hands. She quickly scrambled to close the books and organize some of her mess so Ashton would have a place to sit.

"Hey, figured you might want something to drink and a break. I sure as hell need one."

She moved her notetaking supplies into a pile and took the glass from him before he sat in the space she'd cleared.

"I do, thanks. I didn't realize it would get this hot when I came out here, and I didn't bring my water bottle."

"No problem. Where's Serena?"

Thenia grinned over her glass. "My kitchen."

Ashton raised an eyebrow but continued to sip his tea.

"She's making you an apple pie."

"Wait, really?" When Ashton beamed, nearly ear to ear, it made Thenia laugh.

"Yes, why is that surprising? You mentioned it last week. She's been harvesting apples every afternoon since then."

Ashton stared at her for a minute more before his shoulders relaxed, and he chuckled. "That woman, I swear."

Thenia nodded in agreement. Serena was an amazing person. She was warm and caring, and once she'd felt more comfortable around them, she'd begun to open up. From the moment Thenia first met her to now, the increase in how often Serena laughed was unmistakable, not to mention how much less time she spent staring at her feet or the floor compared to the beginning.

"She still sleeping as a snake?" Ashton asked.

"Yeah. I offered her one of the couches or even to share the bed, but she said she was more comfortable sleeping as a snake."

Ashton sniggered, and Thenia narrowed her eyes.

"What do you know that I don't?"

"Nothing for sure, but I would guess she's embarrassed."

Thenia rolled her eyes. "About what?"

"Wanting to sleep next to you."

Thenia snapped her mouth closed, but Ashton's expression was genuine, and when Thenia realized he wasn't teasing her or Serena but commenting on something deeper, Thenia blushed and looked away.

"Oh."

"I wouldn't let it get to you. She'll get there eventually." Ashton patted Thenia's knee. "Besides, she—"

Thenia and Ashton jumped when his cell phone began making a shrill screeching sound from his pocket.

"What the hell is that?" Thenia asked, trying to calm her heart, but Ashton was on his feet, pulling his phone from his jeans, and didn't acknowledge her question.

He quickly set down his cup, sloshing some of the tea onto the table.

"What is it?" she asked again.

His reaction was tense and instant, so she set her cup beside his and climbed off the bed.

"Someone at the gate."

Thenia snorted. "That's what your system does when someone is at your gate?"

"No," Ashton said flatly.

She watched as he placed his palm on his phone's screen and shut his eyes. They were only closed for a few seconds, but

Thenia's stomach sank when they opened. His eyes were a mix of anger, pity, and regret—all directed at her.

"He found me," Thenia stated, taking a step backward.

"I'll take care of it," Ashton said, turning to walk toward the front of the house.

Thenia's brain caught up when Ashton was only a few steps away, and she caught his arm. "No. Don't."

Ashton glanced over his shoulder at her, and she swallowed roughly as he seemed to be examining her state of mind.

She cleared her throat. "I'll do it. I need to make it clear to him. He needs to leave me alone."

"Thenia—"

She shook her head. "I can do this. I'll be fine."

It seemed like Ashton was going to argue with her, but after a few seconds, he sighed and relented. "Alright."

He briefly shut his eyes again, his phone still in his hand, and when he opened them, he asked, "May I come with you? I opened the gate."

"Please, do," Thenia said, relieved, yet her voice still had a minor wobble to it.

"Okay. You lead. I'm here if you need me, but you're right. You can do this." Ashton quickly kissed her cheek and then stepped out of her way.

Thenia took a deep breath and walked along the porch and around to the front of the house, Ashton silently behind her, providing his quiet strength and reassurance.

By the time they reached the front steps, Lucus was coming into view as he walked up the driveway. Thenia wasn't sure why she was surprised, but he looked exactly the same as he always had. Maybe because she'd changed so much in recent months, she'd expected him to have changed too. The thought made her chuckle, and she saw Ashton glance at her when she made the sound, curiosity in his expression.

When Lucus was nearer to them, she saw that he still wore

his typical black slacks, shined-to-a-mirror-finish dress shoes, and an intentionally cuffed dress shirt. It was his standard uniform whenever the man wanted to give off the air of working hard while still being professional and polished. His black hair was slicked back, and he wore his contacts instead of his glasses, along with one of his many fancy watches.

"Thenia, sweetie!" Lucus' voice practically purred with the tone he reserved for addressing her with when they were in public.

"Interesting," she muttered. If he was using that voice, apparently, Lucus felt like he needed to impress either her or Ashton. That, or her ex felt threatened by one of them.

"Lucus."

Thenia crossed her arms and stayed at the top of the stairs, the vantage point requiring her to look down at him. Ashton stopped a few feet behind her and remained silent.

"You haven't been answering my calls. I was worried."

Lucus stopped at the base of the steps. His eyes skimmed them, and a muscle in his jaw twitched when he saw there wasn't any room for him and that he'd have to stay beneath her.

"No phone," Thenia said, clipped. "Besides, I think we were both pretty clear the last two times we spoke. There's nothing more I have to say to you."

"Don't be like that, sweetie. I told you, I thought it over, and I was wrong."

Thenia failed to suppress a brief laugh. Lucus was *never* wrong. That simple admission explained why he'd come to find her, and it was highly informative. For once, she had the power, not him.

"Wrong or not, the answer is no. I'm not going back to you, nor am I moving back to New Jersey. So, you've wasted your time coming here," she smirked, "and we both know how much you hate a time waste."

If the man's eyes could have slapped her for her insolence, they would have.

"Indeed. You know me well, that's why you should come home. We belong—"

"Where I belong is of no concern to you anymore," she cut him off, and again, she saw his jaw clench at her outburst.

"But I care about you. You should be at my side, not in some small town with your hands in the dirt."

Ashton scarcely shifted behind her, but his movement caught Lucus's attention, and his cold eyes focused on the man behind her.

"Who's this, sweetie? Introduce me to your *friend.*"

"Ashton," he stated, still behind her.

"I see, well, I suppose I should thank you for looking after my Thenia here—"

"I've looked after no one. Thenia is her own woman and takes care of herself."

Ashton had cut Lucus off, and for the second time, Lucus looked ready to explode, and Thenia was starting to enjoy herself.

"Lucus. We have nothing to discuss. Leave."

"We have much to discuss, but this is between you and I. Why don't we let *Ashton* here get back to his day? I'm sure he's got more important things to do than listen to our conversation."

"Nope. I'm free all afternoon. Carry on." Ashton smirked at her and then casually put his hands into the back pockets of his jeans.

"Thenia," Lucus said a bit firmer.

"Enough, Lucus. You are not welcome here. I am not leaving. Frankly, if I never have to hear your name or see your face ever again, I will die a happy woman. If you have one last thing to say, say it, but then get out."

Thenia had never spoken back to Lucus before, never told him no, never second-guessed him, and definitely had never stood her ground against him. Now that she had, she saw the man she'd been dumb enough to waste a decade of her life on turning an excellent shade of white. So white, she was mildly concerned he was going to pass out from shock.

Except, then he regained his composure and stood up a bit straighter, his eyes narrowed at her. "I spoke to your parents."

It was Thenia's turn to go pale, and she involuntarily shuffled back a half step and bumped directly into Ashton, whose hands were instantly on her waist to steady her.

"You did what?"

Lucus sneered smugly. "They were quite worried about you when I told them how things ended between us and how upset you were when you left. You hadn't even told them why you walked out on me." He tsked at her. "Shame on you. We only want what's best for you."

Ashton stiffened behind her but stayed silent. Warmth radiated from his palms against her sides, soothing her rapid pulse.

"You had no right."

"Sweetie, I'm your fiancée. I have every right."

She shook her head. "No. Not anymore."

"You will be leaving here with me, Thenia. It's what's best for you. You know that. Where else will you be as safe and loved as you are with me? You get to be yourself, have anything—"

"Myself!" she shrieked.

Something in Thenia seemed to awaken after hearing Lucus gaslight her for what felt like the millionth time. Her fists clenched by her sides, and then she erupted into laughter.

"What fucking planet do you live on, Lucus? I was never allowed to be myself with you. You dressed me, fed me only what you wanted me to eat, took me out only to show me off, and made me suppress who I am and my magic for years!"

Lucus rolled his eyes and crossed his arms. "Oh, not this again. Sweetheart, magic isn't real. You aren't some powerful plant witch or whatever you think you are. You're just sick, but it's fine. I'll get you help."

"Oh, really?" Thenia smirked. "Want to test that theory? Why don't we find out which of us is the crazy one? The one who thinks magic is real, or the one who refuses to accept what's in front of his face."

"Stop this. This is crazy, you're not a w—"

Thenia whispered under her breath the command to manipulate water droplets. Thanks to the wetter summer they were having, there was plenty of moisture around them for her to use in making her point. She raised the nearby droplets and dew from the plants she could see into the air.

Lucus had continued talking even as she'd tuned him out, continuing to gaslight her about how mentally ill she was and how he was the only one who could save her. She ignored him and focused on moving the water she controlled to hover in front of his face. He immediately stopped talking and stared at it in disbelief. It wasn't until she began shifting the liquid into the form of a snake that he stepped back in horror, his palm coming up to cover his mouth.

"I believe the lady has proved her theory," Ashton quipped and bent over to pick up Serena, who had slithered to their feet while Thenia was focusing. He stroked the top of the green snake's head and held her up to Thenia's shoulder, where Serena curled her tail around her neck and then brushed her head on Thenia's chin.

"Th-this is impossible," Lucus stuttered.

"Is it?" Thenia challenged as she walked down the steps and towards her ex.

Lucus stepped back reflexively, and she grinned.

"Oh, you get it now. All those years, I suffered in silence. Trying to be the doting girlfriend you wanted. The trophy partner for everyone to see, so that you could advance your career. I abandoned my magic and watched daily as strangers tended to my family namesake. Forgetting who I was, what I enjoyed, and what I hated. You did that. And for what? So you could get promotion after promotion. Lucus, you are a selfish, self-absorbed, and arrogant fool, and I'm done being your picture frame's stock photo family. This is the last time I will tell you to leave me alone. The next time you fail to listen, you may also get to see what Ashton and Serena are capable of."

Ashton chuffed behind her, still on the porch. "Do I have to wait?"

Serena rose to her full height on Thenia's shoulder and hissed at Lucus.

"Get. Out," Thenia demanded. "Do not call me again. Do not come back, and do not contact my family again. It's over. Go home and find some other lonely woman to be your ladder-climbing prop."

Lucus opened his mouth to say something, and Thenia made the water snake's form hiss just as Serena had a moment before. Lucus snapped his mouth shut, glanced at Ashton over her shoulder, and then turned and walked toward the car he'd left outside of the property.

Thenia never took her eyes off his back, but she moved the water snake to eye level with Serena and flicked its tongue at her. When Lucus was out of view, Thenia turned to look at Ashton, who, as expected, had his eyes closed and was speaking with the security system.

Nearly a full minute later, he opened his eyes and nodded. "He's gone."

Thenia moved the water snake over to the plants and released it, thanking it as she did. When she was done, Ashton walked towards her with a proud grin.

Serena bumped her head against Thenia's cheek, which made her giggle. "Thanks, Serena. Both for the assist and the courage."

The snake licked her cheek, and Thenia looked up at Ashton when he stopped in front of her.

"Well..." Thenia said stupidly.

"Well."

"Did I, um...do alright?" she looked away.

"Beautifully."

She glanced at him, but Ashton was smiling at Serena. "I hear there's apple pie."

Serena nodded and then slithered her way down Thenia's arm, hip, and then her leg until she was back on the ground.

Thenia stared down at her and shook her head. "I'd have helped you down."

"Want a head start?" Ashton asked, and Serena nodded before quickly slithering off into the plants.

Once she was gone, Ashton checked on Thenia. "Was that what you wanted?"

"What part? Pie?"

He smirked at her. "Who doesn't want apple pie, but no, I mean with Lucus."

"Not to be with him. Yes. Hell, yes."

"Are you sure? Not that I, personally, would have wan—"

Even though she was pretty sure she knew where Ashton's sentence was headed, she wanted to tell him what she was thinking first. Except, instead of using her words, one minute, she was listening to Ashton being silly and supportive, and then the next, she was on her tiptoes, arms around his neck, kissing him. The warmth that spread through her when he pulled her closer to himself felt like ten years of shadows were chased away in an instant, and she genuinely loved every minute of it.

When she pulled away, he was staring at her, his eyes sparkling in the sun, his lips and cheeks slightly flushed.

"I'd like to stay here. Will you let me?" she asked, still holding onto him loosely.

"As long as you want, Thenia. Not a second longer."

She smiled and stepped further away and out of his grasp. "Deal, but one condition."

"What is it?"

"You have the same rule. When you want me to leave, tell me. Don't do what I did and waste time on something that doesn't make you happy."

Ashton placed his palm on her cheek, his thumb gently grazing her skin. "I understand, and I promise."

"Thank you," she said, closing her eyes. She leaned into his palm, enjoying the feel of his skin against hers.

"Thenia."

She opened her eyes and saw that Ashton was suddenly very serious. More so than she'd ever seen.

"What is it?"

"Serena," Ashton pulled his hand away from Thenia and put both of them into his pockets.

"Ah, yeah," Thenia looked away.

"You know how she feels about you, right?" Ashton asked, and Thenia nodded. "I don't want to hurt her."

"Me either," Thenia looked back at him, "but you care for her, too. It's not just me, is it?"

Ashton sighed and scratched his neck, a mannerism that seemed to show up when he was uncomfortable, from what Thenia had observed.

"Ashton?"

"Yeah?" he replied hesitantly.

"I do, too."

His hand froze, and he glanced at her. "Oh, well, um...."

"Does that make this easier or harder?" she whispered.

He sighed and held out his hand for her to take, which she did.

"Both. I think."

Thenia took a deep breath, then exhaled, and nodded.

"I think so, too."

Ashton gently squeezed her hand in his, and they began

walking back toward her tiny house, where the pie made by an amazing woman awaited them.

A woman whom Thenia refused to hurt.

Serena Ainsley

When Thenia and Ashton returned to the garden house, it was obvious that something had changed between them in the short time that Serena had been apart from them. She saw the difference in how they looked at each other and how they sat a bit closer than before.

Her heart ached, and she was surprised by how much. It was only then that she realized her true situation—once again, she was in the way and would soon be forgotten.

Meaning it was time for her to leave.

"Serena, are you up for a walk? I think it's a full moon tonight," Thenia said as she dried a dish Ashton had just washed and handed her.

"Um, you two go...."

Ashton glanced at her over his shoulder before adding to Thenia's request, "Please come with us, Serena."

She stared at the floor until she saw Thenia's toes when they stopped in front of her. "I don't want to get in the way."

"Serena, you're not in the way. You never are. I promise. Please, come with us? Your pie was delicious, and after the adrenaline and then the sugar rush, I need to move around a bit."

"Please?" Ashton asked again as he turned off the sink.

"Okay...."

"Thank you," Thenia said, kissing her cheek. Then, she walked past her and up the steps to the bedroom.

Serena hadn't moved when Ashton's feet replaced Thenia's in her line of vision only seconds later.

"I'm going to grab something from the main house. I'll catch up."

Then Ashton kissed Serena's other cheek before he left the small house.

Unexpectedly alone, she stared at her hands, one of which was picking at the skin on one of her fingers. When she stopped, both hands shook slightly. Then, she realized how quiet it was around her, and she suddenly felt light-headed and too warm.

She needed to be outside.

Serena rushed to the small house's back door and onto the porch. She closed her eyes and inhaled the fresh air as deeply as she could. The urge to shift back into her beast form felt overwhelming, and had Thenia not opened the back door, Serena likely would have given in to it.

"Serena, are you alright?"

When she didn't answer, Thenia stepped out and shut the door. Then she draped the sweatshirt Ashton had given to Serena over her shoulders.

"Still up for that walk? The fresh air will make us all feel better, I think."

Serena turned away but nodded. When Thenia took her hand and laced their fingers together, Serena finally looked at her again and was surprised to find Thenia practically beaming at her.

"Ashton head up to the main house?" Thenia asked.

Serena nodded and let Thenia lead her along the path that wound around the back of the house, meeting up with the path in front.

"Okay, he was going to grab a change of clothes. Are you up for a movie night?"

Serena didn't answer, and Thenia didn't ask again, but they continued to walk. A few minutes later, Ashton was walking towards them, a small bag over one of his shoulders. His bright smile was captivating, and Serena pulled her eyes away from it and back to the floor.

"Got everything you need?" Thenia asked him.

"Yup, all good. You want to pick the first movie, Serena?"

She shook her head and tried to pull her hand from Thenia's, but she held her tightly.

Serena's voice was barely audible when she said, "I should go."

"Serena?" Ashton reached for her free hand, lacing his fingers with hers. She was now between him and Thenia, both of them squeezing her palms and watching her.

"Thenia and I don't want you to go anywhere."

"It's not home without you, Serena," Thenia added.

Serena's world went blurry, and she dropped her head, shaking it.

"I'll just be in the way, and then you'll forget about me, and I'll be alone again. I should just leave now and—" she hiccupped and sniffled.

"Oh, sweetie," Thenia said, but then flinched. "Okay, never mind on the sweetie part."

Serena felt the woman shudder, and Ashton chuckled.

"Yeah, can we make that rule number two?" he asked. "No, sweetie."

Thenia giggled, "Yes, please."

"Serena, do you want to know what rule number one is?" Ashton asked.

"What is it?" she sniffled again.

"No one stays when they don't want to. We won't force you to stay with us, but I really hope you'll decide on your own that you want to be here."

"You make our days brighter, Serena," Thenia added. "I could never forget about you, and I'd be upset to find you no longer with us."

Serena stared at the two hands holding hers, and Thenia brushed her free hand over Serena's cheeks, wiping away her tears.

"Come on. Tonight, let's watch a movie and eat more of your pie. Tomorrow, the next day, or the day after that, you can think about it more and decide. That fair?" Thenia asked.

Serena was disoriented, but she managed a nod. That seemed to placate them enough, and they all resumed their walk. Neither of them ever let go of Serena's hands, but both loosely held on to her, giving her a sense of choice. The conversation was light, and she offered very little to it, but they gave her the space to be quiet or participate as she felt comfortable.

By the time they had returned to the small house, Serena had made her decision.

She'd watch a movie, and once Ashton and Thenia were both asleep, Serena would say goodbye and leave before she inevitably became invisible to them.

Just as she had to everyone else that she'd loved.

Chapter 10: Sunrise and Secrets

June 2024, Maine, USA | Ashton Giri

A hushed shuffling sound woke Ashton from where he had fallen asleep on the couch at some point during the movie he'd been watching with Thenia and Serena. He cracked his eyelids open just enough to see Serena leaning forward on the couch, her elbows on her knees. She looked upset, and based on how her eyes flicked between him and Thenia and the back door, Serena looked nervous and weighed down.

Ashton kept watching her as discreetly as he could manage, even though he wanted to offer to help her however he could. It was clear his and Thenia's admissions earlier in the day had confused Serena. When she'd immediately reverted to the timid woman who endeavored to take up as little space as possible, Ashton knew they hadn't gotten through to her.

When Serena's gaze lingered on the darkness outside the back door again, Ashton forced his eyes shut so he could feign being asleep as she tried to figure out what she wanted to do.

Thenia shifted in her sleep, her head against one of the couch arms, her feet draped over his lap. When he heard Serena sniffle, he knew she was looking away from them, and he opened his eyes just as a tear rolled down Serena's cheek. He forced himself not to move and observed her reflection in the window.

"I'm sorry," Serena whispered to the two people she believed were still sleeping.

Then she carefully got to her feet, trying not to jostle him or Thenia. Ashton used the opportunity to shift a little so he could better conceal his face, allowing him to watch her without Serena knowing he was doing it. She started to take his sweatshirt off but stopped midway and tugged it back on. The hesitation gave him hope that he'd be able to get through to her, but for now, he remained still.

Serena tiptoed past him, her soft footsteps making virtually zero sound, even in the quiet house. Once he heard the front door open and then the soft click of the lock, he opened his eyes fully.

Ashton shimmied from beneath Thenia's legs and then picked up his phone from the table to check the cameras. His hunch was that Serena would say goodbye to his Pops before she left, and when he saw her walking toward the pair of headstones along one of the farthest parts of the property, a grin filled his face.

"See, you don't want to leave either," he whispered softly enough not to rouse Thenia.

Ashton decided to follow Serena's lead, and he yanked on his shoes before slipping quietly from the house and into the dark gardens. He gave her a few minutes of privacy, but when Serena had had nearly ten minutes alone, Ashton followed the trails through the grounds that would lead him to the two graves on the property.

She was still kneeling on the grass in front of Pops' headstone when Ashton stepped through the trees, and even from across the garden, he noticed her shoulders rising and falling as she cried.

Ashton bit his tongue to keep from cursing. It wasn't until then that he understood her earlier comment about people leaving her and the fear associated with it. In a way, that's precisely what Pops did, even if it wasn't by his own choice. Serena had lost the only people she cared about, just as he, Eileen, and Xander had. Except now, Serena thought that she was alone again while he and his siblings had each other.

Ashton crossed the small clearing in the foliage and saw Serena stiffen when she finally heard him behind her. Before she moved, he stopped where he was.

"Serena, they may be gone, but they didn't leave you, and you'll never be alone here."

She sniffled and shook her lowered head. "You're wrong."

He forced his voice to remain gentle, even though he felt more like screaming at her to actually listen to what he was saying. She was likely unable to because of the depth of fear she seemed to carry, but getting frustrated with her wouldn't help her understand.

"Alright, say I believe you. Explain why you think that."

"I'm no one. Not important—the," she cried harder, "one that no one needs."

He closed the distance between them and stopped behind her, where he barely pressed one of his knees to her back, needing to feel some point of contact with her.

"None of that is true, Serena."

She continued to cry while nodding and burying her face in the sleeves of his sweatshirt that she wore. Ashton lowered himself to the grass behind her, his legs stretching to either side of hers. When she didn't react, he gently tugged her to lean back against him, and then he held onto her, his arms around her, as tightly as he dared.

"What about Pops?" he asked, his voice hushed beside her ear.

"What about...him...."

"He needed you. He wouldn't have asked me to talk to his green snake friend if he didn't care about you."

She didn't say anything, and he rested his cheek against her hair, the subtle perfume of the shampoo he'd given her filling his senses. It had been one of the only things she'd requested from him.

He'd been interrupted while working one afternoon when he heard someone sneezing repeatedly in the living room of the main house. When he'd gone out to see what was up, he discovered Serena puffy-eyed and clutching a box of tissues. Apparently, she'd borrowed Thenia's shower products, and even though they were only lightly fragranced, it was too much for Serena's sense of smell. She'd been waiting to ask him if he could help her get something unscented the next time he went into town because she didn't want to offend Thenia with her request. When he'd left the room to grab a few bottles from Eileen's bathroom and then returned to Serena, she looked pale as a sheet.

He'd settled the spare bottles on the kitchen counter for her to take back to the garden house with her, and then he'd shooed her off to his sister's shower to rewash her hair and rinse out the more fragrant products. When he exited his office again a few hours later, there was a plate of cookies where the bottles had been on the counter and a simple note saying thank you.

"Serena, Thenia, and I need you, too."

"Why?"

"Why, what? Do we need you?"

She nodded against him.

"Because you're you," Thenia voiced from behind them.

Ashton held one of his hands up, and a few seconds later, Thenia clutched it and sat beside him and Serena before she nestled into the woman's flank.

"Are these your grandparents?" Thenia asked him.

"They are," he answered, but left it at that.

"Serena, will you tell me about Arthur?"

"He was outside...in the plants...no matter what the weather was like." Serena sniffled. "Even if it was raining, he'd sit on the porch with books, learning more about them."

"Is that where the notebooks came from?"

Serena nodded. "He took notes."

"Lots of them, apparently," Ashton teased.

"Dense notes," Thenia added with a smile.

"He...told me it was for Sue."

"Oh," Ashton said, "in what way?"

"He knew she spent so much time with her computers, locked in a room without windows. He...wanted her to have a beautiful place to be outside when she could."

Ashton's throat constricted, and he squeezed his eyes shut, and it was his time to sniffle.

Growing up, he, Eileen, and Xander had never lacked love. Even as children, they knew their Gram and Pops' love for each other was incredible and ran deep. Ashton had always been willing to bet the pair were soulmates, but they laughed him off and said their three grandchildren were their soulmates.

Thenia released his hand, and he watched her shift to scoot closer to the headstone that was his Pops' before lowering her head.

"Thank you for loving this garden so much. And your wife and family, both the blood-related and the two who are not."

Ashton smiled, knowing she'd included Serena and Xander in her statement.

"Thank you for leaving a legacy that I will try to be worthy of tending to. I hope the angels were swift in retrieving you and your wife, and you spend your days watching those you care for live long and fulfilling lives."

When Thenia was finished, she raised her head and pressed the tips of her fingertips to the stone. Only a second later, she gasped and leaned forward to look at the inscription.

"Thenia?" Ashton asked, concerned by her change in demeanor.

"What is this?" Thenia indicated to a portion of the message on the stone, but she hadn't taken her eyes from it.

"I think it's the language that the mechanite use," Serena answered.

"Yeah, it's the language of the mechanical. Why?" he confirmed.

"Because I've seen it before."

He shook his head. "Highly doubtful. We keep it very—"

Thenia swiveled and glared at him.

"Where?" he asked, figuring the worst he could do was humor her. She wasn't an Outsider, so it was *possible* she'd seen it, even if highly improbable.

"One of his journals."

Serena shook her head. "He didn't know it. I never saw him use it."

"I swear," Thenia grumbled and got to her feet.

"I believe you," Ashton said, gazing up at her, "but Serena's right." Ashton detangled himself from Serena, got to his feet, and helped Serena up. "Pops was human, remember?"

"Fine. I'll prove it." Thenia practically groaned before she jogged off, not even bothering to see if he and Serena were following her.

Ashton peeked at Serena, who grinned as she watched the other woman vanish among the trees and into the sunrise.

"Well, I guess we should follow her, shouldn't we?" he said.

Serena glanced up at him, and her smile receded.

"Serena," Ashton brushed a strand of her hair back from her cheek. "Give us a chance. Let us prove how much we want you to stay with us."

After a few agonizing seconds, she nodded the barest amount, and he leaned in to brush a soft kiss on her lips.

"Thank you, Serena."

"I...I'll try...."

He nodded and then playfully took her wrist, spinning himself around before crouching with her standing at his back.

"Come on, hop up. I don't know my way around the garden this far out, but I can jog, and you can point."

Serena stared down at him, but he gently tugged her, and she hopped on his back. He stood up and resituated her, making her giggle, which made his heart threaten to drop them both to the floor.

"Alright, Navigator! Where to?"

She held on tighter around his neck, and he felt a slight brush of her lips on his cheek. Then she pointed in front of them.

"Go straight and turn left at the apricot tree. There's a shortcut back to Thenia's."

"You got it!" Ashton grinned and began jogging.

Thenia Loris

Serena's laughter made Thenia pause, and through the loft window, she glimpsed Ashton, giving a giggling Serena a piggyback ride. The intimate moment between them made Thenia's heart race, and unlike earlier that morning, this time, the feeling didn't make her want to sob.

When she had woken up alone on the couch, the sun just rising, she'd rushed to tug on her shoes. By the time she'd reached the short wall around her home's garden, Thenia had caught sight of Ashton's back before he stepped into the trees and made his way through a portion of the garden she knew was wilder, and she had not ventured far into it yet. She followed him as quietly as she could, and when Ashton had finally begun to get through to Serena, Thenia couldn't merely observe anymore.

Seeing the two of them being silly with each other now, it looked like their conversation may have helped. Only time would convince Serena that she and Ashton had meant what they'd said.

Thenia tore her gaze from the pair and back to the books on the desk strewn in front of her. It didn't take her long to find the one she'd been reading the day prior, so she brought it downstairs and placed it on the kitchen counter as the other two opened the front door. Serena's cheeks were flushed, but her smile was so large that her eyes were practically closed. Ashton lowered her to the floor and reached behind her to shut the front door.

"Thanks for the ride. I'm lighter as a snake."

Ashton chuckled but kissed her forehead. "Anytime, and either form is fine."

Thenia smiled at both of them but shoved the book toward them once they focused on her.

"This one."

Ashton sat at one of the kitchen stools while Serena skimmed the book over his shoulder.

"Go to the section about roses," Thenia clarified.

"I remember when he wrote that section," Serena added while Ashton flipped to it.

Once he was on the correct page, Thenia watched as both frowned at it.

"Oh, that wasn't there before." Serena cocked her head and then leaned around Ashton to inspect it closer.

"You're right, Thenia. It is the mechanite language, but you're wrong about Pops writing it." Ashton peeked up at Thenia and grinned. "It's Gram's handwriting."

Thenia nodded before brewing coffee for Ashton and tea for her and Serena. "Okay, that makes more sense. Not a lot of sense, but more, at least. What does it say?"

"My name."

Thenia spun around and stared at him, Serena doing the same at his side.

"Why would she write your name in Arthur's book?" Serena asked before Thenia could.

"I have no idea," Ashton stated, flipping through more of the book. "This is the only place you've seen those characters, Thenia?"

"So far, yeah. I think I've at least skimmed all of the books, so I'm pretty confident saying that's the only place, too."

"Interesting."

Ashton set the book on the counter and continued thumbing through it, his finger holding the page where his name was. Serena touched his wrist gently, then she moved to the fridge, pulling out milk, butter, and a loaf of sourdough bread.

"I'll make toast. Peanut butter, Thenia?"

Thenia took the milk and butter from her and smiled. "That's perfect, thank you."

The three of them were silent as Ashton read, Serena fixed a light breakfast, and Thenia finished brewing coffee and tea for them all. Once everything was prepared, she told Ashton to put the book away, but he didn't seem to hear her. She grasped the book, still in Ashton's hands, and tapped her finger on it until he looked up at her, and she smiled.

"Eat. It will be here after a little food. Besides, I made you coffee."

Ashton's eyes darted around the kitchen, and then he chuffed. "Sorry. Guess I was pretty focused."

Thenia placed the book on the counter, away from their food, and then claimed the last stool, which happened to be between him and Serena. "Not a big deal. Did you think of anything?"

Ashton shook his head, his mouth full of buttered toast.

"I wonder why she wrote on that specific page," Serena said while sipping her breakfast tea.

"No idea," Thenia shrugged. "Were roses her favorite flower or special to her for some reason?"

"Nope," Ashton answered. "Far as I know, she loved tulips."

"Yup," Serena confirmed.

"Hmm...." Thenia chewed on her peanut-buttered toast

while she stared at the journal across the room as if willing it to speak to her. "Wait," she said abruptly, stopping the other two mid-bite or slurp. "Roses."

Ashton chuckled, "Yeah, established that part."

Thenia smirked and elbowed him. "No. Roses. All plants are thought to have a meaning or represent something."

"What do roses mean?" Serena asked.

Thenia grinned. "Secrets."

Ashton's eyes widened as his brain caught up with her unspoken hypothesis.

"The letter," Serena vocalized.

Thenia nodded. "Eat. Then we go check out this rose garden."

All three of them resumed eating, their urgency compelling them to chew faster than they had a few minutes earlier.

Thenia wasn't sure what they would uncover in the rose garden, but she knew that whatever it was, just the idea of its existence made Ashton uneasy. He'd drunk his coffee and devoured his toast in less than five minutes. Then, he went to the loft to swap clothes while she and Serena finished their breakfasts.

"I'll wash dishes if you want to go change, Serena. I left a clean T-shirt and your jeans out when I put my stuff away yesterday. They're on the dresser."

"Oh, thank you."

Serena carried her plate and mug to the sink, and Thenia touched her arm as she neared her.

"Serena?"

"Yeah?"

Thenia tugged her arm gently, and Serena stepped closer so Thenia could hug her. Because Thenia was seated, she tentatively snuggled her face into Serena's neck, who, to her relief, hugged her back.

"Thank you for staying," Thenia muttered before she drew away and smiled at her.

Serena glanced away, her cheeks pink, but she nodded. Thenia released her arm and stood up, gathering her dishes.

"Thenia?" Serena asked softly.

"Hmm?"

When Thenia glanced back at her, Serena gave her a feather-light kiss before practically sprinting up to the bedroom. Thenia smirked and shook her head at the woman's timidness, but let her be and washed up all the breakfast dishes.

A minute later, Thenia heard Ashton skip down the loft steps and back into the kitchen.

"She's changing clothes," Thenia said when she saw Ashton in the window's reflection as he frantically looked around the room.

He exhaled heavily, "Ah, got it. Thanks."

"You doing alright?"

Ashton nodded and came to stand beside her, leaning on the counter. "Yeah. More confused than anything, honestly. My Gram wasn't very secretive—well, I didn't think she was. She never withheld anything. We asked, and she'd answer."

"What if it was about work or something, and she wasn't allowed to tell you? Would she still have told you?"

Ashton nodded. "We knew better than to ask things that might put her in a tough situation, knowing she'd not lie to us. If we did stumble on something, we'd tell her to forget we asked and then walk away."

"Well, this must have been pretty important then." Thenia turned off the faucet and dried her hands on a nearby towel before kissing his cheek. "Let me swap clothes, and then we can play super sleuth."

She walked to the bottom of the bedroom stairs and called, "Serena, may I come up and change?"

"Yes, I'm finished."

When Thenia reached the top of the steps, Serena glanced at her, but her cheeks reddened again instantly, and she looked away.

"Ashton's ready. Would you mind keeping him from running off alone while I change?"

Serena giggled and nodded. "Yeah, thank you for the shirt."

"Anything you need. Let me know if you want to go shopping, okay?"

"Okay…." Serena said tentatively but rushed back to the kitchen without saying anything else.

Thenia began digging through her drawers for fresh clothes and was redressed and downstairs in less than five minutes.

"You two ready?"

"Yup." Ashton pulled open the front door half a second later.

Thenia stifled her laughter, but Serena couldn't, and Ashton rolled his eyes at them. "I know, I'm being impatient."

"It's fine," Thenia teased, poking his bicep as she passed him and left the house, Serena following behind her. "Where we headed, Serena?"

"Almost dead center of the west gardens."

"Interesting. That's the English-style garden, right?" Thenia asked.

"Yeah."

Ashton ambled behind them, his gaze on the ground, his hands in his pockets, and his focus unquestionably in his head.

Thenia looped her arm with Serena's and leaned to whisper in her ear. "You think if we went to the wrong section, he'd even notice at this point?"

Serena grinned and shook her head.

"Probably shouldn't, though."

"Another day," Serena said softly. "What do you think we'll find?"

"No clue," Thenia replied at a normal volume again.

"You think we'll find something, though?"

"Feels like it, but really, you two knew them better. For all I know, they were practical jokers, and we could be on a goose chase to find a rubber duck or something."

Ashton chuckled from behind them.
Serena smiled. "I think we'll find something."

Chapter 11: Buried in the Darkness

June 2024, Maine, USA | Ashton Giri

A few days had passed since Ashton had identified the mechanite symbol in Pops' notes, but they were no closer to an explanation of what it signified than the day they found it. Thenia had guided them to the rose garden, but when they got to the correct section, the plants were far too overgrown to search through. Instead, Thenia spent two days trimming, pruning, and tending to the plants. Even if something were hiding among them, she refused to chance harming them to uncover it—not if she didn't have to, and Ashton wouldn't have asked her to.

Now, the three of them were, once again, standing in front of the breathtaking rose garden. Thenia was undoubtedly a master at her craft and quite literally a plant whisperer, with her proficiency demonstrated in each section of the garden she'd cultivated so far, and the roses were no exception.

The three of them had been surveying spiky bushes for over an hour with nothing to show for it, and Ashton was starting to think they'd made a big deal out of nothing.

Ashton squatted down next to Thenia, who was lifting snake Serena to lie on her shoulder. She'd switched to her beast form a half hour earlier to search lower down along the ground, just in case his Pops had hidden something for her to find, not him.

"No luck?" he asked, and the snake shook her head.

"Damn," Thenia frowned and sat cross-legged on the gravel path.

"It was a long shot anyway," he admitted.

"I guess. I was really hoping there was some significance to the choice of roses, though." She chuckled, "Well, at least I know what the symbols mean and can stop trying to guess. Not to mention the roses are taken care of now."

"What did you think the symbols were?" he asked, stroking the top of Serena's head with his fingertip.

"Oh, anything and everything. Watering routes, planting bed patterns, even—"

"Wait!" Ashton smacked his forehead, the abruptness causing Thenia to jerk. "Thenia, you're brilliant. Flower beds."

She smirked sideways at him. "Not following."

"Can you do your dirt thing? Like when you get your key from the flower bed in front of the house. See if anything is buried under the flower beds." He grinned as her eyes widened and Serena started to wiggle.

"That's…of course! Why the hell didn't we think that they'd bury something?" Thenia peeked sidelong at Serena. "Staying or wanna wait with Ashton?"

Serena extended toward Ashton, and he beamed as she slithered onto his outstretched palm.

"Okay. Ashton, go stand over there," Thenia instructed, pointing a way down the trail, so far away that she'd indicated at the next garden section by a jasmine plant, not a rose. "I'm going to aerate all the soil at once and see if there's anything foreign."

"Got it."

He hustled to do as requested, and when she knelt on the edge of the path and stuck both of her palms into the topsoil, he smiled at Serena, and then they both watched Thenia.

From how far away they were, Ashton couldn't hear the words that Thenia spoke, but he could see her lips moving. A few seconds later, the ground around Thenia seemed to shimmy. There was a faint rumbling sound, and then the leaves of the nearby plants grazed against one another, creating smooth, wispy sounds. The entire process lasted only a minute. Once everything had calmed back down, he waited patiently for Thenia's conclusion.

When she rotated and grinned, his blood rushed to his toes.

"Did you find something?"

She didn't answer him but instead leaned towards one of the bushes and groped under it, the leaves skimming her ear because of how far she had to reach. A few seconds later, she jogged over and held out her palm.

"Mean anything to you, Mr. Mechanite?"

Ashton carried Serena in one of his palms, but he reticently picked up the small USB drive tucked into a clear plastic film container from Thenia. Her dirt-shifting magic had cleaned the canister off, and he popped it open. The drive within looked pristine and relatively new. He narrowed his eyes at the device, but when he flipped it over, he identified the symbol.

"Oh shit."

"I take it that's a yes?" Thenia questioned proudly.

Ashton's eyes snapped up to hers. "Come with me?"

She smiled. "Still here, aren't I?"

He closed his fist around the drive and yanked her to him, kissing her deeply but briefly before he then held Serena up so they were at eye level.

"You two are fucking amazing. Thank you. Both of you."

Serena seemed unfazed by his impulsive kiss with Thenia, at least, he thought so, but she stretched forward and licked his cheek, making him laugh.

"Wow, that tickles."

Thenia chuckled lightly and agreed. "It does, but it's sweet."

Serena wound her way up his arm to drape herself around his neck.

"It is. Come on," he grabbed Thenia's hand and thankfully didn't have to drag her since she had hastened her pace to match his. "I think I know what this is."

She laughed as he started to jog, compelling her to run behind him as they navigated the myriad gravel trails until they reached the paved one that guided them to the porch. He released her hand, skipped up the steps, and held open the door for her. After closing it, he ushered her down the main hallway to his office.

"This was Gram's office," he said, pulling her into the dimly lit room.

Thenia gasped when she stepped inside, and he watched her eyes skim everything around her. From his shoulder, he saw Serena doing the same thing.

"Serena, are you staying in that form? You're welcome to do whatever you want, but you can use one of the rooms in the house if you want to shift with a bit of privacy. My room is two doors down to the left."

Serena started heading down his arm, and he knelt to make it easier for her to slide off him and onto the carpet. Once she was there, she scurried from the room and headed in the direction of his room.

"Ashton, this is incredible," Thenia said as she continued to stare from the doorway where she'd stopped.

He smirked, but to a non-mechanite, the space probably did seem that way. To him, a dozen monitors, multiple machines, the blue glow, various keyboards, and the warmth of the room, combined with the steady hum, were normal and felt like being wrapped in a soothing blanket. The fact that it was his Gram's office made it even more so, with the tiny touches of her everywhere. A throw pillow on one chair, framed photos on the walls, a bookshelf with some of her favorite books, and even a few potted plants, though all of them were silk.

Her computer had hardly been used since she passed, and he'd made little to no changes to the room when he inherited it. He'd added his desk, chair, and a few computers and servers, but that was it.

"Shit," Thenia said abruptly, "weren't we not supposed to come in here?"

He smiled and shook his head. "It's all good. I'm not logged into the database right now."

She nodded and then glanced over her shoulder as Serena came running down the hallway and into the room, nearly colliding with Thenia, who had never stepped more than two feet over the threshold.

"Sorry, Thenia."

Thenia giggled and steadied the other woman. "Don't be. I'm the one being a roadblock."

"Okay, sorry that took me so long," Serena apologized.

Ashton glanced at his watch, and then at Thenia, and then back at Serena. "You were gone for less than five minutes. That's slow?"

She shrugged.

"I guess I have something else to hold over Xander's head."

Serena giggled. "He slower?"

"Not all the time, but he's a panther. As a kid, there were some days when I swear he was nothing more than a lazy house cat."

Thenia's laughter was so abrupt that she coughed, and Serena gently patted her back but continued to laugh with her.

Ashton held the thumb drive up, his palm open. "Okay. So, this."

He walked over to Gram's desk and plopped into her desk chair. He took a deep breath and stared at her computer tower. As he wavered, he felt slender hands on each of his shoulders and looked up to see both women standing side by side behind him. He nodded, leaned forward, and pressed the power button.

It only took her computer half a minute to turn on and display the login screen. He pulled the keyboard forward and then froze.

"Shit. I don't actually know her password."

"Wasn't in a will or anything?" Thenia asked.

"Nope. All I know is the password for the basic household profile."

"Can you just...ask it to unlock?" Serena said, her cheeks flushing.

Ashton chuckled. "Technically, yes, but there's a code between mechanites. Basically, we don't mess with each other's shit. So, yeah, I could break in, but I won't. No matter if she's gone or if that means our lead ends here because of it."

"Got it," Serena said.

"Will it lock if you guess a few times?" Thenia asked.

"Probably."

He squinted at the keyboard for a minute and then typed in Pops' birthday. The input window wiggled and cleared. Ashton tested a few more birthdays, their anniversary, and even his parents' birthdays.

"Damn," he bent forward on his elbows and put his face in his palms.

Serena's hand slid from his shoulder, and he glanced from his position of pity to see her wandering the office, looking at things as she went. She wouldn't do any harm, so he let her be.

"What if you put the thumb drive in before you tried to log in?" Thenia asked. "Would that make a difference?"

"Possibly, but I don't want to chance it infecting her setup if it's malicious. I was hoping to find a file or some explanation first. I can build a rig isolated from the rest of the network and try that, but I don't want to if I don't have to."

"Gotcha," Thenia squeezed his shoulder and left to roam the room with Serena.

Ashton pulled out his phone and texted Eileen.

You have any idea what Gram's password is?

He placed his phone on the desk to wait for her reply and returned to his brooding position.

"Are you sure you need to be on her computer?" Serena asked.

"Yup. If she went to all this trouble to hide this, I can't see her putting it anywhere else."

His phone vibrated, and as predicted, his sister didn't know the password either.

"Oh, you have a keyboard with those symbols on it," Thenia remarked, and he saw her bending over it, her hands behind her back while she studied it. "It's an interesting language. There are so many letters. Is letter the right word?"

"Yeah, completely different than English..." Ashton suddenly raised his head, twisting to look at her. "Thenia, unplug that and bring it over here."

She processed his request for a second, but then she jumped to do as he'd requested while he rotated his grandmother's computer tower to the side so he could plug in the augmented keyboard. Once the peripheral was plugged in, the two women gasped, and he smirked at the screen.

"Damn, Gram, really?"

The dull grey background image and black-and-white text window appeared to glitch, but then the background shifted to a scrolling set of blue mechanite words, and a new text input box popped up over it.

"What is that?" Serena whispered.

"It's an entirely different operating system. I'm guessing it's only activated when the mechanite keyboard is attached."

"Clever," Thenia said.

"We still have the password issue, though," Serena said.

"Ashton, try your name. From the book."

"No harm in trying."

He quickly tapped the six keys that spelled his name, and before he could press the Enter key, the screen transformed again. The input box faded and was replaced with the outline of a palm.

The intention was clear.

"Well, then. Alright, Gram, but only because you asked me to."

Ashton closed his eyes and placed his palm on the screen over the outline. When he merged with the machine, he discovered two options.

Destroy; compromised and *Activate.*

He trusted his Gram with his life, so he told it to activate and pulled himself from the machine. When he opened his eyes, he heard the muted scratching of a mechanical motor, and all three of them shifted to scrutinize the bookshelf on the opposite side of the room. He paled when the bookshelf slid to the right, revealing a space behind it.

"Is that—" Serena closed her mouth and tipped her head to the side as she stared at the opening.

"I think it is," Thenia answered.

Ashton, dumbfounded, got to his feet and walked over to the wall, or where a wall had been, but instead, he stared through a doorway that led down a flight of stairs and into the dark. Presumably, it led down to a level of the house he'd not known existed—through a door that shouldn't have existed either.

"Wow, Gram." He smiled over his shoulder at the two astonished women. "Anyone up for an adventure?"

Thenia and Serena glanced at each other. Serena clutched Thenia's hand, and they both looked back at him.

"If you're sure you're okay with us coming, too," Thenia said.

Ashton thought about it for only a few seconds before exhaling deeply. "The system trusts you both, or it wouldn't have opened while you were here."

"Then, yes," Serena said with a radiant smile.

Chapter 12: Generations Passed

June 2024, Maine, USA | Thenia Loris

Thenia wasn't sure what she'd expected to happen when Ashton had plugged in the USB drive she'd found under the roses, but a secret door to a dark set of stairs and a basement not even Ashton had known about wasn't it. If Serena and Ashton's expressions were anything to go by, both of them were just as astonished.

After navigating through a narrow, darkened hallway, they descended a flight and a half of cement stairs before arriving at a steel door with a biometric lock. Ashton had placed his thumb on the pad beside the door, and then he scared the crap out of her and Serena when he yelped. Apparently, it was a blood lock, not a thumbprint scanner, and Ashton had quickly stuck his thumb into his mouth and rolled his eyes.

Then the door had slid open.

Now, all three of them were standing, dazed, in a hidden room beneath the house. The walls, floor, and ceiling were made of metal plating, giving the space a science-fiction vibe. They were now staring up at two large, darkened screens, mounted where the blank walls met the ceiling. The only other object within the room was a short podium in the center of the space with a teeny red light at its base.

Ashton was currently standing at the podium and frowning down at the device. She and Serena stood on either side of him, remaining silent while he scowled at the keyboard set atop the podium, with more mechanite symbols on the keys and a single empty USB slot.

"Can we help?" Thenia offered after a few minutes of stillness.

Ashton scratched his neck and then sighed, focusing on Serena. "I have no idea what this is, but I have to trust her, don't I?"

Serena nodded and wrapped her arms around Ashton's left arm, but still made sure he had room to maneuver. Ashton took a deep breath, glanced at Thenia, and she smiled reassuringly. Then, he pressed what would have been the location of the spacebar on a standard QWERTY keyboard.

Behind them, the metal door slammed shut, causing them to yelp. Six blue lights clicked on from their positions in the ceiling. Next, both monitors began to glow but remained dark and slightly fuzzy.

Thenia clutched her chest as her heart attempted to escape from her ribcage, and when she checked on Serena, she didn't seem to have fared much better.

"Flair for the dramatic your Gram had," Thenia teased with a soft laugh.

Ashton chuckled but concentrated on the two screens as a duplicated message slowly emerged on both of them.

Insert the drive and activate it using the Key, Ashton. Trust me.

Thenia glimpsed Serena's grip on Ashton's arm tighten, and Thenia placed her palm on Ashton's other forearm, drawing his attention.

"Do it, Ashton. It's your, Gram, right?"

He studied her for a moment, but ultimately pivoted to get Serena's opinion, too. She smiled sweetly, and Ashton removed the USB from his pocket, frowning at it between his fingers. Then, he inserted it into the pedestal and pushed the key on the keyboard that corresponded with the icon on the drive.

Thenia reflexively covered her ears as a deafening, unnatural humming filled the room. Her bones felt like they were vibrating, and she glanced at Serena, who was in a similar protective position. All three of them flinched when the two screens flashed white. The light flooded the space, and Thenia was compelled to shut her eyes when they started watering from the harsh change in light level.

By the time she was able to reopen them, Ashton's eyes were fixed on the screens. When the oscillations finally died down and the screens dimmed to a less painful brightness, Thenia looked up at them.

Two different faces, one on each monitor, began to emerge on the grey screens, and finally, they solidified into identifiable figures comprised of thousands of flickering, blue mechanite symbols.

Serena gasped and covered her mouth while Ashton remained stunned, his eyes having yet to blink.

The bust on the right screen slowly fluttered its digital eyelashes as if waking up from a nap. Then, it smiled down at them.

"Hello, Ashton," a feminine voice said from speakers tucked out of sight within the room.

"G-Gram?"

Her already wide smile grew wider, and then she flicked her gaze over to the other screen, and her digital eyes rolled. "Arthur, stop teasing him. We both know you're awake, too."

The male bust cracked one eyelid and then pouted. "Take all my fun, Sue." Then the male face grinned down at Ashton, and his cold digital visage somehow conveyed the man's warmth. "Long time, kiddo."

"This...you...did you? How?" Ashton stammered.

The male image skimmed first Thenia, and then Serena. It wasn't a surprise when his smile grew even larger as he examined Serena, his wife, looking on with a pleased expression.

"It's wonderful to see your human form, Serena. I'm only sad I wasn't given the privilege while alive."

Thenia watched as the young woman began to tremble. Instinctively, Ashton tucked her into his side when she began to cry. Still in shock, he continued to stare at the monitors, so Thenia stepped forward.

"Hello. My name is Thenia. I'm the elemental witch who's had the privilege to continue tending your gardens. Water and earth, by the way."

Both faces shifted their focus to her, and the man's digital eyes seemed to glow a bit brighter as he spoke. "It's nice to meet you, Thenia. Thank you for taking care of everything for me. I hope you found my journals helpful."

She snorted. "Extremely." A laugh she couldn't hold back escaped, and she beamed at the man's image. "Won't lie, a bit dense, but wonderful once I am able to get through them."

Sue rolled her eyes at her husband for a second time while Arthur's hearty laugh bounced off the cold walls around them.

"I'm very glad, and thank you for looking after these two for us, as well."

Thenia nodded but extended her hand behind her for Ashton to take, which he did. Ashton's grandmother smiled at him and Serena before she spoke again.

"I'm sorry we left you so abruptly. Things...escalated faster than I anticipated." Sue's voice sounded exhausted, and Thenia saw Arthur peek over at his wife's screen, a frown on his lips.

Ashton finally shook off his mental paralysis, along with Thenia's hand. He held it up, his other hand still rubbing Serena's back. "Wait, wait, wait. Beginning. Start at the beginning, Gram."

"Of course, my dear," she smiled, but it was no longer as large as before. "It's a long story, but I must ask one thing first."

"Alright," Ashton said.

The woman shook her head. "Sorry, dear, not of you."

Sue studied Thenia and then Serena.

"While we know what relationship you three have, and I expect the answer to be yes, I won't involve either until you're aware of the magnitude of what we're about to tell Ashton."

Thenia met Serena's eyes and nodded to Sue, "Alright."

"This information is known by fewer than ten beings outside of those directly affected. It's highly dangerous to simply know that it exists, and learning about it will put you at incredible risk should anyone discover that you've been added to that small group of informed individuals. If you would rather keep that safety and ignorance, Arthur and I will understand, and I'm sure Ashton will as well, once we've informed him of the information. If your choice is to leave, I will open the door, and you may exit now."

When Thenia's eyes connected with Serena's gaze, all she saw was determination. Serena sniffled, and then she addressed the screens.

"We'd like to stay. If Ashton's alright with it."

Ashton retook Thenia's hand and laced his fingers with hers before sweetly squeezing it. "It's your decision, but I would really appreciate not being alone in whatever this is."

"You're never alone, kid," Ashton's grandfather reassured lovingly, "but we get it. Alright, my dear. You heard 'um, from the top."

"Alright. Then let's begin. This all started with Ashton and Xander's parents."

"That far back?" Ashton frowned.

"Yes. The last mission they were assigned to was to retrieve a thumb drive that the angels had confiscated after they'd found it on a murdered human woman. Before they were able to identify what it was, the drive was stolen. The angels were interviewing the poor soul in order to investigate her suspicious death before putting her to rest, and we have no information on how they allowed it to be taken. The thief left no trail or evidence that the angels had ever held the drive. It was as if it had never existed. The accepted theory was that a sanguiste conducted the theft...in the middle of the day."

"Wait, sanguiste, like human vampire myth, sanguiste?" Thenia asked, confused. "But I thought they couldn't go in the sun. Not that they'd explode into a ball of flames or anything, but still."

"You're correct, Thenia," Arthur confirmed. "Sanguiste are indeed what humans based their vampire legends on. Very few know that in the beginning, sanguiste were not affected by the sun as they are now. The intolerance to the sun and the crippling pain it causes them are the effect of the Original's blood diluting along the generations."

Thenia's eyes widened, and she swallowed roughly. "Okay, um, thanks. Sorry, please continue."

"No problem, my dear," Ashton's Gram said fondly. "Ashton, you and Xander's parents were sent to find the drive and retrieve it."

"Well, it looks like they did, but what went wrong? How'd they get it back to you but then didn't make it back themselves?"

Both digital images looked at each other, and computer code or not, Thenia could sense their grief.

Sue continued. "Yes. They retrieved the drive, and yes, it's the same one before you."

"Okay...." Ashton prodded.

"It was Xander's mother," Sue said, her voice breaking. "She alone survived their mission and was able to get the drive out. However, the thieves followed her. When the original owners of the drive finally caught up to her, she'd already set in motion for the drive to be returned to us, but...."

Ashton sighed, "It didn't matter. They didn't care."

"Precisely," Arthur said. "She gave her life to get it back to us, as well as to protect you, your sister, and her son."

"How?" Ashton asked.

Sue's expression lightened, and Thenia could see the woman's pride for her deceased chosen daughter in her slight smile.

"She didn't send the drive directly to us. She knew they'd be watching and would come for it if they suspected we'd received it. She wanted to keep all five of us safe, so she sent it somewhere else. It took over ten years for the drive to resurface and return to me. By then, those looking for it believed we five knew nothing— and to be fair, we didn't. I was not briefed on their mission before or after their deaths. I only learned the basic details of the case after the drive finally arrived."

Ashton sighed. "Well, Alexia did a good job then. Impressive."

Arthur snorted. "They weren't the AIS's top operatives for nothing, kid. Those four were a team unrivaled, and their deaths shocked not just your Gram and me but the entire magical world."

"Guess that's where Eileen and Xander get it from, then," Ashton said with a slight smile.

"Presumably," Sue agreed. "Once the drive made it to me, I realized it was damaged, likely during the original struggle with your parents. It took me another ten years to restore the original data."

"Ten years! Gram!" Ashton blurted, making Serena squeak in surprise, and Ashton clutched her closer. "Why didn't you ask for help?"

Thenia squeezed his hand, "Ashton, hear her out."

"I would not risk you without knowing what was involved. I refused to lose the three of you like we did your parents."

Arthur cleared his metaphorical throat to silence his wife before adding, "We wouldn't have survived the loss, Ashton.

With your parents, we had you three to look after. That was more important than grief or revenge."

Thenia stepped closer to Ashton's side in the hopes that her soft pressure would help comfort him. From behind his back, Thenia felt Serena's arm slip around his waist before she grabbed Thenia's shirt hem.

Ashton groaned. "Fine. Keep going, please. Can I assume whatever is on this drive is how you two ended up like this?"

"Smart kid," Arthur smirked.

"Correct." Again, Sue made eye contact with Serena and then Thenia. "This is the last chance, do either of you want to leave?"

"No," Serena said quickly.

"Please, continue," Thenia agreed.

Sue nodded. "Are you aware of what a transmogromorph is?"

"Shapeshifters? Human, specifically?" Serena asked.

"Correct. The history of how their kind came into existence is pretty simple. A young princess wasn't fit to rule her people, and when she attempted to hurt a foster girl, her sister, she was stopped by an older man. As told, he used some form of magic to switch their souls within each other's bodies. From then on, the young princess looked like her foster sister and was never able to rule her people. The foster girl wore the face of the princess but was granted the ability to change her appearance at will, and she used it and her pure heart to rule the people in her care in a just and thriving way."

"Okay, so the foster-turned-princess was the first transmogromorph?" Ashton confirmed.

"Yes. However, that is only how the magical world believes transmogromorphs came into existence."

"Sounds like there's more to it than that," Thenia scoffed.

"Yes, the only true part of that story is that an interloper took over ruling instead of the ruthless and narcissistic sociopath that was the original princess."

"So, what's the real story? That's the dangerous part, right?" Serena questioned.

"Indeed." Ashton's grandparents glanced at each other and then back at the three of them before Sue resumed speaking again.

"That foster girl was an operative from this planet's future. She was sent back in time to the point where the end of humanity, magic, the planet, and multiple other planes of existence had been set on an unavoidable path of utter annihilation."

Thenia glanced at Ashton and Serena, and was relieved when they stared back at her in confusion, then at each other. Then, they all looked at the screens and said, "Wait, what?" in unison.

Ashton's grandfather laughed, amused by their synchronized response, and his grandmother smiled.

"Okay...." Ashton released Thenia and Serena so he could step in front of the podium, where he began to pace. "So, you're saying that not only is time travel real, but those in the future messed with the timeline to stop some uber-destructive outcome that essentially ends multiple worlds. Now, those who were sent back are what we know as transmogromorphs?"

"Yes, dear," his grandmother said.

Ashton ceased his pacing and stared at the screens. Thenia could barely make out his profile, lit by the screen's glow, but he didn't look upset.

"Well, that's fucking nuts."

"Language!" his grandfather scolded.

Thenia had just listened to the wildest story she was likely to ever hear in this lifetime or the next, and when she realized it, she felt a bit guilty about how she'd treated Lucus regarding her being a witch. With how she felt at that moment and how he probably felt similar disbelief and confusion, she understood. The difference was that she already believed them.

Then she registered that a computer...or something, of

Ashton's grandfather had just scolded the grown man for saying the word fuck. Thenia burst into laughter so strong that she had to bend over to hold her abdomen while the other four gaped at her in shock.

She held up her hand and tried to catch her breath, but only managed to wheeze out, "Sor...sorry."

Serena released Thenia's shirt and tickled her side, reigniting her fit of laughter. Once Serena stopped, Thenia caught her breath and wiped the tears from the corners of her eyes.

"Sorry. It's just that after everything that we just heard, you scolded Ashton for cursing. I have no idea what you are, sir," Thenia grinned up at the screen, "But I think I'm even more upset now that I never met you."

The older man's image laughed again while his wife nodded in agreement.

"Well, now you have," Arthur said.

Thenia slipped her arm around Serena's waist and stepped into her side before she leaned over to whisper in her ear, "You alright?"

"Yes, thank you," Serena said under her breath, snuggling closer to Thenia.

"What did you do, Gram?" Ashton snapped.

Everyone instantly refocused on him, and Thenia saw his fists clenched at his side. Sue ignored his enraged tone and spoke to him just as she had earlier.

"Part of what was on that drive was the code needed to back up the original programming of the user sent back in time. Within it was a version of an artificial intelligence model that merges the soul with the programming to create an augmented version or a soul-software hybrid of the person. In the future, they can replace that AI in the body and store the source soul. I assume. Clearly, we do not have that technology, and from what I was able to piece together, I believe those in the future have extremely extended lives compared to ours. We have yet to reach that point as a collective, so I did the next best thing, considering our bodies were failing."

"Um..." Serena interrupted tentatively, and Thenia saw her staring at the floor.

"Yes, dear?" Sue said.

"Does...does that mean that when you...died...together...."

Thenia watched Ashton's head fall forward and into his palms as he made the connection. "That's why you died together. It wasn't in your sleep. You transferred your souls."

"Correct, dear. Though, to be fair, I was quite sick. It was only a matter of time."

Ashton's head snapped up. "What! Why didn't you tell us?"

"Kid, what would you have been able to do? Time is time, and we cannot control its flow," Arthur said.

Thenia tsked. "Apparently, we can. Those in the future did...will do? Not to mention, you're still here, so...didn't you as well?"

"Touche, young witch," Arthur chuckled.

Ashton resumed his pacing in a circle again, except this time, it seemed more anxious than introspective.

"This is insane. Eileen. I need to call Eileen. Xander, oh, what the hell am I going to—"

"Ashton," Thenia barked, and he ceased pacing.

She squeezed Serena gently before leaving her side and standing in front of Ashton. He gazed down at her, and she could see the agony in his eyes.

Thenia looked up at the screens. "Would it be alright if we took a break?"

"Of course, dear," Ashton's grandmother said. "Now that you've woken us up, we will be here. I've added your and Serena's information to the door lock, so please feel free to come back when you're ready. With or without Ashton."

"I don't even want to know how you have our blood profiles, but thank you," Thenia said and looked back at Ashton. "Come on, let's go upstairs and get some fresh air for a bit. We can come back after lunch if you want."

Ashton's eyes searched her face, and for a second, she thought he'd argue with her, but then he relented.

"You're right." He looked up at the screens, "Thank you for telling us. I'll come back later, and you can tell me the rest."

"Sure thing, kid," his grandfather said and then looked at Serena. "It's your turn to visit me, little green snake."

Serena sniffled and nodded, "Okay."

Thenia lovingly shooed the pair toward the door, but she was forced to stop when both of them refused to walk and rotated around to face the screens again. Thenia couldn't see the screens behind her, but she noticed that Serena had taken Ashton's hand.

"We…we missed you…" Serena admitted in hardly more than a whisper.

"We missed you, too," Arthur said. "We'll be here when you get back."

Serena nodded and dropped her gaze to the floor while she and Ashton made their way to the door. Once they were near enough to it, the blue lights in the room, along with the monitors, dimmed, and the room returned to the darker, single red-light-lit room. Then, the door slid open, letting them out.

Thenia ushered the two of them up the stairs and out of the office. Then, she led them to the porch and to the bed swing, where she kissed both of them on the cheek, leaving them together while she went back into the house to get them something to eat and drink before they started sorting everything out.

Ashton Giri

"Ashton…" Serena said in a small voice.

"Hmm?"

He felt her scoot closer to his side on the swing bed, and

when he glanced over at her, her eyes shimmered with unshed tears. Ashton opened his arms, and to his astonishment, she practically crawled into his lap and hugged him tightly. He wrapped his arms around her and closed his eyes, resting his cheek on her hair.

"I'm sorry, Serena. I wish I had known you were out here sooner. You wouldn't have been alone so long."

Her hot tears rolled down his neck, and he felt like a jerk. He also wanted to yell at his Pops for not coming right out and telling him about Serena in the first place.

"I wasn't...alone..." Serena muttered. "You were here."

He kissed the top of her head and squeezed her a bit tighter. "You're right. I was, and I always will be, okay?"

She nodded against him, and he carefully shifted them to sit further on the mattress, where she cuddled further into his side. They both closed their eyes, and eventually, he felt Serena's breathing even out as she fell asleep. He thought about Thenia, who had gone inside, but before he'd decided to get up and help her, he, too, was asleep.

Ashton roused when a breeze blew across his cheek and used a strand of Serena's hair to tickle him. The two of them were still on the swing bed, so he gradually sat up, trying not to disturb Serena in the process. The table beside them had two bottles of water and a plate with another one upside down on top of it, protecting whatever Thenia had brought them to eat.

He peeked at his watch, and the digital screen showed they'd slept for nearly three hours. Ashton pressed the heels of his hands into his eyes but took a deep breath before slowly getting off the bed while attempting not to jostle it too much. He snagged one of the water bottles on his way past it as he headed inside.

Once in his office, Ashton put his hand into his pocket, touched the tips of his fingers to his phone screen, and sent

Eileen a message she'd see later. Then he went to his Gram's computer, triggered the disguised door, and descended the stairs.

After his identity was confirmed, the lower door slid open and shut behind him as he approached the podium. Before he reached the keyboard, the room's lighting switched to blue, and the screens flickered. When his Gram and Pops' digitally recreated faces smiled at him, Ashton dropped to his knees when his body became too heavy to carry.

"This really happened. You're real."

"We are, kid," Pops said.

"Why?" Ashton looked up. "How? What do I do now?"

His Gram smiled. "First, you take a deep breath and drink some of that water. Then we'll talk."

Ashton stared at her for a handful of seconds, but in the end, data or flesh, it was his Gram, and he listened to her and did as he was told. Once the bottle was half empty, he replaced the cap and stared back up at her.

"Good. Now, let's answer your first question first. Why?" She glanced over at her husband on the other screen. "A few reasons. Some noble, some selfish."

Ashton scoffed, "Doubt it."

"Ash, I was dangerously close to not finishing the programming before my body gave out. It would have meant I'd spent decades, and they'd all have been wasted."

"Wasted how?"

"I refused to do this alone. Your grandfather's program was more complicated considering his human nature."

"Ah," Ashton smirked at Pops. "Got it."

"The rest of the why is simple," she continued, "because you'll need us."

"For what specifically?"

His Pops answered this time, his tone low and weighty. "Something is coming, Ash. Even as a human, I could feel it. Can't you?"

Ashton stared at them for a few heartbeats, but then he closed his eyes and focused on where his watch rested against the skin of his wrist. As he merged with the machine, it buffeted him with news articles, local radio broadcasts, television anchors, social media, and finally, information from the magical community. All of the data shouted to him at once, and he had trouble filtering through it. Then, the information started to coalesce, and he began to catch fragments of what he was being shown.

Long-lost city rumored to be off the coast of Africa.

Rise in the Gothic movement and young people pretending they are vampires.

Local medium dead after seance gone wrong.

Man swears he saw an angel at his son's bedside after cancer claimed his life.

Ashton couldn't speak. There was too much. Too many articles and instances of their world catching the attention of humans—Outsiders. At the rate things were going....

Keeper.

Prophecy.

Unification.

Ashton gasped, ripped himself from the circuits, and fell to his hands and knees on the cold metal floor, his breath coming in ragged gasps.

"Do you remember a few years ago, Ash, the night that the sky turned red?" his Gram asked, and he looked up.

"No, it was blue."

She shook her head. "It was by the time you saw it. Prior to ice...it was blood."

"Then it's true? The prophecy was triggered. The Final Keeper reigns?"

"She does. For now, we have nothing to be concerned with, and while I'm no truth seer, I have a feeling you will cross paths eventually."

"She's in Alku, then?"

"With Stephan, yes," his Pops answered this time.

"Eileen and Xander," Ashton swallowed roughly, the water in his stomach turning to acid.

"Are safe and will continue to be. You know Stephan, he may be an ancient sanguiste, but his honor and morals are unquestionable."

Ashton nodded and then forced himself to drink the remainder of his water before continuing. "So, what does this have to do with us?"

"The transmogromorph truth. When we were uploaded, the data spike wasn't disguisable. They know I had it and will come for it, Ashton."

"Already have."

He pulled the card from his back pocket and held it between his pointer and middle finger.

"I know. We were dormant when you received it, but when you woke us, we absorbed the camera feeds and history that we missed since our upload."

Ashton nodded and flicked the card to the floor.

"Ash," his Pops said abruptly. "You need to protect each other —all three of you. They won't hesitate to remove anyone who gets in the way of what they want."

Ashton scoffed. "No shit, Pops. Isn't this why we don't remember our parents? I'm aware."

"Ash…." Gram said.

"It's fine," Ashton staggered to his feet. "I hear you. We'll be fine. I refuse to be like them."

"Ashton," his Pops snapped.

"What! You think I—we," Ashton pointed to the closed door behind him, "Aren't paying for their failures? What about Eileen and Xander? All of us. They'll be in just as much danger once linked to this."

"Ashton Giri," his Gram scolded.

"I could have pretended none of this existed. Told whoever it was that I had no idea what they were talking about. Convinced them to leave us alone. Now, I have to deal with two generations of this nightmare!"

He glowered at his grandparents, the best and only parents he'd ever had, but for a moment, he wanted nothing more than to walk out the door and never come back.

"Ash," his Gram said in the soothing, mothering tone she used when any of them as kids were injured. "Get Thenia and Serena cell phones. We'll watch over them. For now, go get some rest. Thenia is looking for you, and judging by her hand-wringing, she's extremely worried."

Ashton's stomach sank, and he immediately bolted to the door. Thenia's distress was the only thing that mattered. He expected the screens and lights to shift when he reached the door, only they didn't.

"I'm sorry…Ash…" his Gram whispered, but when he turned around, everything had dimmed, and they were both gone. The door slid open for him, and he took the stairs two at a time without looking back.

His thoughts were solely on how he could get to Thenia faster.

Chapter 13: Different Languages

June 2024, Maine, USA | Thenia Loris

After discovering Serena and Ashton asleep on the swing bed, Thenia quietly slipped away and roamed the gardens for a while to help clear her head. So much information had been shoved into it in a short period of time, and even after a few hours of wandering and tending to the plants, she didn't feel much less overwhelmed. Eventually, she gave up and returned to the tiny house to get cleaned up and eat lunch before she headed back to check on the other two.

When she finally returned to the main house, Serena was still sleeping on the swing bed, but one water bottle and Ashton had been nowhere to be seen. After briefly searching the house, Thenia guessed he'd gone back downstairs to talk more with his grandparents. She didn't want to intrude, but she couldn't shake the ominous feeling that had formed in the pit of her stomach. When she'd returned to Ashton's office, the door was closed, and she'd remained in the hallway, pacing back and forth and murmuring to herself.

Thenia wasn't sure how long she'd been standing there, but when Ashton threw the door open and saw her and her anxious expression, he had her in his arms before she could blink.

"Are you alright?" he asked. His breath against her cheek made her shiver when it tickled her skin, but he didn't notice.

"Yes. I was…worried about you."

Ashton's muscles negligibly slackened, and she hugged him back and ran her hands up his back to soothe him. He squeezed her a bit tighter.

"I'm fine."

Thenia shook her head against him. "No, you're not. Ash, talk to me."

Ashton froze, and she drew away from him to observe his face better. His eyes were closed, and it was obvious that he was struggling with something.

"Hey, what—"

He stepped back and entirely out of her reach. Then, he turned away before she could place her raised palm on his cheek. She wasn't sure what she did, but she'd very clearly done something, and she dropped her hand.

"I'm sorry," Ashton said.

"For what?"

"You just—" he cleared his throat. "Only Eileen and Xander, call me Ash. Well, and Gram and Pops."

"Oh, I'm sorry, I don't even know why—"

"Thenia?" he asked in a hesitant voice that was more suitable for a frightened child than a grown man.

"Yes?"

"Thank you."

She tilted her head and smiled at his back. "For?"

Ashton pivoted to look at her again, and he affectionately ran his thumb over her cheekbone, as his carefree smile returned.

"Being you. And trusting me enough to allow me to see it."

Thenia felt her cheeks heat, and she wanted to run and hide as she sensed things shifting around her. Instead, she nodded almost imperceptibly and saw when Ashton's eyes were drawn to her lips. He met her eyes again, and he must have seen something in them because he drew her against him and stole her next breath with a kiss.

Ashton caressed her lower back with one palm, as the other tangled in her hair. Thenia stepped up on her toes and nestled further into him. The contrast between the feelings of Lucus and Ashton shook her, and she realized how foolish she'd been for the past ten years. What she'd had with Lucus hadn't been love. Not even close. But Ashton....

He tore his lips away and rested his forehead on hers. "Thenia...."

"Hmm," was all she managed, her eyes still shut, a smile on her lips.

"Stay with me?"

She opened her eyes, and Ashton's apprehension and grief caught her off guard. Thenia tilted away from him to get a better look, but he misunderstood her movement as rejection and averted his eyes.

"Sorry, I—"

"Yes," she said before he could rescind his request.

Ashton's eyes returned to hers, and she continued. "On one condition."

"What is it?"

"Tell us what's got you so upset. It doesn't have to be now, but...don't deal with this alone."

His smile was bashful this time, but his eyes seemed to brighten. "I promise. I need to talk to you and Serena any—"

Ashton cursed and immediately released Thenia, stepping away from her and resting his back against the wall.

"Crap. How do we do this? I don't want to hurt her by being with you or make her feel like we are excluding her."

Thenia chuckled, and Ashton blinked at her, perplexed by her outburst.

"Sorry. I think she was planning to explain it, but Serena

gave me permission to tell you if the topic or situation came up before she could."

"If what came up?" Ashton asked as he scratched the side of his neck.

"You've kissed Serena, right?"

He nodded.

"Well, Serena is ace, so she and I have already talked about..." Thenia felt her cheeks flush, and she glanced away, suddenly embarrassed. "You and I."

"As in asexual?"

Thenia nodded.

"Shit, did I make her uncomfortable? Should I apologize?"

The concern in his voice distracted Thenia from her discomfort over revealing something so personal to Serena without her there. Thenia walked over to Ashton, and he spread his feet wider so she could step back into his arms.

"No, to both questions. But that's the limit that Serena will be comfortable with when it comes to the subject. With either of us."

"Okay, I can respect that."

"However, she understands that I am not, and I apologize since I assumed neither are you."

Ashton shook his head. "Sex has never been something that's run my life, but I'm definitely not ace."

"Same. There's nothing wrong with her being so, but we will both have to learn how not to make her feel left out, but I think we'll manage." Thenia snorted, "She did request that we still invite her to snuggle."

Ashton stared at her, laughed abruptly, and dropped his head to rest on Thenia's shoulder.

"Honestly, how the hell did I get so lucky with you two?"

Thenia caressed her fingertips up the back of Ashton's neck. "From the sounds of it...I think she and I are being rewarded for surviving the first thirty years of our lives."

Ashton turned his head just enough to press his lips to her neck, and she felt him smile against her skin. "Let's make the second thirty better, then?"

Thenia laughed and shifted to wrap her arms around his neck. "That sounds wonderful."

Ashton drew her lips back to his, and their conversation appeared to have set his mind at ease, considering he felt more relaxed than he'd been moments earlier. His arms were draped around her waist, but when he slid one palm beneath her shirt and rested it on the skin of her lower back, Thenia fought to suppress a shiver.

She hadn't hidden her reaction well enough, because Ashton smiled around their kiss, and she felt his hand press more firmly. When his silky tongue brushed hers, she was thankful for his grasp on her since one of her legs wobbled. Ashton didn't only smile this time, but he laughed against her lips, and she pulled away so she could glare at him with a playful smirk.

"Something to say?"

Ashton's skin was flushed, and his eyes were slightly far away when he shook his head and strained to maintain a straight face.

She released her hold around his neck, drug her hands down to his chest, and gently pushed against him to put some space between them. Her gaze dropped to her fingers, but she felt one of Ashton's slip under her chin before he guided her eyes back up to his own.

"I'm sorry, I wasn't laughing at you."

She shook her head. "It's my fault. I've always been weak and —"

"Thenia," Ashton snapped, and she glimpsed an anger in his eyes that she'd never seen before. "Don't."

"What?"

"Leave the first thirty, remember?"

She observed him as she tried to decide whether to believe

him, but before she could make up her mind, he stood up straighter and bent to whisper in her ear.

"There's not a single thing about you that's weak, Thenia. Trust me, I'll be the one struggling, not you." He kissed her cheek but didn't step away. "Come with me?"

Thenia endeavored to remember to breathe, managing only to squeak out an agreement, and followed Ashton down the hallway, their fingers laced together. He ushered her into one of the bedrooms, and when they were inside, he closed the door behind them.

The room was deep blue, with dark carpeting and painted walls. The space was decorated with ebony wood furniture, dark blue linens, and accents. Compared to the brilliant man standing beside her, the room he called his own felt bleak and slightly cold, and the contrast was staggering.

"Not what you expected?"

"No," she muttered as she continued to explore everything that filled the room. All of it felt like it would belong to someone significantly different from the man standing beside her.

"Eileen and Xander are the outgoing ones," Ashton chuckled. "Always laughing and getting into trouble. The physical manifestation of light in the family."

Thenia peeked at Ashton, who was smiling fondly at the memories of his siblings that he carried with him.

"But you're not?"

He met her gaze and shook his head. "No. Not compared to those two, and..." he blushed, "it's only recently that things have changed."

Thenia pivoted to face Ashton, searched his face, and then sighed.

"You didn't want to come back home, did you? You did it for Eileen and Xander."

Ashton hardly looked surprised that she'd figured out what he'd been thinking when he answered, "Yes."

"You traded your happiness for theirs."

"Always will. Besides, I can work from anywhere."

Thenia knew better than to judge a book by its cover, yet she'd known Ashton was lonely and assumed it was because of the recent deaths. Sure, that was part of it, but his longing for companionship was far more complex than that. Truthfully, they weren't so different. Serena, too. All three of them. They may be of different races, but in that way, they were all still human.

"I'm glad you came home, Ashton," Thenia admitted, her voice faint.

Ashton caressed just below her ear with his thumb, and she leaned into his touch.

"Me too."

Thenia allowed Ashton to tug her back to him and into his arms. She focused on the heat of his palms and the thump of his heartbeat beneath her hands, but she forgot all of it when he captured her lips. Ashton teased her tongue with his own while his hands heated the skin on her back. When he trailed his kisses to her cheek, then jaw, and down her neck, Thenia inhaled sharply.

With a delicate nudge, Ashton made her step back. Once, then again. After a few more, she felt the softness of the bed behind her thighs, and she stopped. Ashton's teeth gently nipped her neck, and she shivered.

"Thenia, you're sure?" Ashton whispered.

"Extremely," Thenia said, her voice breathy and hushed.

"Okay. Anything you don't like or I should avoid?"

"I…" she hesitated. She wasn't sure how to articulate what Lucus had done to her, but she felt uncomfortable just thinking about it.

"Thenia?" Ashton tipped her face up to look at him.

"Ah, sorry. I was trying to figure out how to phrase it."

Ashton nodded. "First thing that comes to mind?"

"Lucus."

Ashton's eyes darkened, and she was relieved to see they were enraged, not jealous.

"Enough said." Ashton kissed her softly. "Didn't need long with him, but I understand."

"Thank you."

He kissed her again, but it was brief. "Condom?"

"Doesn't matter. IUD and I was tested after our breakup." The IUD was one of Lucus' demands, but truth be told, she would have thanked him at that moment.

"Alright."

Ashton skimmed his thumb over her bottom lip, and Thenia closed her eyes, focusing on the sensation. When his mouth replaced his thumb, she let out a verbal reaction, and then Ashton lifted her to sit on the bed. He didn't break their kiss while he pulled off her shoes. When one of his fingers skimmed the bottom of her foot, she ripped herself away, overcome with laughter.

"Foot, sorry," she gasped with another giggle.

"Ticklish there, too?" Ashton grinned as he unlaced his shoes and yanked them off along with his socks.

"Mmmhmm." Thenia's laughing fit subsided, and she flopped onto her back and clutched her side.

Ashton knelt on the bed to one of her sides and leaned over her, placing his hands on the blankets, caging her between his arms and torso.

"I'll keep that in mind."

She sniggered, "I warn you, I kick."

Ashton shook his head, his smile amused. Thenia reached up and ran her fingertips down his cheek and over his jaw, which had the barest trace of stubble. When Ashton closed his eyes to savor her touch, she nearly blurted out what she'd been thinking. Instead, she drew him lower and proved it through her kiss. Ashton made a sound that was a mix of a moan and a groan.

"Thenia…."

His voice was practically begging, and hers would have been too if she'd spoken. Instead, she tugged at the hem of his t-shirt, and when her palm brushed his stomach, he hissed. Then he sat up, quickly yanked the shirt over his head, and dropped it beside the bed. The man was beautiful. His skin was one solid color, not a single tan line, likely from the tremendous quantity of time he spent indoors. He was trim and not overly bulky or muscular. What caught her attention was a scar on one hip that ran upward more than six inches and wrapped around his side.

He noticed her staring and smiled, but rolled his eyes. "Shit forgot to warn you about that. I'll explain later, but it's fine."

Thenia smiled and held out her hand, which Ashton accepted, and then he proceeded to demonstrate his earlier point about weaknesses.

Thenia was cozy and weightless, cradled in Ashton's arms.

He tipped her chin up and kissed her lazily. Then, he kissed the tip of her nose, making her smile. He tightened the comforter around them, and she closed her eyes.

"Ashton?"

"What's up?"

Thenia brushed her finger against his wrist. "Set an alarm. I'm too tired to move but want to snuggle with Serena, too."

Less than a minute later, he kissed her again. "Absolutely. I set them for thirty and forty-five. Just in case."

"Thank you."

Serena Ainsley

Serena was roused from her nap when the back door to the main house shut. Ashton was nowhere to be seen, but considering they'd fallen asleep unintentionally, Serena thought it was sweet of him to let her sleep longer.

She stretched and noticed a covered plate and a water bottle on the side table. She sat up to drink some water, forgoing the food for later. When finished, Serena climbed off the swing, stood up, and stretched again. It was becoming easier to remain in her human form, but she did long for her snake form. Being a snake was just...more simple.

Serena quietly opened the house's back door and wandered the rooms before eventually going to the hallway. If Thenia had gone looking for Ashton, or they had gone back into the room downstairs, maybe they wouldn't mind if Serena went with them. Before she entered the hallway, she heard Thenia and Ashton speaking, and their tone made Serena pause. She tucked herself around the corner and remained out of sight.

"Tell us what's got you so upset. It doesn't have to be now, but...don't do it alone." Thenia said, making Serena smile at her use of the word *us*.

"I promise. I need to talk to you and Serena any—" Serena heard Ashton curse after saying her name, and she covered her mouth with her palm to remain silent.

"Crap. How do we do this? I don't want to hurt her by being with you or making her feel we are excluding her."

Serena seized the table beside her with her free hand and held her breath. She'd known the conversation about her sexual boundaries was going to come up at some point, which is why she'd spoken to Thenia about it a few days earlier. She wasn't sure why Thenia seemed safer to talk to about being asexual, but Serena assumed it was the gender aspect. Not that it mattered. The discussion would have been challenging for her regardless of who it was with.

Thenia laughed softly, and Serena squeezed her eyes closed, bracing for the judgment and humiliation.

"Sorry. I think she was going to explain it, but Serena gave me permission to tell you if the topic or situation came up before she could."

"If what came up?" Ashton asked.

"You've kissed Serena, right?"

Serena felt herself redden, but she couldn't move, her fear keeping her in place.

"Well, Serena is ace, so she and I have already talked about…" Thenia paused, "You and I."

"As in asexual? Shit, did I make her uncomfortable? Should I apologize?"

Serena gradually opened her eyes when she heard genuine concern in Ashton's voice.

"No, to both questions. But that's the limit that Serena will be comfortable with when it comes to the subject. With either of us."

"Okay, I can respect that."

Serena held her hand over her mouth but tiptoed backward and away from the hallway as stealthily as possible. Once she was back outside on the porch with the door closed, she sprinted down the steps and through the gardens. Her feet propelled her forward, and she let them guide her to wherever they wanted, her mind too preoccupied to care. It wasn't until she entered the section where Arthur and Sue were buried that she slowed down and approached their headstones.

She sank to her knees before them and dropped her head into her hands. When Serena felt her cheeks lift against her palms as she smiled, she lowered her hands and laughed.

"I…They…."

Serena flopped onto her back in the grass and gazed at the trees above her. She wasn't quite thirty yet, but she was confident she would never meet anyone like Thenia and Ashton again.

They genuinely accepted her. Respected her. No one was forcing her to procreate. They didn't ridicule her or call her names for being different than them.

She rolled her neck and grinned at Arthur's headstone. "Thank you. I'm glad I stayed."

Serena giggled, her cheeks flushing at the oddity. She sat up and spoke to the headstone again.

"Well, we didn't eat the snack Thenia brought. I bet they'll be hungry. I know it's strange that I'm talking to you here when I could—"

Serena snapped her mouth shut. Her eyes skimmed the plants around her, and she thought better of completing her sentence aloud. She looked back at the headstone and rested her palm on it.

"Just, thank you."

Serena got to her feet, brushed the grass and leaves off her jeans, and headed back to Thenia's. Just because Serena wasn't interested in a sexual relationship didn't mean she wasn't aware of how one worked, and it was apparent that the pair needed some time to themselves. Hopefully, Thenia would honor Serena's only request. Before she let herself stress about it, she remembered the conversation she'd overheard and ceased her line of thinking. Serena trusted them both. It would be fine.

"I think I can make a pizza in her oven…" Serena mused as she strolled up the short garden walkway. "Should be big enough."

Thenia had helped her make dough from scratch the day before, and Serena wanted to surprise Ashton with it. Today had been a long and emotional one for all of them, and cooking would help calm her, and the food would hopefully relax Ashton.

She smiled as she stepped into the kitchen and closed her eyes. The house smelled like Thenia's delicate perfume and Ashton's laundry detergent. If Serena focused, she could smell only the barest hint of the bath products Ashton had given her mixed in amongst the others. Serena opened her eyes and grinned at the oven.

"I can't give them that, but…maybe dinner would show them how I feel."

She nodded to no one and got to work.

An hour later, Serena turned off the oven and slumped forward onto the counter, her cheek pressed against the cool surface. Everything was cooked and smelled terrific.

There was no way that she was going to interrupt Ashton and Thenia, but hopefully, they'd be done—

"Serena!" Thenia shouted as she threw open the front door, scaring the crap out of both of them.

Serena jumped up from the counter with a squeak, while Thenia jerked back into Ashton, who grunted when Thenia elbowed him in the stomach.

"What's wrong?"

Thenia rushed across the room and squeezed her into a hug that almost knocked Serena over before she constricted her arms around her. Ashton smiled and shut the front door as Serena hugged Thenia back. The woman's hair was damp and smelled like Ashton's soap. Serena closed her eyes and smiled at the fragrance.

"Are you okay?" Thenia whispered in her ear.

"Yes. Should I not be?"

"I just...we just..." Thenia trailed off.

Serena nodded against her and said in a whisper, "Thank you for telling him."

Thenia's embrace managed to tighten even further. "You're alright with this?"

Serena opened her eyes and noticed that Ashton was still across the room. One hand scratched his neck, and he frowned and looked anywhere but at her.

"Yes."

"You're sure? You don't feel....left out or anything?"

Ashton's eyes finally met Serena's after he heard Thenia's comment, and Serena hoped her expression would put him at ease.

"I don't. Thank you for coming back. I...made dinner...."

Thenia chuckled in her ear before she drew back and kissed Serena's cheek. "It smells wonderful. This the dough from yesterday?"

Serena nodded.

"I'm excited to try it." Thenia brushed a strand of Serena's hair behind her ear. "Thank you for thinking of us."

Serena nodded again.

"I'll plate," Thenia said, walking further into the kitchen. "Go tell Ashton to breathe," she teased.

Serena glanced at him from where he stood in front of the door, looking too nervous to come closer. He smirked at Thenia's teasing, but when he looked at Serena, she noticed he was upset.

"Um, Thenia, can we eat out back?" Serena asked.

"Sounds perfect. You two go make sure the table is clear."

Serena had to walk past Ashton to get into the living room. When she approached him, she stopped. "Would you, um, come with me?"

"Of course," he followed her outside and to the cozy seating area.

"Um, Ashton?"

He sighed. "Yeah?"

She rotated to face him but couldn't look him in the eyes. "Are you...mad...at me?"

He placed his palm on one of her upper arms but didn't force her to look at him. "No. Why would I be mad?"

"I— cuz I'm...."

Ashton dropped his hand and drew her against him, then ran his hand through her hair.

"I'm not mad. Truthfully, it's none of my business. You get to decide who you are. Not the people you're with. I'm just...afraid."

"Of what?"

"Screwing up. Hurting you. All of it." He held her a bit closer. "I don't want you to think I—*we* care for you less."

"I know."

"But, I also don't know how to make sure…well, honestly, I'm not sure."

Serena tipped her head back, resting her chin on his sternum. "Different language."

He smirked down at her. "What?"

She smiled. "I just speak a different language. Earlier, when we took a nap, you stayed with me. That um…shows me how much you care."

Ashton blinked at her a few times and then ran his thumb over her cheek. "Alright. I get it. Just…promise you'll teach me? What you like, don't like, boundaries, all that. Okay?"

She nodded and stepped up a little higher on her toes so she could peck him on the lips. "I will. Thank you…for… understanding."

"I'll try."

"And um…" she glanced away again, "not um…forcing me… to, you know…do other things."

"Serena, I'll speak for both of us. If either Thenia or I ever make you feel like we are forcing you to do anything, tell the other, or hell, tell Pops. He'll set us straight."

Serena giggled and nodded. "Okay."

"Serena…one more thing."

"What is it?"

"You mentioned force. Has anyone…."

Serena rapidly shook her head. "No. I, um, left…home…before that could happen."

Ashton's eyes darkened with outrage, and she pressed her forehead against his sternum again, not wanting to see anymore of his reaction after her words fully sank in.

Luckily, the door opened behind them, and Thenia stuck her head out.

"Hey, slackers, someone come help me carry plates."

Ashton rolled his eyes but smiled. "Yeah, yeah. I guess we did flake on your snack earlier."

"Yes, you did," Thenia teased. "I slaved for multiple minutes to cut that fruit."

Ashton kissed Serena briefly and then released her. "I'll go help. Can you turn on the lights and heater?"

"Sure."

Serena glimpsed Thenia smiling at them. When she saw Serena watching her, Thenia nodded and then took Ashton back inside, leaving Serena alone again.

"Nope. Not alone," she smiled to herself.

Chapter 14: Gifts and Grief

June 2024, Maine, USA | Ashton Giri

Ashton exited the back door of the main house and made his way to the path that led to Thenia's. In one hand, he held a paper shopping bag. In the other, his cell phone, and on its screen, a waveform pattern disguised his Gram's image and distorted her voice.

"You're worrying too much, Ash. You said Thenia didn't want a new phone because of Lucus. Didn't you two solve that issue?"

Ashton chuckled. "Pretty sure I just stood there."

"Wasn't that helping? Sometimes what we don't do is more impactful than what we could have chosen to do."

He shook his head but couldn't keep the smile from his lips. "Even now, you still verbally kick my ass."

His Gram's laugh was soft. "Don't you let Arthur hear you cursing. We both know we won't hear the end of it."

Ashton groaned. "Never gonna drop that, is he?"

"Hasn't yet. I wouldn't get your hopes up, my dear."

"Are you sure he's alright watching after the other two?"

"It was his idea, Ash. We both agree it would be good for them to have someone in case of an emergency, and truthfully, I think the old flirt misses his snake. Not to mention, Thenia is the protege he never had."

Ashton scoffed. "Well, he'll keep them busy."

"Which will also keep him out of trouble. Just as in life, so as in…second life?" His Gram chuckled, "You know what I mean."

"I do," he smiled down at the screen, knowing she could see him through the camera even if her image wasn't visible.

They exchanged small talk and caught up more as he walked through the gardens. All of the plants seemed to be standing taller with brighter blooms as they reached upwards to the clear sky above them. The sun was shining and warm, evident by the slight itch on the extremely fair skin of Ashton's neck. His walk through the gardens practically seeped into his bones, and he understood why his Pops had cultivated the space so diligently. It was the perfect escape and contrast to a mechanite's mainly interior existence.

He was glad his Gram had pushed him to do this now. She had informed him that neither Serena nor Thenia had left the tiny house yet that morning, so Ashton knew to head there and didn't have to check the cameras or wander aimlessly around the grounds searching for them.

Since the day he and Thenia slept together, the three of them had been playing a chaotic version of musical beds. One night, all three of them stayed at Thenia's with Serena in her human form, snuggled between them. Another night, Serena was in her snake form and stayed at the main house with him. Last night, he was alone in his own room, being driven crazy by the smell of them both on his pillows, but neither within reach.

Even when he'd been up at the house or working, Thenia would email if something came up, and Serena even sent him a few messages when she was bored while Thenia was in the garden.

Ashton had done as his Gram and Pops had suggested and ordered both women a cell phone. When they arrived that morning, Ashton spent a few hours setting them up. He ensured Gram and Pops could access both devices and, hopefully, set up the programs and features that would make them as useful as possible for their new owners. Now, he just had to hope they'd accept them.

When he approached the house and went down the short walkway, he noticed the property hummed with tranquility. He knocked lightly on the front door in case either of the women was still sleeping.

"You don't need to knock, Ash," Thenia called from inside.

He snorted and opened the door, but the kitchen and living room were empty.

"Loft," Serena answered before he'd even had to ask.

When he reached the top of the steps, Thenia was at the desk with three of Pops' notebooks open in front of her. Notetaking supplies and plant clippings were scattered everywhere as Thenia was head down, scribbling in the margin of her own notebook. Movement from across the room drew Ashton's attention to where Serena was sprawled on the couch with a novel in her hands.

"Morning," he kissed Thenia's cheek, but she was extremely focused and seemed to barely register him. Serena shifted so he could sit beside her on the couch. He kissed her briefly and then leaned in to whisper in her ear.

"What's she so focused on?"

Serena shrugged. "Been like that since after breakfast."

He frowned but cleared his throat anyway. "Uh, Thenia, can I interrupt you? Just for a few minutes?"

She didn't answer for nearly a minute, and right before he was going to ask again in case she hadn't heard him, she held up her finger. Another thirty seconds later, she lowered it and rotated in her chair to face him and Serena.

"Sure, sorry about that. Arthur was *incredibly* thorough."

He smirked. "Yeah, well, I may be able to help with that."

Thenia crossed her arm and studied him while Serena cocked her head to the side.

"You been holding out on me?" Thenia asked with a smirk.

"So, um…well…." Ashton said and scratched his neck.

"Oh, for goodness' sake, Ash. Just let me talk to them," Gram said from his pocket.

All three of them stared at his hip, and one by one, they each burst into laughter.

"Um, Ash…you need to tell us something?" Thenia teased.

He rolled his eyes and pulled out his phone. "No, I did not surgically attach Gram to my thigh. Imagine the nagging."

With his phone out, he smirked at the front screen as his Gram's digital face emerged from the black with pursed lips but an amused twinkle in her eye.

"The sass."

"Hi, Sue," Serena said, leaning into Ashton's side so she could see the phone screen better.

"Hello, Serena. You look lovely, dear."

Serena blushed and murmured a thank you as Thenia came over to sit on Ashton's other side.

"So, you're mobile now?" Thenia asked.

"In a way, yes. There are some ground rules for everyone's safety. Within your home and the main house, we won't need to hide our forms or distort our voices."

"We?" Serena asked.

"Yes, dear," Gram said, smirking at him. "What Ashton is trying to avoid telling you both is that Arthur and I have requested Ash to get you each a cell phone. That way, Arthur and I can be with you and assist if something arises. Since we are directly integrated with the ground's systems, we can also trigger needed alarms or inform you of anything that could be worrisome."

"Oh, that's not a bad idea," Thenia agreed.

"Hmm," Serena said with a slight frown. "I'm not sure how

that will work when I'm in my snake form, but we can try it. I've never had a cell phone."

"Xander does," Ashton added. "He said if it's in his pocket, it goes wherever all your clothing, jewelry, and stuff go when you shift. He's never explained more than that, though."

"Well, that's cool," Thenia said to Serena. "Where does it go?"

Serena blushed and looked at her fingers. "Long story."

"Fair. Maybe over cocoa?"

Serena looked back up, more relaxed, likely because Thenia didn't press her for the information. Serena nodded and then kissed Ashton's cheek before she turned bright red.

"Thank you for the phone."

"You're not mad?" he asked her, and then, Thenia.

"Why would we be mad?" Thenia asked while Serena shook her head emphatically.

"Well, you said you didn't want a phone...."

Thenia rolled her eyes. "Is that why you've been worrying over this?"

"Yes, he has. For days," his Gram answered more truthfully than he'd have liked.

Ashton groaned, "Really, Gram?"

Thenia shifted on the couch so she was facing him. "Why?"

"I, um..." he rubbed the back of his neck, but when he tried to look away from Thenia, Serena was in one direction, and his Gram was in the other. "I didn't want you to feel like I was forcing you to have one...like Lucus."

Thenia playfully shoved his arm. "As if. Ash, you're nothing like Lucus. Besides, you're not forcing me, and even if you are, why did you get one for me?"

"Because it'll keep you safe? Make your life easier?"

She smiled and kissed his cheek. "Exactly. The intention is completely different."

"I tried to tell him," his Gram said with a wide smile. "Boys. Always making things more difficult than they have to be."

Both Serena and Thenia nodded, and Ashton scoffed. "I'm feeling incredibly outnumbered."

"You remember that, Ash," his Gram teased playfully.

"Noted."

He handed his phone to Thenia for her to hold and dug through the bag he'd put at his feet.

"This one is for you, Serena."

She took the small white box from him and pulled off the lid. Inside was a small phone with a green case close to her snake's coloring. Serena smiled up at him, resting her temple on his shoulder as she turned it on and began to explore it.

Ashton kissed the top of her head before swapping a second box with Thenia for his phone. When she opened it, she saw a larger phone than Serena's, with a deep purple case and multiple cameras on both sides of the device.

"It's a bit bigger, but the cameras are excellent, and I figured it might help with your notes and stuff."

Thenia sniffled and nodded. "Thank you. It's perfect."

Ashton glanced at his Gram, who looked pleased. She nodded slightly at him, and then she cleared her throat.

"Ashton already set them up for you as much as he could. So you'll be able to access the property's cameras and most of the system, along with a few other helpful things. That said, Arthur has volunteered to stay with you girls."

"Wait, really?" Serena grinned.

"Hello, my little green snake," Pops' voice said as his image materialized from the darkened screen.

"Arthur!" Serena giggled happily.

"I hope you don't mind having me tag along. I would love to continue our conversations. If you're up for it?"

Serena nodded excitedly and nearly knocked Ashton over and into Thenia when she launched herself at him for a hug.

"Thank you!"

Ashton chuckled and hugged her back tightly. "You're very welcome. Don't let him talk you into too much trouble."

"Oh, hush, kid," his Pops said from Thenia's phone behind Ashton.

"Hello, Arthur. Nice to see you again," Thenia greeted with a slight wave.

"Hello to you, too, Thenia. I was hoping you might let me accompany you in the garden. I do miss the sun and the plants."

Thenia grinned. "Of course! You're always welcome to come with me when you and Serena aren't busy."

He grinned, his eyes crinkling in the corners.

"Actually!" Thenia exclaimed, jumping to her feet before hurrying over to the desk and sitting back down. "Maybe you can help me with something. I was trying to…."

Ashton smirked at Serena, and both of them covered their mouths to hold back their laughter at the pair and their overwhelming display of energy and focus.

"Well, can't say I am surprised," Gram said softly. "Why don't we three leave them to their botany lesson, and we can go talk a bit more? Would you join us, Serena?"

"Sure." Serena marked her place in her book, put it on a low shelf beside the couch, and then tucked her phone into her sweatshirt pocket. "Thenia made iced tea. Want some? I'll bring her up a glass, too," Serena asked.

"Works for me. See you in a few, Gram," Ashton said, and after she nodded and faded from the screen, he put his phone away and followed Serena. However, he did stop to kiss the top of a very oblivious Thenia's head.

Serena Ainsley

She'd never had a cell phone before. A perk of being a snake was no bills, no technology, and being able to go where you wanted to. One could also consider it a downside as well. No money for human food, no way to contact others, and no home to curl up in a soft bed at night's end. Now, Serena was spending more and more time in her human form, and the few times she'd emailed Ashton from Thenia's computer, she'd found it relaxing, which surprised her.

"Here," Ashton said, sitting beside her on the living room's couch and handing her a steaming mug of hot chocolate.

"Thanks. I'm cold. Tea sounded good, but this sounded better once I saw it."

She stuck her nose over the cup, closed her eyes, and breathed the sweet steam. When she opened her eyes, Ashton watched her while he drank what smelled like coffee.

"What?" she blushed.

"Nothing. You look happy."

"I am. Should I not be?" Serena asked.

"Of course you should be. I just worry."

She cocked her head to the side. "Why?"

Ashton sat back and cradled his mug between his hands in his lap. "You've had a lot of change in the last few months. I just…hope you know you can talk to us if you want to. Or Pops, or Gram. They'd both be willing to listen if you needed it."

"I," Serena lowered her mug and gazed into it, "I know I'm the youngest, and I, I know I act even younger than I actually am, but, um…I've never been able to, uh, be myself…before now. It's nice. I like reading books, and writing you emails was fun. Cooking you sweets and spending time with Thenia in the gardens. It makes me happy."

Ashton placed his hand, palm up, on her knee, and she put her own into it. "I'm glad. Would you tell me how you ended up here? If it's something you're comfortable with."

She lowered her head but held on to his hand tightly. "Uh, sure, but it's not really that bad."

"That's good."

"I'm one of a lot of kids. My parents, well, you saw in my file, right?"

"Only basics, but yeah, two parents, still alive. What was it… twelve siblings?"

Serena nodded. "Yes. My family—my parents are very religious. They believe that it's every paranam's role to breed so that more worthy animal spirits have a chance to ascend into paranams."

"Ah, interesting. Does it actually work like that?"

Ashton's question was a good one and an innocent one for a non-paranam. Even with his brother being a paranam, Alexander was clearly not forced into a breeding program by Sue and Arthur.

"It does, but while I believe in our deity and the cycle of beast spirits, I also believe in the Fates and free will."

"Understandable."

"I am the youngest. The thirteenth. By the time I was born, my parents were…." Serena hesitated, not wanting to talk ill of her parents but also wanting to be honest with Ashton. "Overburdened."

"I can imagine. That's a lot of mouths to feed."

Serena shook her head. "It's not…when you're a snake."

"Is that why you prefer your snake form?"

"No. I guess I should probably hate it. I spent most of my childhood as a snake. Always…forgotten. The last one for everything. Food, clothing, school, all of it."

Ashton sighed, rested his head back against the couch pillows, and closed his eyes. "That's why there were so many blanks in your file. Did you ever even officially register at the age of maturity?"

Serena shook her head. "No. Only at birth. My parents did that. After I left…I spent maybe…three months as a human."

Ashton's eyes snapped open. "Wait, during what duration?"

"Um…until I came to get you…When Nia was sick."

Ashton suddenly dropped her hand before he got up and walked across the room, his back to her.

"Ashton...."

"Give me a second, please."

Serena nodded and returned to gazing into her cocoa.

A few minutes later, Ashton cleared his throat, and his voice was tight when he spoke. She wasn't sure if he was angry or something else, but she'd never seen calm Ashton so...hard.

"Serena, you're telling me that a paranam spent ninety days out of their thirty-year life in their beast form? When typically, paranams spend a few days every month or so as their beast, and the remainder of the time as a human."

"Yes," she said softly.

"Because your parents had some messed-up belief that some other beast's soul was more important than feeding and caring for the souls they'd already brought into the world."

Serena felt tears pooling in her eyes, and she forced herself to nod, but when she realized Ashton couldn't see her, she managed to whisper, "Yes."

"So, how'd you end up with Pops?"

"I um," Serena cleared a little of the emotion from her throat, "left. Home, I mean. Wandered."

Ashton nodded and drank some of his coffee, his back still to her. "How'd you learn to read? Or write? Hell, anything. Cooking, speaking, all of it."

Serena winced. "Um...watching...others."

Ashton set his cup on the table in front of him, then he walked over, took hers from her hands, and set it aside while she watched his feet. Then he knelt to her level and pressed his warm palms to her cheeks.

"Serena, if I make you uncomfortable, pinch me."

Before she could ask what he meant, Ashton pulled her forward and into his grasp and kissed her. She felt warm as she tasted the coffee on Ashton's tongue. One of his arms was on her thigh, and the other was still on her cheek. Just as she worried she was kissing him wrong, Ashton pulled them apart and pressed his forehead to hers.

"Serena, you are incredible—every piece of you. I am so proud of you. I'm not sure, after all that, that I would be even half as kind, caring, and intelligent as you are. I *hate* that you went through that, but selfishly, it brought you to us. Thank you for telling me."

She nodded against him and sniffled. Ashton didn't release her, and Serena was content to stay where she was, but gently pushed herself away from him anyway, not wanting to overstay her welcome.

"Would you like more to drink? I'm going to get a little more."

Ashton wiped under both her eyes with his thumbs and then kissed her lightly. "Sure, thank you. We probably should talk to Gram, too. I think she wanted to discuss something specific."

Serena's eyes widened. "Oh no, I forgot. Yes, you talk, and I will refill our cups."

"Alright. Come back and cuddle after?" he smiled.

She nodded, and then he stood up and helped her to her feet. After she collected their mugs, she returned to the kitchen, poured a bit more milk into the pan on the stove for her cocoa, and turned it on. Then she tiptoed up to the loft, where Thenia still talked animatedly with Arthur. Her glass of tea was empty, so Serena took it downstairs, refilled it, and then placed it back on the desk. When she turned to leave, Thenia caught her wrist.

"Serena?"

"Hm?"

Thenia narrowed her gaze and seemed to be inspecting her, but then Thenia's eyes softened, and she gently tugged on Serena's wrist. When she got close enough, Thenia kissed her lightly and smiled.

"Thank you for the tea."

Serena felt her cheeks flush, but she nodded, and Thenia released her wrist. When Serena returned to the kitchen, she topped off Ashton's coffee and added milk to her existing cocoa, which was heated enough to re-warm what she had remaining in her mug. When she entered the living room, Ashton moved over and pat the cushion beside him with his free hand while the other held his phone. She set his mug on the table in front of him but still within reach.

"Alright, that makes sense, but I have to tell them something," Ashton told Sue.

Serena sat beside him and tucked her legs beneath herself before she scooted further into his side.

"Yes, I agree. I believe it would be safe to tell both Eileen and Xander about your grandfather and me, but we should keep the method and circumstances to ourselves. For now, at least."

Ashton groaned. "I get it, but you understand that both of them will know the moment I try to lie to them."

Sue smiled. "Yes, they are quite the pair. Exceptional skills."

Serena saw Ashton roll his eyes, and she looked at Sue. "Um, can I ask why you don't want to tell them about the rest of it?"

"You know of the work they take on, correct?" Sue asked.

"Yes, nothing specific, but Arthur talked about them."

"Yes. He and I feel that it would put them in more danger knowing the full situation than not. If you three, along with our help, can deal with this mess, it won't add an additional target on their backs for every job they do."

"Do you honestly think those who matter won't just *assume* they know everything, Gram?" Ashton asked.

"We'll need to make it convincing," Sue nodded.

Ashton looked at Serena, then dropped his head back on the couch and groaned. "This is gonna be impossible."

Serena rested her head on his chest and watched Sue, who merely nodded in agreement.

Chapter 15: Unexpected Conversations

July 2024, Maine, USA | Ashton Giri

The gentle and soothing glow of Ashton's office twinkled all around him as he leaned back in his chair and stretched with a loud groan. Before he managed to get his arms entirely over his head, a chat message popped up in his work profile.

Thanks for the quick turnaround, Ashton. I'll get these IDs and licenses over to the relocation department in the next few minutes. Let's hope the next young fire witch doesn't decide to experiment in the dry California hills. At least she was able to put it out...eventually. How's the family? Sue's really missed, not that you don't already know that. Let's grab drinks the next time you're in LA.

Ashton smiled at the young and very chatty mechanite's message. He was a newer recruit, but the kid was smart, fast-fingered, and incredibly empathetic, which is probably why their boss started having him interact with those needing assistance, and not Ashton. Ashton was too quiet, too...gloomy. It didn't help to put a rain cloud over already sodden folks.

He glanced at his phone a few seconds before it started to ring, Eileen's caller ID blinking on the screen.

"Hey, Eileen," he answered with a smile.

"Ash!" his sister screamed excitedly, and he could hear Xander laughing nearby.

Ashton shook his head at his sister and decided speakerphone was safer. Not only was it safer for his hearing, but he got up and went to his Gram's computer and hit a few keys. Her digital visage appeared from the black, and Ashton put his finger to his lips. Gram nodded in understanding.

"How are you, Ash?" Xander said you'd texted the other day. You want us to come home?"

"To clarify, I want you to stop at home when your assignment is completed. There's no rush, but Thenia wants to show Xander the gardens, and Serena is anxious about meeting another paranam, and the sooner those two meet, the better."

"What about you?"

"Me? Well, I did find something I'd like your opinion on, and before you ask," he cut off his sister, whose mouth was likely already open, "No, I can't send information about it to you."

"Is it work?" Eileen asked cryptically.

Ashton glanced at his Gram and then hoped for the best. He was a transparent pane of glass to his sister and Xander most days. It was even worse when they could see his face, so hopefully, neither of them would catch his lie over the phone as quickly.

"Ah, no. Think more along the lines of...family heirloom. One that Gram wants—would want to stay out of the ones and zeros."

Ashton rolled his eyes and scratched his neck, irritated at his slip-up but really hoping Eileen just assumed he missed their grandparents and wasn't used to using the past tense yet. When Eileen hadn't said anything by the time Ashton was done kicking himself, he knew she'd caught it.

"Eileen?"

"Yes. Fine. We'll be home in a bit over two weeks, then. Is that soon enough?"

"It will be here when you get home, so yes, that's fine. Thanks, Eileen."

"Of course, Ash. Don't think we don't know that you're hiding something."

His gaze darted to his Grandmother, who was straining not to laugh, but he couldn't help but smile at the entire situation.

"Yeah, well, let's just say when you see what I'm talking about, you'll understand why."

Xander laughed in the background again, and then Ashton could hear his voice, though it still sounded far away. "Were you trying to dig that hole deeper, Ash?"

"Apparently."

Eileen laughed. "Well, let's change the subject before you just come out with it, and then I'll feel bad."

Ashton scoffed. "Have mercy."

"Tell me about the other two. How's it going? Any developments?"

"They're fine. Getting used to the changes."

"Just the move? Well, and Serena being in her human form more often?"

Ashton flopped back into his desk chair. "Yeah. Mostly."

"And you?" Eileen prodded.

"What about me?"

"Ash, being in love with one person is complicated enough. Two is exponential."

Ashton chuckled. "You're making a big deal out of nothing, Eileen."

"Why? You don't love them both?"

"I—" Ashton glanced at his Gram, smiling warmly at him. "I care about both of them, yes."

"Have you slept with them?"

"Eileen!" Ashton scolded.

"What? You're an adult, and so are they. So, have you? You know we'll know when we get home either way."

"Oh, for fuck sake, Eileen," Ashton snapped, leaning forward to drop his head into his hands. "Look, I'm only telling you this because if I don't, you'll make Serena uncomfortable, and then I'll have to sic Xander on you."

He heard Xander's snort in the background, but Ashton knew the panther would have his back. Especially if Eileen truly did make Serena uneasy.

"Yes, I've slept with Thenia, but I am telling you now, do not make a big deal out of it around Serena, and don't ask me why. It's her information to tell."

"Oh," Eileen sounded thoroughly scolded. "Ash, I'm sorry. I was only teasing you, but I swear I won't say anything to Serena. Will you answer me one thing, though?"

"Maybe," he chuckled.

"Whatever the reason is, it was her choice, and you respected it...right?"

"Eileen," Xander hissed, "I'm going to use all of the hot water tonight and leave you with a cold shower. What the hell are you asking? You're talking to Ash. Not some lusted up sanguiste."

"Sorry, sorry. I know. You're right. I'm sorry, Ash."

"It's fine, but he's right. Thenia and I talked about things beforehand. She knew more information than I did at the time, but I was ready to take a cold shower had I not learned what I did."

"I know. I'm sorry. It's not you. This job has just been...."

"Eileen?" Xander said, his voice getting closer to the phone.

"Fine. Sorry."

"Need to talk about it?" Ashton asked, his Gram's face now mirroring his own worried expression.

"No. Well, maybe, but let's wait until I get home. It's not important."

"You sure?"

"Yeah. Just...Ash?"

"Yeah?"

"I love you. Thank you for being my brother."

Ashton frowned at his Gram, and he nodded his head, his Gram's face fading away as she understood and went to investigate the job Eileen and Xander were on.

"Of course, Eileen. I love you, too. Both of you. You'll be home soon."

"Yeah. You're right."

"Xander?" Ashton asked and then waited for Eileen to pass him the phone.

"What's up, man?"

"How rare is it for a paranam to stay in their beast form more than their human one?"

"Personal preference. I've known a few who swap when their beast form would be helpful, as I do. I don't think I've heard of one staying in their beast form over their human form as their normal state, though. It could be that some do and are just in their beast form, and we don't hear about it."

"Fair, makes sense."

"Why? Serena, I assume."

"Yeah. I told you she prefers her snake, but she told me something a week ago, and I wasn't sure what to think about it."

"If you're comfortable, you're free to ask. Not that I guarantee I'll know the answer."

"Yeah. Less of a question, more of a...fact?" Ashton stood up and grabbed his phone, turning speakerphone off. He paced the small room, his anxious energy needing an outlet.

"Okay."

"She's apparently only been in her human form a few months."

"Makes sense. You said she—"

"No, Xander. Not like the last few months. I mean, from when she left home until the night Thenia passed out. Serena had been in her snake form for all but three months of her adult life and most of her childhood."

"What the fuck? Why?"

"Youngest of thirteen. Parents were more worried about serving your god and getting more souls into the world than caring for the ones they already had."

Xander cursed, and Ashton's eyes went wide, and Eileen asked if Xander was okay.

"Dude, I fucking hate those types of fanatics. Give her my number. If she wants to talk, I'm here." Xander groaned, still worked up.

"Thanks. I will. She and Thenia went into town to get some clothes for her. I'll tell her when they get back."

"Good. Be careful with her, Ash. Parents like that...they leave some deep scars."

Ashton sighed. "I know. I've found a few already."

Thenia Loris

It was a gorgeous day, and Thenia was relishing her time in town with Serena. After much convincing, Thenia got the shy woman loaded into Ashton's car and they headed into town to do some clothes shopping for both of them. They decided to stop for lunch before running past the market and were now walking arm-in-arm along the sidewalk toward where Thenia had found The Crow's Nest many weeks earlier.

"I've...never been to a coffee shop," Serena admitted shyly as they approached a sandwich board sign on the sidewalk in front of the shop's glass window.

"Don't worry, it's not just coffee. I've been dreaming about their iced tea since I had it."

Thenia smiled at the sign and pat it as she walked by. "I owe those two pieces of wood a lot. Damn thing tripped me. That's the only reason I noticed the shop was here and went in. I never would have seen Ash's flyer had I not."

Thenia pulled open the door for Serena, who was giggling as she entered but stopped in awe, scarcely over the threshold.

"Serena," Thenia teased, tickling the woman's sides from behind. "It's even better further inside the door."

Serena's neck turned pink, but she laughed into her palm and stepped further into the shop so Thenia could join her.

"Miss Loris, how nice it is to see you again," Crow said from behind the counter. Their long, shimmering hair was again pulled back into a tidy ponytail, and their dark eyes smiled more than their lips.

"Hello, again."

Thenia took Serena's hand and led her to the counter. Quite a few patrons were at tables around the room, but the bar counter was free. Before they'd even taken their seats, Crow placed two iced teas in front of them with a small nod.

"You remembered," Thenia smiled.

"Of course, Miss Thenia," Crow said, looking at Serena. "Hello to you, too, Miss."

"Serena," she said shyly. "Thank you...for the tea."

"My pleasure. Let me know if you'd prefer something different."

Serena shook her head. "No, thank you. This is perfect."

Crow switched back to Thenia, and their endless dark eyes scanned her before they nodded. "Looks as if you've found your place to root."

"I have. Thank you for that push."

Crow shook their head, but a small, knowing smile was on their lips. "Think nothing of it. You're the one who took the first step."

Thenia chuckled. "Yes, directly into your sign outside, as I was telling Serena."

Crow's smile widened, and their eyes briefly flicked toward

the shop's door. "I'll make sure to scold it later, but then subsequently thank it for you."

Serena laughed again, and Crow reached below the counter, handing each of them a short menu.

"Would you like something to eat?"

"Hey, why didn't I get a menu last time?" Thenia questioned.

"Because you didn't need one," Crow smirked.

"Yes, please," Serena said with a smile.

Thenia held up her hand and shook her head. "You win. I'll have the grilled cheese, please."

"Enjoyed it?" Crow asked.

"Yes, it's perfect with your iced tea."

"Glad to hear it." Crow focused on Serena and waited for her to read the menu and decide.

"Um...."

"Might I suggest this one?" Crow pointed to an item, and Thenia leaned over and read the description for the chicken salad sandwich with cranberries and candied walnuts.

"Oh, that sounds delicious. Sure, um, thank you." Serena handed them her menu, but jumped and pulled her phone from her pocket when it began to vibrate.

Thenia observed Serena, who frowned as she read the message.

"Everything alright?" Thenia asked.

"Ash. Just asking where we are."

Thenia saw Crow smirking as they left them and walked into a back room.

"Tell him we stopped at Crow's."

Serena nodded, and once she was finished, she placed her phone on the counter.

Thenia sipped her tea, and people watched as Serena began to do the same once she'd gotten more comfortable. There was a couple in a back corner talking over their coffee, and the woman would occasionally speak to the empty chair beside her, making her and the other man laugh. Thenia frowned at the oddity, but then she saw a man in his early twenties, with his back to her, and a small bird perched on his shoulder. The bird was eating the seed from the man's sandwich bread when he held it up.

"Oh, I'm an idiot," Thenia mumbled, acknowledging what she was seeing.

Serena looked over and cocked her head.

"Sorry."

Thenia glanced from Serena to Crow as they returned with their plates and set them on the counter in front of them.

"Crow, may I ask you something?"

"Of course, Miss Thenia. Though you already know the answer to your question."

Thenia chuffed. "Understood. Thank you."

Serena glanced between them, still confused, but Crow smiled, and Thenia clarified.

"Nothing, sorry. I only now just realized that our, um...kind...are safe in here." Thenia said semi-cryptically.

"Indeed. Never anything but," Crow added and then wandered further down the counter to clean a complicated brass coffee maker.

"Oh," Serena glanced around at some of the other patrons, but then she refocused on her lunch and smiled. "It looks tasty."

"Swap a bite?" Thenia asked, holding out her sandwich. Serena grinned, took a bite, and then held her own up for Thenia to do the same. They both chewed happily and broke into a fit of giggles as they tucked in to enjoy their lunches.

Thenia pulled Ashton's car up to the gate in front of the house, but it opened before she could roll down the window. She smiled as her eyes darted to her phone on the charger.

"Thanks, Arthur."

"Absolutely, my dear," his distorted voice replied.

"Serena, I'll park and then go get the mail. Would you bring our clothes back to the house? I'll grab the groceries on my way over."

"Sure, no problem."

Thenia drove up the driveway and parked in front of the garage, where she grabbed her phone and tucked it into her jeans. Then, she walked back down the driveway and out the still-open gate to retrieve the mail. While she ambled back up to the house with it, she sorted through the stack. Most of it was junk mail, but when she saw a handwritten envelope addressed to her, she stopped and opened it.

Inside was a blank white card, and Thenia immediately pulled out her phone.

"Arthur, close the gate and get Ash. Now."

"Done," Arthur said less than two seconds later.

She flipped the card over and felt the blood rush from her face.

We know he has it. He returns it, or we come to get it.

"Thenia!" Ashton shouted as he ran towards her, Serena trailing behind him, equally as concerned.

"Ash," she handed him the card as he reached her.

"What is—"

When he saw the card and read the words, his eyes snapped to hers just as Serena made it to them.

"Take Serena and go to your house. Stay there." He stepped backward, but when she didn't move, he pointed in the direction of the tiny house. "Thenia. Go. Now."

"Ashton, I—"

"Later."

He turned and sprinted back into the house without saying anything else or looking back. She could hear him arguing with Sue as he ran, but his words were too obscured to understand.

"Thenia, do as he says," Arthur's distorted voice said, snapping her out of her daze as she stared after Ashton.

"Nia?" Serena asked, confused.

"Sorry. We need to grab the food and get home. I'll explain when we get there."

"Thank you, dear," Arthur said. "Hurry now."

She looked at Serena, and they both jogged to the car, grabbed all the bags they could, leaving only a few non-food items in the trunk, and then walked as fast as they could toward the smaller house.

"Nia, is Ash okay?" Serena asked as they approached the house.

"Yeah, I'll explain when we get it. I think he's...."

"Scared," Arthur finished for her.

Thenia opened the front door, and they settled all their bags on the counters and kitchen floor. Their clothes were still in the bags from earlier, where Serena had placed them beside the stairs, ready to be taken up when one of them went. Once Serena had closed the door, Thenia tugged her into a hug, rubbing the stressed woman's back.

"Okay. So, we got another letter from whoever knows about, um...yeah."

"What did it say this time?"

"Well, it was addressed to me this time, not Ash."

"Why? Do they know that we—"

Thenia stepped back and shook her head. "No, I don't think so. It mentioned that Ashton knew about it and that he needed to give it back, or they'd come to get it. The letter made it sound like they wanted me to run scared to him and convince him to give back whatever they want."

Serena's eyes went wide, and she groped behind her for the bar stool but missed. Thenia caught her and carefully steadied her on the stool.

"Serena, it'll be okay."

"It will be, my dear. Ash and his grandmother are discussing it now. Don't worry."

Thenia pulled her phone out, Arthur's image now on it. His voice had returned to normal since they were inside the house, where they'd not be overheard. She set him on the counter, leaning against a bag of potatoes.

"Serena, talk to Arthur for a few minutes while I put the food away. Okay?"

"Sure."

Thenia kissed her lightly on the lips and then put her palm on her cheek. "We'll figure it out. Okay?"

The woman, even more pale than usual, nodded, as Arthur began talking to her about a recipe for carrot cake, and Thenia left her in his capable...pixels. She couldn't deny that her life had become more chaotic since she'd moved into the small cottage, but she wouldn't have changed a minute of it. When Serena's soft laugh interrupted Thenia's thoughts, she smiled.

"Not a minute of it," she whispered and then began putting groceries away.

"Serena, would you like to take a bath?" Thenia called up the bedroom stairs.

She barely heard Serena's light footsteps as the woman hurried to the top of the steps and stared down at her. A pair of pants was in her hands, and she'd stopped mid-fold.

"A bath?"

"Yeah. We did a lot of walking today, and if my legs are sore, I imagine yours are, too. A bath would help your muscles."

Serena blushed and looked away. "I've...well, I guess I probably took one when I was little, but I can't remember it."

Thenia smiled up at her. "Would you like bubbles?"

Serena didn't look at her, but she did nod.

"Okay. When you're finished, come down. It'll take a few minutes for a bathtub that size to fill up."

"Thank...you."

"None needed."

Thenia returned to their bathroom, turned on the taps, and ensured the water was warm but not scalding. She added copious amounts of bubble bath from the bottle of lightly scented soap that Serena preferred and then grabbed two towels and put them in the dryer to warm up. By the time she'd gotten everything ready and the water was nearly full, Serena quietly stood in the bathroom doorway. Thenia shut off the water and got to her feet from the small stool she'd been resting on.

"Alright, you've got bubbles galore and warm water, and I put towels into the dryer for you, so when you get out, they'll be nice and toasty." Thenia tucked a strand of Serena's hair behind her ear. "Do you need anything?"

"Um, I don't know...."

Thenia kissed her cheek. "I'm going to make a fresh batch of iced tea, so I'll close the laundry room door. You can shout if you need something. Does that work?"

Serena paused but then nodded.

"Enjoy your bath."

Thenia exited the laundry room, closed the door behind herself, and went to sit on one of the bar stools. Her phone was still propped up against the bag of potatoes. Arthur's image smiled up at her.

"She's a good girl."

"She's wonderful...it's just the things she says sometimes. I wonder what her childhood was like, but then I see her expression and don't want to open any old wounds."

Arthur nodded. "A wise choice. She told Ashton a few things the other night when he asked. Sue said he was incredibly upset by what he learned."

Thenia sighed. "Thanks. Now, I'll make sure not to ask her. She doesn't need to relive it twice."

"Remember, Thenia. Sometimes, the scars aren't the important part to focus on. Instead, focus on not inflicting more of them. Then, one day, you'll find the old scars may have faded enough that they are mere memories."

She beamed at one of the kindest souls she'd ever had the pleasure of knowing. "Thanks, Arthur. You're right. Can I ask how Ashton is?"

"Still with Sue. I'm staying out of the way."

"Is he...has he calmed down?"

"A little. Sue talked him down, but I believe that until he has something he can actually affect, then he'll likely continue to feel helpless."

Thenia glanced at the laundry room door. "Yeah. I get that."

"N...Nia?"

Thenia blinked, breaking her blind spacing out.

"Yes?"

She hurried over to the laundry room door and cracked it open. From there, she couldn't see very far into the bathroom, but she could hear Serena.

"Um...would you...could you...um...." Serena paused, and Thenia heard her take a deep breath. "If you're not busy, would you come talk...with me...."

That was the last thing Thenia had expected, but she couldn't hold back her smile. "Sure, give me two seconds."

Thenia returned to her phone, said goodbye to Arthur, and set it on the counter nearest the bathroom so he could alert her if needed. Then she knocked softly on the laundry room door before making her way to the bathroom doorway.

Serena was chin-deep in bubbles. Her knees were up, and her arms wrapped around them.

"Are you okay?" Thenia asked.

"Yes, just...Well, I was thinking, and..." she trailed off and looked into the bubbles.

"Ah, silence. The enemy of a busy mind." Thenia smiled, sat on the stool from earlier, and leaned against the wall.

"Yes."

"Mine does that, too. Would you tell me what it's like when you're in your snake form?"

Serena hesitated but then nodded. "Okay. What do you want to know?"

"Anything you want to share. I have no idea what to think."

Serena talked her stress away as she explained her life as a small green snake, Thenia listening with genuine interest and curiosity. It was the most Serena had spoken in one sitting, and Thenia was relieved to see Serena's shoulders start to loosen, as she spoke and became less guarded.

Threatening note aside, Thenia's day with Serena had been...comfy, and Thenia was coming to enjoy that sensation of comfort.

Chapter 16: Intimate Moments

July 2024, Maine, USA | Ashton Giri

"Thenia," Ashton called as he stepped over the tiny home's threshold and into her kitchen. "Serena?"

"They are in the bathroom, Ashton," Pops' voice said from further into the kitchen. Ashton found Thenia's phone sitting on the counter by the laundry room door. "Serena is taking a bath and wanted company."

Ashton stopped short, and his mind went in ten directions at once. His Pops clearly noticed, and he laughed so lowly that Ashton wasn't sure he had laughed at all.

"Talking, Ashton. Serena was lonely, from what I can tell."

"Got it."

Ashton sank onto the nearest bar stool and leaned on the counter, his head in his hands. He was only there for a minute or two before he heard the laundry room door click, and he glanced up.

"Ash?" Thenia asked as she shut the door behind herself.

"Hey, sorry. Didn't mean to interrupt."

Thenia shook her head and came over and stood beside him. "You didn't. We were just talking. She was telling me what it's like being a snake."

When Thenia smiled, a brightness filled her features, and Ashton was hit with a wave of envy he hadn't expected.

"Hey, what's wrong?" Thenia rested against the counter, her thigh pressed against his leg. "Is this the letter or something else?"

Ashton shook his head. "Sorry. I'm fine. It was nothing."

Thenia crossed her arms and narrowed her eyes at him.

"Really. I was being...stupid. It's fine. I'm glad you two enjoyed your day together."

Her eyes searched his for another minute before she strode back into the bathroom without saying a word.

"Well, shit."

Before he even had a chance to stand, Thenia was back. She returned to where she'd been leaning against him and the counter.

"Ah..." Ashton asked, slightly confused.

"Later," she said, but then glanced over her shoulder at her phone. "Arthur, can you do me a favor?"

"Of course, my dear."

Thenia smiled. "Can you tell me what the weather is going to be tonight? Serena plans to spend some time in her snake form, but if the weather is bad, I'll worry about her."

"Yes, yes. I see."

Ashton met Thenia's eyes as his Pops began to rattle off the local weather forecast for the night, as she'd requested. She was up to something, but when her gaze flicked to his lips, she blushed and looked away, and he had an idea of what she was planning.

Just as his Pops had finished his readout, Serena opened the laundry room door, hair dripping but cheeks rosy.

"Hi," she said, looking at the floor and smiling.

"How was your day in town?" he asked and pivoted on the stool so he could pull her to stand between his knees when she walked over to him.

"Fun."

He hunched down to look up at her, and he saw Thenia smiling at the two of them.

"I'm glad it was fun. I'm sorry about earlier." Ashton said, looking up at Thenia. "To both of you. I didn't mean to be so demanding."

Serena shook her head. "It's fine. We get it, but...um...."

Thenia shuffled closer to them, took the towel from Serena's hands, and began to carefully dry her hair while they talked.

Ashton sighed, "Yeah. I know. I need to explain."

Serena nodded but giggled when Thenia poked her side and scolded her for moving.

"We're pretty sure it's the same sender. I'm not an expert, but the card and the writing look too similar to be a coincidence."

"That's what we figured," Thenia agreed, squeezing the water from Serena's hair.

"I don't want this on the record yet, so I can't ask anyone from work, but I spoke with Eileen and Xander this morning, and they'll be home in a few weeks. My hope is that nothing will escalate before then. The two of them will know better what to do."

"Is there a reason you're not asking them to come back sooner?" Thenia asked and then started to comb her fingers through Serena's hair.

"Well, I spoke with them before the letter arrived. At that point, I didn't see the rush or the need to hinder their current job. Gram and I still think we should be alright until they are finished."

"Um...Ashton..." Serena asked softly.

"What's up?"

"Does Alexander...I mean...should I..." she sighed. "Paranams can be, um, territorial, and um, this is his home...."

Ashton smiled and shook his head. "Opposite. He asked me to give you his cell number this morning. He wanted me to tell you he's there if you want to talk to someone other than the two of us. Not to mention the two meddling grandparents made of ones and zeros he doesn't even know about, yet."

"I heard that young man," his Gram chided from his pocket, before his Pops laughed from Thenia's phone still by the laundry room.

Ashton smirked but focused on Serena. "He's looking forward to meeting you. They both are, but I think Xander is looking forward to having someone else in their beast form around. He's a panther without a pack."

"I don't think that's quite true," Thenia scolded, "but I understand what you meant. Though I'd bet he'd disagree with you."

"Sure," Serena said, nibbling on her lower lip. "Please, um, I'd like that."

"Consider it done," Pops said. "Eileen's has also been added. Just in case. To yours as well, Thenia."

"Thanks, Arthur," Thenia said and tied the end of Serena's braid.

"Thank you," Serena said over her shoulder to Thenia, who kissed her cheek.

"Alright. Well, if we're safe for now, relatively speaking," Thenia added, "I'd like to shower. Drawing Serena's bath made me jealous."

"Go for it," Ashton said, and Serena nodded in agreement. "Won't take me long."

With one last look at him, Thenia nodded and left the room.

Ashton ran his thumb and forefinger over the end of Serena's braid, and she smiled. "So, you met Crow."

"I did. They were very nice. I didn't know there were places for our kind like that."

Ashton snorted. "Well, I'm not sure how many there are, at least ones so overtly in the middle of the Outside world, but yeah, Crow's is special."

"I like the sandwich I had. They gave me the recipe."

"Rad, I always liked their food. Gram and I used to go visit them when I was younger."

Ashton smiled at the memory. He must have made a face because Serena hugged him, her arms around his neck. She was still warm from her bath and faintly perfumed by the soap he'd given her.

"I'm sorry about the letter, Ashton," she mumbled.

"Not your fault."

"I know, but still."

"I just want you both safe. That's all. I'm sorry you got dragged into this."

She stepped back and smiled down at him. "We're not. Nia and I talked about it today. We're glad you're not dealing with this alone."

Ashton's stomach flipped a few times inside his torso. Eileen's earlier remark about loving the two women came back to his mind, and he drew Serena down to him and kissed her lazily. He wasn't sure where her boundary was, but he wanted to show her how much she and her words meant to him. He just wasn't sure how to.

He pulled them apart and kissed her cheek. "Thank you. I'm glad you're here, too."

Serena blushed but nodded.

"Serena, can I ask you something?"

"Sure."

"You're going to be in your snake form tonight, right?"

She turned her head and shifted uncomfortably in place. "Um, yeah, uh...."

"What can we do for you?" he asked, but then quickly shook his head. "Sorry, I didn't phrase that well. Uh...."

He didn't want to come right out and say, *you won't sleep with us, and that's fine, but what can we do instead?* That would only make her uncomfortable, not to mention he'd feel like a jerk for saying it.

"Look, I understand your preferences and boundaries, and I'll respect them. Obviously. But how can we..." he groaned. "Damn, I feel like an ass."

"It's fine," she assured him. "Different language, remember?"

He looked at her and saw she was studying him, and her fidgeting had stopped.

"You're right. Would you translate for me? What can I do that will show you I care about you in the same way as I do, Nia?"

Serena glanced down at her fingers, but he gave her space, and she hadn't pulled out of his arms yet, so his question didn't seem to make her too uneasy.

"Um, tonight...after, when you and Nia are...Can I come home, and will you stay with us tonight?"

Ashton put his palm on Serena's cheek and made her look up at him, though she didn't offer much resistance.

"First, this is your home. I never want you to feel like you can't come home. Do what you want and need to. Even if that's banging pots and pans until you get your point across. Being with Thenia is important to me, but no more so than spending time with you and not at the expense of your feelings. Understand?"

She nodded but said nothing.

"Secondly, I'd be happy to stay here tonight. Would you be up for reading more of that novel we started?"

"Okay."

"Serena, do you know what Nia said to me the last time she and I were together?"

"No...."

"She asked me to set an alarm so we could come snuggle with you." He smiled. "Just because you're not with us doesn't mean we aren't thinking of you."

Serena's eyes began to shimmer, and he tightened his arms around her again.

"Thank you for understanding, Serena, and for translating. I'm looking forward to reading more of our book."

He felt her sniffle against him, while he hoped his honesty hadn't made things worse. He wanted to respect her boundaries, but he also needed to show her how much he...Ashton rolled his eyes and mentally cursed his sister with a smile.

He needed a way to show Serena how much he loved her, even if he had to show it differently than he did with Thenia.

"Tell me more about your day. Did you go clothes shopping?"

Serena leaned back against the counter but lingered between his legs, his palms resting loosely on her hips.

"Yeah. Nia bought me...." Serena hesitated, and a frown crinkled her brow.

"What's up?"

"It was expensive."

Ashton slightly squeezed her hips. "Does that bother you?"

Serena sighed. "Yes. I don't have anything to contribute—"

"Ah," Ashton interrupted her, "I don't think that's accurate."

"But I don't have any money, and I can't even get a job."

"Okay, let's look at this one piece at a time, alright?"

Serena nodded, and he leaned forward to kiss her briefly, bringing a blush to her cheeks.

"First, the job. Do you want to get one?"

He watched as she considered his question, emotions passing through her features as she did.

"Um, not really. I don't think I would be comfortable around people for that long, and my snake...."

"We could always find you something to do from home, but I hear you. As for your paperwork, I can help you update your registration, and we can get you an ID, passport, and other stuff if you'd like. It's probably a good idea anyway."

"Okay..." Serena agreed.

"Next, the money part. Serena, both Thenia and I have plenty of money to support you. Really. Between her inheritance, my job, and the investments I've made over the years, we'll be fine. But why don't we figure out a different way for you to contribute? You already know that your cooking is our favorite, not to mention how often Nia and I both forget to eat or are too exhausted to cook."

Ashton watched as his words sank in, and Serena's eyes narrowed in concentration.

"I guess that's true, and I think I'm getting better...."

He chuckled, "Considering you were fantastic to start with, I don't think you should worry about that part."

Her cheeks flushed deeper, and Ashton brushed his thumb over the pretty shade of pink. "So, how about we start with food then? You're welcome to still ask for help and take nights off, but why don't you be in charge of cooking? Would that make you feel better?"

She nodded, and he pulled her lips back to his own. After a minute, Serena's grip tightened on his forearms, and he pulled away and smiled at her, appreciative of her unspoken enforcement of limits.

The anonymous letter returned to the forefront of Ashton's mind, and he rested his forehead on Serena's sternum. He needed to figure out who was behind them and fast. Thenia and Serena deserved to live their days without having to look over their shoulders, and he would make sure they could.

Serena's fingers affectionately ran through his hair, and he smiled against her.

Yup, his sister was right. He loved them both. She was wrong about the complications, though. They'd figure it out.

Thenia Loris

By the time Thenia had dragged herself from the warm water and out of the shower, it sounded like Ashton was still in the kitchen, cooking something, and Serena had likely gone out for the evening.

Earlier, when Thenia had seen Ashton's look of hurt, longing, and slight discomfort, she'd talked to Serena and explained the situation. It was Serena's suggestion that she spend some time in the garden and give them some time together—not Thenia's. Serena had assured Thenia she was okay with it and understood Ashton's need for that form of connection. To Serena's credit, Thenia believed their third partner was genuinely alright with the solution.

The two of them had spoken a lot over the weeks about their complicated relationship. The one thing Thenia learned for certain was that Serena struggles to open up, but once she does, she is sincere in what she reveals. So, if Serena said she wasn't upset about Thenia and Ashton sleeping together—she wasn't.

Thenia pulled a set of lounge clothes from the clean laundry bin, and when she was dressed, she went out into the kitchen. As she'd guessed, Ashton was cooking a salad that looked to have been made from every color of the rainbow, and she could smell garlic roasting somewhere out of sight.

"Hey, that smells amazing," she said, peeking at the salad bowl around his back.

Ashton smiled but continued to chop a fresh cucumber. "It's nothing fancy, but Serena said you'd gotten some fresh stuff and suggested a salad might be good for dinner."

"Where's the garlic smell coming from?" Thenia said and glanced around before her eyes landed on the oven.

"Made croutons."

Thenia's mouth watered, and she went to the fridge, pulled out a chilled bottle of white wine, and asked, "Up for a glass?"

"Sure. Want help with the cork?"

"Nope, all good. I may not have been allowed to drink, but I still had to host." Thenia scoffed. "Ass."

"Can't disagree."

"Doesn't matter anymore." Thenia reached around Ashton for two glasses in a cupboard above him and stopped to kiss his cheek as she did. "Just gonna think of it as a life skill and call it good."

Ashton smirked and shook his head, but leaned over to kiss her lips as she passed him once more. "Silver lining, I guess."

Thenia focused on uncorking the wine, but couldn't help but feel Serena's absence from the room.

"So, Serena, head out?"

"Yeah. We talked for a bit, but she was going to go downstairs to talk to Pops about Xander and then spend some time in her beast form. It's been a day or two that she's been in her human one, right?"

"It has. She was telling me about her beast form earlier during her bath. It wasn't difficult to tell that she missed it. I can't help but feel she's staying in her human form more for us than herself."

"Of course she is, but she'll find the balance."

Ashton tossed the last of the produce into the bowl, dried his hands, and pulled a baking tray with freshly made garlic croutons from the oven.

"I think talking to Xander will help. I wasn't just trying to make her feel better. It was his idea to give her his number."

"I'd imagine so. Sounds like he's that type of person from what I've heard of him from you four."

"Oh, speaking of Gram and Pops," Ashton said while plating their food. "I talked to Gram about eavesdropping."

Thenia laughed. "Ah. Yeah. Not much privacy when they are literally in everything with an electrical pulse, huh?"

"You have no idea," Ashton smirked. "But yeah, we decided to treat them a bit like Panama's AI assistant, Ziggy. When we ask them to, they'll step back a bit, and we can use a command word that they'll react to and come back."

"Makes sense. What's the word?" Thenia said, setting both glasses on the counter beside their plates.

Ashton glanced at their phones on the counter, his now resting beside hers. "Um...the name of the plant we found the drive under."

Thenia grinned. "I see."

With her hands now free, she pulled herself into Ashton's arms, and he tightened his arms around her.

"They sleeping already?"

He bent down and whispered against her lips, "They are. Well, with Serena still, but will be fully after she leaves, yes."

"Well, as much as I'd like to say forget dinner, I'm starving, and I wouldn't give up those croutons for anything."

He chuckled, but she quieted him with a kiss. When he pulled away, he was still smiling, and he kissed her lightly once more before nudging her toward her stool.

"Considering I barely ate today, you're probably on to something."

She rolled her eyes but pushed him gently into his seat. "Eat."

"As you wish," Ashton grinned, but stuck a forkful of salad in his mouth.

Thenia popped a crouton into her mouth with a similar smile.

"I, uh, talked to Serena about handling the cooking in exchange for us paying for things."

Thenia's fork stopped halfway to her mouth before she sighed and lowered it back to the plate. "Ah."

"I think she's good now."

"Okay," Thenia nodded. "Thank you."

"It's fine. You handled the sex conversation. I got this one." He smirked at her, and Thenia couldn't hold back her laugh.

"Fair enough."

They ate and exchanged details about their day for a while, but Thenia couldn't ignore it any longer.

"Ash, the letter...."

He sighed but sipped his wine and shoved his empty plate away.

"Yeah."

"Do you think it's fair to assume they know of our relationship?"

He swiveled on the stool to lean against the counter and cross his arms. A minute later, he nodded.

"And what about Serena?" she asked.

"Well, it's safe to assume they know you and I have a relationship. I don't think we should assume they know it's more than a working one, though."

Thenia put her fork down and cuddled closer to Ashton's side. "Do you really believe that?"

Ashton was silent for so long that Thenia sat back to see his face, a frown on his lips.

"I'd like to."

She chuffed. "Well, yeah, me too, but I don't think we can."

He sighed, wrapped his arms around her, and tugged her closer. "Yeah, I know."

"We'll just have to be more careful."

Ashton tucked a wispy strand of Thenia's hair behind her ears and then captured her lips with his own. There was no hiding his unease from her, and Thenia fell even more in love with the caring man beside her.

When she pulled away and got to her feet, Ashton cocked his head. She held out her hand, and Ashton seized it.

Chapter 17: Sugar

July 2024, Maine, USA | Ashton Giri

Ashton grumbled and shoved his chair back from his desk, then stood up and paced angrily.

"Ash, we'll find something," his Gram reassured from her monitor.

"Will we? They clearly know how to go untraceable to a mechanite. Hell, even their handwriting isn't identifiable by any database."

"I know, but you know as well as I do that everyone slips up at some point."

He stumbled over his shoe and caught himself, but had to resist the impulse to scream. Instead, he roughly sat back down and slumped forward.

"I have to find something. It's been a week since they sent that letter to Thenia, and they are going to show up in person eventually. I can't let them catch us off guard."

"Why don't you take a quick break, and then we can start again?"

"Where are Thenia and Serena?"

"Serena is sunning herself in the apple orchard, and Thenia is nearby tending to a berry bush. I think?"

Ashton glanced at his Gram and smirked. "You think?"

"Yes," Gram rolled her eyes. "Your Grandfather never digitized his garden layouts."

Ashton chuckled at that and shook his head. "Ask Thenia. She'll do it. It might be a good idea to have around anyway, and chances are, she's already done most of the mapping that Pops hadn't gotten to. If there was any."

"Likely correct. I sent her an email. No sense in bothering her right now."

"Couldn't you just wait until later and ask her?"

"I could have, but she and I have been emailing back and forth, since I'm more often with you."

Ashton cocked his head. "Wait, really?"

"Yes, really," she laughed. "Why?"

"No reason. I just didn't know."

His Gram said nothing and merely smiled, but he took the hint. Not his business.

"Okay, well, I'll take your advice. I need a break. I'll grab a water and be back in a few."

He got to his feet and locked his devices while his Gram nodded and faded from her machine's login screen. Forgoing his cell phone for a quick trip down the hall, Ashton wandered towards the kitchen but stopped in the hallway to examine a piece of art hanging on the wall. His grandparents loved art, and they often went to local galleries and showings as a family when Ashton was a kid—another thing he missed.

Shaking off his sadness, he went to the fridge and pulled out a cold bottle of water. He'd drunk nearly half of it when he felt his watch vibrate on his wrist, and he peeked down at it.

Ash, find Thenia. Cherry tree. Run.

The notification was from his Gram, and Ashton dropped the bottle he'd been holding and sprinted to the front door. He mentally cursed himself for leaving his phone behind, but truthfully, with his watch and Gram, there wasn't much need for him to carry it other than habit. He vaulted down the front steps, circled the garage, and raced deeper into the garden behind it. Just when he began to glimpse the top of the enormous pink cherry tree coming into view, he heard voices.

"Lucus, we've discussed this. Leave," Thenia said sternly.

Ashton slowed his pace and attempted to look casual when he walked around a large shrub and joined them in the cherry tree garden.

"I know we did, but I wanted to try again. Won't you give me a second chance?" Lucus' voice was practically pleading, but he met Ashton's eyes when he entered the garden, and Lucus' expression shifted. "Oh, it's you."

"Ashton," he voiced, but said nothing else.

Ashton moved to stand beside Thenia, who met his eyes and seemed to be calm. This made him wonder why his Gram had sounded so panicked.

"Whatever," Lucus snapped and refocused on Thenia. "Come home. I miss you."

Thenia crossed her arms and rolled her eyes. "You expect me to believe that? You don't miss me. You miss your picture-perfect fiancé. Well, find another one. I'm not going anywhere with you."

"But I do miss you. Don't you remember the good times we had together? The governor's ball last spring. How about that? You looked beautiful."

Ashton struggled to maintain a neutral expression, but he was rather confident he'd seen a picture of the two of them from that party when he'd investigated Lucus. It was one where Thenia had been holding a glass of wine.

"Exactly. I looked pretty. Nothing but a charm on your arm," Thenia said with a self-hating laugh. "You call those good times? Maybe for you, but certainly not for me."

Something about Lucus felt off, and between the bizarre feeling Ashton was getting and his Gram's message, he wanted to test something.

"Thenia," he said before Lucus could say anything else. "Wasn't that the event you told me had an amazing wine that you enjoyed? The one you wanted me to order."

She narrowed her eyes at him, but only a fraction before Lucus spoke up.

"I remember that. See, you still talk about our time together."

Ashton beamed. He was right. This wasn't Lucus, and undoubtedly, Thenia made that same determination.

She glanced back at Lucus and lowered her hands to her sides. "I quit drinking, Lucus."

The impostor nodded. "Well, that's good. Healthier for you that way anyway."

Now that they'd identified the transmogromorph for what they were—because that was the only possibility, Ashton needed to figure out what the hell to do about it. He strayed a few steps away from Thenia, feigning curiosity in a random plant that he didn't even know the name of, but in doing so, positioned himself nearer to the fraudulent Lucus.

"I agree. You know what's also better for me?" Thenia baited.

"Coming home with me?"

Thenia scoffed but met Ashton's eyes, and he glimpsed her fingers start to move ever so slightly.

"No. Making sure that I never go anywhere with you. Ever. You *or* Lucus. Shifter."

Before Ashton had an opportunity to think or come up with a strategy, the fake Lucus bolted toward Thenia, but he only closed half the distance to her when the earth began to shudder beneath all three of them.

Serena Ainsley

Serena was enjoying herself, napping in the sun on a flat rock, when she heard Thenia call over to her.

"Be right back, Serena. Running to the garage for something."

Serena bobbed her little head in acknowledgement.

"Actually, I'm going to work over by the cherry tree for a bit. You look comfy, so don't feel the need to join me. I'll come find you when I'm done, okay?"

She watched Nia's small wave, and then her back as she grew further and further away.

The sun was exceptionally warm, and Nia was correct. Serena was comfy. Serena rolled onto her back and then completely extended her lengthy body before coiling back up on the center of the rock slab. Her eyes were shut for only a few minutes when she heard a rustling in a nearby tree, and she glanced up as a large, dark beast dropped to the floor near her. The feline was sleek and seemed to be made of nothing but muscles, and all of it was beneath a black coat that glistened in the sun.

"Serena, I'm Alexander, don't be frightened."

She nodded and raised her head. "You're back early. Ash didn't expect you until next week. Wait," she extended her body even higher, "why are you in your beast form?"

"Eileen and I followed behind a car when we got here. It stopped at the gate and looked suspicious, so we watched."

Serena knew Ashton hadn't briefed Eileen or Alexander about their current situation, so whatever had them suspicious was unrelated. Hopefully.

"It's Lucus. Thenia's ex."

Serena uncoiled and stretched her body to its full height. Not that she was imposing or anything, considering her size, but now she was closer to eye level with Alexander. "Where is he?"

"Eileen is tailing him. Ash doesn't know we're home yet. When you didn't respond to my text, I came to find you and hoped you were in your beast form."

"Why?"

"I need information. Eileen tried to talk with the system, but she said it locked her out."

Serena nodded. She assumed it was Sue who'd kept Eileen

out.

"Last we heard from Ash, Thenia had told Lucus to leave. Did something change?"

"Not that I know of. We haven't heard anything from him. Unless she didn't tell us, but I think she would have."

"Agreed. Alright. Do you want to come with me? I need to find Eileen."

"Yes," Serena said, but Alexander dropped his head before she could slither to the garden's bed.

"Climb on, I'm faster."

She hesitated. Even as a child, Serena understood that different paranam beast types had various forms of propriety, and in general, practically all of them embraced a reticence to intermingle more often than not.

"I'm fine with it if you are, Serena. I told you before that this is just as much your home as mine. Besides, I don't do that animal kingdom hierarchy crap. We're all paranams."

She nodded and took him at his word. He was Arthur and Sue's son and Ash's brother. Serena trusted them, so she'd trust him.

Alexander took a step closer to her, and she stretched her body out and slithered atop his back and up to his neck, where she could see over his head.

"Is this alright?"

"Fine with me, as long as you're comfortable. Can you hold on well enough?"

"Mostly. If you need to run and can't warn me, it's fine. I've fallen from higher."

"I'll do my best to warn you then."

After that, Alexander lowered his body and walked into the plants as he cut them across the garden.

"Where are you going?" she asked.

"Front garden first. I assume he entered via the gate, so I'll be able to catch his scent there, and then we can decide where to go after that."

"Makes sense. Will Eileen be alright alone?"

Alexander chuffed, and then she felt him purr beneath her scales. "More than fine. Ash has told you what we do, right?"

"Nothing specific, but generally."

"Don't underestimate Eileen. I may have teeth and claws and be the larger human, but that woman has taken me out in either form on more than one occasion."

"Oh." Serena had listened to Arthur talk about the two of them constantly, but frankly, she'd assumed he was boasting about his children.

"Ah, I hear voices," Alexander informed before he quickly and virtually silently padded across the driveway and into another cluster of plants on the opposite edge. "Female. Thenia, I assume. Two men, one is Ash."

"Lucus, then. What are they saying?"

"She just mentioned she stopped drinking after they separated."

Serena tensed. "Wait, alcohol?"

"Sounds like it from what little context I have."

"Thenia wasn't allowed to drink when she was with Lucus."

Serena sensed Alexander stiffen, and then he stood up to his full height. She was able to hear a bit more of what was happening since they'd gotten nearer, and eventually, she could make out Thenia's voice.

"You know what's also better for me?" Thenia asked.

"Coming home with me?" Lucus said.

"That's Lucus' voice," Serena relayed to Alexander, but before she could convey more, the ground began to vibrate beneath them.

"Shit. Hold on!" Alexander warned, and Serena managed to wrap herself around his neck, not entirely, but sufficiently that she didn't tumble off when he started sprinting through the garden and then leaped over a manicured hedge.

Everything erupted into chaos. It looked like Lucus had been trying to attack Thenia, but he was still ten feet from her, his hands out, struggling to keep his balance as the earth shook. Behind him was Ashton, who was equally unsteady. When he noticed Serena and Alexander rushing toward them, his gaze widened, and then he grinned, his eyes darting around the area. Serena ignored him now that she knew he was safe and instead concentrated on Thenia.

She had her hands at her sides and was scowling at Lucus, her lips moving as she whispered. It was undoubtedly Thenia manipulating the earth, but when she glimpsed Alexander out of the corner of her eye, she faltered and lost focus. The ground ceased shaking, but before Lucus could regain his footing, Alexander flew them past Thenia and pounced on the man.

As his paws left the ground, Serena hurled herself off Alexander's back, and then the panther's body collided with the human's, both of them toppling over and into a large hedge.

"Serena!" Thenia cried and dove forward with her palms out, catching her tiny body before she hit the ground. Sure, Serena would have been fine, but she appreciated Thenia's sharp reflexes nevertheless. Though if Serena had been in her human form, she'd probably have been bright red from embarrassment.

"Damn," Ashton said, jogging over to Thenia's side. "Good catch."

Thenia rolled her eyes and nodded, but raised Serena to her shoulder. Serena curled around her neck and rubbed her head on Nia's cheek before licking her and making her laugh.

Ashton refocused on Lucus and Alexander, but everyone's attention was drawn to the foliage behind them, where a lithe, blonde woman emerged from the greenery with so little sound or disruption to the plants around her, it was as if she were made of mist. Her features gave away her relation to Ashton, and Serena knew from photos in the main house that the woman was Eileen. Her mid-length hair was in a severe ponytail, which made her appear even more intimidating when she stopped beside Lucus, her arms crossed in front of her chest, and scanned the man currently pinned beneath Alexander. The black panther's jaws were around the man's neck, but it didn't look like he'd broken the intruder's skin with his teeth—yet.

"Ash, explain," Eileen stated.

It wasn't Ashton who answered. Instead, Thenia spoke up, "That's not Lucus."

Eileen's eyes narrowed, and she studied Thenia, then the imposter, and finally her brother.

"You're sure?"

Ashton nodded. "Positive. I'm sure you heard the conversation. The real Lucus forbade Thenia from drinking."

The woman's eyes narrowed as she stared at the wide-eyed man, practically shivering at her feet.

"Alright. What do you want us to—"

"Wait." Before she could finish, Ashton raised his palm and checked his watch. "Let him go."

"Why?" Eileen snapped, and even Alexander's eyes glanced over to Ashton before they landed on Serena.

Serena stretched over and read a message from Sue on Ashton's watch, and Serena relayed it to Alexander. "He got a message. We'll explain later, but Ash is right. We need to let him go."

"Ash, why the hell—"

"Eileen," Ashton barked. "Listen to me."

"Ash doesn't normally speak like that," Alexander admitted. He gradually backed off the stranger's throat, but still held him pinned beneath him. "He better have a good reason for this, but we need to listen to him, right?"

"Please."

"Fine. I'll tell Eileen."

Alexander's tail flicked back and forth a few times, drawing Eileen's attention. She stared down at him, and they looked at each other for a few seconds before Eileen rolled her eyes and groaned.

"Fine. Let him go."

As Alexander drew himself off the man, Eileen bent to get into the intruder's face.

"You only get one chance. Get off the property, or I'll ignore my brother, and you'll regret your decision not to leave. Understood?"

When she stepped back to stand beside Alexander, the man clumsily got to his feet and ran toward the front of the house.

Serena looked up at Ashton, who had his eyes closed as she'd expected. She saw Eileen was observing her brother, too, and from the expression Eileen was giving him, she was furious. A minute later, Ashton opened his eyes and nodded.

"He's gone."

"What the hell, Ash!" Eileen snapped, but when she advanced toward him, Alexander stepped in her path, and she glared down at him. "Don't tell me you're not just as angry as I am."

From where Serena was, she could only see Alexander's back, but she could tell the pair was completely concentrated on each other.

Then Eileen hissed, "Fine. I'm going to unpack." Without a backward glance, she marched toward the house.

"I'll deal with her. Check on yours, and once Eileen's calmer, we'll come see you guys at the guest house." Alexander said, and Serena nodded before he bounded after his partner.

"Um…Ash?" Thenia asked tentatively.

"Sorry," Ashton looked from Serena to Thenia and then frowned. "Are you alright?"

"Yes. Thank you. I knew something was wrong, but I couldn't figure out if he'd had a come to god moment or a lobotomy. Never even occurred to me that he'd be a transmogromorph."

"Yeah. We'll have to tackle that issue, too, but for now, I need to see how bad Eileen is."

Serena exaggeratedly shook her head, and they both looked at her, Thenia doing so out of the corner of her eye.

"No?" Ashton asked. "What, no?"

"Wait, can't paranams speak to one another when they are in their beast forms?" Thenia said.

Serena nodded, and Ashton sighed.

"Ah, Xander wanted us to do something?"

Serena nodded and then poked her nose against Thenia's cheek.

Thenia smiled. "Does he want us to go to our house and give them a bit?"

Serena nodded her head and then rubbed it on Thenia's cheek again. She wasn't sure how Thenia understood her from the slight movement of a snake, but it worked, so Serena didn't care.

"Well, I guess I can't blame him." Ashton massaged the back of his neck and then exhaled a deep breath. "He'll talk her down. Fine, let's go then."

Thenia grasped Ashton's hand, and Serena took the opportunity to slither down Thenia's arm and coil herself around where the two hands were joined, making them both laugh.

"Thank you, Serena," Thenia smiled.

Serena licked her wrist and then Ashton's before she got comfortable and settled in for their walk.

As they made their way back to the tiny house, Serena closed her eyes and determined that where she was, easily beat her sunning rock as the best sunning spot she'd found yet.

Chapter 18: Back in One Room

July 2024, Maine, USA | Thenia Loris

Thenia poured coffee over ice and passed the glass to Ashton, who was sitting at her kitchen bar with Serena. His phone was propped up, Serena's beside it, with Sue and Arthur's faces on each, respectively.

"Why did you want us to let him go, Gram?"

"Because your sister and Xander were involved. If we hope to keep them out of this, we need to make sure as little attention is brought to them as possible."

"Why are they even here?" Ashton bemoaned, rubbing his hands over his face roughly. "She said two weeks."

Thenia handed Serena a glass of iced tea before taking one for herself and leaning on the counter.

Thenia noticed Arthur's gaze drop, and Sue pursed her lips, glancing over at her husband with what looked to be a mix of frustration and relief.

"Ah, that would be my fault," Arthur admitted.

"How?" Serena asked.

"I, um, sent them an email and asked them to come back sooner."

"What?" Ashton's head snapped up to glare at the older man's image.

"Don't worry, Ash. I've scolded him already, and he knows I will lock him out of all systems if he meddles again." Sue sighed, "But he's correct."

"So they know you're…alive?" Thenia asked carefully.

"No," Sue shook her head. "Arthur sent it from Ash's account."

Ashton groaned and slumped forward onto the counter, his entire upper body on it, looking like the will to live had been dragged out of him.

"Fuck sake, Pops."

Thenia saw Arthur's regretful frown deepen, and considering he hadn't scolded Ashton for his language, the man knew he'd screwed up.

"We have a code, Pops. You can't do that."

"He's aware now, Ash. I'm sorry. I should have discussed it with him sooner. Truthfully," she smirked sideways at her husband, "I didn't think he knew how to do it, or I would have."

Serena stifled a laugh, and Arthur glanced at her and smiled as little as he probably could.

"Fine, fine. Whatever. It's done now," Ashton whined into the counter.

"So, what do we do?" Thenia asked before sipping her tea and running her free hand over Ashton's back.

"Well, the first thing we need to do is explain about us," Sue said. "I had to lock your sister out of the system when they arrived earlier, and she's already jumping to massive conclusions."

Ashton groaned. "You did what?" He pulled himself upright and was now glaring at his grandmother.

"You know your sister's capabilities, Ash. We need to talk to her first, not have her stumble up to your grandfather and me accidentally and without explanation."

"No wonder she was so upset earlier and gave Ash that look," Thenia scoffed.

Serena nodded in agreement. "Yeah, Alexander said she'd been locked out and was confused by it."

Ashton groaned again. "This is a nightmare."

"It'll be fine, Ash," Sue replied in a low volume, drawing all three of their attention to the phone just as their screens faded to black.

"What—" Ashton said, but was interrupted by a soft knock on the front door before he paled. "Oh, shit."

"I'll get it," Thenia offered and nodded to Serena, who took Ashton's hand in silent support.

Earlier, Thenia had only seen Eileen from across the garden, but now that the woman was out of traveling clothes and less upset, not to mention only a few feet from her, Thenia realized that she was stunning. Her shoulder-length blond hair had been pulled from its perfect ponytail and now fell in soft waves, framing her bare face and beautiful skin. She wore a casual pair of jeans and a plain T-shirt. Eileen was captivating, looked exactly like Ashton, and had the confidence to match, which she rightfully deserved from the sounds of it.

A step behind her was a broad-shouldered man with the darkest, most beautiful skin that Thenia had ever seen. He, too, wore jeans and a T-shirt, but the approachable clothing didn't lessen his demanding presence. He smiled at her with a slight nod, but when Thenia looked at Eileen, she seemed unsure or uncomfortable.

"Hello, come in," Thenia said, stepping aside. "Obviously, it's a bit of a tight squeeze, but do what you need to and make yourself at home. Do either of you want something to drink? Iced tea or coffee?"

"Iced tea would be amazing," Alexander requested.

"I'm alright, but thank you," Eileen added, immediately walking over to Ashton and stopping in front of him.

He still held Serena's hand but glanced up at his sister then and immediately looked away.

Thenia saw Eileen hug Ashton from the corner of her eye, as she passed them and returned to the kitchen to pour Alexander his tea. It wasn't until his glass was placed on the counter that Eileen finally released her brother.

"You have a lot of explaining to do, little brother," his sister scolded, but she already looked lighter than when she'd first entered the house.

"I'm aware. For now..." Ashton got to his feet to give Eileen his stool, and he hugged Alexander while she got comfortable. "Hey, man. Good to see you."

"You too, Ash. Looks like we came home right on time."

Thenia glanced at Serena, and they both grinned but said nothing about Arthur's intervention—well-intentioned but against the rules either way.

"Apparently," Ash agreed, but turned to Serena. "This is Pops' green snake, Serena, though you two have met already."

Alexander shook Serena's hand and smiled. "We did. Thanks for the earlier assistance. It's great to finally meet you. I've heard a lot about you over the years."

Serena flushed and nodded. "Me too. Arthur talked about you two a lot."

Eileen snorted. "Meddling old pain in my ass," she said with a smile. "He should have just told us you were here. What was he so afraid of?"

Serena shook Eileen's hand, too, but then looked away anxiously.

"And this is Thenia," Ashton interjected, his attempt at pulling attention from Serena evident to no one but her and Thenia.

"Welcome home," Thenia smiled, shook Eileen's hand, and then Alexander's. "Ash talks about you both a lot, and I know he's missed you."

Eileen and Alexander looked at Ashton, and Thenia realized she'd shortened his name out of habit.

Ashton scratched his neck, picked up his coffee, and tried to hide his blush behind it.

"Oops," Thenia chuckled, pulling the group's stares back to her. "Well, we know you're already aware of our relationships, but please, if I make you uncomfortable—"

"Or…" Serena added quickly, "me.…"

Thenia smiled at the shy woman and set her palm on her shoulder. "Just let us know."

"You won't." Both Eileen and Alexander said together.

Eileen continued, "You're right. Ash has told us the basics, but truthfully, I'm glad he's got people who care about him and are with him when we can't be."

"He does," Serena said softly while staring into her tea.

Alexander gently elbowed Ashton in the side with a smile. Eileen smiled at her brothers, but her smile dropped, and she narrowed her eyes at Ashton again.

"Alright. I want to talk more about everything else, but right now, I think you owe us an explanation for what just happened, Ash."

Ashton nodded and finished his drink before setting the glass on the counter. "Well, it's a pretty long story, so.…"

Tension had started to fill the cramped space, and Thenia cleared her throat softly. "Ash, why don't Serena and I make dinner while you three go talk? We'll use the main house, and when you're finished or need a break, we can eat." Thenia offered, and Serena nodded in agreement.

"Sounds like a good plan to me, Ash," Alexander agreed, glancing between his siblings.

"Yeah…I'd prefer to talk at the main house anyway…" Ashton retrieved his phone from the counter and stowed it in his back pocket.

"Anything specific you want or don't like to eat?" Serena asked Eileen and Alexander.

Alexander shook his head and smiled. "Anything is fine with us, thank you."

"Fine," Eileen said, responding more to Ashton and Alexander than Serena's question. Wasting no time, Eileen got to her feet and headed for the door. "Let's go."

Alexander rolled his eyes at her back but put his arm around Ashton's shoulders, leading him after Eileen. "Come on, you know how she gets."

"I heard that, Xander," Eileen said from further ahead of them and already outside the house.

Thenia looked at Serena, and they both laughed into their palms as the three siblings left the small home and closed the door behind them. Thenia waited a moment more and whispered into Serena's phone, which was still on the counter.

"Arthur?"

"Yes, I'm here," his image appeared on the screen, his features marred by a deep frown.

"How do you think that went?" Thenia asked, sitting beside Serena.

Arthur sighed. "As good as it could. Eileen and Xander are very perceptive, and even weeks ago, they knew Ash was hiding something. He's going to struggle with only telling them half the truth."

"Should we have gone with them?" Serena asked.

"It would have been fine if you had, but I do think this is better. Even though Eileen was acting cold, she really is supportive of you three. This way, she won't hold back on what she's thinking for fear of making a bad first impression. They'll work this out faster that way."

Serena nodded.

"Well, any idea what we should cook?" Thenia asked both of

them.

"I do believe they'd enjoy one of Serena's homemade pizzas. There's still dough in the fridge, right?" Arthur asked.

"Yup," Serena answered and got up to get it.

"That's easy, and I'll make a salad from the last of our produce. We'll need to run into town tomorrow. Especially if there are two more mouths to feed." Thenia said as she gathered ingredients and stuck them in a bag to bring to the main house.

"Yup, and unlike Ash, Eileen and Xander would often eat for six instead of just two," Arthur heartily chuckled.

"Really?" Serena asked. "She's so thin."

Arthur snorted. "A bit of that is genetics, yes, but Eileen works hard at keeping herself that way. She burns the calories she eats to make sure she's fit for her job, but that, in turn, makes her eat more."

Thenia laughed. "Oh, the life of a woman. Add in the demands of her specific job, and I get it."

"Exactly." Arthur nodded but then stopped. "Oh. I need to go. Ash is going to bring them downstairs. I'll be here if you need anything, though. Just call."

"Thanks, Arthur," Serena said, and Thenia waved as his face faded into black.

Thenia sighed. "Well, all we can do now is make sure no one ends up hungry on top of being angry, I guess."

Serena giggled and added the three containers of pizza dough to the bag on the counter. Then she walked over, stopped in front of Thenia, and studied her face.

"Nia, are you alright?"

She was. Genuinely. "I am," Thenia smiled. "Thank you for coming to my rescue."

Serena's ears turned pink, and she looked away. "I didn't do anything."

"Not true." Thenia tugged on one of Serena's blonde braids.

"You were there when I needed you. That's a lot. Especially to me."

The other woman's ears went a deeper shade of red, but she eventually looked back at Thenia, who smiled and leaned down to steal a kiss. In recent weeks, it had become increasingly apparent to Thenia that she was very much in love with both Serena and Ashton, but something still held her back from saying anything. Lucus' face flashed in her mind, but whether Serena had noticed or done it coincidentally, she leaned further into Thenia right as Lucus' presence had been intruding where he didn't belong, and Thenia shoved him from her thoughts.

Thenia pulled their lips apart and hugged Serena tightly. "Really, Serena. Thank you."

Serena nodded against her and snuggled her nose into Thenia's neck, making her laugh. The action in Serena's human form reminded Thenia of when Serena's snake tongue would tickle Thenia's cheek.

"Ug, now I just want to lie on the couch and not cook," Thenia whined, making Serena laugh.

"Me too, but maybe if we feed Eileen and Alexander, they'll get sleepy, and we can steal Ash back."

Thenia snorted. "You sneaky snake." She kissed Serena lightly and then smiled. "Let's do it."

Ashton Giri

Eileen led him and Xander through the gardens and up the back deck before entering the main house.

"Are you going to tell us everything, Ash?"

"I'll tell you what I can."

"Ashton," Eileen snarled, pivoting to glare at him with her fists on her hips.

"Stop it, Eileen," Xander scolded sharply. Ashton would need to thank the dude later for having his back.

"Hear him out first. You know he'd have a good reason for keeping something from us. Stop acting as if you don't trust him."

"It's not about trust," Eileen hissed.

"You're right. It's about your guilt," Xander shot back.

Ashton stood wide-eyed between his two siblings, who rarely, if ever, fought with one another. That said, clearly, Xander hit a nerve because Eileen turned her back on them both and crossed her arms without saying a word. Xander frowned at Ashton but nodded.

"Both of you, come with me. Someone else may be able to convince you better than I can that it's better this way." Ashton brushed past his sister and headed for the office.

He was relieved when he heard Xander whispering to Eileen, and then two pairs of footsteps followed behind Ashton. When he led them into the office, he waited until they were inside, then shut the door behind them. Then he went to his Gram's computer and caught Eileen's frown.

"I thought you didn't know her password?"

"I don't. For this, I don't need it."

He followed the protocols his Gram had walked him through and triggered the mechanism to open the concealed door behind the bookcase. He couldn't hold back his smirk when his sister and Xander were as shocked as he, Serena, and Thenia had been when they'd first found the hidden room.

"Uh, Ash?" Xander said while Eileen held onto his wrist, her mouth open in shock.

"It's fine. Just come with me." Ashton headed for the door, and Eileen seized his arm as he passed.

"Ash, what did you do?"

There was genuine fear in Eileen's eyes, and he tried to smile as reassuringly as possible when he answered. "I didn't. I'll let them explain. Come on."

"Them?" Eileen said, but Ashton ignored her and led the way down the stairs.

When they reached the door, he keyed them in via the blood lock and jumped as he always did at the small prick.

"Okay, I'm starting to freak out now, Ash," Eileen said, and when he glanced at her as the door opened, she was indeed extremely pale.

"I know. Almost there."

"Where the fuck is there?" Xander asked as the door closed behind them and the lights in the room changed from the single red one to the multiple blue ones.

"Watch your language, young man," Arthur's voice scolded.

Ashton groaned but saw Eileen had begun inspecting the nearly empty room after instinctively slipping into her training. Meanwhile, Xander was wide-eyed and staring at the still-black screens.

"Pops, really?" Ashton chuckled.

His grandmother's sigh echoed in the room as the two monitors flickered on, and their images faded into view.

Ashton watched the two living beings in the room as they shifted their attention from the screens to him and back to the screens, before finally focusing on each other.

"Arthur. You menace," Gram teased, but she smiled.

"What? I figured we should just rip the band-aid off. Ash tortured them enough."

"I wasn't trying to torture anyone, but you heard them! I can't keep anything from these two. So, now you get to explain what's going on. Consider it punishment for hijacking my email, you meddling AI," Ashton sassed with a smile.

"I'm…" Eileen started, "Wait…what? Gram?"

"Yes, dear. We have much to tell you, and I'm sorry I locked you out of the system earlier, but I couldn't risk you finding us before we were in a safe space to talk."

"What exactly are we seeing right now?" Xander muttered, glancing at Ashton.

"Well, turns out, Gram here had a secret. A pretty big one."

"Apparently," Xander chuffed.

"I'll let them tell you, but you're looking at the first two trans-mechanite AIs in history. That we know of." Ash walked over to a wall and leaned against it. "That said, they can talk themselves out of this mess."

His Pops narrowed his eyes at him but smiled. "Oh, kid, you watch it. Don't make me change the thermostat in your room tonight."

Xander snorted and rubbed the back of his neck. "Well, that's Pops, alright."

Ashton nodded with a grin. All the drama, threats, and secrecy aside, Ashton was standing in a room with his family, which was something he thought would never be possible again, a few weeks earlier. What he hadn't expected was to feel like there was a snake and a witch-shaped pair of holes on either side of him.

Eileen stepped forward, still frowning. "Explain. All of it."

Their grandmother shook her head. "No, dear, we will not. As Ash has told you, we will share with you what we can, but I warn you right now that we have all agreed that either of you knowing the full story will put you both at too much risk."

Eileen opened her mouth to argue, but Gram cut her off.

"Do not argue with me, young lady. You know we would never do anything to exclude you unless it was for your own safety. You will not convince us otherwise. So don't bother trying."

Eileen stared at Ashton, and he held his hands up and shook his head. "Nope. I'm with them. Sorry."

"Do not pressure your brother," Gram gently scolded. "He knows the importance of this, but you also know that he cannot lie to you. Do not put him in an unfair position."

Eileen stared at the screen for a few more seconds before turning to look back at Xander. Then she walked over to him, and he put his arm around her shoulders, pulling her into his side.

"Alright. We're listening," Eileen said to the screens.

By the time Eileen and Xander heard the extent of the situation they were going to be informed about, Ashton was hungry and slightly short-tempered. He was tempted to leave Eileen in the basement room and lock the door behind himself on his way out.

"Really, Gram? I can't believe you kept this from us," Eileen scolded.

"Give it a rest, Eileen," Ashton hissed, but turned away guiltily.

Ashton had been no less frustrated with their grandparents when he learned about everything, but he had the benefit of knowing the whole story. Eileen only knew half the story while being forcibly kept in the dark about the other half.

"Ashton," Pops said in warning.

"Yeah, sorry." Ashton scratched his neck. "I'm going to go check on dinner. Come up when you're done. Gram will lock up after you."

"Thank you for escorting them down, Ash," Gram said.

He nodded, and once the faces had faded from the screens and the door opened, he exited. He didn't look back at his sister or Xander as he shut the door and made his way back up the dark stairway.

Once Ashton was back in the office, he heard plates and general cooking sounds coming from the kitchen. He didn't want to take his sour mood out on Serena or Thenia, so he quietly slipped from the office and made his way down the hallway and into his bedroom, where he shut the door and flopped onto his back on his bed before closing his eyes.

He must have dozed off because he jumped when there was a soft knock on his door sometime later.

"Come in."

Without lifting more than his head, he saw Serena enter the room and rush to close the door before standing in front of it and looking at her feet. Ashton lifted his hand and held it out, and she shuffled over to the bed and took it. He tugged gently, and she climbed up and snuggled into his side.

"Are you alright?" she practically whispered.

Ashton answered with a groan, and when she giggled, he smiled reflexively, already feeling better.

"Yeah, I'm fine. I just hate lying to them, and frankly, I suck at it."

Serena shifted to look up at him, her head on his upper arm. "You're not lying. They know there's more, and you aren't keeping the rest from them because you want to. You're doing it because you care."

"I know," he smiled at her. "Still sucks."

"Yup, but don't forget, you're not the only one. Four other people also chose to put Eileen and Alexander's safety over their curiosity."

Ashton stared down at Serena, apparently for too long, because while she didn't move, she shifted her eyes away.

"Serena?"

"Hmm?"

"If I don't immediately pass out after food, would you like to read tonight?"

He watched as a slight pink hue faded up her cheeks, but she smiled and nodded. Ashton shifted and snuggled closer to her, making her giggle.

"Can I close my eyes for a few more minutes?"

"Sure," Serena said, running her fingers through his hair.

Ashton made a silly purring noise, making her laugh and him feel lighter.

Chapter 19: Star Filled Skies

July 2024, Maine, USA | Serena Ainsley

When Serena's eyes fluttered open, she was snuggled deeply into fluffy blankets in the darkened bedroom of the tiny house. Ashton was on one side of her, and she'd been using his arm as a pillow. Behind her was Thenia, her arm over Serena's waist, along with one of her legs. Both of them breathed softly in their deep sleep, and if Serena focused, she could hear crickets and frogs singing outside in the gardens.

The moon shone in from one of the bedroom windows, and from her vantage point, the sky looked clear and star-filled. Nothing specific had woken her up, but either way, Serena was awake, and she carefully extricated herself from the two warm bodies on either side of her. She had only made it down to the foot of the bed when Thenia lifted her head and blinked in the moonlight.

"Serena? Are you alright?"

"Yes. Going to get some water. I'll be right back."

Thenia nodded and put her head back down but snuggled her face into Serena's pillow instead of her own. Serena smiled but finished shuffling out of bed and tiptoed down the stairs and into the kitchen. While she sipped some water, she gazed out of the kitchen window and did her best to look up at the stars, but the roof line made it nearly impossible. She downed the last of her water and set the glass in the sink before dragging on Ashton's sweatshirt and then exiting the house and wandering through the front gardens.

The night was comfortable, and it was a good thing, considering she'd not put on shoes. The stone path was still slightly warm on the soles of her feet, and she couldn't help but wiggle her toes as she walked. She tucked her hands into the sleeves of her sweatshirt and then stuffed them into the pockets before meandering through the plants with her head tipped back as she studied the stars above her.

"Couldn't sleep?" Eileen said from somewhere in front of Serena.

Serena glanced around. She'd walked nearly back to the main house, where Eileen was sitting on the porch steps. "I'm sorry, I didn't mean to—"

"Nope. None of that. You're not a bother. This is your home, too." Eileen patted the step beside her. "Come sit for a bit? Do you know anything about the stars?"

Serena did as requested and then glanced up to where Eileen was pointing.

"Any idea what that grouping is called?" Eileen asked.

Serena tipped over to see more in line with Eileen's view and nodded. "Yeah, that's Virgo."

"Damn. I was wrong again," Eileen laughed. "Xander knows a lot about the stars, but I can't seem to learn them. I group too many into one giant uber blob and make the equivalent of cloud animals."

Serena giggled into her sleeve.

They continued to stare at the sky for a few minutes until Eileen sighed. "I owe you an apology, Serena."

"Why?"

"I was frustrated and angry earlier and took it out on you

three. What we found when we came home was...unsettling. I'm not normally like that, but...."

"It's okay. We understand."

"It's just...Ash is my baby brother. And unlike Xander and I, he's more suited to being behind a keyboard, not knocking out intruders. If we hadn't been here...."

"It would have been fine. Thenia would have taken care of it, and we would have been there to help her."

Eileen peeked sideways at her, and Serena glimpsed disbelief in her eyes.

"Doesn't matter though, you were here," Serena conceded. "It was easier with your help either way, so thank you."

Eileen returned to staring out into the gardens. "Perhaps you're right and she could have handled it, but you're welcome."

Serena stuck her nose into one of the sweatshirt cuffs and leaned against the porch railing's banister.

"How's he doing? For real, I mean?" Eileen asked after a few minutes.

"Ashton?"

Eileen nodded.

"Better now that Thenia's here."

"And you."

Serena said nothing. She'd been here the whole time, but it wasn't until Thenia showed up that Ashton had begun to smile again.

"It wasn't just Thenia, Serena. Ash talks about you as much as he does her." Eileen snorted. "Hell, he threatened to sic Xander on me over you."

Serena cocked her head to the side.

"Ah, well. I asked him something...um, personal, and then teased him about it. He got defensive of you."

"Oh," Serena stared at the floor, where she wiggled her bare toes.

"He didn't tell me anything, and you shouldn't feel the need to either, but if you ever want to talk, I'm here if you need someone. Sometimes, a girl needs to vent about their partner with another girl." Eileen smiled. "And I can see you not wanting to bring some things up with Thenia either, considering the situation."

"Thank you. I, um…."

"Remember, don't feel like you need to tell me anything, Serena. How about this? We'll be here for a few weeks. If or when you feel ready, let me know. Okay?"

Serena nodded. "Thank you."

"Of course," Eileen smiled. "Contrary to my bitchy attitude earlier, I'm not like that unless I'm playing a role."

"He scared you."

Eileen nodded. "He did. You all did."

"Did talking to Arthur and Sue make you feel better?"

"A little," Eileen sighed. "I wish she had talked to us. Maybe we could have helped her."

Serena saw Eileen spinning a ring on one of her fingers and recognized it as Sue's. "Oh, Ash gave you Sue's ring."

Eileen smiled down at the white gold band that had a few blue stones set into it. "Yeah. It feels a bit odd wearing it now, though. Considering she's still around."

"Does he have Arthur's?"

"No, Ash gave it to Xander."

Serena smiled, remembering when she'd spoken with Ashton about it. He felt Eileen and Xander deserved the couple's bands considering their relationship, even if they never acknowledged it to themselves or anyone else.

"Where's Alexander?"

"Sleeping, probably. After dealing with me all day, he needs it."

"I doubt it," Serena said, realizing she'd spoken aloud.

"No?" Eileen asked, looking at her out of the corner of her eye.

"Ah, sorry. Um, it's not hard to see how much he cares."

"Yes, well. For better or worse, he's stuck with us now. The three of us are all that are left."

Serena shook her head. "That's not true. Sue and Arthur are just different now. And…" She felt her cheeks heat, "Nia and I are here, too."

When Eileen turned to face her, Serena dropped her gaze to the floor.

"Well, I guess I need to adjust my perspective. Thank you for correcting me. You're right."

Serena nodded but got to her feet. "Um, I should get back before one of them wakes up and worries."

Eileen seemed lighter than when Serena had initially sat down, and it made her happy to think maybe she'd helped her in some small way.

"Thank you for sitting with me."

"Yup. Goodnight, Eileen."

"Goodnight, Serena." She was only a few steps away when Eileen added. "I'm glad you're here, Serena."

"Me too," Serena said softly and then continued her walk back to the house.

It didn't take her long to reach the small garden, but before she could grab the door handle, it was ripped away from her as Thenia and Ashton raced out and directly into Serena.

"Serena!" Thenia gasped, squeezing her in a hug.

"Hi, what—"

"We saw you were gone, and…" Ashton blushed and glanced away, "we were worried you'd left."

Serena's eyes widened. She'd not given any thought to what it would look like if they'd awoken to find her gone. She smiled and tightly hugged Thenia back.

"Nope. I just went for a walk and talked with Eileen for a little bit."

Ashton frowned. "What's she doing up?"

"She was on the porch looking at the stars."

He nodded, and Thenia finally released Serena but held on to one of her hands.

"Are you okay?" Thenia asked.

"Yes. I was coming back to bed. I'm sorry I worried you both."

"It's fine, come back inside," Ashton said, ushering them into the house and closing the door behind them.

Ashton Giri

After getting Thenia and Serena back into bed and listening to their breathing even out, Ashton was still wide awake. He'd had a long day and more than a few times wished he were still in bed where he'd woken up that morning, wrapped around Thenia with a snake on his shoulder.

Ashton's involuntary sigh ruffled Serena's hair from where she was tucked against his neck, and he pursed his lips to keep from doing it again.

A faint vibration on his wrist made him tense, but he tried to relax as he merged with the device. He followed the digital pathway that led to his more secure messaging system, where he found a message from his grandmother.

Can't sleep? she asked.

Second wind, but I don't want to wake them by getting out of bed.

What's on your mind, Ash?

He wavered before replying because what *wasn't* on his mind? *All of it? Do you think Eileen will let this go?*

Doubtfully.

Ashton respected his grandmother's honesty, even if it didn't help him to feel better.

Ash, we have said our part and told them what we can. From this point on, leave their decisions to them. Focus on controlling what you can control.

So...nothing?

It was difficult to overlook the silence from his Gram, so he continued.

We have nothing, Gram—two stupid slips of paper and an old thumb drive. We're nowhere closer to finding out who these assholes are than we were the day I got the first letter.

On the contrary, we know who they're not.

Oh, good. That narrows it down.

Ashton, we'll find something. I'm still searching databases and the dark web and putting some hooks into the blue web.

Is that safe? What if another mechanite retraces your steps?

The blue web was the magical world's version of the dark web, one distinction being that not everything on it was nefarious. There were message boards for safe communication between the diverse species and races, a digital newspaper, and a whole host of other resources that needed to remain away from an Outsider's judgmental gaze.

They'll find what looks like any other mechanite's footprint if they do. I was a mechanite for over seventy years, Ash.

Sorry, yes. I know. I'm just....

Stressed, scared, and worried. I know, dear.

Do you know who Alexia initially sent the drive to?

Yes, but I won't tell you who because we're not secure enough here, and I'm not willing to risk them.

If we're not secure enough here, Gram, we're screwed.

I'm working on that, but for now, this is fine.

What...does "working on that" mean, exactly?

It means I've got it covered, and you needn't worry, Ash. You don't have to take everything on yourself.

You sound like Eileen and Xander.

Where do you think they learned it, Ash?

Fair point. Can I at least ask if the person who had it is safe? You implied it, but....

Yes.

Okay.

Ashton felt himself dozing, so he slipped from within the machine and found himself blinking up into the dimmed room.

"Ash?" Serena whispered, her breath tickling his cheek.

He tipped his head down and saw her gazing up at him, not looking asleep or sleepy in the slightest.

"Did I wake you?"

"Kind of. Are you okay?"

For a moment, he considered lying, but ultimately shook his head.

"Me either."

"What's wrong, Serena?"

She snuggled closer into him, tucking her head beneath his chin in a way that he'd begun to equate with her looking at the floor. The position provided her with a similar level of metaphorical obfuscation.

"Worried about you and Nia, I guess."

Ashton pressed a kiss to the top of her head.

"I'm sorry. I'll figure it out."

"No, *we* will figure it out, right?"

His cheeks lifted in a smile as his chest warmed. When he went to agree, he had to clear the emotion from his throat first.

"You're right—we."

Chapter 20: Powders and Mist

July 2024, Maine, USA | Thenia Loris

Thenia stood beneath the overhang outside the Crow's Nest while Ashton and Eileen were still inside, saying their goodbyes to the shop's mysterious namesake.

Thenia tipped her face to the sun and beamed up at it. The sky was clear, and the weather was beautiful, a balm to her happy yet weary soul. When a gentle breeze drifted past, carrying the smell of freshly brewed coffee and something sweet, she felt her mouth begin to water.

Eileen and Alexander had been home for nearly a week, and it looked like they and Ash had worked out most of the tension that had hung over the beginning of their visit. Alexander and Serena had spent a few days talking, both in their human and beast forms, and each afternoon when Serena came home, she looked brighter and more vibrant than when she'd left earlier in the day. That, coupled with her diet and the increased time she spent in her human form, meant the younger woman gained some muscle mass and looked healthier overall.

Ashton had stopped avoiding his sister a few days earlier, and they seemed to have agreed on what he could and would tell her about their situation. What his sister would have been able to coerce out of him had become off-limits in discussions because if she tried, Eileen would get him to crack with her sisterly powers. After that, the two spent a significant amount of time in the basement with Sue. Some days, Arthur or Alexander would join them, but for the most part, the former kept Thenia company in the garden, and the latter was with Serena.

Their days were quiet and relaxed, and Thenia had to admit she was already upset that Eileen and Alexander would be heading out for their next job in a few weeks. The house and grounds would fall dormant again, but the pair promised to come home more often in the future. They couldn't take Sue or Arthur with them, so they'd have to return home to speak with them, and Thenia would wager that this detail massively impacted their decision-making.

The only concession Ashton had made was email. He made a deal with Arthur, and the two AIs now had their own email addresses in Ashton's name so they could freely email Alexander and Eileen—no moral code violations necessary.

Thenia pulled headphones from her purse and put one into her ear.

"Hey, Arthur."

"Hello, my dear. How's your trip in town going?"

Eileen had suggested that when they were public, they could use headphones to speak with either of the AIs, hopefully helping to conceal the truth from passersby.

"Fine. We stopped by Crow's, and Ash and Eileen are inside talking with them. I stepped out to get some sun. How are the other two?"

"Fine. They are still in their beast forms, flitting between sleeping under the apple tree and talking."

Thenia grinned. "I'm glad."

"Me too. Perhaps I made a mistake not telling the others about Serena sooner...." Arthur's voice sounded pained, making Thenia frown.

"I don't think so. In my opinion, she wasn't ready. I'm not sure whether it was because I was there, someone needed help, or she finally trusted Ash enough. Either way, I think you being her friend while not forcing her to be something she felt she was not, was exactly what she needed."

Arthur was quiet momentarily, and Thenia pulled her phone out to ensure it hadn't died.

"Thank you...for saying that, Thenia. I hope you're right."

Motion out of the corner of Thenia's eye caught her attention, and she saw Ashton and Eileen exiting the coffee shop.

"I believe we're nearly done here. We'll see you soon." Thenia relayed, and after Arthur said goodbye, she put her headphones and phone back in her bag.

"Everything alright?" Ashton asked, his hands tucked into the back pockets of his jeans.

"Yes. Just chatting. All finished?" she asked, glancing from Ash to Eileen.

Eileen pulled her phone from her pocket and nodded to Thenia. "We are. Sorry to make you wait for us."

"You didn't. I just came out to stand in the sun. Oh," Thenia gestured to Eileen's phone, "They are in the gardens. In case you were checking on Alexander."

Eileen snorted. "I was. Thank you." She briefly read something, then put her phone away and looked at Ashton. "What else do we have on the list for this afternoon?"

Ashton shook his head. "Nothing. That was it. Unless either of you needs to do something."

"Nope, I'm good," Thenia replied.

"Would you mind if we stopped by the local jewelry store?" Eileen asked.

"No, but why?" Ashton asked, his head cocked in confusion.

"I want to get Gram's ring sized down a bit. I don't want to chance it slipping off."

"Makes sense," Thenia said. "Doesn't bother me."

"Alright." Ashton turned in the opposite direction. "It's this way, right? I'm not sure I've ever been in it, to be honest."

"Yup," Eileen said, gesturing for Thenia to join Ashton and lead the way down the sidewalk. "Short walk. You mind?"

"Nope," Thenia took Ashton's hand when he reached for hers and laced their fingers together.

Eileen walked a few paces behind them, the two siblings chatting as Thenia listened in, but she didn't feel the need to participate much. Two blocks later, they stopped in front of a small-town jeweler, and Thenia's phone vibrated in her bag. She pulled it out and saw a new text from Eileen.

Can you take Ash while I go in? Gram asked me to do something for him.

Thenia immediately turned the phone screen off and tried not to look suspicious when she stuck it back in her bag and looked at Ashton.

"Shoot. Ash, while Eileen's in there, would you mind running into the bookshop we passed a few buildings down? I told Arthur I would find a book on plants native to Maine." Thenia smiled at Eileen, "Do you mind?"

"Not at all. I can meet you there when I'm done here. Shouldn't take me long to drop this off."

"You sure?" Ashton asked Eileen.

"Positive. See you in a bit." Eileen nodded to Thenia as she passed and entered the shop.

Thenia redirected Ashton back the way they'd come. "Sorry about that. I forgot I'd mentioned it to him."

"It's fine. I'll see if there's something Serena might like."

"You two almost done with that fantasy novel you were reading?" Thenia asked.

"Yeah, only a few chapters left. She reads so much faster than I do," Ashton chuffed, "Not that she'd say anything about me making her wait."

Thenia chuckled, "Nope, she wouldn't. I'm glad you two have that. It's cute."

Ashton smirked at her. "Different language, as she keeps telling me."

"It is. You two have that, and she spends time with me in the garden as my additional hair tie—one that occasionally tickles my ear. I have to admit, I like her language."

"Agreed," Ashton squeezed Thenia's hand gently. "Doesn't bother you, right?"

Thenia shook her head, "Nope. Not in the slightest. I enjoy looking up from those journals and seeing you both reading the same book. Selfishly, I feel less guilty if I zone out while you two are around, but focused on each other."

Ashton snorted, "Yes, you sure know how to focus."

She elbowed him gently as he opened the bookshop's door for her. "Quiet, you. As if you're not the same in front of a keyboard, Mr. Sixteen-Hour-Days without food."

They both entered the shop, and Thenia stopped, shutting her eyes, and a smile crept onto her lips. "Old book smell."

Ashton chuffed but said nothing as they passed over the threshold and deeper into the store. Thenia began to browse, now that she had a book to find for Arthur.

Ashton Giri

Ashton pulled the car into the driveway and shifted into park.

"I'll grab the mail, Ash," Eileen said, holding her hand out for the keys, which he gave her after turning the car off.

"Thanks."

"We'll start unloading," Thenia said, climbing out of the back seat and heading to the trunk as Eileen opened the hatchback for her with the push of a button.

"Thanks, Thenia. I'll be right back to help."

Ashton pulled his phone from the car's center console and frowned at the weather forecast on the lock screen.

"Summer storm rolling in the next few days, Nia."

"Damn. Okay, I'll swap some of the beds I tend tomorrow. A few will need some extra support in higher winds."

Ashton climbed out of the car and helped Thenia carry their bags to the porch in batches. With Xander and Eileen home, their grocery order had increased by more than twofold.

"Where the hell is Xander?" Ashton laughed. "He should be the one hauling the army's worth of food we just bought."

"He's probably still with Serena," Thenia said, passing Ashton a few bags before returning to the car for even more.

He grumbled but smiled as he did it. His complaints were all in jest, and he was more than capable of doing the chore himself, but it was more fun to razz his brother.

"Fine, I'll make Eileen do it."

"What am I doing?" Eileen called from down the driveway, sorting the mail as she walked.

"Helping carry the—" Ashton stumbled back a step as Xander, in his panther form, streaked past him at full speed.

Thenia gasped, drawing Eileen's attention, and she stiffened, focusing solely on Xander.

"Xander?"

From where he was, Ashton could see Xander's hackles raised, and he was focused on the mail in Eileen's hands.

"Fuck." Ashton was pretty positive he already knew the answer to his question, but he asked anyway. "Eileen, is there anything in the mail that is hand-addressed?" He saw Thenia glance at him and then frown, so she had followed his train of thought, too.

"Um," Eileen started riffling through the envelopes, but Xander growled, and she stilled again. "Xander, what—"

It happened so fast that Ashton nearly missed it when Xander swiped his paw out and ripped the mail from Eileen's hands, and it fell to the stones in a shower of papers.

"Ashton, something's not right," Thenia commented and began hesitantly walking closer to the pile of mail. She only made it a few steps when Xander spun on her and hissed. Thenia froze.

"Alright, we get it, Xander. Leave the mail alone." Ashton said, holding out his hand for Thenia to take as she walked back over.

Eileen was investigating the scattered envelopes from where she hadn't yet moved. "Yes, Ash. That yellow one is handwritten. I think."

"Shit. Well, that makes this more complicated." Ashton sighed before addressing Xander. "Look, this isn't the first one we've gotten, so...."

Before Ashton had finished his sentence, Xander had lowered himself into an offensive crouch, ready to pounce.

"Ash, what's going on?" Thenia asked softly.

"Not sure, but I don't think that's the same envelope as before. The color alone is different, but Xander isn't one to freak over nothing."

"Xander," Eileen said calmly, "we won't touch the letters, go change, and then explain."

For a few seconds, it looked like Xander would listen to her, but a slight breeze swirled around them, lifting the fallen papers and picking up the yellow envelope, which flipped over onto its front, the flap unsealing. They all watched as the breeze blew a fine powder from within the envelope in Eileen's direction.

One minute, Eileen was standing, and the next, she was beneath Xander, his body shielding hers and her face forcibly buried in the fur of his neck.

"Eileen!" Ashton and Thenia shouted but didn't move for fear of splitting Xander's focus.

"Ash, Serena!" Thenia said and pointed down the driveway,

the direction the wind had blown from. Serena was still in her beast form, watching what was happening, but Ashton had no idea if she'd heard the first part of their conversation and knew to stay back.

"Crap, Serena, stay there," Ashton yelled before shaking his head. "Actually, no, go back down the driveway and follow the garden wall back to Thenia's. We got another letter."

Serena nodded and then watched Xander and Eileen, who were still tucked up together with him, protecting their faces. She slithered a bit further away from them but didn't leave.

"Xander, how can we help?" Thenia asked. "I assume because it's airborne, we shouldn't inhale it."

Even from where they were, Ashton heard Xander growl and saw him flick his tail. "That's a yes."

"Okay, don't turn around and keep yourselves covered. Will water make it worse?"

Ashton glanced at Thenia, but she quickly returned her attention to Xander, who hadn't moved.

"I assume that's still a no, right, dude?" That time, Xander's tail flicked, and Ashton nodded to Thenia. "Water's fine."

"Got it. Neither of you move, just give me a second. Keep yourselves covered."

Thenia rushed over to a spigot that his Pops used to hook up his hose when he needed to water the gardens located in front of the house. Thenia wrenched on the valve, and water splashed loudly directly onto the rocks below. Ashton watched as she closed her eyes, and her lips began to move in sync with her fingers, as if she were a puppet master.

A second later, the water vaporized, and the heavy fog it had become floated over to the mail and followed the path the powder had taken. It wrapped around Eileen and Xander, enveloping all that was exposed, drawing most of the dust off of them. After the cloud of water vapor had collected all the particulate in the air, Thenia directed the cloud back over to the pile of mail, where the envelope still lay open and was likely not yet empty. Then the vapor condensed into an orb of cloudy liquid water and lowered to the mail before breaking apart and soaking everything beneath it.

Ashton looked from Serena to Xander but saw Thenia's movement from the corner of his eye. When she wavered, his feet started moving on their own.

"Thenia!"

"Fine, just—" Thenia's eyes closed, and Ashton barely caught her before her knees hit the stones beneath her. "Tired...."

"Thenia!" Serena shouted from behind him, and Ashton heard the woman's shoes striking the stones as she sprinted to them. When she knelt beside them, her hand went to Thenia's forehead.

"Fine. Sleepy...." Thenia muttered, her eyes still closed.

Ashton dropped his head and groaned as the adrenaline still flowed through his body. Eventually, he glanced over at Xander and Eileen without letting go of Thenia. Xander's fur slightly glistened, but Eileen looked dry, just rumpled.

"Eileen," Serena said. "Follow Alexander. You need to shower to ensure there's no more of the powder on your clothes."

"Thank you," Eileen mumbled through a mouthful of fur before she carefully got to her feet. She was only vertical for a second before Xander shoved his head into the back of her thigh to spur her forward faster. "Yes, Xander. I know, I heard her. I'm going. Pushy house cat."

Xander growled low in his throat at Eileen's teasing nickname for him, and then he nodded to Ashton as they approached him. Before Xander followed Eileen into the main house, he glanced from Serena to Thenia. Then he pressed his forehead into Thenia's cheek for a few seconds before he followed Eileen.

Ashton saw Serena's worried expression as her eyes roamed over Thenia.

"Gram, can you start looking into what's going on with

Thenia and see what Xander and Eileen know after they finish?" Ashton asked aloud.

His grandmother's distorted voice replied from his watch. "Yes, take Thenia home. She needs sleep, but she will be fine. From what I've found, that bit of magic likely took a lot of effort to control. Your sister and Xander are in the master's shower, and I'll inform you once they are settled."

Ashton exhaled, "Thank you."

"Are you going to carry her?" Serena asked softly.

"No other option."

"House is pretty far, can you make it?"

Ashton thought about it, and he'd likely be fine, but if he wasn't going to make it, Serena wouldn't be able to help him, and they'd end up stuck in the middle of the gardens until Xander could bail him out.

"Bed swing," Ashton suggested, and Serena nodded before she helped shift Thenia so he could lift her into his arms more easily. Thenia wasn't overly heavy, but as Eileen often pointed out, Ashton was made for a computer desk, not lifting shit.

"I'll bring some of the bags in," Serena said.

She walked away, and Ashton checked her expression in the window's reflection as he passed it with Thenia still in his arms, but Serena's back was already to him as she went to retrieve their shopping.

He focused on Thenia, got her to the bed, and settled atop the blankets. Like Serena, he checked her temperature, and Thenia felt normal, nor was she flushed or pale. She honestly just looked as though she were sleeping. Extremely deeply, but only sleeping.

"Hey, Serena?" Ashton called behind him.

"What's up?"

"Can you come sit with Thenia? I'll bring the rest of the stuff in and deal with the mail."

Serena came around the corner of the house thirty seconds later, frowning at him. "Is that safe?"

"No, likely I'll pull a muscle, but you saw the number of bags. Xander will probably be done showering, and I'll still be bringing food into the house." He smirked and was relieved when Serena's lips curled into the hint of a smile at his silliness. "I won't do anything with the mail until we know for sure."

"Promise?" she asked, sitting beside Thenia and taking one of her hands in her own.

"Promise." He leaned down to kiss Thenia's cheek and then briefly kissed Serena. "Shout if you need me, but I think Gram's right. She's just really, *really* asleep."

Serena nodded, and once she'd refocused on Thenia, he left to continue with the groceries. Only now Ashton was even more aware that Xander wasn't helping carry stuff in, but Ashton chuckled and returned to the front porch anyway.

Serena Ainsley

Serena stood outside of Eileen's bedroom door, too hesitant to knock. She'd been standing there, torn between feeling like she'd be interrupting the woman and trying to remember what Eileen had said the night they looked at the stars together.

When Serena finally decided she'd only be bothering her, she turned to leave, but the door opened. Eileen smiled, her hair still in a towel, but she wore comfy-looking pajamas and a sweatshirt.

"Come in," Eileen said, stepping aside.

"Oh, um. Thank you."

Serena entered the bedroom and glanced around the brightly colored space, full of Eileen's energy and vibrancy, evident in everything from the wall color to the trinkets on the shelves.

"Do you mind if I deal with my hair while we talk?"

"No," Serena shook her head.

Eileen walked through the room to a small doorway and into a bathroom. "Everything okay? How's Thenia?"

"Sleeping still."

Serena wandered over to Eileen's bookshelf and saw multiple books on art and past artists. There were also numerous shelves of novels with well-worn spines.

"I assume she'll be alright, or you wouldn't be here, and Ash would be freaking out."

Serena smiled. "Yes. Sue looked it up. I guess turning water into fog is complicated, and then Thenia controlled the fog after she formed it."

"Anything we can do?"

"No, but thank you. If she isn't awake by morning, we'll know something is wrong." Serena frowned, her reflection staring back at her from the window's glass.

"Where is she now? Ash get her home?"

"We moved her to the bed swing. I think Ash is asking Alexander for help moving her now. I wouldn't have been much help if he needed it halfway there."

Eileen stepped into the doorway, a hairbrush in her hand. "We all have our strengths." She smirked, "Neither yours nor mine might be actual strength, but I have no doubt you have others."

Serena tilted her head to the side. "Alexander said you could beat him, though."

"Oh, I can. But not through physical strength, but thankfully, it's not the only kind of strength." Eileen ran her fingers and then the brush through her damp hair. "I'm faster than he is." She smirked, "Well, I'm faster than his human form. Can't beat a panther, obviously."

Serena giggled and shook her head, "Yeah, probably not."

"When he's in his panther form, though…" Eileen grinned, "I have thumbs."

"True, but he has a better sense of smell and hearing, right?"

"He does," Eileen nodded. "As a human, my eyes are worse than his, but my ears are better, and I can use my speed and slight build against him. Actually," Eileen wiggled her fingers in Serena's direction. "It's a bit like your snake form. I'm hard for him to hold on to."

"Oh." Serena frowned but thought about it, and in a way, it made a little sense. "Um…if you think it might be helpful, um… if I can help with something…I'd be happy to."

"Wait, really?" Eileen stopped with her brush midway through her hair.

"Sure."

Eileen grinned ear to ear, and Serena was pretty sure Eileen was excited, which Serena hadn't expected.

"Please! Xander and I have worked together for years, and truthfully, I tend to fight with many cat-like qualities, but there's a ton you could teach me."

"I…well, I'm not an aggressive person…or snake…."

"Aggression has nothing to do with it."

Eileen disappeared back into the bathroom, but only for a second. Then she walked over to where Serena was and pulled a heavy book off a shelf.

"Take art, for example." Eileen flipped to a page about a third of the way into the book. "Do you know who Botticelli is?"

Serena shook her head. "No, I don't know much about art."

Eileen pointed to an image of half-nude women in a forest. The colors were soft, and the fabrics were flowy. It was a beautiful piece.

"See how soft the painting is? You can't see any brush strokes, right?"

"It looks…blurry? But…intentionally, I think," Serena said honestly.

"How about this one?" Eileen flipped further into the book.

The image was of a pair of ballet dancers. The colors were

more blocky, and the brushstrokes were definitely visible. "Oh, lots of paint marks on this one," Serena said.

"Exactly. The image is beautiful, too, right? The dancers are delicate, even if the brushwork is more aggressive. Degas painted many dancers over his career. Some of my favorite pieces are by him."

"They are beautiful."

"Do you see what I'm saying, though? Both delicate and aggressive brushwork are stunning. You don't have to be aggressive to be effective. It could be helpful for me even if I only learned more about how you move as a snake." Eileen smiled at her, and Serena saw her sincerity.

"Okay. I'll help. I'm the one who offered anyway," Serena smiled back.

"Thank you," Eileen said, setting the book on a nearby desk. "You're free to come in here whenever, by the way. Clothes, books, and a quiet space away from the other two, if needed. Xander would likely say the same, but I think my space might suit you better."

Serena giggled. "Clothes would fit better, too." Which she knew firsthand, considering she'd been wearing a set of Eileen's clothes every day since Thenia had passed out and Serena had revealed herself.

Eileen laughed. "True. I always look like I'm a toddler when I wear his shirts. I always have."

Serena watched as Eileen retrieved a small cosmetic bag from her nearby suitcase and started digging through it.

"Actually, the three of us did discuss the house the other day," Eileen said. "Even if Gram and Pop are still here...sort of? This is our house now. Well, yours really, so we think the five of us should reshuffle a bit."

"What do you mean?" Serena sat in the nearby desk chair while Eileen applied lotion to her face.

"Well, Xander and I aren't here often anymore, so we

thought I might move into Ash's room since it's attached to Xander's and is a bit smaller. Then Ash could move into the master, and the three of you would have more room."

Serena hadn't thought about the main house and the living arrangements, but maybe she should have. In reality, she'd invaded Thenia's space and kind of never left.

"Then, you could have my room. If you wanted it," Eileen said, drawing Serena's attention back to their conversation.

"Ash is okay with this?" Serena asked softly.

Eileen sniggered. "Mostly. He's a bit weirded out by moving into Gram and Pop's room, but that's because they are still here. Otherwise, yeah."

"And Alexander?"

"Honestly, half the time we are home, one of us ends up in the other's room. We always share rooms on the job, and we used to sneak into each other's beds as kids. I kind of hate sleeping alone." Eileen blushed slightly and looked away.

"Yeah. I understand. Even the nights I'm in my beast form… it's hard to sleep outside anymore."

"At least you're smaller in that form. Xander's already huge. He literally gains more feet and a tail. Total bed hog," Eileen said.

When Serena looked up to see if she was kidding, Eileen barely held in her laughter.

Serena giggled into her palm, and Eileen gave in to her own laughter. Which is what they were both still doing when Alexander and Ashton returned from the tiny house.

Ashton Giri

With Thenia safely tucked into bed and her phone propped up for Arthur to watch over her, Ashton and Xander returned to the main house, where they were greeted by the sound of muffled laughter.

Ashton hadn't heard his sister laugh that relaxed in a long

time, and he'd never heard Serena express herself that freely. Apparently, Xander was also a bit off balance because he turned to Ashton with an expression that screamed, *What the hell?*

All Ashton could do was shrug and mouth, *I have no idea.*

As they grew closer to Eileen's bedroom, he could hear their distorted conversation and even more laughter. Xander rapped his knuckles on the door, and after another outburst of laughter, Eileen told them to come in.

"You two seem to be having fun," Ashton teased as he leaned on the door frame.

Xander crossed the room and plucked a bottle from Eileen's hands before dispensing a blob of the lotion into his palm and rubbing it into his hands and forearms while muttering something about scalding water.

Eileen snorted at his theft of her product but rolled her eyes and ignored him. "We were discussing the habit of bed-hogging that is so prevalent in this family."

Xander met Ashton's eyes, and they burst into laughter before Ashton choked out, "Accuses the family's number one blanket burrito."

Serena chuckled, and Eileen had the grace to smirk. "I get cold."

Ashton shook his head at his sister but gave all his attention to Serena when she walked over and stopped in front of him.

"How's Nia?"

A strand of Serena's hair fell across her cheek, and he couldn't stop himself from reaching out and running it through his fingers. Of course, that made Serena blush, but she didn't pull away from him.

"She's sleeping with Pops watching over her. He'll let us know if something changes or she wakes up."

Fear and worry filled Serena's features, and Ashton gently tugged her into his arms. She stiffened for a moment, but then she relaxed, wrapped her arms around him, and held on tightly.

"Did you take care of the mail?" Eileen asked.

"Yeah. Xander said the water was enough to neutralize it, and then we got rid of all the mail just to be safe."

Eileen pursed her lips, and Ashton watched Xander observe her profile.

"And none of the other letters had anything in the envelopes?" Eileen finally asked.

"No. Just the letters," he answered.

"They're escalating," Eileen stated, and Xander nodded in agreement.

Ashton heard Serena sniffle, and he held her tighter.

"I know we got lucky. If Xander hadn't identified it in time, all of us would have been really uncomfortable."

Eileen sat on the foot of her bed, her legs crossed beneath her, while she continued to process. "What was it, Xander?"

"Cruopoena."

Eileen's frown deepened, and Serena shifted just enough so her shaky voice was audible, "What is that?"

Xander sighed and went to sit in Eileen's desk chair, where he leaned forward, his elbows on his knees. "It's one from our world. Herbalists still cultivate it."

Serena nodded against Ashton's chest.

Eileen made a huffing sound, and everyone refocused on her. "They didn't want to kill us. That plant in powder form would have made us all incredibly sick for a few weeks, but it's not fatal."

Ashton glared at his sister when Serena squeaked and reburied her face in his sweatshirt.

Eileen winced, "Sorry."

"So, they wanted us out of the way, but not permanently," Ashton hypothesized.

Xander sighed. "Yeah. Because with us incapacitated, they would have been able to do whatever they wanted. Search the house, split us up, anything. In case they didn't find what they wanted, though...."

"We'd still be alive," Ashton noted.

His sister and Xander's eyes connected, and they both said, "Exactly."

"Now what?" Serena asked, her voice barely above a whisper.

"Well, they are probably already aware that their plan didn't work and are regrouping," Eileen answered.

Ashton nodded. "Hey, Gram, was there anything on the external cameras?"

She answered from his watch, not his phone, considering she knew he'd refuse to let Serena go to fish it out of his pocket.

"Unfortunately, not. Only our normal mail delivery carrier has been delivering mail every day since the last time you emptied the mailbox."

"What about the annexed plot?" Eileen asked. "Not the mail, but the property. They would have to be somewhere close by to know they failed."

Ashton had truthfully forgotten about the smaller plot of land connected to one side of the main one. It had once been part of the main house's land, but many years ago, his grandparents had legally carved off a portion and given it to their best friend. He and the system still monitored the land and property, as it was currently empty, but it was always an afterthought.

"Good idea," Gram said, "but no. Nothing."

"Damn," Eileen groaned and flopped onto her back on her bed.

"So, that leaves us with…" Ashton said, but he was pretty sure he already knew the answer.

"Nothing," Xander confirmed.

"Perfect," Ashton said bitterly before he buried his nose in Serena's hair and closed his eyes. "Just perfect."

Chapter 21: Specialties and Strengths

July 2024, Maine, USA | Thenia Loris

Thenia awoke to the quiet whispering of voices. She attempted to roll over, but when she moved, Ashton's arm tightened around her waist, and he snuggled his face into her hair, his chest pressed against her back. Even without opening her eyes, Thenia could tell it was light outside, which meant she'd likely slept through the night.

"You okay, Nia?" Ashton muttered sleepily.

She yawned and reluctantly opened her eyes, into what was indeed a sunlit bedroom. "Yeah, fine. Just heard voices downstairs."

Ashton lifted his head, his eyes still shut, and a few seconds later, he dropped it back onto the pillow.

"Xander, talking to Serena," he said before his yawn escaped.

"Are he and Eileen alright after yesterday?"

Thenia knew that manipulating the amount of water she had, in addition to the water's form being fog, would exhaust her. She'd been hoping to at least make it back to the house before passing out, but it looks like that hadn't happened. The last thing she remembered was her body feeling heavy and her legs giving out while she was still in front of the main house.

"Everyone's fine. Xander and Eileen showered immediately after you passed out, and then he helped me get you back home and into bed. Thank you, by the way."

Thenia wiggled out of Ashton's hold enough that she could roll over in his arms and face him. His drowsy face was always more relaxed than the one he'd slide into place throughout the day's progression; the stress of his day ahead of him had not yet awoken with the rest of his body. He blinked sleepily, and a lethargic grin crept onto his lips.

"You're welcome," she said, leaning forward to kiss him lightly on the lips. "I'm glad I could help and that everyone is alright. How's Serena?"

Ashton yawned and nodded. "Fine. You scared her, though. She was in her human form and across the driveway by the time I'd caught you."

"Wait, she shifted there?" Thenia whispered.

Serena had conveyed to her that most paranam preferred to swap forms in private. There was nothing gruesome, secret, or frightening about it, but it was when most of them spoke to their God and treated the time as a sort of ritual.

"She did. All three of us were too preoccupied to notice, but yeah. She did."

Thenia frowned, and Ashton reached up, softly running his pointer finger down her forehead to the space between her eyes.

"Don't overthink it. Serena's fine. I checked."

Thenia nodded and closed her eyes. "Okay. Thank you."

Ashton removed his finger and tucked some of her hair behind her ear before rolling to his back and pulling her closer to his side. He kissed her forehead and rested his cheek on the top of her head.

Everything had changed for Thenia with a single email to Ashton all those weeks ago. She never considered she'd find someone she felt so safe and seen with. And she'd never have expected to find two of them. If you'd told Thenia that she'd be caught up in some complicated covert history between decades-dead mechanites and a secretive transmogromorph kabal living in a home on the same property with two of the world's first artificial intelligence programs with souls, Thenia would have backed away slowly and then run. That thought alone now had her chest aching even if it was only hypothetical, and Thenia resisted the impulse to rub her sternum.

The sound of the front door shutting echoed loudly in the quiet house, its sound bouncing off the many hard surfaces. Shortly after, the coffee maker beeped, and Thenia heard a kettle get set onto the stove. A few minutes later, Serena tiptoed up the stairs, and Ashton and Thenia held their free hands out to her.

They both sleepily laughed, but Ashton poked Thenia in the side with the arm he still had curled around her.

"You're supposed to be sleeping," he scolded.

Thenia opened her eyes and rolled them after seeing Serena at the foot of the bed, fighting to hold back her laughter. After the three of them had begun sleeping together in the tiny house, Thenia moved all the furniture back to its original position so that no one had to crawl over each other to get in or out of bed.

She and Ashton wiggled their fingers, and Serena walked to Ashton's side of the bed and grabbed each of their hands in her own.

"I put coffee and tea on. Alexander was just here. He and Eileen are going to run into town. There's a storm warning, and they want to pick up a few things."

"Sounds good," Ashton said.

"Thank you. Now come back to bed for a few minutes."

Thenia gently tugged Serena's hand while squirming backward to make space for Serena between her and Ashton.

Serena looked hesitant, but Ashton released her hand to cover his yawn before he agreed with Thenia by lifting the edge of the blankets. Thankfully, Serena relented, carefully crawled over Ashton, and cuddled between them. Her blonde hair was splayed over Ashton's arm, and one of her hands still held Thenia's, where she was tracing silly shapes into her palm with her thumb.

"Are you feeling better?" Serena asked.

"I am. Thank you. I'm sorry I worried you. Again," Thenia smirked.

"It's okay, um, Sue helped. She told us what she could about what happens to an elemental witch when they overextend."

"Good. I must admit, I haven't done that since I was a child. I forgot how exhausting it was."

"Play with fog?" Ashton asked.

Thenia chuckled. "Well, yes, that too, but I meant overdoing it. I think I was in high school the last time I went that far."

"What happened?" Serena asked with unmasked curiosity.

"Ah, well. I was a lot more outgoing and confident as a kid, and I had a friend who was an artist. She specialized in watercolor paintings of local landscapes. I was spending an afternoon studying with her while she painted on this ridge overlooking our town when a storm rolled in out of nowhere. By the time we realized it, we knew we wouldn't make it back to the car before the rain started."

"Rain, watercolor, yeah…" Ash slurred. "Yup, bad mix."

Thenia smiled. "Exactly. What made it worse was that the painting was her final project, and if it were destroyed, she wouldn't have had time to redo it."

"What did you do?" Serena asked.

"Well, thankfully, she is a spirit whisperer, so she knew I was a witch. While she was frantically packing up her supplies, I focused on turning the water above and around us into steam before it fell far enough to reach her canvas."

Thenia looked over at Serena, who was staring at Ashton, the latter abruptly shifting to sit up and frown.

"Nia, how far was the car?" he asked tightly.

Of course, Ashton knew where she'd been heading with her

admission. Thenia glanced away and smirked, but felt her cheeks flush.

"Nia…" he said a bit more forcefully.

"Ah, yeah, um…a mile."

"A mile!" Ash screeched loud enough to make Serena wince.

"Or…two…."

This time, it was Serena's turn to groan, and then she peeked over her shoulder at Ashton. "Well, I guess we should be happy that she only made fog for a minute or two yesterday."

Thenia choked back a laugh but caught the other two glaring at her from the corner of her eye.

"It's fine. I was fine. Like yesterday, I slept it off and recovered."

"Didn't Sue say something yesterday about an elemental witch's power capacity being hereditary?" Serena asked Ashton, who nodded.

"They are," Thenia agreed. "Elemental witches inherit their power from the generations before them. Each witch is born with their own reserves, but when their elders pass, we perform a rite to transfer their power to the next generation down."

"What happens if there's no next generation?" Ashton asked.

"Then it's returned to the source, and another bloodline is born. At least, that's the theory."

Serena's eyebrows were furrowed, and she'd begun chewing on her lip as she considered something.

"Serena?" Thenia asked, breaking the woman's focus.

"Oh, sorry. I was just thinking that it's kind of similar to paranams."

Ash leaned his chin on Serena's side. "From what I've learned from Xander over the years, I agree. Very similar. Both of your magics are…additive?" he said tentatively. "You're given or have something added to yourselves in the form of magic or power or whatever."

"Yup," Thenia agreed.

"Mechanites don't. Just because you're born a mechanite doesn't make you a master of anything. I still had to learn programming, digital forensics, and all the other things. The only difference between us and traditional humans is that we have the instinctual knowledge of how to communicate with the mechanical, but that only gets us so far."

"Oh, interesting," Thenia admitted. "I didn't realize that. I'm not sure what I thought, actually, but I guess I never really thought about it at all."

"Yeah, Eileen and I have degrees in computer science, and I have a masters in digital forensics, cybersecurity, and networking."

"Wow. Makes my schooling look elementary."

Thenia noticed Serena shrink into herself a little, and Ashton had too, judging by the look he shot Thenia over Serena's side.

"I was wondering, Serena," Ashton said, poking her cheek with his nose, "Would you be interested in taking cooking classes?"

Thenia smiled first at him, then Serena, who had rotated to look at him in bewilderment.

"What?"

"If you don't want to attend in-person classes, there are online ones, too. It can be as formal or informal as you want. Either way, it was just a thought."

"I…um…well…but I…."

The coffee maker beeped downstairs, and Thenia was appreciative of its timing.

"I'll get coffee poured and tea steeping." Thenia crawled out of bed and pulled on a sweatshirt from the dresser nearby. "Don't be too long, or it'll go cold."

She nodded to Ashton and left him to chat with Serena, who was still processing his suggestion.

When Thenia entered the kitchen, the tea kettle had just begun to whistle, so she turned off the burner and pulled three cups from the cupboard. Her cell phone, which was charging on the counter by the laundry room, made her smile.

"Good morning, Arthur, Sue."

"Good morning, dear. Feeling better?" Arthur asked.

"You gave us all quite the scare yesterday," Sue added, "but thank you for protecting Eileen and Xander."

"None needed, and yes, I feel back to normal. Thank you for teaching them about elemental witches, Sue."

"My pleasure. Once they knew you just needed sleep, everyone calmed down."

Thenia smiled as she poured the boiling water over top of her and Serena's favorite tea. It was a blend that Serena had put together after Thenia had offered her some of the cuttings from the garden when she'd finished pruning the herb garden one afternoon. The lavender and chocolate mint mixed well with the few chocolate curls in each scoop. Because of that extra sweetness, it was a tea that didn't require sugar and was exceptionally good with a splash of milk.

"Serena said a storm was in the forecast?" Thenia asked the couple.

"There is," Arthur replied. "Not until tomorrow afternoon, but they are advising not to underestimate it."

"Makes sense. I'm not super familiar with the weather here, so I appreciate the warning. Is there anything you suggest I do to prep the gardens in advance?"

Thenia looked up as Serena and Ashton made their way down the steps and into the kitchen. She handed them their mugs, leaned on the sink, and cradled her cup between her fingers.

"Only a few things, but Xander will help you," Arthur said.

"With the trees?" Serena asked, standing beside Thenia and resting her head on her shoulder.

"Yes. He's been helping me since he was a cub."

Ashton laughed into his coffee from one of the kitchen bar

stools. "I'm pretty sure he wasn't helping. I think he just can't resist the opportunity to climb trees."

Arthur and Sue's sweet laughs filled the kitchen, and Thenia wondered if this was what most homes were like on lazy mornings. Her parents were wonderful, loving, and supportive, but they'd been on separate continents for most of Thenia's life. At sixteen, Thenia already lived alone in her childhood home with a few reliable neighbors to support her. Not that she was complaining. She'd been content and learned independence at a young age, but it had been lonely at times.

"What does he actually help with?" Serena asked. "He only mentioned he'd find Thenia when they got home to help her with it."

Ashton grinned. "He knocks out the deadwood and anything loose that could fall and cause damage or hurt someone."

"Well, that is extremely helpful," Thenia chuckled.

"Very," Arthur agreed. "Though I would agree with Ash, good kid or not, he's still a panther, and keeping him out of the trees was always a struggle."

"Or off the roof," Sue added.

Thenia nearly choked on her tea, making the four of them laugh.

"Well," she coughed, "I will make sure to keep an eye on him then."

"Good luck," Ashton and Arthur said in unison.

Ashton Giri

His sister groaned, and when Ashton glanced over, Eileen was sitting on the office floor, leaning against a wall with her laptop open on her outstretched legs.

"You good?"

Eileen's head thumped against the wall before she rolled it from side to side.

"Nope. I don't understand. How is there just *nothing*?"

Ashton swiveled his chair around and leaned back in it. "We warned you," he said, indicating their grandmother's image on her computer monitor.

"I know you did. I was hoping you'd messed up or missed something. Which was dumb considering it's you."

His sister smiled at him, and Ashton felt his cheeks heat. He'd always been the one to have his eyes on a screen, but that didn't mean Eileen wasn't a brilliant mechanite, either. She'd branched out into physical combat and espionage, so over the years, he'd surpassed her in various areas regarding the machines.

"I'm not infallible. It's good to have a second," he glanced at his Gram, "or third set of eyes."

"Yeah, but when the first set belonged to the AIS's top forensic expert, what did you honestly expect me to find?"

Ashton rolled his eyes. "Ug, stop with that crap. I'm the top of nothing."

He watched his sister and their digital grandmother's eyes meet, and then they both stared at him, each with one eyebrow raised in nearly identical expressions, making it his turn to groan.

"I know they want to make you the department head, Ash. Why aren't you taking the offer?" Eileen prodded, shutting her laptop and pulling herself to her feet for a stretch.

"Because I like my hands on the keyboard, not in personnel files. I want to do the work, and managing the department means I don't do casework."

"That's not true, Ash," his grandmother said. "You may not own a case end-to-end anymore, but there were many times when my department manager was in the code with us."

"Exactly. You should take the offer, Ash." Eileen agreed, pulling the second desk chair over to him so she could flop into it before putting her feet on his chair beside his thigh.

"Meh, it's not for me."

"What do the other two think?"

When Ashton looked away, he caught Eileen glancing at their grandmother again, who'd pursed her lips in disapproval.

"Wait, you've not told them?" Eileen accused, poking his torso with her toes.

"There's nothing to tell. I don't want the job."

"What about just talking through it with them? Maybe they'll see something you won't."

"There's nothing to talk about. Just drop it. Please."

Before Eileen had a chance to argue, a window popped up on Ashton's screen, and a chime pierced the air. He gently shoved his sister's feet away so he could rotate back towards the desk and roll closer to it.

"What is it?" Eileen asked, sidling her chair closer to him.

"I wrote a crawler to search the databases at the AIS for any mention of instances where people actively tried to circumvent being traced by a mechanite and using traditional post to do it. It found way too many instances to be helpful, so I added the use of poison, toxins, and powders as a pivot point."

Eileen snorted, and Ashton saw his sister roll her eyes again.

"What did it find, Ash?" his grandmother said from across the room.

"You're not looking?" Eileen asked.

"No. I don't want to chance someone tracing anything back to me. Arthur and I are staying on the intranet, internet, and home network for now. We're spoofed to look like any other human user."

"One that wouldn't have access to the department's systems. Gotcha."

"Ash?" his Gram prodded a second time.

"Sorry, yeah. It found three dozen instances. Fourteen are from before mechanites evolved, but I think we should still look into them."

Eileen nodded. "Makes sense. Just because computers exist

now, doesn't mean who or whatever is behind this hasn't existed for longer."

"Yeah. Another twelve appear to have occurred overseas and never in the states, and nine are considered closed cases with resolution."

"Interesting," his grandmother hummed. "So, out of thirty-six results, thirty-five are likely irrelevant."

"And the last one?" Eileen asked.

Ashton looked around his sister and at his grandmother's image, and when their eyes met, the digital woman sighed.

"Ah. I was afraid of that."

Eileen scowled and then crossed her arms over her chest. "Another thing you two are going to keep from me?"

"I need her help, Gram." Ashton admitted but hastily added, "Not the why, just the what."

The AI woman stared at him for a minute, then her expression softened, and she looked at Eileen and nodded. "Fine, but not the why. I won't risk her or Xander with this."

Eileen groaned. "Do you all think that little of us? That we can't take care of—"

"Don't," Ashton nearly growled, cutting her off. "Eileen, the last result was the case that killed our parents."

To her credit, Eileen shut her mouth as her eyes widened, and she stared at him. Finally, she relaxed, nodded, and stood up.

"Alright. I hear you, and I won't ask again. I understand." She looked at their grandmother. "Thank you for telling me this much. I'm going to go for a walk. When I get back," she pointed at him, "we will start going through your results. I can look at the other thirty-five. That will keep me out of the last one and should help with your concerns. That work?"

Ashton frowned up at her but nodded. "Are you alright?"

"I am. Needed a break before your search results came in. Now I need two." She chuckled softly. "I'll be back in fifteen. Need anything?"

He shook his head, and she turned, leaving the room and shutting the door behind her. Ashton looked at his gram, who was equally confused.

"I can't tell if she took that well or badly," he admitted.

"Both. Let her go talk to Xander. That should help, but she's right. Have her work on the other results. You can verbally ask her for help on the other one if you need to, but keep her out of the database."

"Understood."

Ashton stared at his screen, which displayed the list of case files and code names. His eyes found the twenty-ninth one, and his pulse quickened.

"Gram, can we really end this without anyone else getting hurt?"

When she didn't answer him, Ashton sighed and leaned back in his chair.

"Yeah…that's what I was afraid of."

Chapter 22: Only Ever One Seat at the Table

July 2024, Maine, USA | Serena Ainsley

There had been no preparing Serena for the silliness that was Alexander in his panther form, climbing trees and knocking branches to the ground below. Add to that the water net that Thenia was controlling to catch the branches so that Serena could pull them over to the paths before they crushed the plants below, and their three-person tree trimming was the most entertaining thing she'd seen in a long time. Arthur, too, was laughing from Serena's cell phone in her pocket as he watched them from the ground's cameras.

Once Alexander and Eileen had returned from town, Alexander had swapped to his panther form. The car had been filled with everything from extra fuel for the generators, food, water, and plywood in case of damaged windows. When Alexander followed her and Thenia, Eileen followed Ashton into the house. That had been just after noon, and now the sun was starting to go down.

"How many are left, Nia?"

Thenia pointed to a tree beside the one Alexander was currently in. "That one and then the large one in the front of the house by the garage. That's it. Why? What's up? Getting tired?"

"Nope," Serena said, grabbing a long, thin branch from the water and pulling it over to the knee-high bundle of wood already stacked on the path. "Sun's starting to go down."

Thenia looked up and then smiled. "Ah, yeah. Guess it is. Hey, Alexander!" she shouted up to the panther, who looked down at her. "The one to your right and the large one by the house, left. You good to finish them up, or should we do them tomorrow? It's getting late."

The panther nodded before leaping to the tree that Thenia had indicated, and he began testing the branches with his paw.

"Guess we'll finish up," Thenia laughed.

Serena hauled another branch out of the water and added it to the latest pile. While she'd put on some weight and muscle in her recent time in her human form, the exertion was beginning to get to her, and Serena's arms were starting to ache.

"Arthur, how many piles do we have to move? I lost track of my count," she asked while simultaneously flexing her fingers.

"Seventeen of various sizes. However, only the one by the Chestnut Oak will need to be cut into smaller pieces. I think the rest should be manageable without."

"Thank you."

She picked up a few branches that had missed the water and landed amongst the foliage, but they were more twigs than something large enough to damage the plants that had cushioned their fall.

"Is Eileen alright, Arthur?" Thenia asked. "She looked a bit...stunned when she came to see Alexander earlier."

"She's fine. Ask Ash later when the other two aren't around," Arthur responded.

Serena and Thenia made eye contact and nodded in response. Whatever had bothered the woman was about the transmogromorph files. That's the only thing they couldn't discuss unless they were alone with Ashton.

A deafening crack split the dusk, and both Serena and Thenia looked up in time to see Alexander stumble. The branch he'd been testing gave way under his weight, tumbling to the water below it. Serena gasped and covered her mouth as she watched the panther drop a few feet, twist in midair, and grab hold of the tree's trunk with his claws. He scrambled back up onto a nearby branch, only to have it snap beneath him like the previous one had.

"Shit," Thenia hissed and then began rapidly speaking in a language Serena couldn't understand.

The water layer they'd been using to catch the deadwood rose to meet Alexander as he dropped. Leaves and loose debris from the floor below him integrated with the water, further increasing the padding it would provide. Everything slowed the cat's fall until he was only six feet off the ground and able to roll midair to his feet, where Thenia released the make-shift magical airbag with a splash and the thud of dirt and leaves. Alexander landed safely atop it all, his paws squelching in the mud.

Before Alexander stopped to check on himself, he and Serena ran to Thenia, who was doubled over with her hands on her knees.

"Nia!" Serena shouted, Alexander running beside her. "Are you alright?"

Thenia laughed softly and nodded, her labored breathing pronounced. "Fine. Just out of breath from speaking so quickly."

Serena flopped on the floor on her butt and glanced at Alexander, who, even as a panther, was visibly laughing at the woman.

"Sorry, I didn't mean to scare you," Thenia apologized, but inspected Alexander. "You good?"

He nodded and then glanced at his paws, all four of them muddy. He flicked one towards the plants, where some of the gunk splattered.

"Looks like another bath is in your future," Thenia teased.

"Xander!" Eileen shouted.

All three looked up to see Ashton and Eileen sprinting toward them from the main house.

"He's fine," Thenia said, standing up straight now that she'd caught her breath. "Branch snapped. Just a bit muddy."

"Gram said he fell from the top," Ashton said, slowing beside his sister, who immediately knelt to check on Alexander.

"He did," Serena nodded. "Nia caught him."

Eileen glanced up, and Serena saw her pale complexion. "Thank you. That's twice you've saved him now."

Thenia smiled, still clutching her side. "None needed, but either way. Happy to help."

Serena peered up at Ashton, who put his arm around Thenia's waist and kissed her temple. He must have felt Serena staring because he held down his other hand for her to take, but she didn't allow him to pull her to her feet. Now that she'd sat down, Serena discovered how utterly depleted she was.

"Alright, Xander, bath." Eileen directed and stood up. "Ash, we're stealing Gram and Pop's shower again."

"Do whatever, obviously."

"I'll start dinner after I help Nia," Serena offered.

Alexander nodded, and Eileen smiled down at her. "Thank you. I'll come to help you once I get Xander settled."

The two of them walked away, and Serena watched them go. Eileen spoke to Alexander, a smile on her face as she teased the panther who smacked her in the butt with his tail.

"You sure you're alright?" Ashton asked Thenia.

Serena looked up to see her smiling. "Fine. Promise. I was only out of breath because of how fast I had to react."

Ashton nodded and kissed her temple a second time. "Well, thank you again."

"Yes, thank you, dear," Arthur said from Serena's pocket.

She wrestled her phone out from where it was pinched in her hip joint and saw the waveform Arthur used when they were outside.

"Not a problem, Arthur," Thenia replied.

"Alright, well, you three better get a move on it. It looks like the storm will hit just before dawn, and you're running out of daylight."

"Crap. You're right." Thenia stepped away from Ashton and gazed up to inspect the tree Alexander had fallen from. "Arthur, you think we can call this one good?"

"Yes. Even if it isn't, the risk of falling branches is low in this section."

"What about the large one in the front?" Serena asked as Ashton assisted her to her feet.

"I'll go look at it, but I don't think I want to ask Alexander to go back up today. It'll be dark by the time he's finished anyway, and even if *he* can see, I sure as shit can't." Thenia smirked. "Our luck, he'd drop a branch on one of our heads."

Ashton snorted. "Isn't that the truth? Yeah. Let's call it good. Serena, need help with dinner?"

She smiled. "Sure. Thank you."

"You two go. I'll bundle up the deadwood and shower before meeting you in the main house."

Thenia bent beside the nearest woodpile and looked around before selecting an uprooted ivy vine from nearby. Then she wrapped it around the bundle and tied it in a knot. Serena watched as the vine began to rapidly dehydrate, causing it to constrict around its quarry when Thenia extracted the water from it.

Ashton smirked and shook his head. "Resourceful as always, Nia."

Thenia laughed, "Nope, just lazy. I don't feel like going to get the twine."

Serena giggled but seized Ashton's hand. "Come on, help me figure out what to make."

Ashton laced his fingers with hers and let her lead him away.

"Call if you need help!" Serena shouted back over her shoulder to Thenia as they headed toward the main house.

Thenia Loris

When Thenia saw the clock in her bedroom, she winced and quickly skipped down the steps and into the bathroom, where she stopped in front of the mirror and used magic to remove the excess water from her hair. After she instinctively reached for her magic, Thenia acknowledged how much she had started to use it again in recent months. At some point, Lucus' hold had truly loosened, and she was elated to be reclaiming some of herself and the heritage that he'd tried so hard to suffocate.

While she had showered, the rain had started, the sound virtually lost over the shower's spray. A gust of wind blew drops against the bathroom window, overlaying the black backdrop of the night sky beyond it.

Thenia's phone vibrated in the kitchen, and she rushed to retrieve it, smiling at Ash's text message.

Want me to come get you? The rain's picking up.

She warmed at his thoughtfulness, but there was no reason he needed to drench himself by coming to get her.

Thank you, but stay dry. I'm leaving in five. I'll be fine.

Thenia shoved her feet into her boots by the door and drew on her coat. Sure, she could push the water away from her body, but the air was still chilly, and the wind sounded worse than when she'd gotten home.

Before she opened the front door, Thenia texted her friend Sara to make sure she was ready for the storm, too, and then tucked her phone into her coat and stepped outside. While under the overhang, Thenia yanked up her hood and spoke the words needed to ask the water for its assistance. At first, nothing appeared to have changed, but when she stepped out into the rain, Thenia focused on the drops above her, and over half of them avoided her as they fell. The rest landed on her coat, but she could dry them off at the main house, and a little water never harmed anyone. Well, not her, at least.

She pulled her front door shut and hurried down the narrow path. While commanding water the way she was wasn't overly exhausting, there was a risk that the longer she did it, the more she'd slip up and the wetter she'd get. That harmless threat still incentivised her to pay attention.

Lampposts were scattered at various points throughout the garden, but they did little to light her way through the wind and rain. It felt as if the darkness was swallowing up the faint light they had created. Coupled with the howl of the wind, it was a bit eerie if she were honest. Thankfully, Thenia was confident that she knew most of the grounds from memory, so she kept her head down and sped up her pace.

It wasn't until she reached the main house that she lifted her head and saw Ashton standing on the porch, away from the rain. His hands were in his coat pockets, and he smiled at her. She skipped up the steps and stopped in front of him, and then muttered the same request she had in the bathroom to dry her hair. This time, she nudged the water off her coat and plonked it on the nearest plants behind her.

"Clever," Ashton chuckled and reached out to put his warm palm on her cheek before he leaned down gently to kiss her.

She leaned into him and kissed him back until she felt some of the warmth the wind had stolen from her seep back into her cheeks. When he finally drew back, Thenia saw his eyes were sad, and she leaned back to see his entire expression.

"What's wrong?"

He chuckled softly. "Nothing."

She glared at him, and he sighed.

"Sorry, nothing important. I'm just worried."

"About the letters?" she asked, relaxing a little.

"Yeah. Eileen and I looked through some AIS data earlier,

and I'm positive now that whoever is doing this is the same group who killed our parents."

Thenia felt her blood run cold, and she involuntarily shivered. "Okay, so what do we do?"

He shrugged and turned away. "Honestly? I have no idea."

Ashton's profile openly displayed his discomfort and fear, but as he'd admitted, she had no idea what to do about the entire situation either.

"Well, let's eat first, and then we can talk more."

He glanced back at her and kissed her lightly on the cheek before leading her into the house. As soon as the food's aroma hit her nose, her stomach growled loud enough that she blushed.

"What is she making? It smells amazing."

Ashton locked the door behind them and helped her with her coat. "Chicken and vegetarian stew pies."

Thenia's mouth watered, and she practically purred. "Wow, I can't deny that sounds perfect."

"Agreed. Eileen taught her the pastry recipe she knows. Normally, she makes hand pies, but Serena's filling would have been too heavy for that."

When they walked into the kitchen, Serena and Eileen shuffled bowls to the table, and Alexander appeared to be staying out of their way.

He nodded to Thenia when he saw her, but continued his conversation with the others. "I'm fine with moving stuff around tomorrow. We won't want to be outside in this storm anyway. It's only going to get worse."

"You're sure…?" Serena asked, not meeting Alexander's eyes.

"Yeah. We'll move rooms around either way. If you don't want to take Eileen's room, that's up to you, but seriously, Serena, you're not the only reason for the shuffle, so don't feel guilty."

Thenia glanced at Ashton, her eyebrow raised in question.

"Shit, we talked about it while you were sleeping. I'm going to move into the master, and Eileen is going to take my room. She offered hers to Serena."

"Oh," Thenia said to Serena, who was blushing and looking at the floor.

Thenia had been alone for so long and had grown so used to it, yet the thought that Serena wouldn't be in the tiny house with her felt like ice piercing her chest.

"Nia," Ashton whispered to her, "She's already said she doesn't want to leave you. It would just be a space she could call her own."

Thenia met his eyes, and his expression shifted to one of confusion.

"Nia?"

She shook her head and shooed away her issues. "Sorry. Fine. I'll be back in a minute."

Ashton caught her arm before she walked away, and she smiled in a way that hopefully didn't look too forced.

"Just going to wash my hands."

He inspected her for another few seconds before releasing her.

She couldn't deny that she was fleeing the shared space, as she headed swiftly down the hall. When she reached the end of it, she leaned against the wall where she was partly obscured by a bookshelf and the dim light. She closed her eyes and focused on taking a few deep breaths. Being alone wasn't new for her, and even Ash had said Serena wasn't moving out. So, why was Thenia's body reacting as if she were being left behind?

"Thenia?" Alexander asked as he approached her.

His footsteps had been near silent, and he stopped beside her with a concerned frown on his lips.

"Sorry. Just needed a minute," she said weakly.

"Do what you need. I wanted to say thank you. Again," he smirked.

She nodded but said nothing, fearing her voice would waver.

"Thenia, I know we haven't had much time to talk since we got home, but I'm here if you need anything. I wanted to make sure I explicitly said it."

Thenia glanced at him from the corner of her eye and saw his sincerity. "Have they told you much about my past?"

He moved to lean against the wall beside her. "Basics. Bad ex and still finding yourself again. I try to leave Eileen with the more nosy details unless it's imperative I know something."

Thenia nodded against the wall. "Yeah, Lucus, not the one you saw, but the real one, was a manipulative ass. Only took me ten years and his rejection after we were already engaged to figure it out."

"Don't be so hard on yourself. Learning takes time. Often more than we'd like, but you got there."

She snorted. "Yeah. It wasn't until he showed up here the first time and Ashton and Serena stood with me that I confronted him and our past. Neither of them said anything or tried to fight the battle for me. Just stayed with me."

"Sounds like you handled it well, from what I've heard."

"It was fine."

He looked sideways at her but said nothing.

Thenia groaned and shut her eyes again.

"Anything I can do?" Alexander asked calmly.

"Not really. I just need to get over it."

"Get over what?"

She opened her eyes and stared at her feet. "Being alone. If Serena wants to move into the main—"

"Ah, Thenia, you misunderstood. Serena isn't moving into Eileen's room to live. Just to have a space that is hers. She was clear that she wanted to stay with you unless you wanted her to leave."

That was the same thing Ashton had said, so Thenia knew Alexander was telling the truth, and her heart rate began to slow down.

He sighed. "I'm sorry we didn't make that more clear from the beginning. I'm sure she wouldn't have wanted you to be upset."

"It's fine. I jumped to conclusions." Thenia rubbed her face roughly. "I'm not even sure why it bothered me so much. I've been on my own since I was sixteen."

"That may be true, but you seem to have settled well here with Ash and Serena. It's understandable that you wouldn't want to lose that."

"I don't, you're right."

"Well, I don't think you need to worry." Alexander gently placed his palm on her shoulder. "Take your time."

With one final smile, he left her in the hallway to recompose herself.

After a few minutes of breathing, Thenia slipped into the bathroom, washed her hands, and splashed her face. Then she returned to the kitchen to enjoy a delicious dinner made by those who cared about her.

Chapter 23: Stormblood

July 2024, Maine, USA | Ashton Giri

Ashton bent forward, the tips of his fingers grazing the wood floor as he stretched his back. His bedroom was filled with boxes, piles of clothes, blankets, and various other things he'd spent the day sorting through and separating. Eileen had done the same in her room, and Xander was the only one who had gotten out of the monotonous task. Instead, he had been assigned to sort through their grandparents' room and bathroom, along with assistance from Serena and Thenia.

A loud rattling made Ashton jump, a muscle in his back pulling oddly at the abrupt movement. He groaned as he hobbled over to his dresser, where his phone was vibrating atop it. As soon as he saw the AIS logo on the screen, he rolled his eyes. Work had been too quiet, and he'd jinxed it by even thinking about it. When he opened the message, he relaxed, seeing that it was only a report he had asked for and not an urgent job that required him to drop everything to complete.

It didn't take him long to skim through the numerous pages of digital and scanned content. The case was the final one assigned to their parents decades prior. Most of the information

Ashton already knew, but his thumb faltered over one of the last pages in the report.

"Gram, did you see this?" he asked the device.

"Only that it arrived. Why, what have you found?"

"According to this, the two responsible for our parents' deaths were apprehended and sentenced by the angels a few years after the incident."

When his Gram said nothing, he assumed she'd reached the same conclusion.

"If they're out of the picture, then who the hell is tormenting us?"

"I'm not sure, Ash, but I get the feeling there may be more going on here than we first thought."

A loud crash came from somewhere near the front of the house, and Ash dashed from his room, nearly knocking over his sister, who was similarly frantic when she ran into the hallway at the same time he did.

"Sorry, go," Ash said, letting Eileen lead before following her to the front door.

"What the hell was that?" Eileen asked before she ripped open the front door. The wind blowing against it was so fierce that the door was shoved from her grasp. "Shit!"

Ashton caught it with his foot and bit his tongue to keep from yelping at the pain that seared through where the wooden edge had impacted the arch of his shoe and the bone beneath it.

"I have no idea," he said stiffly.

"Ash!"

Thenia rushed over to join him and his sister, Xander, and Serena, following her into the room.

"What the hell was that?" Xander asked, his question directed at Eileen.

"Not sure. It came from out front."

By now, the wind was so strong, and the rain was nearly blowing sideways. Ash had grown up in Maine, and they often had storms, but he shivered as he watched the trees through the doorway as they bent nearly ninety degrees. When he heard the shattering of a terracotta pot and saw a plant blow past him, roots and all, he knew it was time to stop gawking.

He used his entire body weight to shoulder the door shut. "Gram, anything on the cameras?"

"Considering the weather interference, it's hard to tell, but I think something fell on the car."

"Well, that's great." Ash leaned against the door while he attempted to catch his breath. "Can we leave it for now? I don't think we should risk going outside in this."

"Agreed," Eileen pivoted to Thenia and Serena. "Are you two alright staying here tonight? I know we've just made an absolute mess of all the bedrooms, but the couch can fit all of us." She smirked at Xander, "Well, minus Xander."

Ash saw his brother smile before he playfully glared at Eileen's teasing.

"I can switch to my snake form," Serena offered.

"I appreciate it," Xander said, but bumped his hip into Eileen's, "but my room is still in one piece, so I'll be fine."

"I need to run back to the house for a few minutes. Won't take me more than five," Thenia said, and everyone turned to stare at her in bafflement.

"Is that a good idea?" Serena asked hesitantly.

"Yeah, a tree branch just fell on the car," Eileen added. "Do you have to?"

"I need to make sure everything is locked and secure. I don't want to risk a window or something blowing open and damaging anything."

"Is that really worth it, Nia?" Ashton pressed.

"I'll be fine. Honestly, it won't take me more than a few minutes."

"I can go with you," Serena offered, her voice wavering. "Will be faster with two."

"You're sure you can't leave it?" Eileen asked.

"I could, but I'd rather risk a bit of wind and rain to make sure everything is safe tonight than clean it all up tomorrow."

"Do you want me to go with you?" Xander offered, and Ash needed to thank the dude later for watching out for them.

Thenia shook her head. "Nope, but if you could start moving those dressers in the master bedroom, we can help you more after we get back."

Eileen chuffed but waited silently when she saw Xander playfully scowling at her.

"Okay, I can do that, but only if you're sure?" Xander relented.

"We'll be fine," Serena encouraged, wrapping her arms around one of Thenia's.

"Fine, but hurry, and Gram?" Ashton asked, his phone still in his hand.

"Yes, dear. We'll keep an eye on them and alert you if needed."

"Thank you," he smiled at the phone and then put it in his pocket before looking back at Thenia and Serena. "Go out the back. The walk is shorter, and your coat's back there."

"Here, Serena, you can use mine." Eileen walked over to a small closet, pulled out one of her black raincoats, and handed it to Serena. "You'll end up soaked if you wear only a sweatshirt."

"Thank you," Serena smiled and swapped the sweatshirt he'd given her for his sister's jacket. Thenia pulled the coat closed around Serena and tied off the belt. She winked at Serena, and Ashton's heart fluttered in his chest.

"Ready?" Thenia asked as Ashton stepped forward and took the sweatshirt from Serena.

"Yes," Serena answered.

"Alright, let's do this quickly, then. You good to run?"

"Yup."

Thenia smiled at the group and led Serena to the back of the house. Ashton rubbed the back of his neck and glanced from Xander to Eileen. "Anyone else have a bad feeling about this?"

"We're just rattled from whatever hit the car. It'll be fine. Thenia can control water, remember?" Eileen said, poking him in the side. "Come on, let's get a bit more done before we heat up leftovers and call it a day. It's dark outside already, and comfy clothes and a blanket are the only correct choice in a storm like this."

Xander scoffed. "Both of which you'll steal from me."

His sister grinned, her features lighting up as she walked past Xander and back towards her room. "Being next door is only going to make it easier, too!"

Ashton studied Xander, who may have looked unamused by his expression, but his eyes sparkled as he watched Eileen's back disappear around the hall corner.

When he finally looked back at Ashton, Xander groaned and rolled his eyes. "Don't start that."

Ashton held up his hands in surrender. "I said nothing, man."

"Sure. Your mouth may have been silent, but your face wasn't," Xander teased with a grin as he walked back to the master room.

Ashton chuckled softly at his sister and Xander's inability to see what was in front of them or, in the best case, their stubborn determination to pretend it didn't exist.

Thenia Loris

She and Serena were nearly to the tiny house when the night sky lit up. A second later, the earth beneath them seemed to rattle from the power of the thunder above them. Serena's hand tightened around Thenia's, and she glanced over her shoulder to see that the woman's complexion was pale.

"Almost there." Thenia tugged on Serena's hand to make her run a bit faster.

As they were both becoming increasingly waterlogged, Thenia was mature enough to admit that she had been wrong. Whatever damage may happen to the tiny house, it would have been fine. She and Serena shouldn't have left the main house. As they ran, Thenia tried to keep them somewhat dry, but it didn't take her long to drop her focus from controlling the water and instead pay attention to the debris that swirled around them. They'd already dodged two branches, an entire shrub, and at least one bird's nest. The longer they were outside, the more likely one of them was going to end up on their ass on the stone path.

After being hit in the face by a large, wet leaf, they finally reached the cottage. Thenia threw open the door, pulled Serena inside, and slammed it shut behind them.

"Okay…that was…." Thenia wheezed as she tried to catch her breath.

Serena appeared even more pale than she had during their mad sprint, so Thenia guided her, dripping and shaking, to a bar stool.

"Sit here, and I'll go check upstairs. When you're ready, we can go back. Do you want me to ask Alexander to come get us? Or you can shift, and I can put you in my pocket?"

Serena shook her head, water droplets flicking around her. "I'll be fine."

"If you're sure. Think about it. I'll go do the loft window and be right back."

Thenia pulled her coat off in a futile attempt to avoid trailing more water than absolutely unavoidable around the small space. She hung it by the door and dashed up the steps and into the room above. The lights were dimmed, and another flash of lightning brightened the night sky beyond the glass. When the thunder crashed, it was muffled by the house, but its force still rattled the windows in their frames. Thenia paused, but she didn't hear anything from Serena downstairs.

"You alright?" she called.

"Yes."

Serena's answer was clipped, but not frightened, so Thenia returned to what she was supposed to be doing. She tugged on the window and slid the extra bolts in place just in case. The book Serena and Ash were in the middle of reading was on a small table beside the couch, and Thenia wedged it into her back pocket with a smile.

"I'll check the bedroom," Serena shouted up the stairs.

"Okay, thank you!"

Thenia tucked all of Arthur's journals into one of the desk drawers, finished up in the loft, and went down to the bathroom, where she turned on the light with a flick of the switch. Except it lit, and then there was a loud pop, and Thenia was plunged into darkness again.

"Arthur, did we lose power only here or also at the main house?" she asked into the echoey dark around her.

"Both, but the generators will—"

The man's voice distorted before it cut out, and Thenia groaned. "Great. I bet whatever generators we have aren't meant to keep two AIs active on top of everything else." She leaned through the bathroom doorway and shouted into the house, "Serena, you alright? Power's out."

"Yes, fine! Almost do—"

Glass shattered, followed by a loud thud from the bedroom above Thenia, and then Serena's reactionary scream was cut short.

"Serena!"

Thenia sprinted to the bedroom stairs, slipping on the rainwater they'd brought in through the front door minutes earlier. She caught herself after landing on one of her knees, hissing at the sharp pain that lanced up her leg.

"Arthur! Sue!"

When Thenia finally managed to scramble her way up the steps, mostly on her hands and now throbbing knee, the sky outside went white. The outline of the shattered window illuminated Serena's body sprawled on the floor at the foot of the bed. Once again, plunged into darkness, Thenia remained on her hands and knees and shuffled to Serena's side.

"Serena!" Thenia put her cheek to the woman's mouth and felt her breath, but after a few seconds of Serena not responding, Thenia checked her pulse. Thankfully, her wrist beat strongly against Thenia's fingertips.

"Serena, can you hear me?"

Thenia began checking her for injuries when Serena groaned and then shifted slightly.

"Ni…a…."

"Yeah, it's me. What happened?"

"Window. Crash. Slipped." Serena strained to sit up but swayed and put her hand on the back of her head. "Ow."

Thenia steadied her and scanned the area for the best way to move them further away from the glass and the rainwater streaming through the window.

She whispered the command words to ask the water to help her, and it pooled together on the floor before lifting and filling the space where the window's glass would have been. Then it partially solidified as if frozen into place. The continued rain now splashed into the sheet of water and ice, but didn't penetrate through it and into the room.

"Okay, I won't be able to hold that for long. We need to get you away from all of this glass and check out your head."

Serena made a noncommittal sound before leaning on Thenia and using her arm for leverage to get to her feet.

"You stable?" Thenia tested her, but already knew the answer when Serena swayed again. "Nope, got it. Come on, I know the steps will suck, but let's get you to the couch where it's still dry."

Thenia helped Serena slowly get down the steps and over to the couch, where she lowered the shivering woman to sit down. A minute later, ice shattered, followed by a loud splash above them, which made Serena wince, but Thenia waved it off.

"Ignore it. We'll deal with it later. Arthur, you there?"

When silence answered her, Thenia cursed and pulled her phone out of her pocket. "How strange. I thought Ash said there were backup generators."

"He did," Serena said and winced. "Alex…ander checked them this afternoon."

"Damn. Alright, so what would you like to do? We can stay here for a bit or head back to the main house. I don't know if that's a good idea, though."

Serena shivered painfully, then she winced and began coughing.

"Here," Thenia grabbed a blanket from the end of the couch and drew it around Serena's shoulders. "That should help. Can you tell me what hurts?"

"Back of my head and my neck."

Thenia frowned. "Okay. Give me a second to run up and get the flashlight from the bedroom, and then I'll take a look. Alright?"

"Sure."

"I'll be gone only a minute." She kissed Serena's forehead, now coated in a mixture of cold sweat and rain, but Thenia ignored it and ran back up the stairs.

Her knee had begun to throb, but she shoved it aside, pulled open a nightstand drawer, and retrieved a flashlight. When she clicked it on, the room around her illuminated, and she walked over to the window to investigate what had happened.

A quick swipe of the flashlight didn't reveal any branches or objects that could have caused the glass to shatter. She stepped closer, and one of the curtains whipped out at her from the wind, and she caught it and tucked it out of the way. The other one was pulled to the outside of the window and had become snagged on the jagged edge of the glass. Thenia carefully stuck her head out of the considerable opening and searched around. Nothing stood out as odd or responsible for the window breaking, so she left the window alone—her focus was Serena.

Thenia walked across the room towards the steps, but her boot landed on something, and her heart stopped at the popping sound it made. It didn't crunch. When she pointed the flashlight at her feet, Thenia felt the blood rush from her body into her feet.

Shattered under her foot was the glass barrel of a syringe, the needle attached, the plunger fully down.

"Serena!" Thenia screamed as her brain finally caught up to her body, which was racing down the steps. "Serena, let me see your neck!"

Thenia shined the light on the flushed skin of Serena's throat, and there was no mistaking the deep puncture mark for anything other than what it was. She forced the flashlight into Serena's palm so Thenia could fumble for her phone in her pocket.

"What is it?" Serena asked, but her voice cracked, and she swayed in place.

Thenia almost dropped her phone, but managed to call Ashton. She could have sobbed when it began to ring.

"Thenia, wha—"

"Ash! Serena's been attacked."

"What!"

"She was injected with something and—"

"Xander, Eileen!" Ash shouted away from the phone but then returned to her. "We'll be there in two. Keep talking to me."

Thenia glanced at Serena, who was starting to panic. Her eyes were wide and glassy, and her breathing rate had increased.

"I…we were closing windows. She was in the bedroom. It shattered, and I heard a thud. When I got upstairs, she was on the floor."

The roaring of the wind deafened Thenia as Ashton and the others had left the main house.

"Xander, get a board for the window. Eileen, see if you can

reach Gram," Ashton shouted, his breathing becoming ragged as he ran.

"Ash…."

"She'll be fine, Nia. Don't worry."

Thenia looked over at Serena, whose pale skin was pink, her hands were shaking, and blood dripped down her neck in a thin trail from the injection site.

"Ash…" Thenia repeated, choking back tears.

"I won't let it happen again, Nia," Ashton growled into the phone. "I swear."

"Hurry," Thenia whispered, pressing the back of her hand to her mouth to stop herself from crying.

Chapter 24: What Happens in the Dark?

July 2024, Maine, USA | Ashton Giri

Ashton's shoulder collided with the front door to Thenia's home, and if the sounds of wood splintering were anything to go by, he nearly knocked it down.

"Serena!" he shouted into the darkness.

Thenia's strangled reply came from the direction of the living room. "Couch."

He followed the soft glow of a flashlight into the other room and saw Thenia standing by the back door, her arms wrapped around herself. Then he saw Serena sitting on the couch, wet, pale, and shaking.

His vision went red.

"Ash, move!" Eileen snapped from behind him before she shoved him out of the way and ran over to kneel in front of Serena.

His feet had stopped just inside the room. It felt like he was underwater. Eileen's voice sounded muffled, and Thenia moved in slow motion.

"Ashton!" Eileen shouted, now standing in front of him, her face right in front of his, and he blinked a few times. "Focus on getting to Gram. I'll take care of Serena."

He stared at his sister for a few seconds before she squeezed his shoulder and then rushed back to Serena.

"Watch your back, dude," Xander said from behind him, and Ashton narrowly avoided the sheet of plywood his brother was carrying towards the stairs.

"I'll…help…" Thenia said, her voice hitching mid-sentence, but she followed Xander upstairs to the bedroom.

The next thing Ashton knew, he was the sole person doing nothing, and that snapped him out of his paralysis. He ran into the laundry room, dug around a drawer for backup flashlights, and brought one to Eileen, who'd been using her cell phone for light since Thenia had taken the one she had upstairs with her.

Ashton left the two women in the living room and hid in the kitchen so he could focus on his part. If he stayed with Serena, he knew he'd break down, and she needed him to figure out what had happened, not dissolve into an angry mess.

He leaned on the sink and pulled his phone out of his pocket, but didn't bother unlocking it. Instead, he merged with the machine and began filtering through the last twenty minutes of data directly from the property's system.

As wave after wave of images and mechanite characters buffeted him, he searched for the last time his Gram and Pops had been active.

—sh.

Ashton stopped his digging and waited.

—Ash.

Gram?

Stasis. Check…fi…from…parents.

What?

AIS.

Ashton wanted to scream. He sifted through sections of code and tried to claw himself closer to where his Gram's data was flowing from. Much to his frustration, when he saw what looked like a ball of light made from the mechanite language mixed with binary, he hit the equivalent of a firewall and couldn't get any closer to it.

Ashton...need leverage. Blackmail.

What? He begged, seeing that the light was beginning to dim. *What blackmail?*

Protect...them...all....

Then, the light dimmed fully until it was as if it never existed at all.

Ashton forced himself away from the code and ripped himself from the machine. He shouted in frustration before turning to face the counter, where he slammed his phone onto it, hearing its screen shatter beneath his hand. There was a slight movement behind him in the window's reflection, and Ashton turned to attack whoever it was before they could attack him. At the last minute, he realized it was Xander, but his brother had already blocked Ashton's wild swing and was glaring at him.

"Ash, calm the fuck down," Xander snapped. Then he said softer, "You're scaring Thenia."

Ashton glanced over Xander's shoulder. Sure enough, Thenia was standing by the front door, having just come down the steps with Xander from the bedroom. Her entire body was closed off, and she looked as though she was on the verge of bursting into tears.

He closed his eyes and took a deep breath. Only after he had reopened them and Xander had judged him calm enough, did he release his arm.

"I'll check on Serena and Eileen," Xander said and walked away, but he stopped to kiss Thenia's cheek and whisper something to her. She nodded, and then Xander left for the other room.

Ashton pivoted to face the window again and dropped his head, not wanting to see the fear in Thenia's expression. A minute later, he felt her hand on the back of his neck before she wrapped her arms around him. He pulled her closer with one arm.

"I'm sorry. I didn't mean to scare you."

"For you," she whispered.

"Hm?"

"I was scared *for you.* Not of you, Ash."

He opened his eyes and met hers in the dark reflection of the night beyond the glass, but when he only saw honesty, he turned to pull her into his arms. He rested his forehead on her shoulder before burying his face in her neck. The soft scent of Thenia mixed with her skincare products tried to relax him, but he felt how chilled and damp her skin was, and he was reminded once more of their situation.

"It'll be alright, Ash. We'll figure it out," Thenia soothed as she ran her fingers soothingly through his hair.

He held her tighter but knew he'd lose his temper if he spoke. First, his parents, then Xander's, his grandparents, and now Serena. Too many people had suffered over the stupid thumb drive in the basement. He wished the cursed thing had never existed.

How was he supposed to protect them all? He couldn't even protect Serena.

"Hey, Ash," Xander called from the direction of the living room.

"What's up?" Ash replied and lifted his head as Xander came around the corner.

"We need to get Serena back to the main house. You good with me carrying her?"

"Whatever she needs. Can I do something?"

Xander nodded. "Thenia, can you come and help me while Eileen catches Ash up?"

"Of course." Thenia pulled away from Ashton, and he shivered at the loss of her silent strength and warmth. She smiled weakly and kissed him briefly before following Xander from the room.

Ashton frowned at the cracked and slightly bloodied phone in his hand before shoving it into his back pocket and washing his palm. When he noticed his sister in the window's reflection, her face was hard and business-like in a way he'd never seen before.

"Xander is going to run her back to the main house. Thenia is wrapping her in a blanket right now and is going to go with them and help with some of the rain."

He nodded and hissed when he ran one palm over the other and felt a sliver of glass dig itself in deeper.

"I'll go with them, and we can continue to triage Serena, but I need the generators back on. Can you go figure out why they aren't working? Once we get Serena settled, Xander will come help you."

"Got it." Ashton carefully pat his hands dry, knowing that there was more glass in his flesh he'd not dealt with, but it wasn't his priority. "Any idea what they gave her?"

"A few, but I need better light and, ideally, access to the AIS's database of poisons. Any luck finding Gram?"

"No. Well, sort of."

He relayed to Eileen what had happened, and her expression grew even darker as he explained everything to her. They both heard Xander and Thenia enter the room, Serena in the former's arms, and they ceased their conversation.

"Tell me the rest later," Eileen said abruptly, turning away from him to focus on the others. "Are you ready?"

"Good to go," Xander nodded, and Ashton saw him tighten his grip on the cocooned woman in his arms.

"Ready," Thenia said.

Eileen didn't hesitate or waste time. She opened the front door for Xander, who ran out into the rain, followed by Thenia. When they were out of the house, Eileen stared back at Ashton.

"Generators, Ash."

"On it."

Then Eileen was gone. The front door shut behind her, leaving Ashton in the small, dark house with nothing except a bleeding hand, the sound of rain pounding down on the roof, and a weight on his shoulders that was rapidly approaching unbearable.

Serena Ainsley

Everything moved around Serena in a flurry of activity. When Xander laid her down on Eileen's bed, he smiled briefly and then rushed from the room to find Ash and help with their power situation. Or lack of one.

Thenia had been beside her since they'd left the tiny house, and she carefully pulled the mostly dry blanket from around Serena while Eileen disappeared into her closet, which hadn't yet been moved to the other bedroom.

"How are you doing, Serena?" Thenia asked but immediately added, "I'm sorry, it's too dark, so I can't see your expression."

"Fine," Serena said, but her voice shook uncomfortably, and she shut her mouth.

"Here," Eileen said, her voice approaching them. "Change into dry clothes, and by then, Ash and Xander will hopefully have the power back on. I'll give you some space to change, and I'll go find the first aid kit."

Serena felt Thenia tense beside her. "Serena, do you want me to help you change, or are you—"

"Please."

Thenia carefully tapped Serena's arm, along it up to her shoulder, until she found her cheek, where she leaned in to kiss Serena's forehead. "Alright. It feels like Eileen brought you underwear, sweats, and a thermal shirt. That work?"

"Can I have Ash's sweatshirt back?"

"Of course, love. Let's get you swapped, and then I'll go find where he put it after we left, okay?"

"Yes."

Serena's voice squeaked, but Thenia didn't comment on it, and Serena knew that even if she hadn't begun to develop a fever, she'd have been flushed and hot anyway. It was silly, but she wanted the comforting smell of Ash that lingered on his hoodie. Add to that, Thenia was stripping Serena's damp clothes off one piece at a time after calling her love. Even in the dark, Serena felt her self-consciousness rising. She was the heaviest she'd ever been as a human, and even still, she was considered malnourished and underweight. Serena knew she was gangly and emaciated-looking.

"Serena?" Thenia asked calmly.

Serena hadn't consciously meant to curl into herself, but she had and was actively blocking Thenia from taking her jeans off. "Sorry."

"Would you prefer Eileen to help you?"

"No. It's okay."

Serena softly held on to Thenia's shoulder while she tugged her wet pants and underwear off. Then Serena stepped into dry underwear and a squishy pair of pants. Lastly, Thenia helped her pull her shirt over her head, and even though Serena was relatively flat-chested, Thenia giggled when she wrestled the cotton bralette over Serena's hair.

"I'm not sure if you've ever been in a bathing suit, but getting out of a wet one-piece has the same silly feeling shimmy dance," Thenia said lightheartedly.

"I haven't, but I've seen people struggle out of wetsuits before."

Thenia chuckled. "Even worse. I think it's impossible to do it gracefully or with your dignity intact at the end. When the storm passes, we can get you a bathing suit and go swimming if you'd like. I saw a note in one of Arthur's books about a mile-long trail leading to the shore."

Serena opened her mouth to respond, but then she remembered why Thenia was helping her change in the first place. She'd been injected with something. There was no guarantee Serena would survive the night, let alone the entire nightmare they were in, long enough to see the ocean.

"All done," Thenia said, aiding Serena with getting back into bed before pressing her lips to Serena's cheek. "You'll be fine, Serena. We'll figure this out, okay?"

"Sure."

Serena wasn't confident they'd find a way out of her predicament, but she refused to be forced away from Nia and Ash. If she were to leave them in the future, it would be her choice.

"Serena, I promise you," Thenia whispered, her breath tickling Serena's neck. "I won't lose you. I love you too much for that, and I want more time to see you smile, have you hang out in my hair, and taste your incredible cooking. Understood?"

Serena's chest constricted as if she were locked in a snake's coil. Then she sniffled and managed a nod into the dark.

"Okay. I believe you...."

"Good."

Thenia gently pulled Serena's hair over her shoulder and rotely braided it. By the time she was tying the end of it, someone knocked softly on the bedroom door.

"Come in," Thenia responded for them.

"All set?" Eileen checked before entering the room and shutting the door behind her.

"All good," Thenia said, settling Serena's freshly braided hair onto her shoulder.

"Okay, watch your eyes. I found a lantern," Eileen warned.

Serena shut her eyes, and after hearing a click, she slowly opened them to get used to the change in brightness. Most of the room was now illuminated in a soft glow, and Eileen was settling the lantern on a pile of boxes at the foot of the bed, a large metal box in her other hand.

"Much better." Eileen swapped places with Thenia when she moved out of the way for her. "Xander and Ash are trying to see what the hell's happening with the power, but for now, this will work. Anything is better than my cell phone in my mouth," Eileen chuckled.

"Do they need help?" Thenia asked while Serena managed a breathless laugh at Eileen's bedside manner.

"Doubt it. I think it's confusion, not lack of hands."

"Fair enough. Your stove is gas, right?"

"Yup."

Thenia nodded. "Serena, I'm going to make you some tea to warm up. That alright?"

She nodded and then croaked out, "Please. Thank you."

Thenia glanced at Eileen. "Shout if you need me," she said, then left the room, closing the door behind her.

"Okay, are you ready, Serena?" Eileen asked with a warm smile.

"Um...do I have a choice?"

Eileen snorted. "No, because if I don't figure out what is going on, Ash will kill me."

Serena smiled weakly. "Doubt it, but yeah, what do you need from me?"

"Easy stuff first. What hurts, and can you identify what's from the shattering window and the fall you took versus whatever they gave you?"

"Sure. Um, the back of my head hurts from when I hit the floor, a bit of neck soreness, too, but I don't know if that's from slipping or the needle, but it feels more in the back than where you said the injection was." She reached up to rub the base of her skull and groaned. "Yeah, fall, I think."

"Perfect." Eileen opened the mental box and pulled on a pair of gloves. "Let me check your head first. I didn't see or feel any blood earlier, but I'd like to check with more light now."

"Yeah."

Serena shifted to give Eileen a better vantage point, and her hands were soft and careful as she moved around Serena's hair, mussing up her fresh braid, but it was clear Eileen knew what she was doing.

"Going to press a bit harder in this one spot, okay?"

"Okay."

A second later, Serena hissed as the bruise on her scalp throbbed.

"As I figured. Sorry I hurt you. That's the spot you hit, and there's no blood, but you've got a nice lump and, judging by your reaction, a bruise. We'll keep an eye on it."

"No blood's good."

Eileen sat back and nodded. "Yes, it is. It would have made things far more complicated. Besides, Xander is the better one of us with a needle and thread." Eileen shivered, "Ew."

Serena giggled softly.

"But yeah, all good there. That said, would you be comfortable sleeping in here with me tonight? I'd like to stay close in case anything escalates."

"Um, sure? If you're alright with it."

"Very. Thenia and Ash will probably fight me, but I'd prefer to stay with you myself. Not that I don't care about you, but I'm a step further removed and likely more clear-headed when it comes to this type of thing."

"Makes sense."

Serena had heard Ashton's shout earlier, and whatever he'd been upset about had made Eileen tense up. Xander came into the room a few minutes later and said Ash was fine, but neither Serena nor Eileen fully believed him.

"Okay. Is there anything else related to the fall? Cuts, bruises, anything?"

"I don't think so?" Serena said but stopped, "Actually, my ankle was stinging earlier."

"Let's check it. Glass, if I'd have to guess."

Eileen rolled up the fabric covering the leg Serena indicated and then nodded.

"Yup, small slice. Let me clean it up and bandage it." Eileen leaned forward and then pulled the lantern over, inspecting it closely. "I don't see any glass in there. It's barely more than what you might do if you slipped with a kitchen knife and nicked your finger."

She put the lantern back on the boxes and removed a few more supplies from the kit. In a few minutes, Eileen had cleaned and covered the wound.

"Thank you," Serena said softly.

"None needed. You're family, Serena."

Serena felt her cheeks heat, and she looked away. Similar to Thenia's earlier comments, Eileen's made her feel overwhelmed and... full.

"Okay, well, now we have to tackle the unknown issue." Eileen frowned but pulled a disinfectant pad from the box. "Let me clean it first, and then we can go through a few of the more likely possibilities."

Eileen's firm fingers tipped Serena's head back and to the side a bit, and then she cleaned the injection point but didn't bandage it.

"Damn, I really could use a non-shit light," Eileen whined.

Serena giggled, but then both of them yelped, and she shut her eyes as the room was flooded with light.

"Well, ask, and I shall receive, I guess." Eileen chuckled. "Let me look at this real quick. Just in case this light isn't a permanent fix."

Again, Serena tipped her head and tried to watch Eileen's

expression from her peripheral vision. She looked focused for the most part, which was reassuring.

"Interesting. There's no coloring or anything around the wound or immediate area, other than general irritation, but that's expected. I'm going to press, but I'll be gentle, okay?"

"Mmhmm."

As promised, Eileen's pointer finger barely pressed on the entry point. Still, other than a level of pain that seemed reasonable, there wasn't anything on Serena's side that felt overly concerning.

"I assume that didn't hurt much?"

"Nope."

"Good," Eileen said, sitting back and narrowing her eyes at the wound. "I'm going to get extremely close to it, okay?"

"Sure."

Not sure what to expect, Serena had to suppress a shiver and a giggle when Eileen's nose nearly brushed the skin of her neck.

"Sorry," Eileen grinned a moment later when she gave Serena her space back and returned to sitting beside her. "There's no smell, or at least not to my nose. Honestly, it's almost like the needle was empty, but that would make no sense."

A faint knock on the door had both of them glancing toward it before Eileen said whoever it was could come in. Ashton stepped in, and his eyes immediately found Serena's before they went hard, and he looked away from her.

"Need anything?" he asked tersely.

Eileen crossed her arms in front of her and scoffed. "Yeah, for you to pull the stick out of your ass, Ash. You're being a jerk."

Ashton glared at her, but when he opened his mouth to retort, Serena heard Alexander growl from somewhere behind him.

"Remember what I said, man."

Even across the room, Serena could see the tightness in Ash's jaw. He glanced at her one more time before leaving the room without a word. Eileen groaned and dropped her arms as Alexander entered the bedroom and shut the door again.

"Ignore him, Serena. He feels guilty and helpless. He doesn't want to take it out on you, which is why he left. He thinks it's better that way," Alexander said, standing beside Eileen.

"Men are fucking stupid," Eileen said.

Alexander cleared his throat but smiled down at her.

She waved him off. "You're a panther. Doesn't count."

Serena chuckled, and Alexander rolled his eyes.

"So, what's the deal?" he asked, his arms behind his back and his posture suddenly stiff.

"Honestly? Nothing?" Eileen sighed. She pulled off her gloves and collected the soiled medical supplies. "No discoloration, no abnormal pain, and no smell that I can detect. What's the chance that the syringe was empty?"

Alexander stared blankly at Eileen.

"Damn. I didn't think so either," she said before taking the trash into the attached bathroom.

Alexander stared at Serena's neck, and she tried not to squirm under the scrutiny. He must have noticed because his eyes and posture softened, and he sat where Eileen had been.

"Sorry. I know this must be scary."

She nodded and looked down at her fingers in her lap.

"Don't worry. We'll figure out what it was. Once we narrow it down, Eileen and I will probably already know how to treat it."

Eileen snorted as she reentered the room. "Don't let Ash hear you say that. He'll lock us in the basement before our next job."

Alexander smiled fondly. "Yeah. Probably would."

"His point, though, is correct," Eileen said, leaning on Alexander's shoulder. "So far, you're not exhibiting symptoms other than what I'd expect from the rain's chill and your slip."

"Hey, Eileen, can you grab the door?" Thenia's muffled voice called from the hallway, and Eileen ran over and did as requested. "Thanks, I brought you a cup, too."

"Amazing, thank you," Eileen said, taking it from her and getting out of the way.

Thenia brought a cup over and set it on the side table for Serena. "Let it cool a bit."

"Okay. Thank you."

"Anything you need, or I can do?" Thenia asked all three of them.

"I don't think so," Eileen answered, cradling her warm mug in her hands. "Serena's going to sleep in here with me tonight, and I'll keep an eye on her."

Alexander chuffed and looked at Serena before leaning over to whisper, "Warning—she's a blanket hog."

"Watch it," Eileen glared with a smirk.

"Okay, well, if something changes, please let me know." Thenia requested.

"I will," Eileen said, looking at Alexander. "Xander, mind staying with Serena while she drinks her tea?" Then she looked at Serena. "After that, try to get some sleep. The last thing we need is you getting sick on top of all of this."

"Okay," Serena agreed and picked up her tea before blowing on it.

"Yeah, go help Ash," Alexander said, waving both Thenia and Eileen off.

Serena smiled weakly at Thenia before Eileen looped her arm through Thenia's and led her from the room. Once the door was shut, Alexander got to his feet and walked over to Eileen's bookshelf.

"Do you mind if I read while you sleep?"

"No. Can I ask what you're reading?" Serena's tea was cool enough to drink and warmed her to her toes. It immediately soothed her throat, and she took a deep breath of the floral steam, feeling a smile creep onto her lips.

Alexander chuckled. "Promise not to tell Ash?"

"Sure?" Serena said, tilting her head to the side and instantly regretting it.

"Romance novel. I've been stealing them from Eileen since we all hit puberty."

Serena grinned. "Does she know?"

Alexander nodded emphatically. "Oh, for sure. It got easier once digital books became a thing, but before that, she would buy the ones I liked and claimed they were for her."

"That's cute."

His hand hovered over a book's spine on a shelf above him, and Serena saw the smile he tried to hide. Then, he selected a book and pulled it off the shelf before mumbling.

"Yeah, it is."

Chapter 25: Emotional Understanding

July 2024, Maine, USA | Ashton Giri

Ashton knew his sister was right and that he was being an ass, but every time he looked at Serena, he was reminded of how badly he'd failed her. He tried not to stomp his way down the hallway and into his office but stopped and stood in the doorway for a few minutes. Eventually, he shut the door and settled into his desk chair.

He tapped the keyboard to wake one of the two machines still being powered and navigated to the AIS's intranet. In addition to everything else, he had to complete a report informing the department that his rig had potentially been tampered with.

When he and Xander finally found the issue with their generators and backup power systems, there was no way to deny that their entire system had been intentionally taken down. From what they could tell, whoever had done it wasn't a mechanite, or even if they were, they'd opted for a physical solution instead of a code-based one. Unfortunately, when it came to the AIS, it didn't matter. He had to report a sabotaged power line the same way he would a hacker.

It didn't take him long to pull up the correct digital form, and he had it filled out and submitted in just a few minutes. Then he opened the file for the operation their parents had been killed on and tried to find something he'd missed.

"There has to be something. Everyone slips up eventually," Ashton muttered as he scanned through information, his eyes unblinking.

Most of the files had been redacted, but that wasn't surprising. The surprising part was that he was able to access it at all. Luckily, he'd had his Gram because, even with all of the omissions in the file, she could fill in a few gaps, allowing him to see a mostly complete story.

As Gram had said, the drive had shown up on a dead body whose soul the angels were responsible for escorting. During their investigation, the drive was stolen midday, seemingly without a trace or recording on any of the entry or security systems. His and Xander's parents were assigned to retrieve the drive, and the four-person team was sent to an undisclosed location in Europe. There, they lost communication with their team located at headquarters, and it wasn't until Xander's mom escaped that she was able to check in.

Her report was extremely thin, though. She verbally granted custody of Xander to Sue and Arthur, then informed the base team that that was her last check-in and the job had been completed. Before they could ask her anything further, the line had gone dead.

After that, their lives continued. Their family was significantly smaller now that they were short four people, but there was no alternative.

The AIS had offered condolences and support, but his grandparents declined, instead focusing on healing their family on their own. Ten years later, the drive resurfaced, and his grandmother scaled back her work projects, citing age and illness. In reality, she'd begun working on decoding the drive that had finally found its way to her.

As far as the AIS knew, both Sue Giri and her husband passed away quietly at home after she'd lost the battle with a long-term illness, and her devoted husband developed broken heart syndrome.

As Ashton read through the file, his intuition told him he was missing something. He just couldn't figure out what that something was.

Someone knocked on the office door, and he glared over his shoulder. "Who is it?"

"Eileen."

"Come in."

He verified that his department had received his report and then shut down his connection to their systems and his computer entirely. It wasn't worth frying the machine if he and Xander missed some electrical issue. Truthfully, he was lucky it hadn't already fried, considering the sabotage.

He swiveled his chair to face where Eileen had flopped into the other desk chair. "What's up?"

She glared at him and crossed her legs, then her arms, dramatically. "*What's up?* Really, Ash?"

He was unable to suppress his eye roll, and there was no way to miss it when Eileen's temper flared.

"Yes, what's up? What do you need?"

"Ashton, why are you acting like this?"

"Like what?"

"A jerk. You won't look at Serena, you scared Thenia, and you nearly hit Xander."

"Serena needs to focus on herself. I talked to Thenia. I didn't realize it was Xander until the last second."

Eileen stared at him but said nothing. What she did do was stare long enough for him to start becoming uncomfortable.

"If you're done, I have work to do."

He abruptly swiveled his chair back to the desk, knowing that he was lying and he'd already turned his machine off, but he needed to get away from his sister before he said something worse than he already had.

When Eileen got to her feet, he could have sighed in relief at her giving up. Except this was Eileen he was talking about, and before he'd realized what was happening, she'd rotated his chair back to face her, and she bent so she was at eye level with him and nearly nose to nose.

"You haven't even asked what I found during my exam. Don't you care? She could be dying, and you—"

"Stop!"

He shouted and shoved his sister away from him, where she stumbled a few steps backward before landing in the other chair.

"You don't think I know that! I know what's at stake, Eileen! I've been doing nothing for months but reading about how these bastards murdered our parents. *Months,* Eileen! I get it!"

His sister shot to her feet and glared daggers at him, but she kept her distance from him this time.

"Ash, pull your head out of the past and focus on *now.* Serena was attacked, and we have no idea what they injected her with. Our parents are dead. GONE! Do you want Serena to join them?"

"Of course not, that's why I'm trying—"

"And if she dies during the night while you're in here beating yourself up? Then what?"

Ash's skin ran cold, and he must have physically reacted because his sister realized she'd hit her mark, and her tone and posture softened.

"We know you're scared, Ash. We all are. I don't want to lose her either. You know I've always wanted a sister. I may not love her like you do, but she's family."

"So what am I supposed to do? We have no suspects, no poison, no Gram, and no idea what the timeline is. I'm on my own. What do you want from me?"

He shoved himself to his feet and crossed to the far side of the room, his back to his sister.

"Ash, I'm sorry we left you here alone after Gram and Pop died."

He bit the inside of his mouth to stay quiet and not snap at his sister again.

"I don't know when you started thinking you were alone, but we should have been here to see it. You're not alone, Ash. Don't shoulder all of this yourself. If you try to..." she sighed. "If you try to, you'll fail and lose them both."

A handful of seconds later, the office door opened and closed, but he didn't move. He stared at the pictures of his family on the wall in front of him and pulled his phone from his pocket. The damaged screen, with spiderweb cracks and a chunk missing from the corner, was another reminder of how he had lost his temper.

Even through the damage on the glass, he could still see the picture he'd taken of Thenia and Serena one afternoon while they were working in the garden together. Both had dirt on their cheeks, and Serena wore a crown made of vines that Thenia had pruned and then woven for her.

"Shit."

He pressed the heels of his hands, freshly rid of glass shards, into his eyes and struggled to fight back the terror he'd been so desperately trying not to let drown him. When he heard a knock on the office door, he sniffled.

"Haven't you done enough, Eileen?"

When he heard the door creak open, he tensed. He'd really hoped she'd go away and leave him alone. Except when the woman stopped at his side, he smelled the earth, not Eileen's soft perfume. Then he felt Thenia's cool hand on the back of his neck, and she pulled him into her arms and his head down to her shoulder.

"I refuse to lose her, Ash. We'll solve this. Even if I have to find the bastards myself and get whatever antidote we need."

Thenia's voice was clear, without even a hint of a waver.

"I know you're scared, mad, frustrated—all of it. So am I. I had more time to process everything while we waited for you and the others to make it to the house. But at the end of it, I realized something."

"Hmm?"

"That I love her, Ash." She ran her fingers through his hair. "And you. I'm happy and I feel like myself for the first time in a long time." He heard her swallow roughly before she continued. "I'm not alone anymore. Not in a crowded room or an empty one. You're both with me, and I will do *anything* to keep that."

Ashton squeezed his eyes shut so hard that they started to hurt. Without opening them, he tipped his face, kissed just below her jaw, and felt when Thenia smiled.

"I'm…scared, Nia," he said, barely more than a whisper.

"I know."

"I can't let them take any more from me."

"I know, and we won't."

He finally had the strength to open his eyes, and when he leaned back to look at her, he was surprised to see her eyes were puffy and tears stained her cheeks. They'd been so quiet that he'd not even noticed them falling. He stuck his phone back into his pocket and ran his thumbs under her eyes, which brought a small smile to her lips.

"I'm sorry, and I love you, too, Nia. Both of you."

"We know," she said, stepping onto her toes to wrap her arms around his neck and kiss him.

He ran his hand up to the back of her neck and wove his fingers in her hair as he pulled her closer and deepened their kiss. His clothes were still wet from running through the rain and dealing with the generators. Until that moment, he'd not even felt the cold that had thoroughly seeped into his bones. Only now that Thenia was chasing it away was he able to see what he'd been doing to everyone around him.

Eileen had been right. At some point, he'd decided he was a team of one. Alone. Left and abandoned. But he was wrong. There were people in the bed swing again, and life in the gardens. Someone to read with and two siblings to rely on. He was an idiot. The woman in his arms was proof of that.

After a few more seconds of enjoying the feeling of her, Ashton pressed his forehead to Thenia's, his eyes still closed.

"I get it. I'm done being blind."

She laughed, her soft breath tickling his cheek. "You're not blind, just distracted."

He pulled away and scratched his neck. "Guess I need to go apologize."

Thenia took his hand and shook her head. "After. Right now, you are still soaked and need to warm up. We can't have you getting sick either."

When he involuntarily wiggled his toes in his saturated shoes, they squeaked, and both he and Thenia looked down at them before bursting into laughter. He was still clutching his side when she shook her head and led him from the office and into the master bedroom.

Instantly, his laughter stopped, and his eyes scanned the room. Then, Thenia closed the door behind him. It looked nothing like when his grandparents had called it their space. All the furniture had been moved, and some pieces were even swapped with others from around the house. The important items from his childhood room had been moved into this room, and the curtains and linens had all been replaced. The walls were bare, and there were still boxes in the corners of the room, but overall, it was unrecognizable. He was wide-eyed and slack-jawed when Thenia released his hand.

"Different enough for you? Alexander said you felt strange moving into their room with them still around."

Ashton slumped against the door and continued to stare at everything one at a time, which made Thenia laugh.

"I'll take that as a yes. Come on, I'll warm up the shower, and then I'll take your clothes to the laundry room to wash later."

Once Thenia was out of sight in the bathroom, Ashton shook his head and stood back up.

"Be right back, Nia," he called into the other room.

Then he left the bedroom to apologize and thank the three other people in the house he loved more than anything.

His shower could wait.

Thenia Loris

It wasn't until nearly two in the morning that everyone had settled down to sleep for the night. They all hoped that the storm would pass by morning, but now that Thenia was lying in bed beside a sleeping Ashton, the sound of the rain thundering outside hadn't lessened, and she could feel it wasn't ready to move on yet.

She carefully reached over to tap the screen on Ashton's watch and then rolled her eyes when she saw it was nearly four in the morning. It looked like she'd been lying in bed for two hours already, and it was time to admit that she wasn't going to be sleeping anytime soon.

Thankfully, Ashton was so exhausted that she could extricate herself without waking him up. She pulled on a pair of sweatpants and then grabbed a sweatshirt to cover the t-shirt she'd stolen from Ashton. With one more look to ensure he was still asleep, she quietly exited the room, heading for the kitchen.

The house's emergency lighting was on along the baseboards in the hallway, and it gave her just enough light not to trip over her own feet. Before she reached the end of the hallway, a shadow moved in the dark. She opened her mouth to call out for help, but realized it was Alexander in his panther form. From what it looked like, he had been sleeping at the hallway entrance.

She put her hand over her heart and tried to steady her breathing and rapid heart rate.

"Holy shit, Alexander. You scared me half to death."

The cat, nearly invisible in the darkened house, padded over to her, pressed his forehead against the side of her leg, and then sat and stared up at her.

"It's fine. You just scared me. Are you sleeping out here?"

His tail twitched, and she remembered when Ashton had decoded his beast form's replies and guessed that was his version of yes.

"Why?"

He stared at her and blinked a few times, and she laughed softly. "Yeah, not yes or no. Stupid question. Better one, are you alright?"

He replied with a yes, and she smiled and nodded.

"Alright. Well, I can't sleep, and I've been staring at the ceiling for the past two hours. Figured I'd get up and do something with the extra energy."

Alexander nodded and then walked toward his bedroom. He stopped in front of the partially opened door and glanced over his shoulder at her, and then at the floor.

"Um...."

He looked at her again and then at the floor a second time. "Stay?"

Alexander chuffed and flicked his tail before he walked into the other room, the darkness beyond it obscuring him entirely. He returned in his human form only a minute later, wearing jeans and a T-shirt and grinning at her.

"Sorry, I don't want you wandering the house alone tonight."

His devoted nature warmed her, and she walked over to give him a hug. "Thank you for caring," she said.

He hugged her back, then released her and smiled. "You're getting better at understanding me."

Thenia indicated that they should head to the kitchen, where they would be less likely to wake the other three with their conversation. Once they were there, she flicked on the cabinet lighting and put water on for tea while Alexander dug around the fridge for something to snack on.

"I remembered what Ash had said about your tail flick."

Alexander chuffed. "Yeah. We all learned early on that we needed a way to communicate when I was in my panther form. Now Eileen teases me because I'll answer questions even when the other person doesn't realize I am."

"Is that how the two of you communicate so well?"

"Some of it. Some of it is also time. Eileen and I are the same age, so we've been basically inseparable since forever. School, home, sports, all of it."

Thenia leaned against the counter to wait for the water to boil, but then changed her mind and popped onto it to sit cross-legged.

"Must be nice to have someone like that."

"I'm very lucky. I'm thankful every day that Sue and Arthur took me in with Ash and Eileen. As...cold as it sounds, it could have been worse. None of the three of us remembers our parents, so there's nothing to miss or mourn."

Thenia thought of the couple and smiled at her hands in her lap. Then she thought about her parents. They had a love like Sue and Arthur did, but were too free-spirited to stay in one place. When a job opportunity came up on the other side of the world for one of them, Thenia hadn't had the heart to ask them not to go. She'd spent sixteen years watching her parents struggle against being tied down to one place with a child. Telling them not to leave her would have been selfish, so she encouraged them to go instead.

"Thenia?"

She blinked and smiled at Alexander, who handed her a bowl of fruit topped with a dollop of whipped cream and accompanied by a fork.

"Sorry, thanks."

"You okay? Looked awfully far into your head." He stabbed a berry in his own bowl and then stuck it in his mouth, leaving her space to answer.

"Ah, yeah. Was thinking about my parents. I'm envious. I didn't have a Sue and Arthur." She swirled the tines of her fork in the fruit topping but stopped and ate a raspberry.

"You had to have had someone, though. Right?"

She shook her head as she chewed.

"Hmm...."

"A few friends, my parents on the phone, and through letters, and then Lucus. Other than that, it was just me."

"I understand a bit better why you were worried that Serena was leaving the cottage. I think, in a way, you finally had someone at your side and didn't want to lose them. I'd feel similar if someone took Eileen from mine."

"Probably very similar, yeah."

They both ate quietly until the water started to boil, at which point she slipped from the counter and poured them both a cup of hot water. She passed Alexander a small jar of individual tea bags to choose from, and she picked one of the ones Serena had made. Then, she returned to her spot on the counter.

"Thanks for taking care of Ash earlier," Alexander said while he put the jar away.

"None needed. I think...Well, I think he feels like I did about Serena leaving the tiny house."

Alexander sighed but returned to his snack and cooling tea. "We shouldn't have left so soon after they passed. He was so...he seemed fine."

"It's interesting, when I first moved here, I could tell he was hiding a sadness just under the surface. Then we found Sue and

Arthur. It wasn't until then that I realized he hadn't wanted to come home."

"You mean to live?"

"Yeah. He said he did it because his job could be done anywhere, as long as he had his computer. But you and Eileen didn't have that option."

Alexander put his bowl down and crossed his arms in front of himself. "Damn it, Ash. Dude can't lie to us worth a damn, but this he somehow manages to hide?"

"It was important to him. He wanted you to continue living your life as you wanted to, without feeling like you were tied down to a house full of memories."

"I kind of want to kick his ass," Alexander said and then laughed softly. "Eileen's gonna feel even more guilty now."

Thenia put her palm on Alexander's shoulder. "It was his choice. Don't let her invalidate his gift to you both by telling him it was wrong to have given it."

She returned to eating and let Alexander think beside her. The rain outside had quieted, but it was still coming down substantially, and she stared out of a nearby window into the darkness beyond the glass.

"How do we save her?"

When Alexander answered her, she realized she'd spoken the words aloud.

"Actually, I think we have to ask for help. Without knowing what they gave her and without Sue's assistance...not even Eileen and I can narrow down something from nothing. Whatever it was, it's incredibly slow acting. Or possibly something even stranger because, as of right now, Serena seems fine."

"How is that possible?"

"No idea," Alexander blew over his tea and said nothing more about it.

Thenia sipped more of her own and enjoyed the company

beside her rather than feeling the need to talk. At one point, she saw a glint of metal on Alexander's finger, and it made her smile.

"May I ask you something? And feel free to tell me to forget I asked if you'd rather not answer."

Alexander smirked. "Well, with a lead-up like that. Go for it."

"You're wearing Arthur's ring, right?"

He turned his hand over and looked at the band on one of his middle fingers. "I am. Eileen has Sue's."

"I know. Ash told me he was saving it for her."

Alexander sighed and lowered his hand. "To answer your real question, yes, I know why he gave it to me and didn't keep it for himself. I appreciate the gesture, but...."

"It's not hard to see how much you love her, Alexander."

He said nothing in response for a few minutes, but then went to wash his mug and bowl.

"I'm sorry. I didn't mean to make you uncomfortable."

"You didn't. You're right. I do, but that's just not an option."

Thenia slipped from the counter, carried her dishes over to the sink, and rinsed them.

"I understand, and I won't pry, but thank you for telling me."

He smiled weakly and then passed her the kitchen towel to dry her hands.

"Ready to sleep yet?"

She was about to say no, but then she yawned so hard her whole body shook, and Alexander chuckled.

"Guess so," she grinned. "You good?"

"I am. I'll walk you back and then change. I can hear and smell better in my beast form."

"Okay. Thank you for the company."

He gestured for her to lead, and when she was safely back in the bedroom with Ashton, she sighed. Those two would figure out what they were to each other—or they wouldn't, and they'd stay as they were.

Either way, Thenia would leave it to the Fates.

Chapter 26: Access Altered

July 2024, Maine, USA | Ashton Giri

Serena shifted beside Ashton. They sat on the couch in the main house's living room together, his arm around her waist. With her movement, he held on a little tighter, glanced down, and watched as the tips of her ears turned pink.

"I don't think we have much of a choice, Ash," his sister said from the other side of the couch, where she had her feet up and in Alexander's lap.

"I hate to say it," Thenia yawned. "She's right."

Thenia had been unable to sleep the night before, and when she'd left their room, Ashton had been ready to go after her when he heard her talking to Xander. He returned to bed and left her in his brother's care. Now, her head was slumped on her arms, pillowed on the edge of the couch, her body exhausted from the day and night before.

"You don't have to give them many details, I don't think," Eileen added. "You already submitted a tamper report, right?"

"Yeah," he rested his head against the couch and shut his eyes.

When they'd woken up that morning, the storm had reduced

to a normal amount of wind and rain, and the house's main power had returned just after dawn. His grandparents had not.

No matter what he'd tried, their room beneath the house stayed dark, and he and Eileen ran out of ideas on how to get them back. Ashton held on to the hope that when his Gram mentioned stasis, she was talking about themselves. Stasis was something they could come back from.

Serena had woken up with a slight fever, cough, and aches throughout her body. Eileen and Xander had given her a once-over, but they couldn't determine whether she had gotten a cold from the rain or her symptoms were related to the injection. They couldn't say for sure which.

"Ash," Serena said softly.

He looked up and saw she was pointing to his watch, the screen of which was lit and flashing.

He groaned, "Awesome, just what we need."

"What is it?" Thenia asked through another yawn.

"Work," he said before kissing Serena's temple and carefully getting up from the couch. "I'll be back in a few minutes. Hopefully."

The four of them nodded as he left the room and headed down the hallway and into the office. Across the room, his cell phone sat, powered off, shattered, and less than useless. The new one that Xander had ordered for him wouldn't arrive for a few days, so for now, Ashton sank into his chair and logged into his machine and then the AIS system.

As soon as he was verified, the message his watch had notified him about popped up in a window, obscuring everything beneath it. It was a response to his report of the power line tampering.

Ashton Giri,

Thank you for submitting your report. The results of our investigation conclude that your recounting was accurate and complete. Furthermore, we have found no evidence of system breaches or malicious attack attempts on our systems.

Consider this case closed.

"Course it is. All you care about is your system."

He rolled his eyes and closed the message, but an instant later, a second message filled most of the screen.

Ashton,

It has come to our attention that you recently accessed a confidential file pertaining to an operation that concluded nearly three decades ago.

Ashton felt his heart skip a beat. He had the proper clearance level to view that file. There should have been no reason for his accessing it to be flagged as suspicious.

Considering this behavior, other recent database searches, your report of electrical tampering, and Sue Giri's recent passing, we are opening a case to investigate further and assess the risk. Until we reach a decision, consider yourself on paid leave.

Someone will contact you soon to follow up and record a statement.

"You're fucking kidding me!" he rotated to shout over his shoulder, "Eileen!"

He didn't want to risk the message closing if he walked away because he knew that once it did, he'd be fully locked out of the system. The sound of running footsteps grew closer, and the office door opened without a knock.

"Ash? What is it?"

"Hurry up, read this before they lock me out."

Eileen rushed to do as he'd asked, and he watched as her eyes shifted from confusion to shock and then to outrage.

"What the hell?"

"I know. I have clearance for that file. This should be an—"

They both watched his machine as all the windows closed, and his access was revoked. Within fifteen seconds, he was looking at the desktop of his personal machine.

"Well, shit," Eileen snapped and began to pace in a small circle before she shook her head. "Come on, nothing we can do in here now, and you worried everyone else. Come back out."

He nodded and followed his sister out of the room, not bothering to shut the door, as he was now a regular citizen with nothing sensitive or needing to be hidden from those around him.

"Ash, what's up?" Xander asked from the couch, a frown on his lips and brow.

"I've been suspended." Ashton returned to where he'd been sitting earlier, and both Serena and Thenia observed him with narrowed eyes.

"For?" Xander asked.

Ashton glanced at his sister, who thankfully began to explain everything while he tried to think through the reason behind the department's actions and possible solutions.

"Um," Thenia said a minute later, "Doesn't that mean you no longer have access to their poison database, too?"

"Fuck me," Ashton dropped his head into his hands. "I hadn't even gotten that far in my head yet, but yeah."

"Ash," Eileen said, and he glanced up at her. "We don't have a choice now. We need that database. Whatever this is, Xander and I don't know it. Neither does Stephan."

"You told him?" Ashton asked, slightly surprised.

"We did," Xander nodded. "He's not just a client anymore, Ash. We trust him. We'd be stupid not to ask him."

"Who's Stephan?" Serena asked curiously.

"Our main employer," Eileen answered. "Sanguiste. One of the good ones."

Serena nodded.

"Fine," Ashton said, swallowing roughly. "We ask the AIS. I'm just a normal person now, so I'll have to submit through the front door, and I have no idea how long my report will take to be processed."

"Then let's get it over with," Xander said and got to his feet. "Come on, I'll help fill in the details we already know."

With another groan, Ashton got to his feet and smiled weakly at Thenia and Serena before following Xander back down the hall and into the office again.

Serena Ainsley

Once Ashton and Alexander had left the room, Eileen got to her feet, and her eyes flicked between her and Thenia.

"I'm ready for some food, how about you two?"

Serena agreed in a whisper, but Thenia had barely opened her mouth to reply before she yawned again.

Eileen chuckled at her. "You, close your eyes for a bit. I'll make some breakfast."

"Don't need help?" Thenia asked, her words slightly slurring.

"Nope. Keep an eye on Serena for me." Eileen glanced at her and winked.

Eileen and Xander had discussed Serena's condition with her when they woke up that morning. While both of them were confused, they'd agreed she wasn't showing symptoms of anything abnormal beyond getting sick from the entire escapade in the rain. Eileen still wanted to keep an eye on her and continue to look into what she could have been given, but for now, they had nothing to go on. The only oddity seemed to be how quickly she'd become ill, but neither had an answer.

"Thank you," Thenia said sleepily, and Eileen left for the other room.

"Nia?"

"Hmm?" Thenia said from where she was still draped over the arm of the couch.

"Come snuggle?" Serena blushed and looked away, but

Thenia moved, put her head in Serena's lap, and wrapped her arms around her waist.

"Mmm, much better."

Serena stifled her giggle but carefully ran her fingers through Thenia's hair. She was pleased when her shoulders loosened nearly immediately. Only a minute later, her breathing evened out, and she had fallen asleep. Serena rested her head on the back of the couch and closed her eyes, too.

If she strained her ears, she could hear the slight mumble of voices down the hall with the occasional click or clang from Eileen in the kitchen. After all the years Serena had spent in the garden, it was only now that she truly felt at home.

In the past, whenever Alexander returned home, Serena left the property while he visited. Both out of respect and fear, but she kept returning to Arthur's side after the panther had gone.

It hadn't been long since she'd been talking with Arthur as a human, but already, less than a day without him felt...hollow. She didn't understand the AIs like Ashton, but even Serena could tell he was scared for them and that they may never return.

Serena took a few deep breaths, or as deep as her crunchy lungs would allow. She couldn't shift into her base form but felt the urge to be close to her snake. It didn't take her more than half a minute to feel the warmth of her partner's soul flare within her chest. Instead of relinquishing her physical form to it, Serena greeted it like the old friend it was. Her chest hummed as the soul happily returned her greeting.

At this point, if she were comfortable shifting, Serena would have prayed to their god for assistance with the form shift, but she held back from speaking the call in her mind. What she did do was pray.

When she was a child, her parents would force all their children to pray to their god each sunlit hour of the day. Serena never had. While those around her offered themselves to a faceless watcher, she had been mentally slithering through the trees in some made-up forest.

Until a week after she'd left her home.

It had been a full twenty-four hours since she'd slept, and Serena had dozed beneath a shrub in a city garden. She'd felt the warmth of her partner's soul beside her and then heard a voice unknown to her. It only spoke one sentence to her, but it was something Serena would never forget.

You are free, Kin.

Even now, Serena felt a smile on her lips as she remembered the joy and pride she'd felt that day.

Ever since, Serena prayed to her god every few weeks to express her thanks and pay homage to the god who had earned her devotion, not demanded it. It was now that she felt the urge to reach out to the ever-present watcher and offer up her gratitude and fears.

Mother Kin, hear my soul as I provide gratitude for my partner soul and my own. We...are finally home, Mother Kin. I have found those who make me happy and care for me. I have a family and a home...but they're being threatened. I am sick. Eileen and Alexander, another of our Kin, don't know what was done to me.

Serena sniffled and felt Thenia shift on her lap, but she didn't wake up.

I am afraid. I don't want to leave them. Please watch over me, and if...if it is my time, please, keep watch over Thenia and Ashton when I'm gone.

From the heart of the earth, the soul of the Kin, and the body of our Mother. To my partner, I pledge my flesh and accept theirs in return.

Serena didn't finish the words that would begin her shift into her snake form, but opened her eyes and lifted her head. Alexander was seated at the end of the couch by Thenia's feet with one of his ankles crossed over his knee. He caught her staring, and she blushed, lowering her head.

"I spoke mine last night after you'd fallen asleep," Alexander said.

"Hmm?"

He pulled his pant leg up a few inches above his ankle, and Serena saw a glint of metal. "You were speaking to Mother Kin a few minutes ago, right?"

Serena nodded, but lowered her eyes to Thenia's sleeping face, which was snuggled into her lap.

"I—" she swallowed her words instead of voicing them.

"Eileen mentioned that she'd not seen your coin when she examined you. She admitted there were other places you could keep it close to you, but..." Alexander sighed. "She knows of mine and how important it is to me, and expressed concern for your possible lack of one."

"I don't have one. Not anymore." Serena could barely breathe the words, let alone speak them aloud, but Alexander hummed in acknowledgment.

"Would you like one?"

Serena's head whipped up, and she saw Alexander's observant gaze focused on her.

"I—I mean, I don't—" She closed her eyes and took a deep breath before trying again. "I no longer belong in a den. My soul coin was taken from me when I left mine."

"I understand. Would you like a new one, Serena?"

"What do you mean?" she asked, meeting his eyes again.

"If you were offered one, would you want to take it? I know you can shift without it. The myth of us needing our coin is just that—a myth."

"They would never return it to me," she said tightly.

Alexander watched her closely for a minute before he pushed to his feet and left the room. Serena would have called out to him if Thenia hadn't been sleeping peacefully, but she needed the rest. Serena patted the couch around her to find her cell phone and text him an apology, but before she could find it, Alexander returned and walked over, kneeling in front of her so they were closer to eye level.

He glanced at Thenia and smiled warmly, but then he leaned forward and draped a delicate chain around Serena's neck and fastened it. When he sat back, a soul coin was in his palm, threaded on the chain, the face of a panther etched onto the side facing up.

"Neither of my parents ever wore theirs on missions," he ran his thumb over the etching, a sorrowful smile on his lips. Then he smiled up at her. "I'd be honored to join my claw with your den, Kin."

Serena's eyes widened, and she put her palm over her mouth to hold back the gasp that had rushed to the surface.

Alexander gently released the coin, which settled against her t-shirt on her sternum. Then he got to his feet and rested his large palm on the top of her head.

"Don't worry, little sister, we'll figure this out. I promise."

He ruffled her hair just like one would do to a young one, smiled once more, and left the room toward the kitchen.

Serena had no idea how much time had passed before Ashton froze in the doorway and rushed to her side.

"Serena, what is it?"

She shook her head and sniffled, finally lowering her hand from her mouth, but she slipped it down to the chain and clutched the soul coin. Ashton's eyes followed her movement, and the anxiety fled his features.

"Ah. Xander." Ashton smiled and leaned forward to press a kiss to Serena's lips. "I'll go help with breakfast."

She nodded and watched him go, still holding tightly to the small metal coin on a thin chain of gold.

Chapter 27: Sacrifices

July 2024, Maine, USA | Ashton Giri

It had felt as if the rain would never stop. Finally, the day prior, the sun broke through, and the storm passed. What hadn't passed was Ashton's worry because Serena's condition continued to worsen.

The morning after she was attacked, Serena seemed to be on the mend, but later that evening, she began coughing. Then, her fever spiked. By the next day, even Ashton could hear the fluid in her lungs as her breaths grew shorter, and she began to wheeze.

It had been three nights since she was attacked, and so far, all he'd heard from AIS after asking for help was silence. He'd even tried asking some of his coworkers if they'd heard anything about his case, but they'd all said the same thing—nothing. Apparently, everyone had been told that if Ashton contacted them, they were not permitted to tell him anything, or they'd risk their own positions. After someone let that little tidbit slip, he stopped asking and unintentionally forcing his friends into tough positions.

Thenia and Xander had taken turns staying with Serena, though she was asleep most of the time, while he and Eileen had called everyone they knew and searched through every accessible database and resource for more information or anything that might help. In the end, they continued to come up with nothing.

Which was why Ashton was currently moping, his head pillowed on his arms where he was slumped over his desk. He could hear Eileen's nails clicking on her keyboard beside him, but she stopped abruptly.

"Ash."

"What?"

"Look."

He lifted his head to see what she was talking about and saw her pointing to one of the monitors which displayed a live feed from one of the property's cameras. This one was pointed at their front gate, and Eileen was directing his attention to the large, blacked-out sedan that had just pulled up to it.

"Can you make out the plate?" he asked, squinting to see it himself.

"No. Do you think it's the AIS?"

"Possibly, but they would have notified me. Well, I think?"

Eileen got to her feet. "I'll get Xander."

Ashton didn't take his eyes off the screen as his sister left, but when one of the car's rear doors opened, and someone in a dark suit and sunglasses stepped out, Ashton merged with the system and looked through the camera directly to get a closer look. A second person exited the other side of the car. Ashton was positive he knew neither of the strangers, but was also reasonably confident that Eileen was correct and they were from AIS.

The smaller of the two figures had light hair, cut into a severe bob just above the shoulders, and was the one to approach the call box with a stiff, business-like stride. In contrast, the broad-shouldered, dark-skinned, dark-haired man stood at their back with a relaxed yet fully alert posture, somehow managing to look both intimidating and approachable.

Ashton pulled himself out of the system just as the gate's intercom buzzed.

"Can I help you?" he replied through the gate's keypad speaker using the microphone connected to the system's PC.

"We're here about the report from A. Giri regarding the attack that occurred three days ago."

"Understood. I will open the gate, but my sister will greet you. Please have your identification ready. You understand, I'm sure."

"Of course. Sir." The feminine voice was clipped, and if Ashton had to guess, it revealed her annoyance at being forced to prove herself to anyone.

Ashton closed the intercom connection, went to the office door, and shouted down the hallway to Eileen, who promptly popped out of her bedroom.

"Can you greet them? They're here about the report. I told them to present their IDs, but something feels off."

Eileen nodded. "I'll be right back then."

As she walked away, Xander exited his own room, putting his watch on as he went.

"Ash, have Thenia monitor the cameras while we deal with this," Xander instructed and followed Eileen.

Ashton had to admit that having Thenia monitor from the cameras would be extremely helpful and keep her safe and out of the way. He jogged to Eileen's room, where Serena was sleeping, and opened the door only enough to whisper inside.

"Nia, can you help me?"

"Sure."

He heard her get off the bed and set something aside before she met him in the hallway, shutting the door behind herself.

"How can I help?"

He quickly briefed her on the newcomers and Xander's suggestion, and she agreed without hesitation.

"Yes, of course."

She followed him to the office, where he gave her a crash course on all the cameras and instructed her on how to discreetly alert him and Eileen if there was an issue. Then, he demonstrated how to secure the entire system if a major issue arose.

"You're sure you're okay with this?" he asked, frowning at her sitting in his desk chair.

"If this is how I can help, then I'm more than okay. Just be careful."

"I promise." He leaned down and kissed her once before leaving the room and shutting the door. Then he locked her in— or rather, the strangers out.

By the time he'd made it to the front entryway, Eileen was leading their two guests inside, and Xander was coming in behind them.

"Thank you for coming, please come in," Eileen said politely. Her eyes met Ashton's briefly, and she stepped aside for the strangers. "Can I get either of you something to drink or to eat?"

"No, thank you, Miss," the large man said.

Then the agent with the light hair answered, "I'm fine, thank you for the offer."

Xander shut the door and stayed off to the side, his wrists crossed behind his back.

"I take it you're Mr. Giri," the man said, stepping forward to offer his hand.

"I am," Ashton said. "Thank you for coming."

The woman didn't move but nodded once at him while the other man continued talking.

"Not a problem. From the sounds of it, there's been quite a commotion around you lately. We were told that you submitted a civilian report."

"I have. On the morning of my probation. I hadn't had a chance to submit through the internal reporting tool before I was locked out."

"Why didn't you submit it directly after the attack?" the woman accused sharply.

Neither of the individuals had removed their sunglasses, but

Ashton could feel the scorn in the unknown woman's eyes from behind her blacked-out lenses.

"Actually, that's what I was doing. That was the first chance I'd had to report it. After the attack, we were very focused on treating our injured. It was only while my sister," he nodded to Eileen, "had been helping her into dry clothes and doctoring her wounds that I had the opportunity to slip away. That was when I reported the tampering. Before I had the chance to submit another report regarding the attack, I was needed again, and it remained that way until the early morning hours when we all were forced to sleep."

"Forced?" the agent asked, her eyebrow raising behind the frames of her glasses.

Eileen chuckled. "If you don't listen to your body, it will always ensure it's heard. We all basically sat down for a minute and then passed out until morning."

"Understandable," the man said with a knowing smile.

"In the morning, I made sure everyone was safe and as well as they could be, and then I reported the attack. Truthfully, I was sidetracked when I saw the two emails from the AIS in my inbox. I'm sure you're aware that the user is immediately locked out after a suspension notification."

"We are," the man nodded. "Well, all of that checks out, and if your file and personnel report are to be believed, it would have been more suspicious had you filled out paperwork and not taken care of those in need first."

"What does that mean?" Ashton asked, crossing his arms in front of him. Sure, he knew everyone had a personnel file, but he'd never had a run-in with HR, so there shouldn't have been anything except the basics in his.

"You have an extremely positive reputation, Mr. Giri. Your file is filled with feedback from colleagues and those you've assisted over the years."

His sister chuffed and drew everyone's attention, but she

shook her head and smiled. "Sorry, proud sister moment. Nothing important."

The man grinned. "You have a right to be proud."

The incredibly unfriendly woman cleared her throat, and the levity was sucked from the room.

"As much as this conversation is enlightening, I'd like to ask a few questions about the girl who was attacked."

Ashton plastered a plain smile on his face. "Yes. What would you like to know?"

"I need to see her."

"Ah—" he started to argue, but Eileen stepped beside him.

"She's sleeping right now. Her condition has gotten worse. I'm the one who treated her. Perhaps I can help answer your questions."

"Are you a physician?"

"I am not, however, I have—"

"Then I care not for your answers."

Behind the two strangers, Xander shifted from one foot to the other, but the movement was so small Ashton only noticed it because of his familiarity with his brother.

"Of course," Eileen retorted with an exaggeratedly cheery smile. "If you'll follow me."

Ash's watch vibrated once against his wrist as Eileen and the stuffy woman followed her deeper into the house.

"I'd like to ask you a few more questions while they take care of that, if that's alright."

Ashton returned his focus to the other man, who appeared to be fulfilling the good cop role of the pair.

"Sure, would you mind if we went into the other room? Still a bit sore from the storm prep and clean up." Ashton smiled, this one genuine. "I'm better suited behind a keyboard."

The man and Xander laughed, the latter shaking his head but grinning at him.

"Not at all," the agent said.

Ashton led the way to a formal sitting room with a noteworthy fireplace. This room had less of the family charm and more of the "if we invite you in here, do not overstay your welcome" vibes.

Except for when the fireplace was lit, it had been rare for anyone to spend much time in this room other than his Gram. She used to hide out in it when she needed a quiet evening and time away from three chaotic children. Ashton wasn't even sure any of them had even entered the room since their grandparents had passed.

He glanced at his watch as they walked the message from Eileen.

If Xander leaves, don't panic. We'll keep her safe.

Ashton tried not to groan at his sister's attempt at soothing him, but she only succeeded in making him even more anxious. He tried to remember that the two of them were incredible at their jobs, and that this was likely nothing compared to the issues they had handled in the past. Not that that revelation made him feel better, but that was a subject to brood over another time.

"Please, have a seat," Ashton said, sitting opposite the man who lowered himself onto the large couch.

To Ashton's surprise, Xander came to stand beside the chair Ashton had chosen and leaned casually against the back of it.

"What can I help answer?" Ashton asked.

"Well, first, I'd like to offer my condolences," the man nodded to Xander as well, "to both of you. Your grandmother was a kind woman, and though I only crossed paths with her once, she was always warm and willing to assist the new recruit with big shoes to fill." The man smiled with what seemed to be genuine appreciation for Sue.

"Thank you. It's been…."

Xander finished for him, "Difficult, but we'll continue to make her proud. There is evidence of that in Ashton's file."

"Agreed. Well, please know that there are those of us still feeling her loss. Not like your family, I'm sure, but in our own way."

Ashton nodded, his throat thick, and he inwardly scolded himself for losing focus on their current predicament, even if it was only for a few moments.

"Okay, well. Now to the bureaucratic stuff," the agent said, his demeanor stiffening.

It wasn't lost on Ashton that the man hadn't removed his glasses, and he'd bet neither had the woman in the other room. Other than being reasonably confident neither of them had fangs, leaving aside the fact that it was nearly noon and clear skied, Ashton had no idea which of the magical races either of the strangers was. Which meant he also had no idea if one of them was a mechanite, or had green witch hearing, or any other number of capabilities that required them all to be overly cautious.

"I'd like to go over the timeline of events with you. Can you confirm the date of Sue and Arthur Giri's passing?"

"Why is that relevant?" Ashton snapped, but Xander placed his palm on Ashton's shoulder, and he closed his mouth.

"While many considered Sue an honorable and ethical individual, she did have enemies. We are merely trying to rule out possible suspects that would have wanted to harm her and, instead, have gone after you in her absence."

Xander lightly increased his pressure on Ashton's shoulder before removing it again.

"March twenty-ninth," Ashton answered.

"Thank you. Can you tell me how long the woman who was attacked has lived here? I believe her name is S. Ainsley."

"Correct. Serena, her name is Serena. A little over a month."

"And what is your relationship to this woman? She is a registered paranam. Snake, correct."

Ashton clenched his jaw but forced himself to respond, "Correct. I don't see how our relationship is any of your business."

The stranger glanced over Ashton's shoulder at Xander and then back to him. "Mr. Giri, please. I'm only trying to understand the full situation. I'll ask a different version of the same question. Is it possible that Miss Ainsley was attacked because you two are in a relationship, and she can be considered a pressure point on you?"

"That is correct, though we have no evidence of that being the case," Xander answered before Ashton could.

"Thank you," the man said to Xander with an appreciative smile. "In your report, you mentioned receiving threatening letters in the mail. You have no idea who the sender is?"

"No."

"While we have been dispatched to investigate the tampering with your systems and the report of violence, there is also the reason you've been suspended to address. What is the reason you have accessed the file pertaining to the deaths of Alwin and Adeline Giri and Desta and Alexia Yoru?"

"I have every right to be in that file. My clearance is—"

The man raised his palm. "I am not here to discuss that case with you, nor any issue of conduct. I simply need to find out if it's related."

Ashton sighed. "Fine. We didn't know."

"Know what? About the file?"

"About any of it," Xander answered. "We knew our parents had been killed on a job, but that was it. Ashton found a reference to the case in Sue's belongings, and only then did we learn more about the operation."

Ashton looked down at his hands in his lap to hide his expression. Xander hadn't lied, but he'd come damn close, and Ashton didn't want to screw anything up by exposing that with his lack of a poker face.

"I see. Are you aware of the specifics of the operation?"

"No," Xander answered again. "Only what's in that file, which I will note, sounded heavily redacted, but, personally, I've learned enough to satisfy my curiosity and get closure."

"You were shown the file?"

"No. Ashton was careful not to reveal information he wasn't allowed to." Ashton glanced up when Xander laughed softly. "In fact, it drove both Eileen and me crazy, but we respected his struggle and didn't ask anything further. We trust him. If there were more that he could tell us, he would have, but we refused to put him in a position that would compromise his job, ethics, or safety."

"I see. Well, I admit, I'd want to know what was in that file if it had been my parents."

"We were incredibly young. Sometimes, it's better to leave those faint memories as they are," Xander said solemnly.

"Interesting. Alright, well, back to the assault. Do you think the uncovering of your family's past could be what sparked the recent events?"

"No. I received the first letter before I accessed the file," Ashton answered. "I guess it's possible that they are related, but from my perspective, the timing is off."

"Have you been confronted by anyone suspicious recently? Followed in town? Strange door-to-door salesmen? Anything?"

"Yes," Xander answered, and Ashton once again struggled to keep his face blank. "There was a transmogromorph who confronted the groundskeeper a few weeks ago. They were posing as her abusive ex-fiancée."

"You are referring to Miss Loris?"

"Correct."

"And what happened to this assailant?"

"We ran him off," Ashton answered.

The man nodded. "Well, I think that's all of my questions. Oh, before I forget." He reached into his suit jacket, pulled out a sealed envelope on AIS stationery, and held it out to Ashton.

"What is this?" Ashton asked, hesitating to take it.

"Your department head asked me to give it to you. She expressed her regret for not attending Sue's funeral. I gather they were quite close."

Ashton accepted the letter and set it on his lap. "Thank you for delivering it," he said.

"Not a problem." The man hesitated but then glanced over his shoulder toward the entryway and back at them. "If I may offer you one unsolicited piece of advice, Mr. Giri."

Ashton nodded.

"I hear you're on the shortlist for a Director position. As I said, I read your personnel file. You would make a great department head."

"Thank you. I'm not interested, but I appreciate the confidence in me."

The man pulled out his phone, frowned, and looked around the room for something. Xander stepped forward and held out his unlocked phone to the man, who stared at it before nodding. He took it, typed something out, and passed it back to Xander. The device was barely back in Xander's hand before they heard Eileen and the other woman in the next room over and headed their way.

"Thank you for your assistance," Eileen said before stepping into the room and immediately making eye contact with Xander.

"How is she?" Ashton asked.

"I am uncertain," the harsh woman answered. "I have taken a blood sample and will return it to the lab for testing." The agent looked at her counterpart. "Come on, we're done here."

All of them stood and walked the two agents back to the front door, where the woman walked directly out the door held open by Xander without a word. The man paused for a moment.

"Thank you for your time."

"Thank you for coming," Xander said, holding his hand out to shake the other man's. "Mr...."

"Zareb. We'll be in touch." With a final nod to them, the man left the house, and Xander closed the door.

Ashton immediately merged with the mechanics in his watch and accessed the front camera. He watched the two people enter the car on the same sides they'd exited from, and less than a minute later, the car pulled away without incident. When he opened his eyes, Xander held out his cell phone for Ashton to read.

"Ash, I think we need to talk," he said.

Ashton read the two sentences typed on the digital notepad Xander had provided to the male agent.

You should take the job. They won't stop.

Ashton glanced up at Xander and then at his sister. When he saw Thenia enter the room, he leaned against the wall.

"This is all my fault, isn't it?" Ashton asked, his voice scarcely a whisper.

"Ash," Thenia said tentatively. "What was in the letter?"

"Oh," he pulled it from his back pocket and then looked at Xander. "All good?"

"Yes, I don't believe Zareb is anything but a pawn. They wouldn't risk giving anything dangerous to a minion who could screw up and draw attention."

Ashton ripped open the envelope and unfolded the letter. It was handwritten, and he recognized the penmanship from letters his Grandmother had received over the years.

Ashton,

My deepest condolences on your loss, and my apologies for not being able to attend the funeral. Know that I celebrated both Sue and Arthur's lives in my own way, and I miss them dearly.

I hope you know you always have someone here if needed. Your grandmother meant a great deal to me, and I would be more than happy to be an ear or shoulder to lean on should you need one. Now or in the future.

That said, I am aware of your current situation and would like to offer one piece of advice. Be honest. There are far too few people in this world with your morals and empathetic compass. Don't let others' actions taint your goodness. I know you are not naive enough to think there are not those out there who wish only to use you and that kindness. Sometimes, we must do what we do not want in order to protect others.

Be well,

Josephine

Ashton lowered the letter and looked up at the three curious faces staring back at him. He absentmindedly handed the letter to Eileen and opened the front door.

"I need…" he sighed. "I'll be back later."

Then Ashton left the house and started walking.

Chapter 28: 925

July 2024, Maine, USA | Thenia Loris

Thenia felt the bed dip beside her, waking her up. She faced the center of the bed and kept her eyes closed until Ashton settled. Once he had, she squinted through the dark and saw he had his back to her. He was still atop the blankets, his clothes from the day still on. She reached out to rub his back, but she'd barely touched the tips of her fingers to his back when he flinched, and she yanked them back.

"I'm sorry. I didn't mean to startle you," Thenia whispered.

"It's fine."

"Ash?"

He didn't respond, and she moved closer to him. When she rested her forehead on his back, his entire body stiffened. She sighed and then scooted back to her side of the bed and rolled over to face away from him.

"I'm here if you need me, Ash. Sleep well."

Thenia shut her eyes again, her heart breaking for Ashton and the turmoil he was going through. Eileen had informed her about Ashton's job offer and why, months ago, he turned it down. Once Thenia knew the background, she understood why he'd walked out and only now returned. It was evident that the

AIS was using the current chaos and threats to pressure Ashton into accepting the position. And she was fairly certain that now he believed not only that Serena's attack was his fault, but also that he was the obstacle to her recovery with his decision not to take the job.

"Did Eileen tell you about the letter?" Ashton whispered sometime later.

"She did, and the job offer."

They both went quiet again, and she was slipping back into sleep when Ashton whispered into the darkness.

"Protect them all."

Before she could respond, sleep enveloped her in its comforting blanket.

Thenia yawned and sat up in bed. She stretched and wasn't surprised to find that Ash had already woken up and left the room. She just hoped he was feeling better after a good night's sleep. One of her sweatshirts was draped over the end of the bed, and she pulled it over her head. Then she went into the bathroom to wash her face and brush her teeth. When she felt more awake, she wandered into the hallway and paused to listen and see if anyone was up and in the kitchen.

Alexander was speaking in hushed tones to Eileen, and Thenia made a slight noise to alert the two of her presence and cover up whatever they were discussing so that Thenia couldn't accidentally overhear it.

"Morning, Thenia," Alexander said when she entered the room. His smile was bright and far too cheery for so early in the morning. "Feel better after some sleep?"

"I'm jealous. I could use a day to sleep in," Eileen said with a laugh.

"Wait, what time is it?"

Alexander chuckled. "Nearly one in the afternoon."

"What!" Thenia ran over to the other side of the room to see the clock over the stove. "Wow. I haven't slept that long in forever." She chuckled to herself and leaned on the counter.

"Yeah, well, did you wake that brother of mine, or is he still out cold?" Eileen asked, biting into a slice of apple.

Thenia glanced between them, and then Alexander stood up straighter.

"Thenia, Ash isn't still sleeping, is he?"

"N-no. He wasn't. I assumed he was out here."

Eileen cursed and set her bowl on the counter a bit harder than she had probably intended to, the loud crack echoing in the space filled with hard surfaces. Then she ripped her cell phone from her pocket and shut her eyes.

"Alexander…" Thenia asked hesitantly.

"We haven't seen him since he left yesterday."

"He came to bed, but he was still dressed and kept… flinching when I touched him. He asked if Eileen had told me about the letter. I said yes, and then I must have fallen asleep."

"What time was that?"

"I'm sorry, I don't know. I didn't check."

He nodded and watched Eileen, whose forehead became increasingly concerned with each passing minute. Then her eyes popped open, and she glared at Alexander.

"I'm going to fucking kill him myself," she snapped.

Alexander sighed and rested his head back against the cabinet behind him.

"Eileen?" Thenia asked, verging on panic.

"My stupid brother left. He took a flight to Montana just before dawn."

"Montana?"

"That's where the North American office is for the Alii Interface Syndicate and the Invisibles Department," Alexander clarified. He downed the water in his glass and nodded at Eileen, "I'll pack."

"Wait, what?" Thenia said and ran to block the kitchen's exit for both of them.

"We'll go get him. It's fine, Thenia," Eileen assured her.

"No, stop it." Thenia put her hand on her hips and glared at them both. "Tell me what's going on. Why is he going there, and why is that a bad thing?"

"Thenia, we think the AIS is using the attack to pressure him into taking that job," Alexander answered.

"Yeah, no shit. Figured that part out."

Alexander chuckled at her response.

"If they're willing to hold an antidote for Serena over his head, what else do you think they might do?" Eileen asked sternly.

Thenia's stomach sank. "Wait."

She felt the blood drain from her face and felt Alexander's firm grip on her arm holding her upright.

"Thenia, are you—" Eileen started, but Thenia cut her off.

"Book me a flight. I'll go."

"Absolutely not," Alexander and Eileen said in unison.

Everything started to slot into place the more Thenia thought about it. Serena's attack on the night of a storm. The power to the house being cut, and then the backups. A syringe with a mystery poison that didn't seem to have an effect. Sue and Arthur going into stasis on the same night. The night they needed them most. The night when someone had known how to get around a third-generation mechanite's system, was confident enough to break in with a panther paranam on the property, *and* knew to go after the weakest of them.

She tugged her arm from Alexander's grip and stood up straighter.

"Look, I need you to trust me. I understand what's happening, but I need to go after Ash."

"Thenia, no offense, but—"

"Eileen," Thenia snapped. "I get it. I'm not some super-assassin like you two, but I know things about this that neither of you does. You will be a liability to him walking in there with a third of the story. I won't need strength, just the complete set of data."

She watched as Eileen's eyes narrowed, and then she threw up her hands and paced in a circle.

"Hurry up and fucking pack," she said tightly after a minute of the motion. "Xander will get you to the airport. I'll book the flight. You have fifteen minutes."

Thenia nodded to her and then met Alexander's eyes before bolting to the back door and sprinting barefoot down the path to her house. She ignored the mud and burst through the front door of her little house, going directly into the laundry room to grab her bag and some clean clothes from the dryer. Then she rushed up to the library side of the loft, shoved her laptop and passport into the bag, and ran back down the stairs. She set her everything on the kitchen counter and went back into the laundry room to change into jeans and a t-shirt, then cleaned off her feet, pulled on socks, and slipped into her tennis shoes.

With one last look around, she grabbed her bag and hurried back to the main house.

After nearly eight hours, Thenia exited a cab and stared at the hotel before her. Eileen had found where Ash had booked a room for the night, and they were hoping he'd be too exhausted to go to AIS until the next day. It was a risk, but the only thing they had since he'd left his broken cell phone in Maine and was ignoring Eileen's attempts at reaching him—even her more creative and unorthodox ways.

Thenia hefted her bag higher on her shoulder and entered the hotel. She already knew Ash's room number, so she skipped the front desk, acting like she belonged there, and found the bay of elevators. It felt like forever until the doors opened, and even longer before she reached one of the higher floors. When the doors opened on the ninth floor, she took a deep breath and found room number 925.

She lowered her bag to her side and then knocked heavily on the door. It was nearly ten o'clock, but judging by Ash's sneaking out, he was probably awake and still brooding. When she heard footsteps approaching from within the room, she held her breath. The locks clicked, and Ashton opened the door.

"What do you— Nia!"

She glared at him, but seeing him safe and sound made her glare weak at best. Then she gave up and smirked at him instead. "Gonna let me in?"

"What the hell are you doing here?"

Ashton stepped aside to let her through, and when he closed and relocked the door, he rolled his eyes.

"Damn her. Eileen found me, didn't she?"

"She did. What else were we supposed to do? You left without a word." Thenia dropped her bag by the wall and crossed her arms in front of her.

"Yeah, intentionally. She shouldn't have been able to find me without breaking the code."

"And what if she did? Don't you think in a situation like this, fuck the code?"

"No! I left alone for a reason!"

His voice started to rise to match hers, and then, Thenia took a breath and spoke at a normal volume.

"Do you know what it took for me to get her and Alexander to stay in Maine?"

Ashton threw up his hands. "Well, at least I only have one of you to worry about!"

"You're accepting the job. Aren't you?"

"Of course I am! If this is all about me, then what else am I supposed to do?"

Thenia clenched her teeth and tried not to tell him everything she'd learned and planned since she realized he was gone. As difficult as it was, she needed to keep him and everyone else in the dark a little longer.

Ashton sat roughly in an armchair beside a small, conference-style table.

"Nia, I needed you safe."

She walked over and knelt at his knees so she could look up at his lowered face. "And what makes you think I'm safer without you? Hmm?"

"Because all of this stems from me."

"Ash, did you forget that *my* ex attacked us? Or that they hurt Serena in *my* home while she was with *me*?"

"Yes, but—"

"Ashton!"

He shut his mouth, and she stood up and glared down at him.

"I refuse to sit on my ass and watch the world go on around me anymore. I don't need you to protect me—to put me in a glass case, too fragile except for you to take out when *you* feel it's safe."

She watched as he raised his head slowly, understanding creeping into his features before he went pale.

"Not a day longer, Ash. If you can't love me for who I am and treat me like your partner, not your doll, then this isn't going to work."

He stared at her, unblinking, before he tipped forward, wrapped his arms around her midsection, and pressed his face into her stomach.

"I'm so sorry, Nia. I didn't realize."

She rolled her eyes, happy she'd gotten through to him but annoyed she'd even had to pull that card out in the first place.

"It's alright. I came after you, didn't I?"

He nodded against her. "Thank you...for coming to find me."

Thenia giggled. "Yeah, you owe me one. Eileen is scary when she's pissed."

Ashton laughed and nodded against her. "I can imagine. How pissed is she?"

"Alexander forbade her from coming to drop me off at the airport with him, *and* he took her passport with him."

Ashton looked up, his chin still on her stomach. "Why?"

"So she didn't give him the slip and beat me here."

He winced. "Great. He's going to make me pay for that."

She nodded. "Probably."

When he groaned, she didn't rule out assisting Alexander when they got home.

"I hesitate to ask…how's Serena?"

Thenia snorted. "Fucking pissed, but home, in bed, resting where she belongs. I'd be more worried about her tongue-lashing than anything your sister or Alexander have planned."

"Well, that's probably fair," he said with a small laugh.

"Do you have an appointment tomorrow, or are you just going in?"

"Ah," he released her waist and sat back in the chair, looking like a scolded child. "Noon."

She checked the clock behind him, then walked over to her bag and took off her shoes and socks.

"Why?"

"Why, what?" she asked, ensuring her phone was off airplane mode and that she hadn't missed any messages during her travels.

"Why do you ask?"

"I ask because you slipped away the last time I fell asleep." She smiled and walked back over to stand in front of him. "I woke up, after noon, alone, to find you gone."

He turned away, and she carefully knelt one leg onto the chair, outside of his thigh, and then the other, effectively putting herself above his lap. Ashton's gaze traveled from her knees up to her face, and she smirked.

"Not only do I want compensation, but I expect you to be tired enough not to be able to run away this time."

She watched as his eyes narrowed, and then he slid one palm up her thigh and to her hip.

"I won't."

When she sat back, fully putting her weight on his lap, he gripped her other hip with his free hand.

"Good."

She leaned forward but stopped, lips less than an inch from his.

"Nia?"

"Hmm?"

"I love you, and I'm sorry."

"You're forgiven, and I love you, too."

Ashton Giri

Ashton lazily ran his fingers up Thenia's spine, but he stopped when he realized what he was doing. He pressed a kiss to the top of her head where it lay on his chest, her soft, sleeping breaths tickling his exposed skin. His vibrant witch had done as she'd promised, and he was in no shape to run away again—not that he would. Unfortunately, he wasn't tired enough for his brain to stop.

Thenia's accusation that he'd been treating her like glass had been a bucket of cold water to his entire system. As soon as she pointed it out, he knew she was right. It didn't matter that he didn't mean to do it. He still had. Ashton was lucky she came after him instead of walking out.

His watch was still on his wrist, and Ashton texted Xander.

I'm sorry, and thank you for helping Thenia.

It wasn't more than a few minutes later that Ashton felt his watch vibrate.

You have to stop this, Ash.

I think it's safe for me to agree, but what am I stopping?

You're not alone, Ash. You don't have to protect us—especially not Eileen and me. We can take care of ourselves, but more than that, we're all we have left, so knock it off.

Ashton swallowed roughly. *I know.*

There were a few minutes of silence, and Ashton messaged again. *How is she?*

Fucking pissed.

I mean Serena, lol.

Fucking pissed, Ash. You're lucky to have Thenia. Not only did she put Eileen and me in our place, but she convinced Serena to stay in Maine.

I'm sorry.

I'm so pissed off at Gram and Pops, Xander replied a few minutes later.

Uhh...why?

For putting this shit on you. Their attempts to keep Eileen and me safer only put you at risk, and for what? I have no idea. What's more important than your safety?

I know, but there's no reason for all of us to be targets.

Ashton. If this were a job, we would have walked. You don't withhold information about the situation from your protectors—and before you say something about not needing protection, let me say with three decades of love for you—fuck off. We're family, and we protect each other. We need to know.

Ashton read the message from his brother a few times before audibly groaning.

"Ash?" Thenia slurred.

He winced. "Sorry, go back to sleep."

She tipped her head up to see his face and then propped herself up on one arm. "What's wrong?"

"Nothing. Well, just Xander. Nothing's wrong, we're just talking." Ashton held up his wrist, his watch visible.

"And?"

"He wants us to tell him and Eileen the full story."

Thenia frowned and rested her chin on his chest. "What's his rationale?"

"Exactly what you think it is," Ashton said, tracing his finger down Thenia's cheek. "They can't protect us with only half the information."

"Hmm...."

Thenia's brows furrowed as she thought about the situation, and a few minutes later, he watched her expression as she settled on her decision.

"What's the plan?" he asked with a smirk.

"I think he's right. I know you and the others think keeping them in the dark is safer, but we've seen that it doesn't matter."

"Okay."

She blinked at him, "Huh?"

"What? You're right."

"I am?" she said with a chuckle. "You're not going to argue with me or forbid it?"

Ashton frowned, slipped his palm to her cheek, and ensured she was looking at him. "No. I would never forbid anything, even this, but I agree with you. Not only are you a few steps more emotionally removed from the situation, but I never wanted to keep this from them in the first place. Gram did."

Thenia smiled and leaned into his palm.

"One sec," Ashton said, sending his brother another message.

You win. If you can wait until we get home, I'll explain. If not, take Serena downstairs and ask her to fill you both in. Gram's not here, and I never agreed anyway.

Chapter 29: Leverage

July 2024, Montana, USA | Thenia Loris

Thenia and Ashton drove a rented sedan and were nearly to their destination—the AIS's North American headquarters.

"I doubt you'll be able to come with me," Ashton said, breaking the silence.

"We'll see."

"Thenia?"

She glanced over and saw him staring at her, trying to figure out what she wasn't telling him. Eventually, he sighed and refocused on the road.

"Just be careful, please."

"I promise," she squeezed his right hand.

Thenia returned to absorbing the stunning landscapes they were driving through. The location the AIS had chosen to set up shop, however, many decades prior, was far out in the middle of nowhere, Montana. The reason for their visit aside, and the lack of Serena, Thenia was happy to be exploring someplace new again.

"See the arch?" Ashton asked and leaned over to point into the distance. "That's the start of the compound. You'll be able to see the ground-level building in a minute."

Sure enough, a minute later, what masqueraded as a ski lodge appeared on the horizon, and they were soon on a private road after passing beneath the metal arch he'd pointed out. Less than five minutes later, Ashton pulled the car into a free space and turned off the engine.

"Ready?" he asked.

"Yeah. Let's do it and go home." She smiled weakly but opened the car door and waited for Ashton to do the same.

Thenia must have been staring because she heard Ashton chuckle beside her as they walked.

"It's beautiful, isn't it?" he said, indicating to the building.

"It really is."

He opened the door for her, and the view got even better when she stepped into the pristine foyer. A highly polished wooden floor gleamed with the reflection of bright lights and plush seating spaces. On the far side of the room was a reception desk, making the space feel infinitely more like a lodge than a super-secret headquarters for the magical community. The ceilings were high, the windows were enormous, and a quiet fire flickered and crackled in a stone fireplace on one side of the room.

"Hello, may I help you?" a woman in a pressed pantsuit with light wavy hair said from behind the desk.

"Yes, I have an appointment. A. Giri," Ashton responded.

The receptionist typed a few things on the keyboard in front of her, and Thenia noted that she was neither a qondo nor a green witch, judging by her eye color.

"I see it. Thank you," she bent, pulled a badge from beneath the counter, and passed it to Ashton. "Please keep this on you and visible at all times, Mr. Giri."

"Thank you."

The woman switched to Thenia and smiled. "And what can I do for you, Miss?"

Thenia pulled an envelope from her purse and passed it to

the woman without a word. The receptionist set about opening it and reading it while Ashton looked sideways at Thenia while trying to remain neutral about the whole interaction.

A minute later, she re-folded the letter, placed it back into the envelope, retrieved a badge, and handed it and the letter over to Thenia.

"Please, as I told Mr. Giri, keep your badge on you and visible at all times."

"I will, thank you very much." Thenia smiled and then looked at Ashton. "Ready?"

He narrowed his eyes at her but said nothing. Instead, the woman behind the counter pressed a button somewhere, and the heavily carved wooden door nearest them clicked.

"Right through there, please."

Ashton led them through the door and down a long hallway that matched the decor of the rest of the building, before they came to a bank of elevators. He pressed the button to call one.

They said nothing as they waited, and Thenia would hazard a guess that they had been constantly watched and recorded since stepping out of the car—or maybe even earlier.

When the elevator arrived, Ashton gestured for her to get inside, looked at the panel, and selected one of the middle floors. The doors shut, and then a red light filled the car, and she glanced at Ashton.

"Scanning for contraband. Don't worry, this is normal."

She nodded and they began their descent below ground. The panel indicated that Ashton had chosen the Invisibles Department, which made sense considering it was the one he worked for and was likely where his boss was located, but it also worked out well for Thenia. The person she needed to see was also located on that floor.

"They'll already know you're not a mechanite, but to be safe, don't touch anything mechanical," Ashton warned as the car's bell chimed.

"Sounds fair enough. Thank you for the warning."

He stared at her a moment longer, his concern plainly visible, but then he nodded and exited the elevator with Thenia falling in step behind him.

They reached another reception room of sorts, except there were people in small stations that resembled a bank's teller setup than a reception desk. A few people sat in chairs in the center of the room, waiting for their turn, but Ashton bypassed them and went straight over to a single desk in a corner.

"Ashton?" a young man with a bright smile and dark eyes said energetically. "Dude, it's been ages since you've been in. How you been, man?"

Ashton smiled. "Been better, but also worse. You?"

"Fine, fine. Missing Sue's presence, though. How's Eileen doing?"

"She's fine. Same old shenanigans, really."

The man nodded and smirked at Thenia. "Sorry, rude of me. You're both here to see Roma, right?"

"Yes, please. She should have my appointment on her calendar," Ashton responded.

"She does. Saw it this morning. Go on back. It was great to see you. Stop by more often."

The man fist-bumped Ashton and gave Thenia a small wave as he unlocked a door to his side. Thenia followed Ashton into yet another space. This one was full of short hallways with two doors opposite each other at the end of them. The main hallway seemed to go forever, but Ashton randomly turned them right and down a side hallway that was wider than the others and had a few more doors in it. At the end of that hallway was a large frosted glass door. A woman in sunglasses and a dark suit stood outside it, giving Thenia the same impression as the two AIS agents who had come to Maine.

"We're here to see, Roma," Ashton said.

"She's been expecting you." The agent stepped aside, and Ashton thanked her before knocking softly on the glass.

"Come in, Ashton," a female voice said from inside.

Ashton opened the door and let Thenia enter before following her and shutting it again.

"Ashton!"

The coincidence of both her and Ashton needing the time of the same woman was not lost on Thenia.

A matronly woman stood behind a desk, her arms held out, a glowing smile forming as she approached them. She was classically beautiful, with her grey hair pulled into a tight braid that fell down her lower back, but her eyes held a weary look within them.

"Hello, Josephine," Ashton accepted her hug with a slight frown.

Thenia tried to assess the stranger discreetly, but Eileen had assured Thenia that, contrary to office politics, Josephine Roma had been one of Sue's greatest and oldest friends. Both Alexander and Eileen said that Thenia could trust her, but not to trust those around her or the environment itself.

"It's so nice to see you, kiddo. It's been far too long." She smiled and then looked at Thenia. "I'm sorry, how rude. I'm Josephine. Ash's boss, technically, but, more importantly, Sue's oldest friend."

"Hello, my name is Thenia. Thank you for taking the time out of your day to meet with us." She shook the woman's slightly cold hand and smiled.

"Honestly, anything for Ashton. Especially in person, considering how rare it is for him to come in to see us."

"It's not down the road or anything, Josephine," Ashton said with an eye roll.

She waved him off and indicated to a small sitting area. "Let's sit. Would either of you like something to drink?"

"I'm alright," Ashton answered and glanced at Thenia.

"Could I trouble you for some water?"

"Of course, my dear." Josephine walked behind her desk, opened a small refrigerator that sat beside another office door, and pulled out two bottles of water. She returned to hand one to Thenia and opened the other for herself.

"Thank you," Thenia said, accepting the bottle.

"Look, you already know why I'm here," Ashton said abruptly.

"I have my guesses. Have you finally decided to take the Director position?"

He scoffed. "As if I'm being given a choice."

Thenia cleared her throat as discreetly as she could manage, and Ashton continued.

"Yes. I'll accept the position, but I have conditions."

"You know I don't hold all the strings, but I promise to do what I can, provided they are within reason, Ashton."

He nodded. "The antidote—for Serena. I want it before I leave today."

Thenia saw something akin to regret flash briefly in her eyes before she hid it away again and nodded. "I believe it's been synthesized by the labs. Once we're finished, I'll call for a traveling unit."

"I need to stay in Maine. You know how much Gram and Pops loved that house, and Eileen and Xander aren't the type to settle in one place."

Josephine frowned. "Yes. I know. That will be a bit more difficult, but I can advocate for it. Is there a compromise of some sort if I'm rejected? One week a month in Montana or three months out of the year or something?"

"We can talk about it. I understand why wanting me on-site would be a sticking point. I'm not saying no, but I'd need to discuss it with the others first. Can I say yes, with a limit of no more than three months a year total, and then we can figure out the timing of those visits?"

"I think that's fair. As I said, I will try to get you your preference first."

Ashton nodded and glanced at Thenia before continuing. "I'd also like to see my parents' file. The *full* file."

"Provided you accept the position, you will have that clearance level inherently."

He sighed. "Lastly...I need those threatening us taken care of. It's clear we are out of our element, and Eileen and Xander can't be fully read in, which makes them vulnerable."

"You're asking for those responsible for the letters, the tampering, and the attack on Miss Ainsely to be found and for them to be held to account for their actions?"

"I am."

Josephine paused for a moment, but ultimately nodded. "I can take care of that. I can't promise you a timeline, but I will keep you apprised of the progress."

Ashton nodded.

"I have a few of my own negotiating points, Ashton," the woman said.

He glanced at Thenia but then nodded to Josephine. "Alright. What are they?"

Josephine's eyes flicked to the vase of flowers beside her on the table, and then she yawned, raising her palm to cover her mouth. Thenia would bet money that the woman had gestured to something across the room.

"Apologies, clearly I have not had enough caffeine yet today."

Ashton nodded slowly, indicating his understanding, and then Josephine looked at Thenia.

"I understand," she laughed lightly. "I, myself, find I am a slave to the caffeine gods," Thenia smiled.

Josephine chuckled softly and nodded. "Correct, my dear. As I was saying, though, you will need to sign a loyalty clause along with your other paperwork."

"Why? What have I done that warrants that level of distrust?" Ashton said sharply.

"You will have high levels of access, Ashton. It's only standard."

"Have you signed one?" Thenia asked Ashton's boss, who looked taken aback, but nodded in reply.

Ashton crossed his arms in front of him. "Fine, whatever. It's not like I wasn't operating as if I were under one already."

Thenia observed Josephine, who frowned sadly at her best friend's grandson.

"There's something else," Thenia said, speaking up. "What aren't you telling us?"

Josephine studied Thenia and then nodded. "There is." She looked back at Ashton. "You need to turn over the thumb drive and Sue and Arthur's programming to the AIS."

Thenia sighed, having guessed that was what all of this was about, but Ashton had apparently been taken by surprise as he paled.

"Wh-what?"

Josephine nodded. "We know about Sue's programming, and it's too dangerous to be in the hands of one mechanite."

"But the AIS having control over them is safer?" Thenia asked sternly.

"It is."

"No. Absolutely not," Ashton snapped. "I refuse."

"Ashton, I'm afraid my asking was only a courtesy. Whether you leave here with a new role or not, you will not be retaining their programming."

"Try me," Ashton growled.

"Ashton," Thenia warned, placing her palm on his forearm before looking back at Josephine. "Answer one thing for me, if you don't mind."

She looked sideways at Thenia but hesitantly nodded.

"What was Serena injected with?"

"What? How is that—" Ashton hissed, but Thenia squeezed his arm.

"You know what it was, don't you, Mrs. Roma?" Thenia pressed. "Or rather, you know what it wasn't."

The woman stared at her for a second longer before only saying, "Correct."

Thenia could feel Ashton beginning to shake slightly, and she dug once more into her purse, retrieving a second sealed letter.

"Well. Since that's the case, I'll assume that the attacks against us, the tampering Ashton reported, and Serena's fake poisoning were put into motion by the AIS. I think you might want to read this before saying another word."

She held out the letter, wax seal side up, a dark feather pressed into it. Josephine's eyes widened, and she stared from the seal to Thenia, then Ashton, and then carefully took the proffered letter.

"Thenia?" Ashton questioned warily, but she pressed her finger lightly on his arm to quiet him.

Josephine cracked the wax seal, her hands slightly trembling, before she pulled a crisp piece of paper from the envelope and began to read it. Thenia had no idea what Crow had put in either letter, but when she'd stopped past their shop before heading to the airport and told them what was happening, they'd simply nodded. Then they'd walked into the shop's back room and returned with the two envelopes a minute later. One was for getting her into the building, and the other was to provide information to Mrs. Roma if Thenia's hunch had been proven correct.

Once Josephine had read the letter, she folded it back up and returned it to the paper envelope before setting it on her legs and drinking a fair bit of water. Then she addressed Thenia with a nod.

"I understand and will relay the information."

"Thank you," Thenia replied. "Now, considering we no

longer need an antidote and Ashton has concluded his business, I believe we should be going." When she got to her feet, Ashton and Josephine did as well.

"Miss Loris," Roma said stiffly.

"Yes?"

"You'd do well to be careful with those whom you choose to associate with. The AIS *will* recover Sue and Arthur's programming. They will not stop. How many people will get hurt before that happens is up to you."

Thenia smiled. "Actually, I think it's up to AIS. Even knowing Sue and Arthur for the short time I have, I promise you this—they *will* corrupt their programming before they see another person hurt or become slaves to the AIS. You and I both know this, so I suggest that you impress upon those higher up within the AIS the importance of understanding *their* current position. They are not the ones with leverage. Not unless they want a blank, shattered thumb drive as their end goal."

Josephine glanced at Ashton, who was still pale but had taken Thenia's hand and was squeezing it tightly.

"Stay safe, Ashton. I will be in touch. For now..." she glanced at the letter in her hands. "Go home to your family, and...put a flower at Sue's grave for me."

"I will. Thank you," he said, his voice shaking.

Josephine nodded and then walked to her desk, never turning back around.

Thenia gestured to the door, and she and Ashton made their way back through the long hallway, into the elevator, and eventually out into the beautiful lobby, which Thenia was now convinced was a façade for the underground shadow government. When they got back into the car, neither of them spoke, and Thenia resumed sightseeing as Ashton drove them back to the hotel.

Once they were safely back in their room, Ashton put his

finger to his lips and closed his eyes. A minute later, he reopened them and collapsed onto the bed to stare at the ceiling.

"I don't even know where to start," he groaned.

She chuckled, set down her bag, and kicked off her shoes. Then she quickly texted her group chat with Alexander, Eileen, and Serena to say they were back at the hotel and safe. She also informed Eileen of Serena's mystery poison and promised to explain more later.

Then, Thenia set her phone on the table and flopped next to Ashton.

He pulled her into his side and shifted to tip his head down to look into her eyes. "What did you just do?"

She giggled. "Texted your sister?"

Ashton glared playfully at her.

"Sorry, yes. I suppose you have some questions."

Ashton's eyebrows raised. "Some?"

"Before the airport, I stopped to see Crow and told them what happened. Truthfully, I have no idea what they put in those letters. They simply wrote them, told me who to give them to, and when to use them."

"So you have no idea what Josephine's letter said?"

Thenia shook her head.

"Well, whatever it was, the dude's got some leverage."

"Apparently," she agreed. "However, what she said wasn't incorrect. They won't stop trying to get Sue and Arthur's programming."

"I know. I think that's why Gram went into stasis. She obviously knew something about the night of the storm that we didn't."

"For now, I think we just have to wait and watch. It's their move."

"Yeah, I guess it is." Ashton kissed Thenia lightly and then smiled against her lips. "Want to go home?"

"Since the moment I got here," she grinned. "I need Serena cuddles."

"You and me both." Ashton's smile faltered. "Thenia, thank you again for coming to do this with me."

Thenia kissed his cheek, sat up, and held out her hand. "Come on, we've got packing to do and a plane to catch."

Chapter 30: Fall

July 2024, Maine, USA | Serena Ainsley

Serena was wrapped in a blanket, sitting on the couch in the main house, waiting for Alexander to return home with Ashton and Thenia. Tissues surrounded Serena on the floor, her hair barely braided, and she desperately needed a shower.

Eileen was pacing the floor a few feet from Serena and mumbling to herself about how stupid her brother was and how she was going to kill him. Occasionally, Eileen would switch to Alexander and how he'd taken her passport, so she couldn't sneak off to get Ashton herself.

The entire situation made Serena laugh, which, in turn, made her cough. Most of the chaos had occurred while she'd been sleeping, and even though she was pretty sure she remembered Ash coming to say goodbye to her, she wasn't entirely sure it wasn't a fever dream either. Thankfully, the grossness in her chest had begun to break up the day before, and she was already feeling less sick and was now more exhausted than anything else.

The house's security system beeped, and Eileen stopped pacing and shut her eyes. A few seconds later, she opened them and sighed in relief.

"They're home."

Serena nodded because talking still burned her throat a little, and she would cough again until her ribs hurt if she said anything. Eileen was back to looking anxious, and Serena waved to get her attention before making a shooing gesture at her. Eileen had no reason to sit with her and wait for them. Serena would be fine.

"You sure?"

She nodded again, and Eileen rushed off into the other room. Serena leaned her heavy head on the couch and shut her eyes. Her blanket cocoon was doing its job, and she was warm but no longer felt feverish. When she heard voices in the front room, she smiled, but was too tired to move.

The sound of running footsteps was coming her way, and she'd only managed to crack her eyelids when she saw Ashton a second before he nearly tackled her, pulling her into his arms.

"I'm so sorry, Serena. For all of it, but..." he leaned back and smiled, his eyes glassy, "I'm so glad you're alright."

She nodded weakly. "Got the test back. Just pneumonia."

Ashton hadn't laughed so lightly in weeks when he said, "*Just* pneumonia. I'm not sure I've ever been so happy to hear someone *only* has pneumonia."

When she giggled, it made her cough, and he softly rubbed circles on her back. "Should you be out of bed?"

"Eileen said it...was...fine. Until you got home," Serena managed to say between coughs.

"Well, we're home. Can I carry you back to bed?"

She nodded, and he gently pulled her into his lap. Then, he lifted her, cocoon and all, and headed for the bedroom hallway. Thenia was standing in front of Eileen's room, talking to Eileen, but turned to look at her when she heard them coming.

"Serena!"

Thenia rushed over and kissed her forehead before pressing her own against it.

"Missed...you...Nia...."

Thenia smiled before kissing her head one more time. "I missed you, too. Next time, you go with us. It was stunning."

Serena nodded but then rested her head back on Ashton's chest.

"Alright, she needs to get back to bed," Eileen scolded with a smile before lightly shoving Ashton through the doorway. "Sooner she rests, the sooner she's better."

Ashton chuckled but carefully tucked Serena back into bed and kissed her cheek. "Get some sleep, and I'll be back in a bit. Okay?"

Serena nodded, but her eyes were already closing as sleep claimed its debt.

It was after dark when Serena woke up again. She checked to see if Eileen had already come to bed and was surprised to see Ashton asleep beside her instead of his sister. He seemed to be sleeping deeply, so Serena carefully unwrapped herself and hung her legs over the side of the bed.

"Serena? Are you okay?" Ashton slurred.

She cleared her throat and then took a sip of water from a glass on the side table before answering. "Yes. Just going to the bathroom."

"Are you stable to walk?"

"Yup. I'll be right back. I'm sorry I woke you."

"It's alright. I don't mind."

Serena carefully got out of bed and quickly did what she needed to before returning to the bedroom at the same time that Ashton was reentering the room from the hallway.

"Hey, I got you some cool water." He set the glass beside the bed and helped her climb back under the covers.

"Thank you," she sipped it and smiled at how much better she felt.

Ashton got back into bed beside her, looking lighter than she'd seen him in weeks.

"Where's Nia?"

"In the master. Much to her annoyance," Ashton grinned.

"Eileen with her?"

Ashton snorted. "Nope. In Xander's room, probably." He rolled his eyes. "I'm amused that she still thinks no one notices. Pretty sure Gram and Pops knew she was sneaking into his room when she was eight."

Serena remembered her conversation with Eileen and nodded in agreement. "She told me."

"Yeah. I'm happy they have each other. Even though I'm the youngest, I never worried about her. Xander would protect her. Whatever form that took."

Serena put her water back on the nightstand and snuggled deeper into the blankets. "I really like them. She's taken good care of me, and Alexander is easy to talk to. Not to mention..." Serena pressed her fingertips over the soul coin tucked beneath her shirt.

"I'm glad," Ashton brushed a strand of hair off her forehead. His cool hand felt good, and she closed her eyes.

"Serena, can I come snuggle? Or will you be too warm?"

She reopened her eyes. "I don't want to get you sick."

"Compromise? Back to back?" he smirked.

His expression was so hopeful and slightly silly, making her struggle to suppress a laugh again. "Alright."

She rolled over, facing the outside of the bed, and felt Ashton lean over to kiss the back of her head before he, too, shifted to face away from her. Then he wiggled his way backward so their backs were pressed together, and then he tucked one of her feet between his ankles. The entire series of affectionate actions made her grin into the dark room, but she didn't care.

"Um, Ash?"

"What's up?"

She took a deep breath. "Thank you for everything, and...I love you."

He slowly rubbed his ankle against hers. "I love you, too, Serena. Now, get some sleep so you can get better. I'm not the only one who misses snuggles."

Serena closed her eyes, a smile on her lips and warmth against her back as she drifted back to sleep.

Ashton Giri

Ashton lay awake for almost an hour after Serena had gone back to sleep, but his body refused to cooperate and follow suit. Instead, he finally gave up, carefully crawled out of bed, and made his way into the hallway.

The house was silent, and he couldn't suppress the smile that crept onto his lips when he realized everyone was safe and where they belonged—at least for one night. With the issue of the threatening letters and Serena's attack solved, Ashton knew Xander and Eileen would head back out to another job soon.

Ashton made his way into the laundry room to change into jeans and a hoodie. He put on his shoes and picked up his car keys before heading for the front door. It only took him a few seconds to disable the alarm, slip outside, and turn it back on without making a sound or waking anyone up. He also sent Thenia and Serena a silent text with the location he was heading to, just in case either of them woke up.

Twenty minutes later, Ashton pulled his car up to one of the street parking spots outside of Crow's place and walked up to the doors. Unsurprisingly, the lights were on inside the shop, and the door was unlocked when he tried opening it.

"Come on in, Ashton," Crow called to him from behind the bar.

As usual, the barista was wearing black and had a multitude of silver rings, bracelets, and even charms in their flowing, unbound hair that cascaded down their back.

"Hey, Crow."

Ashton chose a stool at the counter and sat down, glancing around the shop before raising an eyebrow at Crow. "You even open?"

Crow didn't answer but merely smiled and asked, "Caffeinated or not?"

"Dealer's choice. You always pick what I need anyway."

His friend nodded and began pulling levers and turning knobs on the large brass coffee maker. "I assume everything worked out with Miss Thenia and your department?"

Ashton couldn't hold back his snort of laughter. "Sure, if you mean she walked in, made it to JoJo with zero blockades, and then provided her with whatever you'd written, and then we just walked out again with everything we wanted...then yeah, everything worked out."

Crow smirked, their reflection visible to Ashton in a brass container on a high shelf.

"Not gonna tell me what you said in your letters, Crow?"

They didn't answer Ashton and instead focused on finishing crafting his drink, and only once they'd set it before Ashton did Crow shrug.

"I said nothing of great importance nor anything they did not already know."

Ashton raised one eyebrow. "Yeah...sure."

Crow laughed softly but then turned and began making a second drink. Ashton sipped his own, the mix of salt and caramel hitting his tongue just before the rich coffee, which was cooled to the perfect drinking temperature by some richly flavored milk.

"Holy crap, this is amazing."

"Glad you like it," Crow said, a huge grin on their face as they peeked at Ashton over their shoulder. Then their gaze flicked to the front door, and Ashton heard it open.

When he shifted to see who was coming in, Ashton rolled his eyes but got up and let himself be pulled into Xander's arms for a hug.

"Should have known I'd not be able to sneak out without waking you."

Xander grinned. "Serena, actually. She texted me before you'd even made it out of the driveway."

Ashton winced. "Shit."

"She's fine. She showed me your message and is already back to sleep."

Ashton retook his stool, and Crow set the drink they'd prepared in front of Xander with a smile. "Nice to see you again, shadow hunter."

Ashton spluttered into his coffee and glanced at Xander, who was grinning before reaching out to clasp Crow's outstretched hand.

"You too," Xander's eyes flicked to Ashton before he finished, "Crow."

"Shadow hunter?" Ashton asked.

Xander sipped his drink, and Crow nodded. "Is it a name that is not accurate?"

Ashton looked between them both and then shook his head. "Fine, keep your secrets."

Xander looked away, and Crow's smile widened before they turned and left for the shop's backroom.

"You good, man?" Xander asked.

Ashton smiled into his cup and then sighed. "Yeah. Couldn't sleep after Serena got up, and I didn't want to spend another hour counting the wrinkles in the plaster."

"Makes sense. Couldn't have made coffee at home, though?" Xander looked up at Crow as they returned to the room. "No offense."

"None taken," Crow smiled before leaning against the counter and sipping from a cup they now held.

"Didn't know I wanted coffee," Ashton admitted. "Came to

thank Crow for their help, and of course, they gave me what I needed."

Xander smirked. "Yeah. Makes sense."

"Jerk won't tell me what they did, though," Ashton growled playfully.

"I think you'll find I did, in fact, tell you."

Ashton rolled his eyes. "Ah, no. You said you told them something they already knew. That's incredibly not helpful."

"Does it matter?" Xander asked, surprising Ashton.

"Knowing?"

"Yes."

Ashton groaned. "Whose side are you on?" he teased. "Fine. You're right. No, it doesn't." He turned to Crow and said, "Thank you. For helping Thenia. Us."

"My honor, Ashton," Crow said with a slight bow of their head.

Xander cleared his throat softly, and Ashton saw that his brother was suddenly angry. "Eileen told me about Serena. What they...did, or well, didn't do."

Ashton sighed. "Yeah. I want to say I can't believe they'd fake poisoning someone to get me to accept a stupid job, but...."

"When it comes to those with power," Crow said, "You'll find that whatever they have is never enough. They will do whatever it takes to own you, Ashton. Do not think that you have won."

Ashton felt his chest tighten, and he wasn't sure if he was still breathing. Not until Xander growled beside him.

"But to one so...innocent. Serena is not a tool for them to wield against Ash."

Crow shook their head. "No, she is exactly that. You all are. You, Eileen, Miss Thenia, and Serena. Even Josephine." They stared into Ashton's eyes, "Even Sue and Arthur. They will use everything and everyone they can to force you to their will. You must be prepared for it."

It relieved him to see that Xander's eyes had widened at

Crow's mention of their grandparents, just as Ashton was sure his own blood had fled his face to take residence in his feet. Crow, being Crow, noticed and smiled softly before nodding and returning to his drink.

"Ah…" Ashton croaked and then swallowed roughly. "So…tell me why I don't just quit and move out into a mountain range somewhere and go off the grid?"

Xander scoffed, "Dude, you'd last two days without the internet."

Ashton elbowed his brother, but couldn't argue with him.

"Because it would not have stopped them, young one. Some things are set in motion by the Fates and cannot be avoided, no matter how much we may wish to."

"Well, then. Fuck." Ashton said, making Xander laugh.

"What have I told you about that language, kid!" a slightly distorted version of Pops' voice said from his pocket.

"Oh, you're fucking kidding me!" Ashton said, ripping his phone from his pocket while Xander choked on his drink through his laughter. "First, where the hell have you been, and *now* is when you decide to come back? Second, I think I deserve a pass on my swearing. Trust me, I'm holding back quite a lot worse right now."

Ashton held up his phone and glared at the dark screen as synthetic wave patterns rippled in rhythm with his Pops' laughter.

"Fine, fine. I guess you can have a pass. Only this once!" his Pops said, a laugh not hidden well in his tone. "Turn me around, I want to say hi to Crow."

Crow smiled, their eyes sparkling as they leaned on their elbows on the counter and waved at Ashton's phone. "Hello, my friend."

"Nice to see you, Crow. I wanted to thank you for helping my kids out. Sue thanks you as well, but she's a bit…busy at the moment."

"You're very welcome, both of you. As I've told them, this will not be the end of it."

"We know."

Xander coughed one last time and glared at Ashton's phone, so he turned it to face the pissed-off panther. "What are you doing, Pops?"

"Don't worry, Xander, Crow's place is safe. Do you really think your grandmother would have let me say anything if we were in any danger here?"

"He is correct," Crow added. "You are not reachable here. You may relax."

"I am so confused," Ashton admitted.

"You and me both," Xander added before downing the rest of his drink in one go.

Crow and Pops laughed while Ashton stared down into his cup, suddenly wishing there was something more potent in it than coffee and sugar.

Chapter 31: Earth, Beast, Metal

August 2024, Maine, USA | Ashton Giri

It had been nearly a month since Ashton and Thenia had returned from the AIS's headquarters in Montana. He was still on paid leave while the higher-ups presumably attempted to figure out another way to compel him to provide them his grandparents' AI files. Not that he'd ever do it. Even if Thenia hadn't been right about his Gram corrupting their files before ever being handed over to the AIS, Ashton and the rest of them would have fought back. Hell, even Eileen had threatened to call in favors if they needed them.

After a week of bed rest, Serena had completely recuperated and returned to hanging out in Thenia's hair while she gardened. If the snake wasn't there, you could find her sunning herself on a rock with Xander while he was in his panther form. Eileen had begun teaching Serena more recipes, and they had cooked virtually all of the group's meals since Serena had recovered.

A few nights a week, Ashton would read with Serena. Xander often teased them when he walked by and found them debating a scene or grumbling about a character's actions.

Similarly, Ashton would spend time independently with Thenia when she wasn't in the gardens gossiping with his Pops or watching movies with Eileen and Xander while they passed copious quantities of popcorn and junk food between them.

Now that Ashton's life had settled into a cozy and peaceful rhythm, he dreaded returning to work, but he had a gut feeling his undesired vacation was reaching an end.

"Hey, Ash!" Eileen shouted from across the garden.

"Yeah?"

"Gram says open the gate. We've got visitors."

"Why didn't you tell me yourself?" he asked the new phone in his hand.

His Gram's delicate laugh made him smile. "You looked very happy. I didn't want to interrupt."

"So you made Eileen do it?" Ashton chuckled before opening the gate as requested.

"No. I did, in fact, ask *her* to open it. Sassy girl."

Ashton erupted into laughter but got to his feet as he strolled along the porch to the front of the house.

"Yeah. She's gone a bit rogue, Gram."

"Hmm, takes after your father."

Ashton stopped at the top of the deck's steps and observed a black sedan as it pulled up the driveway.

"Gram, stasis."

"It's fine, Ash."

He was about to argue with her, but shut his mouth when the driver and passenger doors opened. Much to his surprise, Josephine and Zareb, both outfitted in casual attire, got out.

"Hello, Ashton," Josephine said with a smile. She shut the car door, and he met her halfway, where she squeezed him into a hug. This time, she lingered, and he knew it was because of the difference in location, allowing her to display her chosen family side rather than the one that belonged to his boss.

"JoJo, why didn't you tell us you were coming?"

"She did, dear," his Gram said, causing him to stiffen.

"Don't worry, Ashton," Josephine said. "Sue and I have spoken, and before you panic, it was untraceable and off the record."

He stepped away and glowered at his phone. "What the hell, Gram?"

"Watch your language, young man," Pops' voice said from behind Ashton, where Thenia carried her phone as she exited the house.

"Nice to finally speak to you again, Arthur," Josephine said with a smile. "Thanks for staying by this crazy woman's side."

"Oh, hush you," Sue said.

Ashton glanced over Josephine's shoulder and saw Zareb standing with his hands in his coat pockets, entertained by the banter.

"Hey, man. Nice to see you again. Thanks for the heads up last time, too."

Zareb grinned. "No problem. Josephine will explain more later, but for now, just try to give me the benefit of the doubt. I'm on your side. It's Wyatt, by the way."

"He is," Josephine said firmly and with a nod. "Would you mind if we went inside to talk?"

"Nope. Do you want me to call Eileen and the others, too?" Ashton offered as everyone filed into the house.

His Grandmother answered, "Not for this, Ash, but do call Serena, please."

He and Thenia looked at each other and laughed as a small green snake slithered her way up to the top of Thenia's head and flicked her tongue in Ashton's direction, or more accurately, his phone's.

"Oh," his grandmother remarked before chuckling. "I'm sorry, dear. I lost track of you for a minute there."

Thenia peeked up with only her eyes and giggled when Serena dipped her head down to look at her along the bridge of her nose.

"Yo, Josephine, I'll find Eileen and Alexander while you all talk."

"Thank you, Wyatt. We'll come get you once we're finished."

Wyatt nodded and then let himself back out the front door.

"Ash, please come talk downstairs," his Gram instructed.

"Seriously, Gram. You're killing me. You couldn't have given me a heads up or something?"

Ashton laughed but led the way into the office and activated the secret shelf. When they reached the bottom of the stairs, he unlocked the door with the blood scanner and held it open for Josephine and Thenia to walk in first. Once they were all inside the space, both he and Thenia tucked their phones away as the doors sealed behind them, and the two overhead screens flickered to life.

"Oh, my," Josephine sniffled, putting her hand over her mouth.

"Hello, JoJo. I'm sorry I never told you."

Josephine shook her head and cleared her throat, tears visible in her eyes. "No, it's alright. I understand."

Thenia walked over to Ashton's side and grabbed his hand while Serena rubbed her head on his cheek, making him laugh with her tongue flicking.

Josephine sniffled again and waved her hands in the air in front of her. "I'm sorry. Business first. Ashton, all of your requests have been granted. Along with a few I added on your behalf."

"Oh, alright. Thank you...I think?"

His grandmother chuckled, and Josephine smiled at her monitor.

"First point to address. While I'm here in a semi-official capacity to inform you of your new position and assist with the signing of your contract, Wyatt and I are without machines and, from the AIS's perspective, off the grid at the moment."

"Why?" Thenia asked. "Wouldn't that put you in a vulnerable spot?"

"A bit, but nothing I can't handle. However, that's where some of my own negotiations on your behalf come in. Wyatt will be moving into the cottage on my property to the south of you. He will act as your right-hand man and liaison. He will stand in for any meetings that need to be in person or situations where you cannot be in two places at once."

"Wow," Ashton said, glancing between his grandmother and Josephine. "Thank you?"

Josephine nodded. "Don't worry. As Wyatt said before, he is well and truly on your side. While he may be newer to our department, Sue and I have worked with his father for years. He's a good, trustworthy man, not to mention highly skilled."

"And you will need more people at your back, Ash," his Gram affirmed.

"Feel like there's another shoe…" Thenia smirked.

"Well, yes," JoJo said, glancing at the monitor before continuing. "I have been given a new role, just as you have. In fact, your official job placement will be to take over mine."

"Wait, what? Why? That's way over—"

"Hush, boy. Let her finish," his Pops interjected.

JoJo winked at the older man's image but continued once more. "I told you before, they will never stop trying to get the code for Sue and Arthur's programs."

"Which is why I reached out to JoJo myself," his Gram admitted. "She will be the AIS's sole researcher into trans-mechanite AI systems, working directly with me."

"Is this safe?" Thenia asked the monitors.

His Gram nodded. "We will do our best, Thenia, but this was the right option for now."

"I agree with Sue. I will be relocating to Maine, though not directly next door. As I mentioned, Wyatt will be in my cottage. Someone I trust will remain in Montana and keep us all apprised of the situation there. That and Wyatt will be making frequent trips back and forth and remain in direct contact with that person at all times."

Ashton released Thenia's hand so he could pace, his body needing to expel the anxiety that was beginning to build.

"So, I'm taking your job. I have Wyatt as my second, who is essentially a spy, while he and you are moving here. You are now leading a department of one, researching my grandparents' code while also leaving a second spy in Montana. Did I miss anything?" he stopped and glanced between the monitors and JoJo.

"Correct, but there's one more thing. The other non-negotiable I advocated for on your behalf. All of my research will be conducted in this room and only in this room. There is no direct connection to AIS or between them and Sue or Arthur."

"Well, that's even harder to believe," Thenia said, crossing her arms in front of her. "They agreed to all that?"

"Yes. Let's say between the letter you provided me, my own explanation, and Sue's threat, they came around."

"Threat?" Ashton said, scowling at his Gram.

"Well, dear, I simply informed them that unless they wanted the first, truly sentient AI, new species, and fully conscious beings to reformat their drives, they would do as we said."

"They believed your bluff?" Ashton asked, astonished.

"It wasn't a bluff, Ash," Thenia stated. He looked over and caught her frowning up at the screens. "Was it? That's why you went into stasis. To prove you would erase yourself and that you could. At any time. You left your family on their own against the AIS when they needed you the most to prove a point."

Ashton's gaze flicked between Thenia and his grandparents twice, but it wasn't until he glimpsed JoJo's expression that he realized Thenia had been spot on. They would have erased themselves without a word, and he and the rest of them would have effectively buried their family a second time.

"While Ash and Eileen are proficient mechanites, neither

knows enough about our programming to recreate it from scratch. Those at AIS knew me well and knew that when I vowed to destroy all traces of our programming if my family were even slightly threatened, they believed me."

JoJo smiled. "They did. Some of those pompous pricks made wonderful expressions when they realized it was a conscious Sue speaking to them and not a recording."

Ashton sighed, "Is there anything else?"

"One thing, but it's not a large detail," Josephine answered. "Both Wyatt and I are fully read into your parents' files. So, while you'll not be sharing specifics with Eileen and Alexander, know that the two of us can be sounding boards if you need to talk about it. Once you, yourself, are read in fully, Ash."

He nodded. That made sense, at least.

"Ash," Pops said, gaining his attention. "Don't forget, this is the AIS. None of this situation worked out the way it did by their good graces. You must always watch your back." He frowned down at Thenia and Serena. "All of you must."

Thenia walked over to where Ashton had ceased pacing and retook his hand before she and Serena nodded. "We understand."

Ashton released her hand and drew her into his side instead, sliding his arm around her waist.

He pressed his free hand to one of his temples. "Well, as with every time I seem to come down here, I need some air and space to think."

His grandparents laughed, and JoJo nodded with a smile.

"You gonna stay and talk for a while?" he asked Josephine.

"She is." His Gram was grinning at the other woman, but then she peeked sideways at the other monitor. "Arthur, on the other hand, is going with you."

The old man rolled his eyes but smiled. "Yes, yes. As in life, same after death. Girl time means no husbands."

Everyone chuckled while Arthur nodded to JoJo and faded

from the overhead screen before communicating from Thenia's back pocket. "Shall we return to the daffodils, my dear?"

Ashton snorted but directed Thenia and Serena to the door. Once the remaining screen had dimmed and the door unlocked, he waved to JoJo, shut the door behind them, and locked her inside.

"Bed swing?" Thenia asked beside him. "Sounds like we have a lot to talk about."

"So it seems," he kissed her cheek. "Sounds perfect." He looked up at Serena, still roosting on Thenia's head. "Up to join us? Human form, I mean. I want to hear what you think, too."

Serena nodded, and the three of them made their way up the stairs and back into the office. Thenia dropped Serena off in her new room as they passed it, and they left her to swap forms in private.

"Oh, guess this will be a larger conversation," Ashton said, opening the back door for Thenia.

"Ash!" Eileen said with a smile. "Wyatt's told us the highlights. What are you thinking?"

Xander and Wyatt were leaning against the porch pillars, and Eileen was sitting cross-legged on the bed swing. Thenia climbed up beside her and mimicked his sister's positioning.

"Honestly," he plopped into a nearby chair, "nothing. Still trying to figure out what it all means."

"Don't worry, you've got time, and I'm here to help with whatever you need." Wyatt smiled.

"Mechanite, I assume?" Ashton asked.

"Yup, second generation."

When Serena opened the back door and stepped out, everyone focused on her, and she froze. He reached over and gently tugged her wrist, and she allowed him to pull her into his lap.

"Serena, this is Wyatt," Xander said, introducing the

newcomer.

"Oh yeah, shit. Sorry," Ashton said, having forgotten he was unknown to Serena.

"Language!" Pops hollered from Thenia's pocket.

"Oy, you eavesdropping old man?" Eileen taunted when Thenia retrieved her phone.

"Oh, come on. Those two kicked me out. Don't leave a man with no one to talk to."

Eileen snorted and rolled her eyes, but got up from the bed swing. "Ash, can I borrow you for a second?"

"Sure?"

He kissed Serena's cheek, and she left his lap and went to sit beside Thenia. When Eileen held out her arm for him to take, he chuckled but did as requested.

"Be back in a few," Eileen called back over her shoulder as they walked away.

Xander smiled at them as they left, and now Ashton was genuinely interested in what his sister wanted with him. Once they were out of earshot of the others, he poked her side.

"What's up, Eileen?"

"Well, um," she stopped to face him, but seemed squirrely. "I know why you gave Xander Pop's ring, and he does too."

"Yeah, and?" Ashton crossed his arms and smirked at her. "The two of you have been a pair since day one. Romantic or not. It's better you have them than me."

Eileen nodded, and he saw his sister's ears tinge slightly pink.

He narrowed his eyes at her. "Eileen? What did you do?"

She snorted, removed a box from her pocket, and held it out to him.

"What is it?"

"Open it."

Ashton accepted the long black box, but where he'd expected a bracelet or something longer, there were three shining bands— two thin ones with three stones in each and one thicker one to match. The stones were brown, green, and blue, and they absolutely sparkled.

"It's from the necklace Pop gave Gram for their fiftieth wedding anniversary, and yes, I asked first."

Ashton gaped at the three pieces until his sister's face infringed on his view when she ducked to shove it between him and the box.

"Earth to Ash?"

He closed the box, hugged his sister, and attempted not to sniffle in her ear.

"Thank you, Eileen. It's perfect."

She smiled against him and squeezed him back. "I'm glad you like them. Xander designed them after I found a piece to use. There is one stone for each of you. Earth, beast, metal."

Ashton nodded, his throat thick with emotions. Not only had his siblings accepted his relationships with both women, but they had also welcomed them into the family without a second thought. Eileen had watched over Serena when she was sick, and Thenia had protected Xander more than once. Together, they all felt...right.

"Ash?" Eileen said quietly.

"Hmm?"

"I want you to remember that we love you. You're not alone."

He smiled, this time not holding back his sniffle. "None of us are."

"Nope. We're not. Our family has grown, and I speak for Xander, too, when I say we are three very blessed orphans."

Ashton squeezed the box in his hand tighter.

"Yes. We are."

Epilogue

August 2024, Montana, USA | ???

The sound of stiletto heels clicking on the metal floor beneath her was loud and piercing in the otherwise silent lab. It didn't matter, considering no one was around to hear it except her. To her, the sound was soothing, akin to how a bell's ring projects confidence and power.

When she stepped over the threshold between one of the testing labs and into the empty private lift, lights flicked off from where she'd come and on in the lift's car. After the door slid closed, she selected the lowest floor of the facility and waited.

"You're late," a voice that practically dripped with ulterior motives purred from behind her, and she rolled her eyes in response.

"Considering you're trespassing, I suggest you shut your mouth."

An ebony feather brushed her cheek, and she leaned away from it.

"Move on, Sama. I have more important business to attend to than to waste my time entertaining you, angel."

The voice laughed, but she felt when he'd left and slipped back onto the angel plane. As the lift's sole occupant once more, she rubbed her cheek where the feather had touched her, and she had the sudden urge to walk through a sanitation hallway. Twice.

She dusted the front of her lab coat out of habit and ran her fingers through her fair hair. Neither action was needed, but she was nervous, and she loathed it.

A muted chime indicated she'd reached her floor, and she stared straight ahead as the doors slid open to reveal a large, dark space beyond. Her heels echoed even louder than before in the expansive room as she walked down a thin walkway toward the center of the space and up to the glowing orb the size of a pool ball that rested there.

"You're late, Agent Alpha," a distorted voice, part human, part machine, and part static, snapped.

"My apologies. I made more progress today, but I became lost in the work."

She bowed to the orb when she reached it and stared up at the hologram of an ever-changing face glaring back at her. The features of the face shifted every few seconds. A female set of lips and a male nose, then the left eye went green, and then the mouth became less feminine. Over and over, the image's features swapped, never coalescing into a single visage or staying too long on any single element. It was unsettling, or it had been—but that was long ago.

"Fine. Understandable. What news do you have of the two worms?"

"Roma has been dispatched and will begin studying the two AIs under her own assumptions that we will honor the isolation agreement. We have also received the updated contract for the man replacing her in the Invisibles Department."

"A useful tool. He seems to have great promise for a third generation."

"Yes. Incredibly skilled, and his file is filled with praise and kind words from his coworkers and past assignments."

The face grimaced. "How I despise those who are good to the core."

She said nothing in response and waited.

"Well, for now, I guess we will watch. I've waited this long. He is but a mechanite, and his life is short."

"Yes, as you requested, I will continue with my research and report back with new information once I receive it."

"Good. You may go."

She bowed to the orb a second time and began the short walk back to the lift. She'd only made it halfway when the voice behind her spoke again.

"How fortunate I found you, my corrupted one. Never forget who saved you all those years ago...Princess Esme."

She swallowed hard but lowered her head and continued to the lift, muttering, "I will not," as the door opened before her.

Eliza Leone

Eliza Leone is an author from the Pacific Northwest who specializes is chronicling the stories of her imaginary friends. As a kid, you could find her on the playground with a few kids acting out the stories they'd made up. When she got older and discovered there were entire worlds hidden within the pages of endless books, chances are her nose was in one. Over time, Friday nights were reserved for bookstore runs with her mother and together, they'd resupply for a week of adventures.

Writing had always been a far off dream, her ability to spell and do that grammar thing correctly, severely lacking. It wasn't until her mid-twenties that she decided if she was only writing it for herself, then no one would care about her lack of proper punctuation. Ten years and over a dozen books later, her family, human and fiction, convinced her to finally share her stories with the world.

From short stories and micro-fiction to the entire urban fantasy universe of Alku and its people, Eliza can't wait for you to giggle, sob, and throw your book across the room with her. Just...please don't throw the e-readers.

You can find Eliza Leone on: Discord at https://discord.gg/DvfMefpJAP, Instagram @ElizaLeone_author, and at ElizaLeone.com.

Leave feedback, read exclusive bonus content, and support this project at www.campfirewriting.com/explore/ElizaLeone